MW01632960

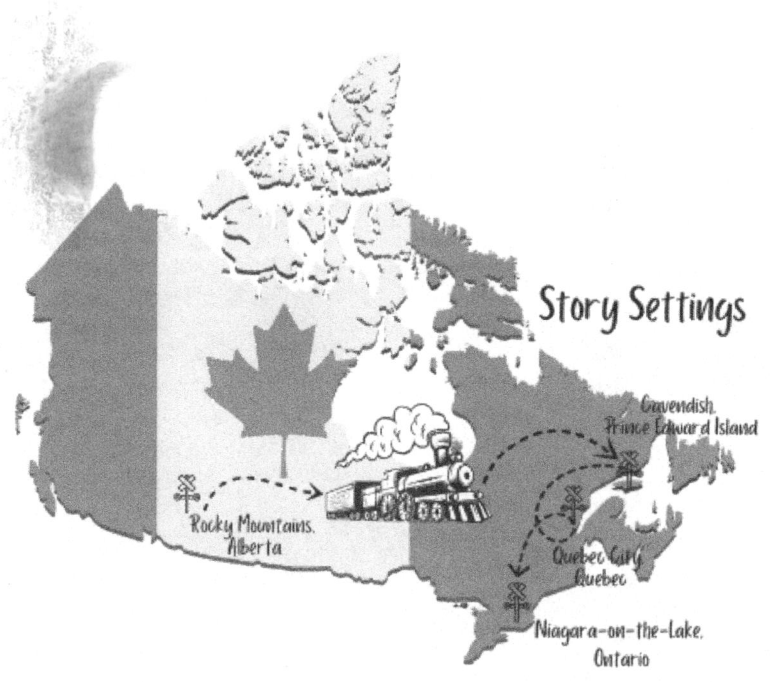
Story Settings
Cavendish,
Prince Edward Island
Rocky Mountains,
Alberta
Quebec City,
Quebec
Niagara-on-the-Lake,
Ontario

Four Contemporary Christmas Novellas of Faith, Hope, Love (and Trains)

I'll Be *Home*

DARLENE L. TURNER * HELENA SMRCEK
MELANIE STEVENSON * SARA DAVISON

ISBN: 978-1-0690162-0-1

Published by Fab Four Press

Cover design by Indie Publishing Services
A Christmas anthology from Fab Four Press

WHO ARE WE, ANYWAY?

We jokingly refer to ourselves as the Fab Four, a group of authors God has beautifully knit together. We have become so much more than writers; we've become dear friends.

We start every day by saying good morning on Facebook Messenger and asking what everyone is up to. We update each other on word counts, manuscript completions, and everything in between.

We cheer each other along the roller coaster of this writing life by celebrating each other's successes, mourning the rejections, and linking arms to hold each other up in prayer. We meet for writing retreats, take road trips together to writer's conferences, and plan events for other writers and readers.

We embrace that each of us is unique both in our writing and our being. We acknowledge that we are stronger together and continually thank God for bringing us together.

Given that, it made sense that we'd unite for this Christmas anthology. We hope you enjoy reading it as much as we enjoyed writing it.

Love,

Darlene, Helena, Melanie, and Sara

Praise for the Novellas in I'll Be Home

"Mistletoe and Mayhem in the Rockies" by Darlene L. Turner

"Darlene L. Turner never disappoints. She writes intriguing characters set in heart-pounding action stories. This vibrant novella was compelling from the first word."
~ Dana R. Lynn, USA Today Bestselling Author

"Across Time" by Helena Smrcek

Pull up a chair, grab a cup of hot chocolate, and settle in for a heart-warming Christmas to remember as love shows up in unexpected ways, proving that even the most obstinate can find happiness...even when they're not looking.
Publishers Weekly Bestselling Author Tabitha Bouldin

"Where My Heart Belongs" by Melanie Stevenson

"Where My Heart Belongs is a joyous, heart-stirring, mug-of-hot-chocolate-with-whipped-cream-and-marshmallows of a story, and a definite highlight of this wonderful Christmas collection. The fact it's set in Quebec is even more special, reviving fond memories for this Canada-loving author and reader. I loved it."
Carolyn Miller, award-winning author of The Original Six and Muskoka

romance series

"Just a Gilbert Blythe Kind of Girl" by Sara Davison"

As a long time fan of Sara Davison, I was thrilled to discover she's now writing romcom, and she doesn't disappoint! Just a Gilbert Blythe Kind of Girl is filled with all the nostalgia and smiles you'd expect from the title."

Angela Ruth Strong (www.angelaruthstrong.com), award-winning author of *Hero Debut, Husband Auditions* (Christy Award Finalist), and Resort to Love Series (*Finding Love in Big Sky* now a television movie)

CONTENTS

Mistletoe and Mayhem in the Rockies

DARLENE L. TURNER

MISTLETOE AND MAYHEM IN THE ROCKIES

Darlene L. Turner

A cozy Christmas on the Double H Ranch in the Rockies... with a twist of danger.

Mystery writer Emory Burke only agreed to her sister's request to spend Christmas at her ranch to get inspiration for her next book. Soon she finds herself at the center of her own whodunit. To make matters worse, her ex-fiancé is among the guests, pulling at her heartstrings. Constable Hunter Knight has worked hard to put the woman he'd believed was his forever love behind him. After a guest is murdered and presents go missing, he and Emory must work together to unravel the tangled web of clues before the holidays are ruined—and the killer strikes again. Can they solve the crime and find their way home—to each other?

For Jeff

My heart is home with yours.

For I know the plans I have for you," declares the Lord, "plans to prosper you and not to harm you, plans to give you hope and a future.

Jeremiah 29:11 (NIV)

~ ONE ~

December 22nd, 1:00 p.m.

Emory Burke stared at the blinking cursor. The white page mocked her stumped creativity. She'd never finish her mystery novel at this rate. Her approaching deadline elevated her blood pressure, and she slammed her laptop shut, focusing on the beautiful snowy landscape zipping by her train window. *Why did I agree to this getaway?*

You know why.

She had a hard time saying no, and she didn't want to disappoint her sister, Autumn Hardy. Especially since their relationship had been strained for too long. Autumn and her husband, Joel, owned the Double H Ranch in Bowhead Springs, Alberta—Emory's destination. Joel recently inherited the struggling homestead, and they'd hoped to turn things around by offering a good ole fashioned Christmas ranch experience for paying guests. Autumn promised Emory it would be fun and help spark ideas for Emory's upcoming Christmas mystery novel.

You better be right, Autumn. I need the inspiration.

The train lurched, bringing Emory back into the stuffy passenger car decorated with garland and battery-operated twinkling lights. She had taken the two-hour train ride to allow her time to think about her plot. A lot of good that did. They were twenty minutes from her destination, and she was no further ahead.

The thirtysomething GQ man sitting beside her leaned into her space and tapped her laptop. "You an author?"

She recoiled from his macho presence and strong cologne. *Did you bathe in it, buddy?* She stuffed her computer into her bag and silently chastised herself for her poor attitude. "I am. What gave it away?" As an introvert, she despised small talk, but it was challenging to avoid in a cramped car.

"The way you stared at the blank page. I've heard writers do that." He slouched in his seat. "Where are you headed?"

"To my sister's for Christmas." Vague answers. Something her cop father always taught her. *Never give anyone details when traveling alone. Makes you an easy target.*

Good advice, Dad.

"What's your book going to be about?" he asked.

"Good question. All my editor asked for was something to do with Christmas." She harrumphed. "You'd think that would be easy when one grew up with the Griswolds."

The man chuckled. "That bad, huh?"

"Let's just say my dad would have given Clark a run for his money." She chewed on her lip. "I only wish it would help me."

GQ man withdrew a pamphlet from his briefcase. "Well, this might give you inspiration. I'm spending the holidays here. Gonna be sleigh rides, bonfire with s'mores, horseback riding. This place has it all." He handed her the brochure. "My name's Cal."

"Emory." She glanced at the information. "No way. You're going to the Double H Ranch? Me too. My sister and her husband own it."

"That's awesome. I think we're almost at the—"

The train wheels screeched, and Emory careened forward. She grabbed the back of the seat in front of her to steady herself. Her heart rate increased with every sway.

Screams filtered throughout the car, and she bit down hard to stabilize her emotions. *God, keep everyone safe.*

The train's brakes screeched like nails on a chalkboard, only more intense.

The screams grew louder.

Emory assumed a crash position, blocking out the panic from the other passengers while she waited for the impact she guessed would come next. *Breathe, Emory. Breathe.*

Their car jumped the tracks and plowed into a snowbank, coming to a full stop. Emory smashed into the train's window. Pain shot through her head as a warm trickle tumbled down the side of her face. Her panic elevated and threatened to consume her body. She gasped for breaths. *Lord, help!*

Sounds muted in the background. She barely registered movement as other passengers straightened, groaning and checking on those they were traveling with.

Cal inched closer. "You okay?"

Was she? The pain in her head escalated with each breath. She inhaled and exhaled slowly to calm her nerves. "I'll be fine."

"You're bleeding." He fished out a tissue and wiped her forehead. "Let me help."

She winced from the pressure he applied and pushed his hand away. "I'm fine. We have to help get everyone off the train." Using the back of the seat in front of her, she pulled herself upright. Her wobbly legs buckled, and she stumbled.

Cal caught her by the waist. "Whoa now. Easy."

Shouts blared throughout the train, followed by pounding footsteps. Employees advanced throughout the cars, helping passengers.

"Everyone okay?" one asked.

Two men emerged from another car. "How can we help?"

"We need to get everyone off in case something else happens." Emory's author research told her that was the best course of action. She thrust her bag containing her laptop over her body but left everything else. No way she'd leave her device behind.

After everyone had evacuated the train, Emory stood beside the others and drew out her cell phone. She punched in her sister's number and waited.

"You at the station, sis?"

"'Fraid not." The frigid temperatures snaked down Emory's neck and she shivered. "Train derailed about twenty minutes outside of Bowhead Springs."

"What? You okay? Anyone hurt?" Autumn fired questions at her like ideas in a brainstorming session.

Emory explained what happened. "We're waiting for authorities to arrive."

Sirens pierced the area, and emergency vehicles barreled toward them, pulling to the side of the road. A truck parked behind them and a man jumped out.

Emory sucked in a breath.

Hunter Knight.

The ex-fiancé she never wanted to see again.

But now couldn't avoid.

Detective Hunter Knight halted at the sight of the beautiful redhead shaking in the cold. *Emory.* He zipped his parka to block out the biting wind but also to hide what lay beneath. The engagement ring she had returned to him fourteen months ago when she thought Hunter had cheated on her. She wouldn't believe him when he tried to explain he was only having lunch with a fellow officer in need of advice. Even Emory's sister couldn't convince her.

Hunter had placed the ring on a chain and kept it hidden from everyone. He had loved her deeply, and the jolt of his heartbeat at seeing her again told him he still did.

She doesn't feel the same. Get her out of your head.

Smeared blood on her forehead propelled him forward. "Emory, are you okay?" He reached up to check her wound.

She swatted his hand away. "Hunter, why are you here?"

He suppressed a sigh. Even after all these months, she still despised being in his presence. "I was in the area and caught the derailment news on my police scanner. I followed the firetrucks here."

"Oh." She pursed her lips.

"What happened?" Hunter examined the train's front car buried in the snow. "Looks like it skipped the tracks."

An impeccably dressed man to Emory's right stepped forward. "Yes, it did."

"And you are?" Hunter held his breath. Had Emory moved on?

"Cal Tracy."

"How do you know Emory?"

Emory folded her arms. "Hunter, Cal is a fellow passenger who helped get everyone off the train."

Paramedics arrived and began attending to the shaken travelers.

"Please tell me you weren't in the first car, Emory. It looks like it's in bad shape." Hunter extracted his cell phone and opened his notes app, waiting for her answer.

She shook her head. "We were in the second one, but I don't think there were any serious injuries. Thank the good Lord."

Cal patted her hand. "Agreed. God kept us safe."

Hunter flinched at the man's obvious attraction to her. *Emory's not yours any longer.* He cleared his throat. "Where were you headed?"

"Autumn's for Christmas. She and Joel are having a special," she air-quoted the last word before continuing, "*Christmas ranch experience* for guests. Autumn promised me the exposure would inspire my next book."

"Wait, that's where I'm heading too. Joel asked me to help with the ranch hands." Hunter puffed out a breath, the vapor lingering in the frigid air. "Sounds like they're playing matchmaker again."

There was nothing Hunter would like more. A snowy Christmas setting with a beautiful redhead.

"I'm going there too, and so are some of the other passengers on this train." Cal eyed Emory, his gaze lingering a little too long.

The man's words and attention to Emory deflated Hunter's hope of Autumn and Joel's plan succeeding.

There was no way Hunter could compete with the handsome Cal Tracy.

"Okay, I'll arrange for transportation for all those headed to the Double H Ranch. First, I want to check with the firefighters." Hunter pointed to a paramedic. "Get checked out by EMS."

"Shall we?" Cal held out his arm.

After a couple of seconds, Emory hooked her hand around it.

Hope sparked again. Had she hesitated because of Hunter?

Cal patted her hand. "I'll take good care of her."

Not what I asked you to do. Hunter gritted his teeth, suppressing his irritation. "Emory, will you be okay?"

She withdrew her arm from Cal's. "Yes. I'm going to call Autumn and have a little chat with her." She trudged through the snow away from both men.

At least she wasn't tied to Cal as much as the man probably hoped. Hunter refrained from gloating as he headed toward the fire chief. "Chief Borden, can you give me an update?"

"Good to see you, Constable Knight." The chief thrust out his hand.

Hunter returned the gesture. "You too. Any updates?"

"We'll know more after further investigation, but it appears the train missed the switch of the tracks. My firefighters are fighting a few flames that erupted in the first car when it slammed into the snowbank, but the immediate danger has passed. You heading up the investigation?"

"Not officially. I'm on vacation." He noted Emory's arm flailing in the air. Obviously, the conversation with her sister wasn't going well. "Let's just say I have a vested interest."

Hunter's cell phone rang. "Gotta take this. Be safe." He hit *Answer*. "Knight here."

"Hunter. It's Joel. You at the train derailment with Emory?"

"Yes. I can tell from her body language she and Autumn are in a heated discussion at the moment. You guys setting us up?"

"What? No. I really could use your assistance, and our excursion will help her get out of her writing slump."

Something in Joel's tone told Hunter he wasn't telling the entire truth. "What do you mean? Last I heard, her books were on multiple bestseller lists."

"Most, but not all. Her agent is breathing down her neck to finish this Christmas mystery story."

"And you both thought coming to the mountains would help." Made sense, but what didn't make sense was the fact they invited both of them when they knew their breakup had been messy.

"Exactly. Autumn is calming her sister, but I wanted to warn you. There's a cluster of intense storms moving in. You best get here soon before you can't get here at all."

"Will do. We should be able to leave shortly."

"See you when you arrive." Joel ended the call.

Dispatch mumbled a message over the radio using Hunter's identifying creds. He unclipped the device from his belt and pressed the button. "Come again, Dispatch. Didn't get that."

"Constable, be warned. An escaped convict was recently seen in your area."

Great, that was all he needed. An angry ex, a pending storm, and a convict on the loose. What else would this holiday season bring? Wasn't it enough God had taken Hunter's mother on Christmas Eve last year? He dreaded the grief firsts, and this one would be the hardest. His Mom had loved Christmas.

How can I get through this season without you, Mom?

~ TWO ~

December 22nd 3:34 p.m.

Snow mixed with ice clanged against the truck's window. The weather had taken a turn for the worse while paramedics were tending to the injured. Emory held her breath as the truck tires swerved on the icy roads. Those destined for the Double H Ranch's Christmas event piled into a van while Emory and Cal drove with Hunter.

An awkward silence filled the cab. Emory sensed a male rivalry brewing. Already. She suppressed her irritation and concentrated on one thing—the deadline looming over her.

Once she reached her sister's, Emory planned on locking herself in her room. She had a date with her laptop and wanted to distance herself from both men.

She didn't need a man, but she also couldn't ignore what Hunter's surprise reappearance in her life did to her insides. They were melting as fast as the wet snow hit the windshield. Not good. *Don't let him in. Don't let him in.* The mantra chimed in her head like the annoying Christmas lyrics playing on Hunter's radio. Over and over.

His shoulder touching hers as the three sat in the older truck's front seat didn't help. Neither did the woodsy scent she remembered all too well—a cologne she'd given to him on his birthday. Right before she caught him having an intimate supper with his beautiful coworker.

Emory studied his profile. "You've let your short hair grow a bit. I like the waves." *Why did you say that?* Now he'd know she had been checking him out.

Hunter rubbed his chin and chuckled. "I've also let this grow a bit too. Thanks for—"

The truck fishtailed, crossing the line into the opposite lane. Emory's muscles locked, and she pressed her hand against the dash.

Cal gripped the door handle.

Hunter swung the wheel to compensate. The truck righted itself moments before another vehicle appeared around the curvy highway.

"That was close," Cal said. "How much longer? I need a shower and a hot drink. My insides still feel frozen."

Thankfully, after firefighters had contained the flames, passengers were allowed to retrieve their luggage. All commuters were currently being transported to their destinations.

"We're only about two kilometers away." Hunter's words came out forced.

Clearly he didn't like that Cal had ridden with him instead of going in the van with the other travelers.

Emory studied the sky. Darkened clouds now blanketed the region. "This storm is moving in fast. How much snow are they predicting?"

"Close to a couple of feet or more." Hunter pointed to the mountains in the distance. "It sure is pretty, though. Look at the peaks."

Emory agreed. She lived in Calgary and rarely traveled to the Banff area. Now that her sister lived closer, Emory had promised more visits, since the ranch was located just outside the town limits. "Hunter, have you been to the Double H yet?"

"Twice. Have you not?"

"No. I know they inherited it a year ago, but with all the renos and my writing deadlines, I haven't been able to get there." Poor excuse. Truth be told, Emory and Autumn had been on the outs lately. Emory hated that her sister had taken Hunter's side when Emory ended their engagement. They'd had a huge fight and then Autumn had blamed her for ignoring them.

"Congrats on making the *USA Today* bestseller list recently." Hunter hit his right signal and turned onto a country road.

So, he was keeping tabs on her. Huh. Interesting. "Thanks." Her last mystery novel had received thousands of reviews, and now her publisher was pressuring her to give them a Christmas bestseller.

But how could she when she hated the season? She bit her lip and rested her head against the seat.

Five minutes later, Hunter stopped in front of the Double H Ranch laneway. The wrought-iron gate remained closed.

"Is there a secret to opening? Some sort of riddle?" Cal leaned forward. "Speak, friend, and enter."

Emory laughed. "This isn't Middle Earth, Cal."

"I'm impressed. You must be a Tolkien fan."

"Sure am. While others are watching all the Die Hard movies at Christmas, I'm glued to the Shire and the one true ring."

Cal tsked. "What? You're not a Hallmark junkie?"

"Not this gal." Even though her publisher wanted a Hallmark type of book this time around.

The gates opened.

Cal clapped. "It worked."

Hunter rolled his eyes and pointed to the camera fastened to the pole next to the gate. "Hardly." He drove down the snowy lane and moments later parked in front of a red barn. "The others should be here within minutes. I'll grab your suitcase, Emory."

Strapping her laptop bag onto her shoulder, she exited the truck and stopped to stare at the log-style home. "It's beautiful."

Hunter lifted all their bags from the back. "I figured you'd like it, since you love log cabins. Didn't your sister send pictures?"

He remembered that? "Of course, but they don't do it justice."

The front door opened, and Autumn bounded down the steps. "Em! You're here. Finally." Autumn practically threw herself into Emory's arms.

Oof. Emory stiffened in her sister's hug. "So good to see you too." *It's been too long.*

Autumn broke their embrace and held her out at arm's length. "Let me take a good look at you. You've lost weight. I thought all writers munched on chocolate while they wrote."

Was that her sister's way of telling her she must take better care of herself? Emory forced a smile. "That's a given. I also write while on my treadmill, though."

Joel appeared from around the barn. "Hunter!" He rushed forward and slapped Hunter on the back. "Good to see you again, bro." He eyed Cal. "Who's this?"

Cal stuck out his hand. "One of your guests. Cal Tracy. Can't wait to get settled in. I'm freezing."

"The others are arriving now. They just drove in." Joel gestured toward the door. "Let's head inside, and I'll show you to your rooms." He gave Emory a quick hug. "Glad you're here, Em."

"Me too, Joel."

Autumn tugged on Emory's arm. "Are you okay? That train crash was scary. Hunter, do they know how it happened?"

"Investigators are still looking into it. I'm officially on Christmas vacation."

The van pulled up, and five passengers climbed out. Giggles and singing erupted from the group, the crash clearly behind them.

Seemed Christmas had arrived at the Double H Ranch.

Two malamutes raced around the corner barking. One plowed into Emory's legs.

"Luna, down!" Autumn ordered. "She's happy to see her aunt."

Emory bent over and ruffled Luna's ears. "Hey, girl." She petted the other. "You too, Nanook. I bet you love your new ranch home."

"They do, but for the Christmas events, they'll be mostly staying in their kennel. One of the guests—Daniel Holmes—is allergic."

"Bummer."

"You haven't met the newest members of the family," Autumn said. "Two tabby kittens. Roxy and Susie."

Emory couldn't wait to meet them. She loved cats. "Cute. Autumn, how many guests are coming for this ranch experience?"

Joel, Hunter, and Cal helped lug the guests' bags into the home. The driver left, claiming he had to return to the depot before the storm fully descended upon them.

"Since this is our first year doing it, we weren't expecting a good turnout, but four more guests registered today, so twelve. Well, fourteen, including you and Hunter." She smirked.

Emory poked her sister. "I know what you're doing, and it's not gonna work."

Autumn tilted her head. "I saw how Cal looked at you, and I think I have my work cut out for me. Hunter better watch out."

Emory rolled her eyes. "Sis, I'm not interested in a relationship. Too busy."

And her heart couldn't take another crushing blow.

Autumn hooked her hand through Emory's arm. "Hopefully you won't have to write twenty-four-seven while you're here." She nudged her forward. "Come on. I want to show you the ranch. This is gonna be so much fun."

Coin-sized snowflakes fluttered around them, giving off a Hallmarky vibe.

Seemed the weather agreed.

Maybe this would lighten Emory's foul mood and be exactly what her Christmas mystery needed.

The perfect setting.

Hunter dropped his armload of wood into the bin beside the gigantic stone fireplace in the main living area. His gaze traveled to the ceiling, taking in the ambiance. Everything about this ranch yelled both rustic and Christmas. Hunter chuckled to himself, picturing Autumn ordering Joel to hang the lights and garland. From what Hunter had seen, there was a Christmas tree in every guest's room. Their job was to decorate their own as they liked. More details would be provided during a country-style supper happening in one hour. Autumn had made sure all the guests knew the plan, checking it off her list. Everyone had arrived except for four. They'd be there in time for s'mores around the fire pit later tonight. If the storm didn't squelch Autumn's plans.

Hunter picked up a log and added it on top, poking the fire. It spat out an ember, and he quickly stomped on the flaming coal.

Joel entered, carrying a stack of boxes. "Little help, bud?"

Hunter hung the poker on the hook and hustled to his friend's side, removing two boxes from his load. "What's all this?"

"Decorations for the trees. Well, for some." Joel nodded toward the long coffee table. "Set them there."

"What do you mean for some?" Hunter placed the two beside Joel's three.

"You didn't hear this from me, but the guests are to make their own decorations for their individual trees and are only allowed to take a few from these that Autumn has collected over the years."

"Interesting. Does she have everything planned out?"

"Yup, right down to the Christmas movies for movie night." Joel moved to the window facing the lake and the back of the ranch. "I'm afraid the storm may squash some of her plans."

"No, it won't," Autumn declared, hustling into the room holding a huge bowl of popcorn. Two tabbies followed, nipping at her heels. "No way would Mother Nature mess with me."

"Heaven forbid," Joel said.

A waft of fried chicken drifted into the room, sending Hunter's stomach growling. "Something smells delicious."

"Supper will be ready in five." Autumn brought out a notepad and short pencil from her back pocket, then scribbled. "Popcorn made. Check."

Hunter smirked at Joel.

Joel shrugged. "Told ya."

Autumn crinkled her lips. "What are you referring to?"

"Nothing, my love." He kissed her on the cheek. "Where's Emory?"

"In her room, settling in."

Or avoiding me.

A timer buzzed from the kitchen.

Autumn snapped her fingers. "Dinnertime." She fished out her phone, tapped on the keys, then picked up a cowbell sitting on an end table. She jingled it.

Hunter's cell phone buzzed, and he swiped the screen. Group text from Autumn.

Supper's ready. Come and get it.

Approaching footsteps told Hunter the others were on their way to the dining room. Emory entered and sat in her designated spot.

Thirty minutes later, after a feast of fried chicken, garlic-roasted potatoes, green beans, and homemade rolls, Autumn clapped. "Attention, everyone."

Hunter finished his last bite and set his fork aside, waiting for Autumn to share her plans.

"I've sent the Double H Ranch's first annual Christmas experience agenda to all your phones." She took a breath. "First up is your tree decorating time. You've noticed you all have a small one in your rooms. The rule is you can take five ornaments from the boxes in the living room, but you must make everything else. I've placed a big bowl of popcorn, thread and needles, and cranberries by the fire."

Murmurs from the group intensified as they discussed possible ideas.

Once again, Autumn clapped. "You haven't heard the fun part. There will be a prize for the best-decorated tree."

"Who's the judge?" Cal shouted from his position on the other side of Emory.

Autumn had constructed place cards for each spot, putting Emory and Hunter together. Cal had been assigned a seat on the opposite side of the table. However, he had switched his card with another guest so he could sit beside Emory, too.

Then he had proceeded to monopolize the conversation, not allowing Hunter to speak a word edgewise.

Hunter had buried his irritation and spoken to the young family of three on the other side of him. The couple and their six-year-old had found out about the ranch Christmas experience online. Ava had begged her parents to bring her, claiming it would be the best Christmas EVER. Gil and Josee Drew couldn't refuse their daughter.

"Judges are confidential." Autumn waggled her index finger. "I don't want any bribery happening."

Emory snickered. "My sister, forever the organizer."

"Has she always been like this?" Cal wiped his mouth with his candy cane napkin.

"Pretty much. I used to find her lists all over the house." Emory picked up Roxy and kissed her face. Susie jumped up on her lap, purring. Seemed she also wanted attention.

Autumn laughed from her position at the end of the table. "Well, someone had to keep the rest of the Burkes in line. You sure weren't gonna."

"You inherited Dad's Griswold Christmas nature." Emory extended her arm, gesturing around the room. "Look at these decorations. Need I say more?"

"Let's just hope there isn't any cat food in our dinner." Hunter couldn't resist bantering with Emory. It had been his favorite past-time when they dated.

"Wait a minute. Aren't you that mystery writer?" Daniel, a thirtysomething geek, stuffed a roll into his mouth.

"She sure is." Cal puffed out his chest as if that would gain Emory's respect and admiration.

Hunter knew better. Emory had often squirmed from the attention her bestseller status threw her way. At the same time, she confessed to being proud of herself for persevering and following her dreams of becoming a published author.

Emory raised her hands. "Let's not get carried away. I've only written a few books."

"A few? I've read every one." Daniel's eyes glistened in the dimmed lighting. "What are you working on now?"

"She's writing a Christmas mystery."

"Cal, I can answer for myself, you know." Emory placed her utensils on her plate.

Hunter covered his mouth to hide a grin. He pictured one imaginary strike against the man, which sent Hunter's hopes soaring.

Well, not that he really expected Emory would let him back into her life.

"Okay, here's what will happen next." Clearly, Autumn wanted to steer the conversation away from her sister. "Dessert will be s'mores later." Autumn's gaze shifted to the window. "Weather permitting."

An older woman stood and began clearing the dishes. "Let's get started so we can beat the heavy snowfall. I love s'mores."

"Ruby, I have it covered. If need be, we'll use the fireplace, so no worries."

Emory pushed herself upright. "Autumn always has a backup plan."

Hunter's cell phone dinged, announcing a text. He swiped the screen. His fellow Constable.

Be warned. A convict escaped a prison transport near the train station. We checked the last public computer that inmate used and found the Double H Ranch in the search history. Prisoner's name is Jess Gardner.

Sending a picture, but the prisoner is known for being a chameleon. Stay on alert.

An icon appeared seconds before *Unable to Load Photo* splashed on his screen. Hunter's pulse elevated as he tapped in a message.

Didn't come through. Try again.

His phone's bars disappeared.

Hunter failed to subdue his gasp.

Emory leaned closer. "What is it, Hunter?"

"Later." No need to alarm the guests, but one thing was for sure.

The convict may be among those seated at the table.

And Hunter had to find a way to interrogate each without tipping his hand.

~ THREE ~

December 22nd 7:15 p.m.

Emory followed Autumn, Joel, and Hunter into the games room after the guests had settled into a routine of making their tree decorations. Hunter had requested he speak with them privately.

"Have a seat." Hunter closed the door and turned. "I wanted to make you all aware of a situation that may affect you."

"Is this about the text you received at the supper table?" Emory plunked into a plush chair.

Autumn took the couch while Joel stood, leaning against the floor-to-ceiling bookcase.

Hunter hooked his thumbs into his jean belt loops. "You always had good intuition. Yes, that's exactly what this is about." He paused.

Gathering his thoughts or stalling?

"Spit it out, bro." Joel crossed his arms. "What's going on, Hunter?"

"First, check your phones. Do you have a signal?"

They complied and shook their heads.

"That happens a lot in storms out here in the country." Joel swiped his screen. "It appears we've also lost our Wi-Fi. The satellite tower was damaged in the last blizzard, so I wouldn't be surprised if it's been taken out completely."

"The snow *was* mixed with ice when we drove here." Emory tucked her phone away. "What did the text say?"

"It was a colleague of mine letting me know that an inmate recently escaped custody and could be among your guests."

Autumn leaned forward. "What? How do you know that?"

"That text was from my partner. A prisoner escaped near the train station, and they found the ranch's name in the search history of one of the prison computers that inmate had been using." Hunter addressed Emory. "The convict may have been on your train. Did you see anyone acting suspiciously?"

"No, just excited Christmas passengers." She crossed her legs. "Wait. Don't you know what he or she looks like?"

"Unfortunately not. The inmate's picture didn't load. All I have is a name—Jess Gardner. That could be a male or female."

Autumn buried her face in her hands. "We're ruined. This was our one chance to get ahead of all the bills."

Joel pushed away from the bookcase to kneel in front of his wife and bring her into his arms. "Shhh...it's gonna be okay. God's got this."

A car door slammed.

Emory stood and peeked out the window. "The rest of your guests have arrived. Hunter, what do we do?"

He tapped his chin. "Let me think about this."

"Well, the storm may answer that question for us." Emory pointed to the light in the driveway. "It's coming down bad now and has already accumulated in the short time we've been here."

Autumn bolted upright, wiping away her tears and rolling her shoulders. "Let's check with the driver on the conditions and go from there."

"Please keep this news confidential, okay? I don't want to scare anyone." Hunter opened the door.

"Will do." Joel and Autumn hurried from the room.

"What are the odds that the convict is really in the group here?" Emory knew her sister, and this would devastate her. Autumn had confided in Emory that all their savings had gone toward upgrading the place, and if the Christmas experience didn't go well this year, they'd have to sell the ranch.

"I don't have any answers, but rest assured, I will be watching everyone closely." Hunter joined her at the window and squeezed her shoulder. "I'm sorry this is happening."

She flinched at his touch, ignoring what it did to her insides. Maybe it would be good if Autumn and Joel canceled, so she could get away from this man.

Before her feelings returned tenfold.

But that would be selfish, and she had to make amends with her sister—even if that meant enduring the man beside her. "Not your fault. Let's go talk to the driver." She rushed to the entrance.

The four guests brushed snow from their coats as the driver tucked two suitcases into the foyer's corner. "I'll get the rest, folks. Just let me catch my breath." The older gentleman inhaled. "It's coming down pretty hard now."

"How are the roads?" Hunter asked.

Laughter filtered in from the living room as Christmas music played softly in the background, reminding Emory of why they were all here—to celebrate the season in a ranch-style atmosphere. She held her breath, waiting for the driver's answer.

"Treacherous. I barely made it." He looked at Joel. "Name's Mike Reacher, and I'm stuck in your driveway. Any chance you have an extra room? No one is going anywhere now."

Well, that answered her earlier question to Hunter about what they should do. At this point, there was little they *could* do except stay put and pray the escaped convict wasn't under their roof. Emory swallowed hard.

Autumn's eyes brightened. "Of course, Mr. Reacher." She turned to Joel. "Honey, would you mind getting these guests checked in so I can prepare the extra room in the basement?" Singing "Deck the Halls," she bounded down the hallway without waiting for her husband's response.

Even with the possibility of a convict on the premises, Emory's sister wouldn't let it dampen her spirits.

And—if need be—Emory had noted where Joel kept his hunting rifles. After multiple research trips to a gun range, she had no problem firing one.

If it came to that.

She prayed it wouldn't.

Emory eyed Hunter. If she was being completely honest with herself, she was more worried about the damage the constable's charm would do to her heart than the convict possibly invading their Christmas ranch experience.

"Take your coats off, folks, and follow me." Joel beckoned them toward his office.

They complied and followed him down the hallway.

Hunter plucked his coat from the wall hook. "I'll help you with the rest of their suitcases, Mr. Reacher."

"Appreciate that. Call me Mike."

"Hunter Knight." He nodded toward Emory. "This is Emory Burke."

"Nice to meet you both." Mike whistled "I'm Dreaming of a White Christmas" as he opened the front door.

Hunter leaned close to Emory. "Keep your eyes open for anything suspicious and report back to me," he whispered. "I know how your mystery writer brain works. You're good at picking up on things others wouldn't. I'm counting on that."

"I've got your back. It will be okay. The convict is probably long gone."

"My gut is saying that's not the case." He trailed out the door after Mike.

A gust of wind mixed with a flurry of snowflakes snaked through the entrance, chilling Emory to the bones and filling her with an eerie foreboding. She hustled to shut the door, blocking the chill.

And the trepidation coursing through her iced veins.

Hunter surveyed each guest huddled around the large fireplace roasting marshmallows as Christmas music played softly in the background. He couldn't get the obvious question out of his head—was the convict posing among those gathered at the Double H Ranch? He viewed them one by one with his constable brain, mentally adding them to his suspect list.

The Drews—a mid-thirtyish couple and their six-year-old daughter, Ava. Even though Gil Drew gave off a secretive vibe, Hunter crossed them off his mental list. No way a convict would bring a child into the mix.

Bucky Fletcher—Joel's lead ranch hand. He lived in a cabin on the property with his two children—Liam and Lacy. The twins were currently intent on making the best s'mores of the group. Seemed friendly enough and was helpful to the Hardys, but how well did they know Bucky?

Ruby Marple—Hunter guessed the woman to be around fifty-five. She had brought her seven-year-old grandson, Eli. He tried to persuade her to make a s'more, but she refused to take part, claiming she had diabetes and needed to watch her sugars. She constantly checked her watch for some odd reason. Weren't they all here to take in the atmosphere and forget about their timetables?

Wilson Spade—appeared to be around thirty-five and was attentive to Ava. Not in a sick sort of way, but as a father looking after his child's well-being. Hunter had observed Wilson carefully scoping the room out with his keen green eyes, but he had claimed he was an antiquities dealer and loved every piece at the Double H Ranch.

Daniel Holmes—the geeky younger man had his nose stuck in a book in the corner chair. Close to the action, but not partaking. Wasn't he here to get that ranch experience? So why would he stay glued to the pages of the latest Connelly novel? And if he was allergic to the dogs, why didn't the kittens bother him? However, Hunter supposed it was possible to be allergic to one and not the other.

The Watson family—Rose Watson clearly had a firm grip on her adult sons, Phil and Dick. Their clothing and jewelry screamed big money, but the brothers' constant bickering elevated them on Hunter's list.

Cal Tracy—of all the guests, Cal annoyed Hunter the most, and Hunter had already put him at the top of the list. Was that only because of Cal's flirtatious attitude with Emory? Right now, he had nestled himself beside her, roasting her marshmallow. Hunter wanted to snatch the stick from his hand and hit him over the head with it. Of course, all that didn't prove the man was a convict.

It only confirmed that Hunter's jealousy had reared its ugly green head.

Mike Reacher—the driver had only arrived tonight and was snow-stayed by the storm, so he was an unlikely prospect. Still, Hunter never crossed anyone off a suspect list.

Fifteen people including the children. Hunter had memorized the names and would add them to an actual list on his phone. Even though he was technically on vacation, as the sole law enforcement officer on the premises and with an escaped convict in the vicinity, he'd just been recalled to active duty. Even if he hadn't been, he wouldn't be able to shut off his sleuthing mind. It was a cop's habit.

"Earth to Hunter."

Emory's voice jarred him from his thoughts. "Sorry, what did you say?"

She held up her s'more. "I asked if you were going to have one. They're delicious." She bit into her treat, mumbling the words between bites.

Roxy and Susie bounded into the living room, chasing each other.

Shoving back his driving need to stay vigilant, he chuckled and approached the fireplace. "Why not?" If everyone there believed he was simply another guest, not a cop, they might relax their guards around him, which would make it easier for him to spot the guilty party if he or she were here. He nabbed a skewer and stuffed a marshmallow on top before kneeling in front of the fire. "The secret is to keep turning while roasting. This will prevent burning."

Cal harrumphed. "Well I, for one, like them burnt."

Of course you do.

Hunter ignored the man and focused on the redhead beside him. She was still as pretty as she'd been fourteen months ago when she stormed out of his life.

"So, Emory, what is your Christmas mystery novel about?" Hunter had to get his mind off their break-up and his list of suspects.

"Good question. I'll let you know when I know."

"You haven't started it yet?"

"Nope, and it's due in a few weeks." She tickled Roxy's belly. "My agent and editor are both pressuring me."

"Maybe this Christmas experience will help spark some ideas." Hunter removed his marshmallow, squishing it between the graham crackers and chocolate. "Ooey-gooey goodness." He bit into his treat and let the chocolate flavor explode in his mouth.

The Christmas music stopped, and Autumn clapped. "Okay, everyone. I need your undivided attention."

The chit-chatting tapered off and soon only the coals crackling in the fireplace filled the room.

"Joel and I apologize that our Wi-Fi and your cell phones aren't working. The storm is playing havoc with the satellite tower. Even so, we're not going to let that stop us from having fun." Autumn held up sheets of paper. "Now that you've had dessert, our festive agenda is about to begin."

"What exactly is on this list?" Wilson asked.

Joel entered the room. "What isn't on the list would be the better question to ask."

Autumn swatted him with the bundle of papers. "Funny guy." She handed the stack to Bucky sitting in the closest chair. "Please pass these along. Since it's now nine o'clock, we'll start with the gingerbread house contest after breakfast in the morning. Right now, you can all take the decorations you made and head to your rooms."

"In other words, get to bed, folks." Daniel snickered.

"Well, I wasn't going to put it like that. I meant time to decorate. Breakfast is served at seven, then for anyone wanting to go horseback riding, Joel and Bucky will get you all set up." She paused. "Depending on the weather, of course."

All the children jumped up at the same time. "Yippee," they shouted simultaneously.

"When do we make the gingerbread houses?" Ava asked.

"That starts at 10 sharp."

Ava tugged on Josee's hand. "Come on, Mama. We need to go. Now!"

The group chuckled.

Rose Watson stood. "I for one don't do early mornings, tree decorating, horseback riding, or gingerbread house making."

"You obviously came to the wrong place," Ruby said.

The older woman's eyes narrowed. "It wasn't my idea." She flicked her hand at the group. "Tata. Heading to bed. Don't wake me at the crack of dawn, or else." She strutted out of the room.

Dick Watson smirked. "Believe me, you don't want to see the wrath of the almighty Rose Watson." He gestured to his brother. "Come on, Phil. We still have some business to take care of before bed."

The younger brother stood, following Dick from the room with slumped shoulders.

Clearly Dick was the domineering one of the two.

The rest of the group dispersed, mumbling their good nights.

Joel slapped Bucky on the shoulder. "Can you check to ensure the horses are comfortable? It's nasty out there."

"On it, boss. Night." He exited with the twins, whistling a Christmas tune.

Autumn gathered the dishes. "I'm going to take these to the kitchen and do the food prep for breakfast. Joel, can you help me?"

Emory popped to her feet. "I can."

"Nope, you're a guest." Autumn kissed her sister's cheek. "So glad to have you home. It's been too long. Have a good sleep." She winked at Hunter and hustled from the room.

"Your sister isn't subtle, is she?" Hunter added another log to the fire.

"Not Autumn. Sorry." Emory peered out the window. "Joel was right. It's gotten worse out there. From the looks of it, the wind has picked up."

"Thankfully, this place is big enough to house all of us."

"Yes, Joel and Autumn had an extension put on, as it's always been his dream to have a big ranch full of children." Emory sighed. "Even after five years of marriage, though, they've failed to get pregnant. Breaks my heart."

"What did she mean by 'it's been too long'? Haven't you seen your sister lately?" She obviously didn't know Autumn's secret.

"No."

"But you don't live that far away."

"You sound like her. I've been so busy." She raised her hands. "I know...that's no excuse. How have you been? I'm sorry about your mom's passing."

"Thanks. I'm okay. Really not looking forward to all the firsts, though." He swallowed the lump in his throat, shoving his emotions aside. "Also busy with lots of cases."

"You really think there is a convict among the guests?" She glanced at the door and lowered her voice. "Everyone seems so nice, except maybe Rose and her sons."

He shrugged. "Not sure. All I know is that Joel and Autumn deserve a great Christmas. I'm keeping a close watch on everyone. Hopefully we'll get cell service back soon in case things get dicey."

Hunter stood at the same time as Emory stepped forward, and she bumped into him. He wrapped his arms around her waist to prevent her from toppling over before releasing her. "Sorry about that. I didn't realize you were so close." Not that he minded. Holding her in his arms—even for a second—was worth the collision.

"It's fine. I'm going to try to get some words—"

The lights snapped off, sending them into pitch blackness.

In the dark, she found his forearm and gripped it. "Great, that's all we need to add into the mix. A storm and no power with a possible convict among us."

Hunter didn't miss the angst in Emory's voice. "Don't worry. The generator should kick—"

The lights flicked back on, and she abruptly released him.

"In. See? All is good." He forced a smile.

But was it? Hunter couldn't help but think the storm and loss of power foreshadowed future events. He was definitely going to have to force away thoughts of Emory and how good her touch felt if he hoped to stay focused on possible threats.

~ FOUR ~

December 23rd 6:15 a.m.

The annoying buzzing woke Emory from dreams of kissing Hunter, and she slapped her hand on the nightstand. Make it stop. She forced herself into a seated position in the bed and turned off her alarm. The empty Christmas tree in the corner called out to her, "Decorate me," and she stared at it a moment.

"Ugh!" She flung the buffalo plaid comforter off. Emory had planned on adding the few decorations she'd made but got sidetracked working on her novel. A story idea had hit late last night, and she had to get the words onto her laptop before they disappeared from her brain.

Had Hunter inspired her? Obviously, their collision had re-sparked something deep inside. Or why would she have dreamed about his kisses?

"You're foolish. He's moved on." Great, now she was talking to herself. Not that it wasn't common among writers. Their characters became real, and she'd confessed to having multiple conversations with them. One reader told her once that she had prayed for the people in Emory's books.

Bacon smells interrupted her thoughts, and Emory sprang out of bed. She drew the curtains back, looking out the window. Snow piled high everywhere. Snowflakes continued to fill the air. When would it stop? She checked her cell phone. Still no signal or Wi-Fi.

At least they had power, but for how long?

Emory snatched the towel from the dresser and entered the attached washroom. Autumn had made sure Emory had the best room in the ranch to give her privacy. Plus, it had an awesome view of the property.

The snow-laden trees in the backyard and at the forest's edge were spectacular. Majestic mountains finished the Thomas Kincade picture beautifully.

Why did people doubt God? His creation spoke volumes, and last night's storm had proved it. He had painted the peaks with a fresh, white blanket.

After showering, Emory put on her Christmas plaid shirt and jeans before heading into the hallway.

"Gil, we can't afford renos for the house. You know we spent a fortune to bring Ava here." Josee Drew's voice filtered through the closed door.

Emory hesitated.

"We have to in order to sell. You know that!"

"The bank won't give us another loan. We need to sell my car to make ends meet."

"Shhh...keep your voice down."

Where was Ava? Emory prayed the little girl wasn't present to hear her parents' heated discussion.

Emory tiptoed by their room and down the steps. On the way past the living room, she caught sight of Ava sitting on the floor in front of the tree. *Good. Stay there, little one.*

Footfalls sounded behind her, and Emory whirled around.

Ruby appeared in her housecoat.

"You scared me." Emory placed her hand on her chest. "You're up early."

Ruby raised a Bible. "Yup. Wanted to get my quiet time in before Eli wakes. God and I need to chat."

"Everything okay?"

The older woman sighed. "Not really. I'm in the process of trying to get custody of Eli. You see, his father is a drunk and has left Eli alone too many nights. Time for me to intervene."

"I'm sorry to hear that." Emory grazed Ruby's arm. "I will pray for guidance."

"Thank you, dear." Ruby smiled and shuffled into the living room.

God, be with Eli and protect him.

The fresh scent of brewing coffee interrupted Emory's silent prayer and lured her into the kitchen like a fly to a trap.

Autumn turned at Emory's approach. "Good morning, Sissy. You sleep well?"

"Yes, must be that mountain air. Glad the power came back on. I see the Wi-Fi is still out." She selected a Christmas mug from the turntable rack and poured a coffee. "What's today's flavor?"

"Your fave. Gingerbread. Which, of course, goes with today's gingerbread house making contest." Autumn giggled and flipped the bacon slices over. "How are you and Hunter getting along?"

"No fights. Yet. I saw what you did last night." She nudged her sister's shoulder. "Stop playing matchmaker. You know what he did."

Autumn waved the spatula. "No, he didn't, and you know it. I think deep down you got scared and pushed him away with your cheating accusations."

Emory sipped her coffee, pondering her sister's observation. Could that be true? She did have a hard time trusting men ever since her high school sweetheart cheated on her with her best friend.

"You two are perfect for each other, and you know it."

"How are you so sure?"

"Because you look at each other the same way Mom and Dad used to." Autumn turned the burner to simmer. "You still have feelings for him. Admit it."

"Admit what?" Hunter sailed into the kitchen and snatched a Christmas mug, whistling "Frosty the Snowman."

"Nothing." Emory took another drink and moved to the festively decorated log table. She picked up a plate. "You changed your Christmas theme this morning. What's up with all the mistletoe? It's everywhere."

Autumn winked. "Nothing."

"Wow. Seems like you two love that word." Hunter added cream and sugar to his coffee.

"And you still load your coffee with junk. It's gingerbread and already sweet enough." Emory sat.

Joel shuffled into the room, carrying another stack of plates. "Found them, hon."

Hunter leaned against the island counter. "Need any help with breakfast?"

Autumn shook her head. "Almost ready. Joel, can you ring the cowbell?"

Roxy and Susie trotted into the kitchen. "What's with the cowbell?" Emory picked up one tabby. "Morning, Roxy girl." She scratched under Susie's chin. "You too, girl." They meowed.

Joel kissed his wife's cheek. "Her idea. Thought it gave off that ranch vibe." He grabbed the bell and walked into the hallway, clanging it. "Breakfast time, everyone!"

Hunter picked up Cal's name card and placed it across the table.

Emory chuckled. "What are you doing with GQ's card?"

"GQ?" He shrugged. "What can I say? He grates on my nerves."

Could it be that, or was Hunter jealous of the man?

"Sissy, can you help me set the food on the table?"

"Sure can." Emory blasted to her feet, welcoming the distraction from the handsome blond constable.

Autumn scooped the scrambled eggs into a Corningware dish and handed it to her.

Emory placed the food in the middle of the table, then topped up her mug with gingerbread coffee. She required more fuel to jolt herself awake. She had to get her word count in today, even if it meant disobeying her sister's Christmas agenda. Her characters were calling.

Cal strutted into the room, appearing fresh and wide awake. "Morning!"

Emory cringed. *Too chipper, Cal. Simmer down.*

Autumn pointed to the coffee bar. "Grab yourself a coffee and have a seat. We're just waiting for the others."

Cal raised his hands. "Nope. No caffeine for me. I'm fully awake."

Clearly.

The Drews entered the kitchen, Ava skipping to the table. "I'm hungry."

Daniel sauntered into the room and plunked down in his chair. "Smells so good. Do we—"

A bloodcurdling scream resonating from upstairs pierced the early morning hour.

The group simultaneously bolted to their feet.

"Stay here, everyone. I'll check it out." Hunter rushed out of the room.

"Not a chance." Emory hurried after him.

Hunter pivoted. "What are you doing?"

"Following you to find out what's going on." She jerked her finger at him. "Don't try to stop me."

He shook his head. "Why do I even bother giving you an order? You never listen."

She raised her hands, palms up. "You may need my help."

"Fine, but stay behind me." Hunter bounded up the stairs.

Emory followed him toward the commotion coming from Rose Watson's room, stopping in her tracks at the entrance.

Rose Watson sat slumped in the chair by the window, a teacup shattered on the floor by her feet. Her face was ashen.

Phil Watson knelt on one side of her, slapping her hand. "Mama, wake up!"

But from the woman's appearance, Emory guessed Rose Watson wouldn't be waking up anytime soon.

She was dead.

"Step aside, Phil." Hunter approached and placed his fingers on Rose's neck. Not that he expected to find a pulse because her mottled skin gave him a clear picture of her condition. The woman had passed. When and how? He observed the room.

Suitcases still packed.

Bed undisturbed.

Open book on the small Victorian table beside her.

Broken teacup on the floor.

If Hunter was a betting man, he'd guess she died late last night.

But he wasn't a betting man and would stick to the cold, hard facts. They were telling him her death wasn't by natural causes. "Phil, did your mother have a heart condition?"

"You mean she's..."

"Yes, I'm afraid so. My deepest sympathies."

The man sucked in a breath. "She was in perfect health." Phil shot to his feet. "Are you thinking murder?"

Hunter raised his hands. "I'm not saying that. Just trying to get a little background on your mother's health."

"Other than her being ornery, she was fine."

The man's admission to his mother's abrasiveness surprised Hunter. He hadn't said anything after Dick's comment last night. "Where's your brother? Did you only find your mother now?"

"Yes. I heard the breakfast bell and came to fetch her." His lip quivered. "I found her like this."

Emory pointed to the teacup. "Who served her the tea, or did she get it herself from the kitchen?"

Hunter guessed what she was thinking.

Someone poisoned the wealthy business woman.

Phil placed his hands on his hips. "Rose Watson serve herself? Hardly."

Hunter noted the heavy sarcasm in his tone. Clearly, both sons held animosity toward their mother. Why?

"Did you bring it to her last night?" Hunter performed a cursory check of the woman's body. No blood or any type of wounds. Emory's silent assessment was a definite possibility.

If this woman was murdered, it could very well have been from something in her drink.

"I brought her the Christmas tea around ten last night after she ordered me to." Phil gestured to the dresser on the other side of the room. "I made her a pot."

"Mom. Phil. You at breakfast?" Dick's loud question boomed from the hallway seconds before he stuck his head inside the entrance. His eyes widened at the group. "What's going on in here?"

"Didn't you hear me scream?" Phil poked his brother in the chest. "Our mother is dead."

Dick's eyes widened. "What? I was in the shower. What happened?" He inched forward.

Hunter moved in front of him. "Don't come any closer. Everyone, we need to step out of the room while I attempt to call 911."

"I need to see my mother." Dick took another step.

Hunter placed his hand on the man's chest. "Mr. Watson, I'm sorry for your loss, but I have to ask you to move into the hallway."

"Dick, someone killed our mother." Phil tugged at his brother's arm. "Do what the man says."

Dick yanked his arm away. "Don't tell me what to do, little brother."

"Gentlemen." Hunter raised his voice to get their attention. "Please. You're not helping matters."

"Well, I for one am starved. Isn't that why someone clanged the terrible cowbell?" Dick stomped from the room with Phil following close behind.

Hunter guessed the two clashed constantly, but would either kill his own mother?

"What are you thinking?" Emory's question pulled him back into the room.

"Same as you." Hunter nudged her into the hall. "That it's quite possible someone poisoned the woman," he whispered. "Did you smell that faint aroma?"

"Almonds. I've done lots of research, and that could definitely suggest cyanide poisoning."

"Possibly."

"What are you going to do?"

"What's all the commotion about?" Mike Reacher shuffled down the hallway, interrupting their conversation. "I heard a scream."

"Mrs. Watson has passed away, and her son found her." Hunter took his cell phone from his pocket and closed Rose Watson's door to prevent anyone from contaminating the scene. "Hopefully the 911 operator can get someone here."

"Not in this weather, they won't." Mike pointed over the railing to the large living room window. "Have you looked outside lately?"

"Mike's right, Hunter. We probably had more than two feet overnight, and it's still coming down hard. I need to update Autumn." Emory descended the stairs.

"Mike, you go get breakfast while I make this call."

The man nodded and followed Emory.

Miraculously, Hunter managed to get through to 911 and explain the situation. "Can you send emergency services here and the ME?" As soon as help was on its way, he'd question them about the escaped convict, get more information.

"Unfortunately, most are out on calls. It's stormageddon out there and supposed to get worse. You need—"

The call dropped.

Great. So much for getting more information on the convict. Hunter would have to investigate the guests himself, both to discover if anyone was a threat and to determine if Rose Watson actually had been murdered. Some vacation. He stuffed his phone into his pocket and made his way to the kitchen where the guests had gathered.

Autumn announced that Emory was the Christmas tree judge, and she had picked a winner.

The chit-chattering ceased with only faint Christmas music playing in the background.

Emory stood. "You all did a great job, but only one can win." She lifted a tiny, grinch-like tree from the island. "The winner is...Ava!"

The little girl squealed and snatched the plant from Emory's hands. "Eli, let's go put it in the living room for now." The kids scrambled out of the room.

Which gave Hunter the perfect segue. He positioned himself at the table, raising his hands. "Folks, sorry for interrupting your breakfast, but I need to inform you of a situation. You're probably aware that Rose Watson has passed away."

The group mumbled among themselves.

"What are we going to do about it?" Dick's question boomed over the chattering.

"Unfortunately, the roads are impassable, and we're cut off from the outside world. My 911 call even dropped. For now, I must ask everyone to stay out of Mrs. Watson's room. It's very important."

"But I need to get my mother's papers," Dick said. "We have an important deal we need to finalize today."

Daniel's jaw dropped. "Really? You're worried about your deal? Your mother is dead."

Dick dropped his knife and shoved his finger in Daniel's face. "That's none of your business."

"Enough, guys." Hunter sat beside Emory. "We can't do anything right now, so let's finish our breakfast."

"Someone needs to arrest the person who murdered my mother." Phil's statement lingered in the air.

Ruby Marple's hand stopped midway to her mouth. She put her fork down. "Wait, someone murdered her?"

"We won't know for sure without an autopsy." Hunter added eggs, bacon, and a croissant to his plate.

"She was in perfect health." Dick turned to Ruby. "So, yes, someone sitting here at this table murdered my mother. That's the only answer."

The group once again murmured among themselves, clearly confused.

Emory raised a brow and leaned closer to him. "Looks like you need to interview everyone, Sherlock."

"Only if you'll be my Watson."

"I thought you'd never ask." She winked, a smile exploding on her gorgeous face.

Great. How would he be able to concentrate and solve a case with this beautiful woman at his side?

~ FIVE ~

December 23rd 10:15 a.m.

Emory followed Hunter into Rose Watson's room, gingerly stepping in his tracks. "Are you sure we should come in here?" The faint scent of almonds wafted, and her gaze flew to the teapot on the dresser. "I still think someone laced her tea with poison."

"That's a definite possibility, yes, although it's important to keep an open mind. That's why I want to inspect her room to rule out any other options."

"Like what?"

"Any type of medication she may be taking." He pointed to the woman's suitcase. "Perhaps she didn't tell her sons everything."

"Why didn't Rose smell the almond odor in her tea?"

"Not everyone can, but if she did, she probably thought it was an ingredient in the Christmas tea."

"Makes sense." Emory placed her hands on her hips. "Okay, where do we start?"

"With her luggage." He passed Emory a pair of latex gloves. "Put these on. I'll check the closet."

Emory obeyed and squatted in front of the large, tapestry suitcase. "Wow, she brought three bags. Why so much?"

"One for each day?" Hunter pointed to Rose. "Look how she's dressed. I'm guessing she has nothing but the best in clothes and jewelry."

"I've heard about the Watson family. From what I understand, they're business sharks and can be ruthless." Emory glanced over her shoulder. "Speaking of her clothes, she's not wearing the pearls she had on last night. Do you think whoever laced the tea also stole them?"

Hunter pulled out his cell phone. "Good observation, Watson. I'll add that to my list of questions."

Emory chuckled and unzipped the suitcase. "Tell me, you dating anyone?" Wait—did she just ask that? Out loud?

"Nope. You?"

"Don't have time for a love life." Not true, but how could she voice what she was really thinking? That no one could ever compare to him.

She cleared her throat, shoving past regrets deeper into the recesses of her mind. Right now, she had to concentrate on the mystery before her. Not the man in question.

Emory rummaged through the woman's bag. "I hate snooping through someone's stuff. It feels wrong."

"I understand. We need answers, though. My gut is telling me someone in this house murdered her."

"And your cop gut is never wrong. Or at least, it never used to be." Emory lifted out a white cashmere sweater. "Yup, Rose Watson sure had the best of the best. This sweater probably cost hundreds."

Laughter filtered up through the staircase.

"I hate missing the gingerbread contest." Emory placed the sweater back into the suitcase.

"Because you wanted to win? I remember your competitive nature."

She resisted the urge to throw something at him. "Funny."

His expression softened. "I know, but we have to get to the bottom of this."

"I'm glad Autumn and Joel agreed to keep their Christmas agenda in play. They really need this." How much should she share? "Has Joel told you about their situation?"

"Yes. He explained that they're in the red and need this event to help get them on their way to recover what they put into their renos." Hunter closed the closet door. "There's nothing in there. She hadn't even unpacked yet." He picked up Rose's makeup bag and placed it on the bed. After unzipping it, he rooted through the contents.

"I'm guessing she also had highly priced makeup."

"Probably. What's this?" Hunter raised a medication bottle. "Alprazolam. Seems Mrs. Watson had anxiety."

"Many people are on that medication. That doesn't tell us anything." Emory shut the large suitcase, and opened the medium-sized one. "High-stake business deals can bring on lots of stress. I follow her on social media, and—"

"Wait, why would you do that?"

"Research. She's a great example to base a character on. Some of her posts about Phil and Dick are condescending." She observed the woman slumped in the chair. "Sad to say, she wasn't a nice person."

"Look at you, Nancy Drew, checking out the players."

"What can I say? Sleuthing is part—"

The door opened, and Phil entered. "What are you two doing in here?"

Hunter pivoted. "We're simply investigating. What about *you*? We told you not to enter."

Phil gestured toward the laptop bag sitting on the floor beside his mother's body. "Dick sent me to get Mom's computer."

Dick—the bossy older Watson.

"You can't take anything from the room." Hunter held up the medication bottle. "Tell me why your mother was taking alprazolam."

The man stumbled backward. "What? I didn't know."

Seemed Rose Watson kept her own secrets. Could they have gotten her killed?

A question about the Watsons' pending business deal rose in Emory's mind. "Tell me, Phil. Why was your mother blocking this merger you're working on?"

Hunter's jaw dropped.

"Ho-how ddddid yuuou knnnow thhat?" Phil's sudden stuttering revealed her question had taken him off his game.

"I read an article on the net a few days ago. She had done an interview."

"N-noo co-co-comment."

Phil reached for the laptop bag, but Hunter stopped him. "That's evidence."

The man huffed and waltzed out of the room, leaving the pungent scent of his cologne behind.

"That sure rattled him." Hunter opened the dresser drawers, rummaging through them. "Any other tidbit you'd like to share about our guests?"

"The Drews are going bankrupt. I heard them arguing earlier about their finances. Ruby Marple told me earlier she's fighting for custody for Eli from his drunken father. Such a sad situation. Let's see. What else?" She tapped her index finger on her chin. "Oh, Daniel is a tech guru. I observed him on his cell phone before we lost the Wi-Fi. His fingers flew across his screen, which gave him away. That's all I've got. If I were able to get online, I could get more information."

Hunter whistled. "You always were good at finding things out."

"I call it research, as you never know what part of their stories will end up in my book."

He raised a brow. "Be careful. I don't want you on the police's radar for researching something you shouldn't."

"I'm pretty sure your colleagues have better things to do than to check an author's search history."

"True." He closed the last drawer. "Empty." He lifted the teapot lid and leaned closer. "Almonds. Which makes cyanide poisoning a strong possibility, although not in the gas form." He turned. "*If* that's what happened, someone must have added it to the pot, and it had to have been a high dosage to cause death. Which rules out accidental poisoning. You know what that means, right?"

"Yup. The killer is in the house."

Hunter's cornflower-blue eyes narrowed. "Exactly. Which would put us all in danger."

An icy shudder crawled across Emory's skin, sending her pulse jack hammering.

They had to solve this mystery before another person was poisoned.

Hunter puffed out a ragged breath later that afternoon after Autumn had crowned the gingerbread house winner and Hunter had interviewed the guests to determine what he could ascertain from them. One thing became apparent.

Each acted suspiciously and held secrets.

He slammed his notebook on the dining room table. "I need a break. I'm tired of people lying to me."

Emory closed her laptop. "How about a walk in the snow? I remember how you used to love that."

Hunter had requested Emory join him as he spoke to the guests. He trusted her judgment. She had studied body language extensively for her books, so he figured she'd pick up on things he may miss. Two heads were better than one—or so they said.

He rose to his feet. "Good idea. A change of scenery is exactly what I need to clear my mind." And a walk with a beautiful redhead was the icing on the proverbial cake. "It will also give me a chance to check the weather."

Five minutes later, after bundling up for Alberta's relentless colossal storm, Hunter and Emory went outside. Heavy snow still pummeled the region, but the wind had subsided—for now.

Emory nestled her scarf closer to her neck. "It's colder out than I thought. Where do you want to go?"

He gestured toward the red barn. "How about the stables? I'd like to—"

"Race ya!" Emory trudged through the deep snow, swinging her arms.

"Oh no you don't." He scooped a pile of snow and formed a ball, then chucked it at her.

Splat!

The snowball hit her square on her back. She stopped and pivoted. "Hey!"

"That's what you get for sneaking a head start in this impromptu race."

Emory bent over and made a snowball. "Two can play at this game." She threw it at him.

The icy ball hit him in the face, and he fell into the snow, faking injury. He played dead, waiting for her to come to his rescue. He liked the fact that she had dropped her frosty guard. Hopefully, her walls stayed down.

"Hunter!" She plopped beside him. "You okay? I'm so sorry."

He turned over and hauled her to the ground. "Gotcha!"

She landed on top of him and slapped his chest. "Why, you little sneak. Some things never change."

"Nope, and you fell for it again."

She hopped to her feet and brushed the snow from her jeans. "You're such a little boy."

He rose. "But a cute little boy. Don't you think?"

"No comment." She plodded through the snow.

Hunter followed, sensing it was time to change the subject. That wall had formed again. "Give me your initial thoughts from our interviews."

"They all are acting shady, if you ask me. Not sure if it's connected to the case or holiday stress. This time of year can be hard on people."

He understood. This was his first Christmas without his mom. "You mean like you?"

She stopped just shy of the barn doors and turned. "You know how I hate Christmas."

"I do, but I don't really understand why. Because your dad made you watch *Christmas Vacation* every year?"

"Partly. But it's more because it brings out the worst in everyone. All the parties, rushing to get the best presents before they're gone, spending way too much, that sort of thing."

Hunter slid open the barn door and gestured for her to enter. "It also brings out the best in people."

Luna and Nanook bounded around the corner.

"Really? It didn't in my family." Emory bent to pet the malamutes. "Hey there. You're both so cute."

They barked as if agreeing.

"Is that why you avoid them this time of year? Joel said you always have an excuse why you don't come home for Christmas."

Emory huffed out a breath. "Too much on the go with my books."

"Your sister needs you, Em."

Her eyes flashed, and she poked him in the chest. "Don't tell me what to do, Hunter."

He took her hand. "I'm sorry. I only want you to make amends."

"Why do you care so much?"

"For one thing. I'm now alone. You know Dad died years ago, and with Mom's death last Christmas Eve, this one will be tough for me." Alone. The one thing he feared the most in this world. It was why he tried to stay connected with friends. Being an only child meant he had spent most of his life by himself.

She grazed his arm. "You're right. I'm so sorry. And the other reason?"

Hunter gazed into her eyes. "Haven't you figured that out yet? I realize it's been a while since we've seen each other, but Em, I still care."

And I want you back in my life.

He didn't miss her long, audible breath intake before she shifted away from his presence and approached the first stall.

Averting the conversation...again. *Figures.* Avoidance was always her way.

Hunter followed. "That's the newest addition to the family. Em, meet Stardust. Isn't she a beaut?" He opened the gate. "Go in. She loves people."

"Hey, Stardust. I'm Em. Nice to meet you." Emory took off her glove and rubbed her hand along the horse's neck, down her back.

Stardust lifted her nuzzle and whinnied.

Hunter chuckled. "She likes you."

"Of course, what's not to like?" A smirk frolicked on her lips.

His pulse elevated.

Her smile had always been his kryptonite, turning him to mush. *Let her go*. Words his mother had engrained into him after Emory walked away. Even so, Hunter had a hard time doing that. She had branded Hunter's heart, and he'd love her until the day he died.

Emory turned from her position beside Stardust. "We should ask Bucky to hitch up the sleigh." Her eyes sparkled despite her earlier agitation.

"That's probably somewhere on Autumn's list."

"No doubt." She checked her watch. "I should try to get some writing in before supper." She pointed at him. "And you have a case to solve."

"Wait, don't you mean *we* have a case to solve?"

"Good point." Emory stuffed her gloves back on. "Break is over then." She ruffled the dogs' fur. "Bye, guys."

Hunter closed Stardust's stall door and followed Emory out of the barn.

A gust of wind assaulted him, stealing his breath as snowflakes hammered the region. Would they be able to go on that sleigh ride?

Hunter pondered his question as he stomped up the steps, silently willing the storm to subside so he could talk Bucky into letting Hunter have a private sleigh ride with his favorite mystery writer.

However, as soon as they entered the foyer, Autumn crashed around the corner, eyes wide. "They're gone!"

Emory tugged off her gloves and coat, tossing them on to the deacon's bench. "What are you talking about? What's gone?"

"The kids' presents I put under the tree this morning."

Hunter's jaw dropped.

Not only did he have a killer to catch, but now a thief, too?

What type of Christmas ranch experience was this, anyway? One thing he knew for sure...

Time to gather the guests and be a constable rather than a visitor.

~ Six ~

December 23rd 4:15 p.m.

Emory sat on the couch beside her sister, who struggled to keep her tears at bay. Who could blame her? Autumn had carefully picked out the gifts to surprise the kids in attendance, and now all was lost. Emory had searched the ranch house with Autumn, but they'd come up empty.

Hunter had gathered all the guests, informing them he had important matters to discuss and their presence in the living room was mandatory. He stood in front of the fireplace.

The guests mumbled, clearly annoyed at their festivities being interrupted.

Hunter clapped. "Everyone, listen up."

The group silenced.

"Tell us what's going on." Cal's voice personified irritation.

Hunter's gaze traveled over the guests one by one before continuing. "As you're aware, Mrs. Watson is deceased, and now we—"

Dick Watson shot to his feet. "Which of you poisoned our precious mother?"

Precious? Emory suppressed the question. The last time he'd spoken about his mother, his words didn't include precious. In fact, he'd been downright hostile toward her. What had changed his perspective? Suspicion niggled at the back of Emory's mind.

"Dick. Sit. Down." Hunter's command stopped any further chatter. "We never said anything about her being poisoned."

The man obeyed.

Phil leaned forward. "Wait, I made her tea. Do you think someone could have slipped something into the teapot after I left her room?"

Simultaneous gasps filled the room, followed by mumblings from each guest.

Hunter raised his hands. "Let's not jump to conclusions. That's not why we gathered you here. We've discovered someone stole presents from under this tree." He pointed to the rustic-decorated Christmas tree in front of the bay window.

"They were for the kids." Autumn's statement squeaked from her mouth.

Gil Drew's eyes narrowed. "Who would do such a thing?"

"You all care about stupid presents when my mother has been murdered?" This time, the younger brother exploded to his feet. "Unbelievable."

"Shut up, brother." Dick hauled him back down. "*Constable*, what do you plan to do about all this criminal activity?"

The man laced the word constable with sarcasm.

"First of all, other than the suspected theft, there is no proof yet that a crime has taken place. The investigation has just begun. That's why I brought you here together. I need to do a thorough search of the property, including your rooms."

Wilson Spade flung out an arm, knocking over his hot chocolate. "You can't do that. You'd need a warrant."

"I was hoping that, in the spirit of Christmas and in honor of Rose Watson, you'd all comply with my request."

Ava raised her hand. "Sir?"

Hunter smiled, his forceful demeanor shifting to one of compassion. "Yes, Ava?"

"You can look in my stuff. I don't steal. It's wrong." She turned to her mother. "Right, Mama?"

Josee patted her daughter's hand. "That's right."

"I don't want him in our room though." Gil scowled.

"But Papa, they have to find the presents." Little Ava's bottom lip protruded, her eyes glistening.

Gil cupped her chin in his hand. "How can I resist that face?" He turned to Hunter. "Constable, you can search our room. The Drews have nothing to hide." He grabbed Josee's hand. "Right, dear?"

She bit her lip and yanked free from his hold. "Of course."

Even though the woman agreed, her body language told a different story. Emory supported Hunter's earlier assessment of the guests. The ranch was full of people holding secrets. Or was it only the stress of the Christmas season?

Emory surveyed them. Each sat with their arms folded, scowling. None wanted their rooms searched.

"Friends, the sooner you let me do the search, the sooner we can get back to Autumn's activity list. You can each be present." Hunter paused. "Or, we can wait for a warrant, and with this storm, who knows when that would be. We'll have to cancel Christmas."

Eli and Ava both jumped to their feet. "No!"

Emory doubted Hunter would really carry out that threat.

Joel rose. "Please." He gestured toward Hunter. "Let my friend do his job."

Josee stood. "Fine. I have to clean up some things first. I left our room a mess."

"Me too." Cal headed for the door.

The others scattered from the room like bees from a disturbed colony. Only the kids, Joel, Autumn, and Emory remained.

Autumn reached for the children's hands. "How about you two help me set the table for supper? Then later, we'll get ready for tomorrow's Christmas cookie baking event. Bucky's children will join us. Do you like Liam and Lacy?"

"Yes," they yelled, skipping from the room.

Over her shoulder, Autumn caught Emory's gaze. "You wanna help?"

"Maybe tomorrow with the cookie event. Right now, I'll assist Hunter with searching the rooms, and then I need to write."

Autumn's shoulders slumped, disappointment washing over her pretty face. "Fine. See you at supper." She marched from the room.

You did it again, Emory. Way to add another brick to their sister-feud wall.

"I appreciate you helping solve these cases, Hunter," Joel said. "I can't believe this is happening. Autumn is putting on a brave face, but she's petrified of losing the ranch if this event fails."

Hunter squeezed his friend's shoulder. "I will do everything in my power to figure all this out as quickly as possible."

"Why haven't you told the guests there's a convict among them?" Joel asked.

"I don't want to scare the others or let the felon know we're on to him."

Emory tapped her chin with her index finger. "It may not be a bad idea, Hunter. You know, study their faces while you tell them. See if any flinch."

"She's right. It might help flush them out." Joel walked to the entrance.

"I don't want to put anyone in danger." Hunter pinched the bridge of his nose. "I'll think about it. Weigh out the pros and cons. For now, let's search their rooms."

Emory trusted his constable mind. But when and how would this Christmas caper end?

Hunter raked his fingers through his wavy hair, frustration setting in. He had searched most of the rooms with Joel and Emory's help. So far, nothing had materialized. Sure, each guest's antsy demeanor cast suspicions, although they'd found no poison or the missing presents.

He pondered Joel and Emory's idea of telling the group a convict lurked among them, but something held him back. Right now, the cons dwarfed the pros, as far as he was concerned. *God, show me what You want me to do.*

Come home.

Hunter stiffened. Where had those simple but complex two words come from? The only home he had was the one he grew up in, and he hated it there without his mother and father. They were both in a better place, although that didn't ease his anxiety. He'd moved in with his mother when her cancer had progressed last December. She had insisted on him moving her bed into the living room so she could enjoy the tree lights each night. Her death on Christmas Eve had rocked his world and put his faith on hold. How could God take her at her most favorite time of year?

However, in her eyes, it was perfect timing. God knew she wanted to spend Christmas with Him and her husband. Still, that hadn't made it easy for Hunter. He had plopped in front of the fireplace on Christmas Day, staring at his family's ornaments, wishing they were there with him, and hating being alone. Emory had broken up with him two months before the season, which had added to his plummet into a pit of despair.

Every day since his mother's death, Hunter had kept himself busy, not wanting to face another night alone in the quiet house. All his life he'd longed for a brother or sister to play with but had to settle for the next-door neighbors' kids. Now that his parents were gone, the desire for connection and family had intensified a hundredfold.

Tonight, Christmas had returned to the group as Autumn led them in an old-fashioned carol sing. Her plan had been to take them through a nearby neighborhood to do the caroling, but the storm squashed that idea. Still, the group made the most of it. They'd ended the evening watching Christmas movies and sipping candy-cane-flavored hot chocolate topped with whipped cream, marshmallows, and sprinkles. She announced they'd bake cookies in the morning for Santa and then have a tree-lighting ceremony in the backyard. Snowstorm or no snowstorm, the event would be at eight o'clock. Sharp. After all, it was Christmas Eve, and they had to get everything ready for Santa.

Even though it was now ten pm, Hunter sat in the dining room and clicked on his cell phone. He wanted to re-check his notes on the guests so he could solve this case. He wouldn't let it spoil Christmas.

I'm not so sure I'd call it spoiled. Being storm-stayed with Emory Burke wasn't a bad thing. At least in Hunter's eyes. Plus, it meant he wouldn't be alone for the one-year anniversary of his mother's death.

"Hunter, I found something." Emory plunked a journal on the table in front of him. "This is interesting."

Emory had searched Cal's room after the caroling. "Cal tucked it under his mattress. He left to take a shower while I finished up my search, so he's not aware that I found it."

"What's inside?"

She sat down and opened the journal, flipping several pages before tapping an entry. "Here. A list of all the guests and information about each."

Hunter scanned the pages filled with details on everyone, including information Cal had obviously found on the internet. "Why would he gather and document his findings?"

"Exactly my question. Also, why would he hide it?" She drummed her fingers on the table. "This screams pre-meditated deceit."

"I guessed something was off about the man." Not that Hunter would admit the real reason—his jealousy toward Cal over his obvious attraction to Emory. He closed the journal. "I guess it's time to—"

"What's the meaning of this?" Cal stormed into the room, pointing at his journal. "I gave you permission to search my room, but that's personal property. You have no right to read it." He snatched it off the table.

Hunter stood, moving into Cal's personal space. "Why hide it and, more importantly, why are you collecting data on each guest?"

"It's not what you think. I'm not a killer. Or a thief."

"Answer Hunter's question." Emory also stood and poked the man in the arm. "You're hiding something. What is it?"

"Okay, okay." Cal glanced at the entrance and then back to them, leaning closer. "I'm an undercover reporter here for a scoop on this place."

Emory's jaw dropped. "What? What story could there possibly be on my sister and Joel?"

"Not them. Their ranch hand, Bucky."

Hunter's muscles tensed. "What about Bucky? I know for a fact Joel vetted him."

"Well, my source claims someone is posing as a ranch hand around this area before stealing from the owners."

"What makes you think it's Bucky, and why write information on the others?" Emory asked.

"Because this conman has a helper who goes to these events to case out the joint." He dropped into a chair. "He or she warms up to the other guests and the owners on a pretense of being friendly. Then scopes out the ranch. This Christmas event is the perfect choice, so my boss sent me here undercover."

Not only did Hunter have a convict and a murderer to contend with but now a con man too? Or a con woman? Could the con artist and the convict be one and the same?

Emory shook her head. "I'm pretty sure Bucky Fletcher is on the up and up. I trust Joel and Autumn's judgment. You're reaching, Cal." Emory yawned. "It's late. Let's—"

Footfalls thudded down the steps, interrupting her.

Dick bounded into the room. "She's gone!"

"Who's gone?" Hunter asked.

"Mom."

What? Someone had taken Rose Watson's body? How?

And, more importantly, why?

A vise clamped Emory's heart, strangling her chest. She willed the rapid rhythm to slow as she followed Hunter and Dick to Rose's room. Phil sat on the edge of the bed, head buried in his hands.

Hunter entered. "What happened?"

Phil pointed to the empty chair. "Someone stole our mother. Why would they do that?"

"Good question." Hunter walked around the chair.

Emory surveyed the overturned suitcases. "Has anything else been stolen, guys? Looks like someone rummaged through those."

The brothers exchanged a glance before Dick addressed her. "Didn't you do that?"

Emory shook her head. "We searched her suitcases but left them neat. This mess was made by someone else. Did your mother bring valuables?"

"Wait." Phil picked up Rose's makeup bag and unzipped the side pocket, inserting his fingers into the opening. "It's gone! She normally kept her valuables here."

"What valuables?" Hunter asked.

"I saw her pack pearls, a ruby ring, and an emerald necklace she planned to wear on Christmas Day." Phil threw the bag on the bed. "They're all gone."

"So, not only is the thief taking presents, but now jewelry." Emory peeked into the dark backyard. A single light from the barn illuminated the area. "My question is, where would they take Rose? The roads are closed, and there's nowhere to run. Doesn't make sense."

"What's going on here?" Autumn appeared in the entranceway, rubbing her eyes.

Joel approached with Daniel, Cal, and Gil behind him.

Hunter raised his hands in a stop position. "Did any of you see or hear anyone in this room earlier?"

"I heard footsteps around 9:30," Daniel said. "I was reading, but I assumed it was just Phil or Dick. Why?"

"Someone took Mama." Phil's voice hitched.

"And stole her jewelry," Dick added. "Was it you, Autumn? I heard you say the ranch was in trouble. Mom's valuables would bring in lots of money."

Joel stepped into Dick's personal space and poked his chest. "How dare you accuse my wife. Next, you're gonna say she killed your mother and stole her body? If the roads were passable, I'd kick you off my property. You disgust me."

"Maybe it was the escaped convict in the region," Daniel said.

Hunter's expression clouded, his lips flattening into a tight line. The cat was definitely out of the bag now, whether or not Hunter wanted it to be.

"Daniel, where did you learn that info?" Emory had to step in, as Hunter had frozen on the spot.

"Read a news alert about it right before the Wi-Fi went out. Was it a secret?" His gaze shifted to Hunter's. "Wait, you suspect the convict is here among us, don't you?"

"What?" Cal's eyes widened. "If that's true, we're all in danger. The convict is the killer, and we're next."

Hunter raised his hand, clearly snapping out of his trance. "Let's not jump to conclusions. Everyone, go to bed. And lock your doors."

"I have to protect Ava," Gil said.

What about Josee? Not her too? Doubts filled Emory's thoughts, and an image popped into her mind.

Josee had recoiled against Gil's touch earlier. Was there more going on in their marriage than their happy-white-picket-fence relationship conveyed?

"Again, we're not sure the convict is here, but that's why I want everyone to lock their doors." Hunter corralled them through the entrance. "Now go."

Joel glanced over his shoulder on the way out. "Hunter, please solve this case. Tomorrow is Christmas Eve, and we want nothing but peace."

"I get it." Hunter gestured toward the darkness outside. "We're not gonna solve anything tonight or find Rose. We'll scour the grounds first thing in the morning."

"Let's pray nothing else happens between now and then." Joel and Autumn floundered down the hallway arm-in-arm, leaving Emory alone with Hunter.

"This case is getting more confusing by the minute." Emory reached for a stray lipstick, but snapped her hand back. She couldn't add her fingerprints.

Hunter unclipped his cell phone. "And the tower is still out. Ugh! I wanted to see that picture." His gaze traveled around the room. "We're not gonna find anything else here tonight. I'm tired, so I'm heading to bed. You?"

"I have to write before then. Haven't reached today's word count."

"Still pursuing your *NY Times* bestseller dream?"

Emory flinched. She had secretly shared her dream of hitting the infamous list and how she'd struggled with imposter syndrome. Her writing friends continually won contests, and while she'd reached her *USA Today* bestseller goal, the sales of some of her books had tanked. Had her readers finally figured out she was a terrible writer?

Hunter had challenged her, stating her writing was a gift from God and to always use it for His glory, not hers. While she believed that, lately she'd lost her motivation to do so. Plus, her muse had dried up.

"Not all my books have done well, so my publisher is pushing for a bestseller."

"And you're struggling with your story."

"You always were good at reading my mind. However, an idea has been percolating, and I need to get writing, so I'll say good night now."

After their snowball fight earlier, and all the happenings at the ranch, her storyline had blossomed. A Christmas Caper. She'd even set it at a ranch like the Double H.

She eyed Hunter.

And she had the perfect hero for her story.

~ SEVEN ~

December 24th 6:00 a.m.

Hunter yawned as he meandered into the dimly lit kitchen, beelining directly to the coffeepot. The aroma had enticed him from his sleep, although he welcomed the interruption. He had been trapped inside a dream of he and Emory getting married. A dream that had once been real, until his stupid mistake of having lunch with a co-worker without telling her had shattered everything. Even though his innocent act of wanting to help a friend had been misconstrued by Emory, he felt responsible for their break-up. He should have been more careful. He'd carried that guilt for fourteen months now, and the heavy load weighed upon him.

After Emory had left to write, he had gone to his room to make notes on all of the guests—and to pray.

Something he hadn't done much of lately. He and God had lots to catch up on, and Hunter finally fell asleep at two in the morning. Four short hours ago.

"You not sleep well?"

Hunter jumped at Joel's question. "Man, you scared me. I didn't see you. Some constable I am." He added cream to his coffee. "Why are you sitting in the dark, bro?"

"The dark is where I do my best thinking." Joel sipped his coffee. "It's where I find the light for my day."

Hmm. Odd statement. Hunter pulled out a chair and sat. "Tell me more. Do you sit in the darkness every morning?"

"Yup. For thirty minutes before Autumn gets up. I make coffee and sit here to pray. God and I have done lots of talking. Sometimes we fight. Sometimes we cry."

"I've wrestled with God ever since Mom died."

Joel blew out a breath. "Death is hard. Still, knowing we'll see our loved ones again if they're believers brings comfort."

"I've been struggling with why God doesn't intervene. Why did He allow the love of my life to walk away? Why take my mom at age 69 when she had so much more life to live?"

Joel squeezed Hunter's shoulder. "I know the past year and a half have been tough for you. God is in control, though. He just wants you to come home."

Hunter paused at his friend's words and took another sip. "I'm trying. Problem is, my path keeps shifting. How can I find the right one?"

"Prayer and faith are the only answers I can give you."

"How can you say that with your most recent loss?" Hunter had kept the Hardys' secret—even from Emory. At Joel's request. Not that it was hard, since Hunter and Emory hadn't seen each other until two days ago. Even so, he hated to see the sisters at odds. They needed each other. He knew for a fact they had been best friends—until Emory broke up with Hunter. Did that have something to do with the sister feud?

The tapping of bare feet sounded in the hallway.

Joel stood. "That's Autumn. Time to help with breakfast and then search for Rose."

"Hopefully the weather will give us a break." Hunter drank the coffee, pondering his friend's words.

Prayer and faith.

Could those be the keys to coming home?

Forty minutes later Hunter added two fried eggs to his plate. "Emory, please pass the hash browns."

She handed the dish over and leaned in. "You okay?"

"Didn't sleep much. Lots going through my mind." He scooped a spoonful of potatoes from a bowl and placed them beside his eggs. "You get lots of writing done?"

"A good start. Finally." She bit into a pumpkin muffin.

Now wasn't the time to talk about his burdens. He had to solve this case before he could put the past behind him. Exactly what his mother would probably tell him to do. In the end, she had been his best friend and confidant.

"Constable, why didn't you tell us there's a convict among us?" Josee asked.

"Mama, what's a convict?" Ava stuffed a fork loaded with eggs into her mouth.

Hunter winced. "Not the time for this discussion."

"I agree." Ruby Marple dished food onto her grandson Eli's plate. "We have little ones among us."

The back door slammed shut. Seconds later, little feet pitter-pattered down the hardwood. A boy and girl skipped into the room.

"Is it time to bake cookies?" Liam ran to Autumn's side. "Mrs. Hardy, is it?"

Bucky entered the room. "Sorry for the interruption, folks. My children are excited. Can you tell?" He tucked one arm around the boy, the other around the girl. "Liam and Lacy, they're eating."

Joel raised to his feet. "Bucky, have some breakfast. There's lots."

"Can we, Papa?" Lacy bounced. "Pretty please?"

"You mean your Fruit Loops weren't enough?"

"That was our first breakfast," Liam said.

Bucky chuckled. "Okay, Mr. Hobbit."

"Have a seat, kids." Autumn rushed to the counter and brought back plates. "Here you go. We need energy to bake all of Santa's cookies."

"Yippee."

Hunter caught Emory's expression.

She'd been staring at her sister, her eyes watering.

Was God softening her heart toward Autumn? Could it be Autumn's gentle manner with Bucky's kids?

"Hey, where's Cal?" Wilson's question broke through Hunter's thoughts.

"Perhaps he's sleeping in?" It was hard not to miss the over-powering GQ reporter, although Hunter assumed the man had chosen to eat later.

"He told me last night he wanted to help search and planned to be up early." Wilson poured cream into his coffee. "I checked his room on my way down. Doesn't even look like he slept in his bed."

"Maybe the convict got him too," Phil said.

Dick slammed his hand on the table, the utensils clattering. "Brother, stop." He turned to Hunter. "What are you going to do to find this criminal before we all end up dead?"

The children whimpered at the man's brass voice.

Hunter stood, eying Emory. "Autumn, can you and Emory take the children into the kitchen and start your cookie baking?"

Emory wiped her mouth with the napkin. "Good idea. We can do that."

Hunter gestured to the men. "Let's go." A thought raced through his mind.

How convenient, GQ man going missing shortly after someone stole Rose's body. Was he responsible and trying to hide evidence?

Hmm...Hunter shrugged off the question and nabbed his coat.

Time to catch this convict and protect the Double H Ranch's guests.

Emory turned up the volume, and "Here Comes Santa Claus" blared in the kitchen. She had longed to be out with Hunter searching the property, but he was right in what he didn't say. She had read the unspoken message in his eyes. Autumn needed her right now, and this was where Emory had to stay. Plus, the two sisters had enjoyed baking with their mother every Christmas Eve morning. Emory loved that Autumn had included the tradition on her agenda.

"This is my favorite song!" Eli did a jig around the kitchen's island, the other children following.

Autumn giggled before holding her spatula in the air. "Okay, kids. Time to get baking. Santa needs his cookies. You all have your directions. Get to it."

They skidded to a stop and went to their assigned spots, prepared to commence their duties.

Two hours later, four dozen cookies covered the countertop, ready for icing. The kids had cut out trees, Santas, gingerbread people, stars, stockings, and candy canes.

"Let's decorate Santa's cookies." Autumn raised her icing tool. "Watch me first and then you design yours. Ready?"

"Yes," they yelled in unison.

Autumn gave them expert instructions on how to hold the decorating bag and apply the right amount of icing onto the cookie. Soon, her Christmas tree took shape. She finished by adding sprinkles on top. "There, done. Now it's your turn."

Emory studied her sister before helping each of the four children hold their bags so they could carefully squeeze icing onto their cookies. It brought memories back of their mother doing the same with them. An icing fight would complete the occasion.

Emory would wait until the kids finished decorating their cookies, though, as she knew how meticulous her sister was in the kitchen. Nothing out of place.

Over the next hour, Emory added notes into her app on her cell phone as ideas sparked from the cookie fun. She took lots of pictures to help give her visuals for the inspiration of the hero and heroine in her story's cookie-decorating fight.

After the kids finished, Emory scooped a finger full of icing and held it behind her back. "Autumn, there's something missing from our cookie-baking event."

The side door opened. Seconds later, Joel and Hunter appeared.

Autumn pursed her lips. "What? I've thought of everything."

"This." Emory plopped the icing onto her sister's nose.

"Why you little..." Autumn took a spoonful of icing, and flung it at Emory.

The children giggled.

Hunter and Joel chuckled.

The kids threw blobs of icing at each other.

Hunter and Joel joined in on the fun, each dipping their fingers into the icing and painting Emory's and Autumn's faces.

Emory scooped a dollop of icing and plopped it on Hunter's stubbled chin. "Take that, mister."

"You'll pay for that." He grasped her around the waist and tickled her.

In her weakest tickle spot. He remembered.

She squealed and ran around the island, attempting to get away from him. Hunter was too quick. He nabbed her again and tickled more.

"Stop. Uncle! I give in." Emory panted for breath.

"That's what you get, sis, for starting the icing fight." Her sister raised her hands. "Kids, fun's over. Time to clean up this mess." She glared at Emory, then winked.

"It had to be done, Sissy. It's tradition." Emory turned to Hunter. "We did the same as kids."

"I remember you telling me." Hunter snatched a dish towel hanging on the oven door and wiped his chin. "Wow, you got me good."

She tilted her head, placing her hands on her hips. "I'm an expert and won every fight."

"She did too." Autumn scraped icing from the counter into the garbage can. "Mom called her the Icing Queen."

Emory bit her lip. "I miss those days."

Her sister's face softened. "Me too."

"Emory, can I talk to you for a sec?" Hunter asked.

"Sure." She washed and wiped her hands.

Hunter guided her into the hallway.

"Did you find Rose?"

"Not yet, but Josee reported that the presents she brought for Ava and the kids have been stolen too. I didn't want to say it in there and disappoint them."

Emory latched onto his arm. "We have to find them. Tomorrow is Christmas day!"

"I know. Santa has his work cut out for him." Hunter gazed at her face and chuckled.

"What?"

"You have icing on your bottom lip." He wiped it off with his thumb, keeping his eyes focused on her mouth.

She drew in a sharp breath as memories of his lips on hers flooded her mind. Truth be told, she had loved his gentle kisses and missed them.

"Em, I..." He inched forward.

What would it be like to kiss him again?

He wrapped his arm around her waist and drew her closer. "I've missed you."

Emory held her ground. *Yes, you want him to kiss you. Let him. What's the harm? After all, it's Christmas and there's mistletoe in here somewhere. That counts, right?* She tilted her chin, silently giving him the okay.

His lips grazed hers as a shock of electricity sparked throughout her body.

I've missed you too.

Pounding footsteps sounded behind them, breaking the moment. "Hunter!"

She pulled back and sighed, clamping her lips into an impregnable seal. It was for the best, anyway. She couldn't fall for him again.

Joel skidded to a stop. "Sorry, didn't mean to intrude."

Hunter shoved his hands in his pockets. "What's up, Joel?"

"They found Rose. Come quick." Her brother-in-law darted out the front door.

Emory grabbed her coat from the hall hook. "I'm coming too." She didn't wait for a reply as she sprinted outside.

The icy wind bit her cheeks, but she didn't care. She had to wipe the feeling of Hunter's lips on hers out of her head. And suppress the disappointment of being interrupted.

What better way to do that than to solve a mystery on a stormy Christmas Eve Day?

~ EIGHT ~

December 24th 11:45 a.m.

Hunter followed Joel and Emory across the yard, stumbling through the deep snow. He banged his fist on his leg. *Stupid, Hunter. You shouldn't have tried to kiss her.* But he couldn't help himself. Being back in her presence proved one thing to him.

He still loved Emory Burke.

In fact, he'd never stopped loving her. The ring around his neck verified that. He hadn't been able to let her go.

Still, the look in her eyes after Joel interrupted them revealed regret. She didn't feel the same.

God, why are You stirring up these feelings again?

Joel beckoned him forward. "Hunter, this way."

Concentrate.

"This is our root cellar." Joel opened both wooden doors and descended into the darkness.

Emory and Hunter followed.

A musky dampness filled the enclosed space.

"I didn't know you had a root cellar." Hunter shivered. "It's definitely cold in here."

"Autumn keeps all her canned fruit and veggies in here. It also serves as a storm shelter in case of bad weather." Joel tugged on a string and light flooded the entrance. "Come."

They followed him down the crushed-stone hallway.

"How did you find her?" Emory asked.

Joel stopped in front of a door. "The cellar is linked to the shed by another entrance. Wilson and Daniel were inside the shed when Cal called out." He opened the door.

"What? You didn't mention you found him too." Hunter stepped into the dimly lit cellar and scanned the room. Multiple jars of veggies and fruit lined the shelves along the wall. Potatoes filled a wooden box to the right of a long table.

Where Rose Watson's body rested.

GQ man sat in a chair, holding his head.

"Cal, what happened?" Emory approached, squatting in front of him. "Are you okay?"

Hunter winced at her attention to the man. *Get a grip. Focus.* "How long have you been locked in here?"

"I'm not sure. Someone hit me over the head in the middle of the night. I had gotten up to get a glass of milk." He gestured toward Rose. "That's the last thing I remember before waking up here, next to her."

A bloody trophy lay discarded on the floor next to Cal's chair.

"I'm guessing that's what the suspect hit you with, but why bring it here?" Something didn't smell right. Hunter turned to Joel. "You recognize this?"

Bucky entered the room. "What are you doing with my trophy?"

"You're responsible!" Cal clambered to his feet and swayed.

Emory grabbed him. "Whoa. Sit back down."

Cal obeyed.

"Nope, wasn't me, man," Bucky said. "I left my trophy in the kitchen, as I wanted to give it a good cleaning. Then I forgot about it. Someone is setting me up."

"Are you sure, Bucky?" Cal once again gingerly touched the back of his head. "Did you take all the gifts too? I heard about your conning ways."

Bucky kicked a stray potato, averting his gaze.

"What's he talking about, Bucky?" Joel asked.

The ranch hand looked at Joel. "That's all in the past, I swear. I would never do that to you."

"Do you have a history of swindling ranchers like Cal claims?" Hunter knelt and eyed the trophy.

"A long time ago. Until I met my wife, and I mended my wayward ways." He glanced at Cal. "You would have known that if you dug a little deeper. I returned all the money I conned those ranchers out of and even served a few years in jail for it."

Hunter planted a palm on the arm of the chair to push himself to his feet.

Cal scowled. "How can we believe you? You're probably the convict among us!"

Bucky walked into Hunter's personal space. "You have to trust me, man. I would never do anything to hurt the Hardys. After my wife died six months ago, they took me and my kids in."

Hunter analyzed the man's face and body language.

He didn't flinch under Hunter's scrutiny.

Hunter nodded. "I believe you. Someone is obviously trying to cast blame on you. Joel, let's get everyone out of here. We need to preserve the scene."

Joel pointed to Rose. "What about her?"

"We leave her too. It's cool in here, so that's good." Hunter motioned to the group. "Let's go."

Joel locked the back entrance leading up into the shed.

Once outside, Joel intertwined the chain into the cellar's handles and padlocked it shut. "We're good."

Emory yanked up her hood. "We still haven't figured out why someone moved Rose."

"We likely won't until we find those responsible." Hunter fished his phone out of his back pocket, checking his screen. "Still no signal."

"I need to check on Autumn and help her finish cleaning the kitchen." Emory trudged through the snow and entered the home.

"Bro, be careful." Joel slapped him on the back. "I saw that almost kiss. I'm not sure she's ready."

"I know. She may never be."

"I explained that to Autumn when she devised her plan."

"Wait, what are you talking about?" Hunter watched a male cardinal fly and land on a snow-laden Douglas fir branch. Its stark red feathers against the whiteness reminded Hunter of a verse in Isaiah.

Though your sins be as scarlet, they shall be as white as snow.

Just like God's love for them. Pure. Redeeming. *Thank You for the reminder.*

The malamutes bounded around the corner, barking. They ran to the duo, their tails wagging.

Joel bent over and ruffled their fur. "Autumn felt if she could get the two of you here for our Christmas ranch experience, it would bring you back together. You know, the romance of the season."

If only.

"I appreciate her trying, but I'm not sure it's gonna work."

"Don't be so sure. After all, Christmas is a time for miracles. Give her time." Joel smiled and gestured toward the barn. "I need to attend to the horses. I'll be in for lunch in about twenty minutes. Come, Luna and Nanook." The dogs followed him toward the barn, jumping at the snowflakes along the way.

Hunter breathed in the fresh, frigid air and scanned the property. "I could get used to living in a place like this."

With Emory by his side.

Like that was gonna happen.

He shook his head and headed toward the ranch just as the door burst open.

"Hunter, come quickly."

Emory's frantic tone propelled him into action, and he maneuvered through the snow as fast as possible.

"What is it?" He bounded up the steps.

"We found the poison." She re-entered the foyer. "At least, Mike did."

He closed the door behind them and stomped the snow from his boots. "Where?"

"In Daniel's room."

The geek? Wow. Not who Hunter would have suspected.

Emory bit her nails, waiting for Daniel to answer Hunter's question. They had brought the twentysomething into the dining room while Autumn and the guests searched for the missing gifts. Only Joel remained behind with Emory and Hunter.

Joel grabbed the young man's arm and hauled him out of his chair. "Answer the question. I'm tired of people deceiving me in my home."

Hunter pried Joel's hand from Daniel. "Bro, we'll get to the bottom of it. I promise." He nudged Daniel back into his chair. "Did you poison Rose Watson?"

"No! Someone is setting me up. I've never seen that bottle before." He meticulously circled his thumb around the armrest, avoiding their gazes.

Emory stepped forward. "You may not have poisoned Rose, but you're hiding something. What is it? Did you take the presents? Don't you want the kids to have a nice Christmas?"

"I didn't take the gifts either…" His sentence trailed off and he looked at Hunter. "I only agreed to it for the money."

"Agreed to what?" Hunter asked.

Daniel bit his lip, dipping his chin toward Emory. "Write an exposé about the famous mystery author. I work for a magazine, and they wanted me to do a write-up on you."

Emory frowned. "How did you know I was coming here?"

"My boss got a tip. I'm guessing from someone within your publishing house."

Hunter raised a brow. "Em, did your editor know you were coming here?"

"Yes, but she wouldn't have let it leak." She threw her hands in the air. "Besides, there's no dirt to get on me."

Daniel sneered. "Everyone has skeletons in their closet."

Hunter's eyes narrowed. "You're a lowlife." He planted his palms on both arms of Daniel's chair and leaned in. "If I see any unkind article about Emory, you'll be sorry. You hear me?"

"Fine."

"Get out of my sight." Hunter pushed up from the chair.

Daniel scurried from the room.

"That was interesting. I'll certainly be contacting my editor about this once our phones are working." Emory pointed to the dark, unmarked dropper bottle sitting on the table. "How did Mike know this was poison?"

"He said he walked by Daniel's room and saw it on the dresser," Joel said. "He was curious and took a whiff of it. I believe Daniel, though. Someone placed the bottle there to set him up."

"No signs of the presents?" Hunter took a picture of the poison.

"None. Autumn is disheartened. When word gets out about what's happened here, no one will want to come to the Double H Ranch." Joel threw up his hands. "Why does God allow so much to happen in one family? First the miscarriage, and now—"

Emory's jaw tightened. "Wait, what? Autumn had a miscarriage and didn't tell me? I didn't even know she was pregnant."

He faced her, his eyes flashing. "It's not like you've been close lately. You're always too busy with your writing and have an excuse. Stop pushing your sister away like you did your mother." He barreled out of the room.

Emory struggled to keep her tears at bay. "He's right. I have been doing that. I get so wrapped up in my deadlines, and I don't take time for family."

Hunter hugged her. "Don't be so hard on yourself. Life has a way of taking over. I know it has for me."

She leaned her head on his shoulder, letting his warmth and kindness wrap her in a cozy blanket. His long arms felt like a teddy bear holding her tightly, protecting her from danger. "I've missed you," she whispered.

"Missed you more."

Did she just say that out loud? She hadn't meant for him to hear her. This man had a way of breaking down her walls. If she wasn't careful, he'd worm his way back into her life.

She stiffened and broke free of his hold. Seemed even her sister was keeping secrets. "I need to talk to Autumn." She didn't wait for him to respond but hurried into the dining room.

Emory halted at the scene before her—Autumn laughing with the kids, showing them how to set the table. Her gentleness broke Emory's heart now that she knew about the baby her sister had lost.

You'll make an amazing mother. Lord, help it to happen soon for them.

Emory advanced farther into the kitchen and dining room area. "Can I talk to you, Autumn?"

She smiled. "Of course. Ava and Lacy, you finish here. Eli and Liam, how about you guys go ring the cowbell, okay?"

The boys jumped up and down, their eyes widening. "Can we?"

"Yes."

They raced from the room.

Autumn faced Emory. "What's up, sis?"

Emory eyed Ava and Lacy. "Let's go back into the kitchen while the girls finish setting the table."

"Sure. I have to put the garlic bread into the oven, anyway." Autumn headed toward the kitchen.

Emory followed, checking over her shoulder to ensure they were out of earshot before stopping next to her sister. "Autumn, why didn't you tell me you were pregnant and that you lost the baby?"

Autumn slapped the garlic bread on the counter. "You haven't exactly been in my life much. I had to practically bribe you to come here for Christmas." She snatched a knife from the holder.

Emory didn't miss her sister's moistened eyes before Autumn looked away. "I'm sorry, Sissy." How could she tell her sister why she'd been so absent from her life?

Tell her the truth. You've kept secrets, too.

The words blasted into her head like a bolt of lightning splitting a tree in two.

Emory took the knife from her sister's hand before pulling her into her arms. "I've failed you and should have been there for you."

Autumn sobbed in her arms. "My baby is gone. Yes, he's with Jesus, but I can't believe He took him before I could even say hello and kiss my boy."

How did one respond to such a heart-wrenching situation? *Be there and listen. Don't make it better with false promises.*

Something their mother always said to them. If only she were here. Doreen Burke always knew what to say in circumstances like this.

Emory held her sister tighter. "I'm so sorry for your loss." She let her sister cry on her shoulder.

After a moment or two, Autumn sniffed and broke free of Emory's embrace. "I need to get the bread in the oven."

"When did this happen?"

"Four weeks ago." She picked up the knife and sliced through the bread.

"Why didn't you cancel this ranch event?"

Autumn stopped cutting. "We need the revenue to keep this place going. You'd know that if you came around more."

Even though Emory lived two hours from Autumn, she could make a better effort to visit. "You're right. I'm sorry."

"It's like you're avoiding me. What did I do to you?"

Emory placed the cut bread onto the cookie sheet, then sprinkled the grated cheese on top. "Nothing. It's me."

"Tell me. I miss the closeness we once had. It's more than your deadlines, Sissy. You can be honest with me."

"You're right. Something I haven't told you is that I almost lost this next contract." She added another slice, placing it close to the first one. "I missed a few deadlines, and my editor threatened to terminate me. Like the ranch is important to you, my writing pays the bills, and I can't miss getting this book in on time. I've barely written on it." Emory fought the tears fighting to fall. "I've lost my inspiration ever since..." She let her thought trail off.

"Your break-up with Hunter?"

Emory nodded. "He crushed my heart, and you took his side."

"I'm sorry you felt that way, but you were wrong." Autumn set the knife down, and placed her hand on top of Emory's. "Stop blaming him for something he didn't do. I realize other men have betrayed you. Hunter's different, though. It's time to let it go."

Emory thought back to their interrupted kiss earlier. "I thought he was the one."

"He is. Can't you see that? You're perfect for each other."

A tear won the battle and slipped down her right cheek. "I wish I could believe that."

"You can." Autumn squeezed her hand. "Let. It. Go. And let him back in. He still loves you."

"No, he doesn't. How could he after the horrible words I said to him?"

"Ask. I think you'll be surprised."

Could it be true, and Emory had been wrong all these months? She had lots to mend, starting with her sister. "Autumn, there's another reason I've stayed away."

"What?"

Emory sighed. "I'm jealous of what you and Joel have." She circled her finger around the room. "All of this."

"Well, there are times I'm jealous of you too." Autumn placed the garlic bread into the oven. "I want you back in my life."

Emory waited until her sister closed the oven door, and then hugged her again. "I'm back, and I'm here to stay. I'm sorry for my jealousy. Can you forgive me?"

"Of course. I love you to the moon and back."

"Love you more." Emory chuckled at their sisterly banter. "I've missed you." How many times would she say those words today?

The cowbell rang in the distance.

Time not only for supper, but for Emory to move on, and the Double H Ranch was the best place to begin her journey.

~ NINE ~

December 24th 7:59 p.m.

Hunter analyzed the two sisters, holding hands and looking up at the large tree in the Double H Ranch's backyard. Something had shifted in their relationship, which had lightened their moods. Emory appeared almost the cheerful girl he'd fallen in love with. The two sisters had been inseparable tonight, ever since Joel had let it slip about Autumn's miscarriage. Their giggles at the supper table were contagious, and soon the entire atmosphere changed. Gone were the accusations, talk of a thief, and any mention of the deceased woman in the root cellar.

Autumn broke free of Emory's hand and moved beside Joel. The group had assembled in the cold to wait for the tree-lighting ceremony. Once again, the snow had increased. Wind gusts circled around the ranch's corner.

Emory made her way to Hunter's side. "Brrr, it's getting colder." She inched her plaid scarf closer to her neck.

"Looks like you and Autumn have gotten closer." Hunter studied her. "What happened?"

"Let's just say we had a long overdue sister-to-sister chat. I should have talked to her ages ago. I blame myself."

"Regret can eat us alive. I should know." He pictured his mother on their last Christmas Eve together, moments before she passed.

Emory hooked her hand through the crook of his arm. "I know tonight is hard for you. Doreen died a year ago."

"I regret not spending as much time with her as I wanted." He pushed back the tears forming. "Family and friends are so important."

"They are."

"Let's get this show on the road." Dick's irritated voice boomed over the wind. "It's cold, and we shouldn't even be celebrating with Mama's murder and all."

"It's for the kids." Joel set the button to light the tree onto the stand he had built for it and turned to his wife. "Let's do this together."

Autumn nodded and placed her hand on top of Joel's. "Everyone, 10, 9—"

The group shouted the countdown.

At one, Joel and Autumn pushed the button.

Multi-colored lights illuminated the darkened back yard, spreading hope and light into the storm hammering the region.

The children clapped and shouted while hopping around in the snow singing "Jingle Bells."

Excitement over Christmas radiated from them. Just like it had Hunter's mom every year.

"Mom would have loved this. She turned into a child at Christmas." Hunter failed to suppress the hitch in his voice.

Emory snuggled closer. "I remember. Her enthusiasm was contagious. She was a beautiful lady, inside and out."

"Definitely. Mom said the same thing about you, and she was right." Hunter took a risk and wrapped his arm around her waist. "You are beautiful. Let that girl out again. The one you've been hiding."

He didn't miss her soft moan.

Had he overstepped?

"I'm working on it, Hunter. Baby steps."

Autumn clapped. "Everyone, the weather is getting nasty, so how about some warm, kid-friendly eggnog to help guide Santa to the ranch?"

"Yes!" The kids bounded toward the front door.

Emory wiggled out of Hunter's hold. "Sounds like a brilliant plan. I'm freezing." She followed the kids, singing "Silent Night."

Hunter's Mom's favorite Christmas hymn.

He trudged through the snow, humming the song, his heavy heart lifting. *Mom, I miss you, but I will get through tonight. I'm surrounded by those I love.*

At least until Christmas was over. He hated the thought of leaving the ranch and Emory behind. For tonight, though, he'd revel in the season.

Thank You, Lord.

9:30 p.m.

Emory finished her eggnog and set her mug on the coffee table. Bucky and his kids had left, promising to be back early in the morning. Liam and Lacy had written their notes for Santa and placed them beside their cookies next to Ava's and Eli's plates. Thankfully, the adults managed to keep the fact that the presents were still missing a secret. Once again, the group had joined forces to find them, including Phil and Dick. Seemed no one wanted to spoil the children's Christmas morning excitement.

Hunter sat in the rocking chair beside the fire drinking his warm eggnog. He and Emory had waited until they searched their area of the ranch before taking delight in Autumn's homemade Christmas treat.

"I'm so frustrated we haven't found the gifts." Emory threw her hands in the air as she paced the room. "It's not like the thief could leave in this weather. Has Bucky searched the grounds?"

"Yes. He even used Luna and Nanook to help. The malamutes, like most dogs, have a keen sense of smell. Of course, the cold weather may have hampered their search."

"What about the barn?"

"Joel and I searched there. Nothing."

Emory plunked into her chair. "I hate that this will spoil the kids' Christmas morning. I know I complained about my childhood Christmases. Deep down I loved spending time with the family, though, opening the gifts."

"Even though you had to endure your father's version of Clark Griswold?"

"Yup. I—"

Dings sounded on both Hunter's and Emory's phones like bells at a Christmas Eve service. Emory checked her screen. "I've got a signal again."

"Me too."

Multiple texts from Emory's editor and agent displayed, checking on her manuscript status. Ugh! She'd tell them later her inspiration had returned, and she was back on track to making her deadline. *Thank You, Lord.*

Hunter grabbed her arm. "I know who the convict is."

"Who?"

He held the picture in front of her. "Meet Jess Gardner aka Wilson Spade."

Emory leaned closer. "Are you sure? That doesn't quite look like Wilson."

"Remember, he's good at disguises. Check his eyes."

She flinched. "You're right. His vivid green eyes are hard to miss. I'm surprised he didn't use contacts to change the color."

"Probably didn't have time. Let's go confront *Wilson Spade*." He air-quoted the imposter's name.

The lights snapped off.

Emory drew in a ragged breath. "Great, the storm has knocked out the power again."

"The generator should kick in."

But they remained in the darkness.

"Generator must be out too, and I'm guessing it wasn't from the storm." Hunter said. "That tells me one thing...we're getting closer to finding the gifts and the killer. And Wilson doesn't want us to."

Not good.

Hunter used the light on his phone to locate the flashlights Joel had left on the living room coffee table and passed one to Emory. "We need to find Wilson and detain him."

Joel and Autumn shuffled into the living room. "Why Wilson? What's going on, Hunter?"

He explained the situation and revealed the convict's identity. "Keep this between us until we locate him and restrain him. Joel, can you grab me some plastic ties?"

"Sure. I keep them everywhere since I use them a lot. There's probably some here in the drawer." He moved to the end table and rummaged through items before lifting the ties out. "Here you go."

"Thanks, bud." Hunter stuffed them into his back pocket.

Autumn's hand flew to her mouth. "Of all the guests, he was the nicest."

"Obviously a good con man." Emory turned on her light. "He fooled all of us."

"Joel, can you check on the generator?" Hunter asked. "I'll find Wilson."

Joel nodded. "Autumn, come help me. I also need to feed the dogs. Plus, I don't want you anywhere near that guy." They left the room.

"I'm coming with you, Hunter," Emory said.

"No, you're not. It's too dangerous." Hunter's hand automatically went to his hip, but his gun was back at the station. "We don't know what Jess is capable of, and I don't trust he won't try to attack us."

Her eyes sparkled defiance in the dim lighting. "You subdue him, but I want to be in the room when you talk to him."

"Fine. Let's go."

Seconds later, Hunter knocked on the convict's door.

"Who's there?" The man's gruffy voice revealed his annoyance.

"Wilson, it's Hunter. I need your opinion on something to do for the kids. Can I come in?" Although he hated to be deceitful, he had to get the upper hand on the man to keep the others safe. Hunter stole a peek at Emory standing at the end of the hall.

He shone a light at her and caught her smirk at Hunter's ruse. He tilted his head and shrugged.

"Fine." The door opened. "Why me?"

"I'll explain." Hunter waited for him to turn around to walk farther into his room.

As soon as he did, Hunter bull-rushed him, tackling him to the floor and yanking his hands behind his back. "You're under arrest, Wilson. Or should I say Jess?"

The man struggled to free himself.

Hunter dug his knee into Jess's back. "Stay put." He withdrew one of the ties and wrapped it around Jess's wrists to restrain him. "You have some explaining to do."

Hunter grabbed Jess by the elbow and hauled him to his feet before nudging him into a chair. "Okay, Emory," he yelled.

She entered the room.

The man's eyes widened in Emory's flashlight beam. "What's this all about? I'm Wilson, not Jess."

"Don't be coy." Hunter withdrew his cell phone and showed him the picture. "This is you. You escaped from the transport bus."

"Tell us why you killed Rose Watson. For her jewelry?" Emory sat on the edge of the bed.

"What? No! I did not kill that woman."

Hunter stuffed his cell phone into his back pocket. "Do you admit you're Jess Gardner?"

He slumped and nodded. "I am, but I didn't kill anyone. I'm a con artist, not a murderer."

"Did you knock out the power?"

"No. Other than disguising myself, the only criminal activity I've done is steal the presents."

Emory got up and paced the room. "Why? Why spoil those children's Christmas?"

"Because I had to get gifts for my kids. My wife just lost her job and told me she had no money for toys. I figured if I surprised them with presents, I'd redeem myself in their eyes. I found out about the ranch's Christmas experience on the internet and guessed there would be presents to steal. So, I faked sickness on the bus. They stopped for me, and that's when I got away. I was going to turn myself in after Christmas." His eyes never wavered from Hunter's glare. "I. Did. Not. Kill. Rose." He paused. "I swear on my boy's and girl's lives."

Hunter examined the man's face and body language. Nothing screamed deceit.

Jess Gardener was likely telling the truth.

Emory moved closer. "Tell us where you hid the presents, Jess."

The man's lips quivered.

She squeezed his shoulder. "I'll make you a deal. You tell us where they are so the kids here at the ranch can have a nice Christmas, and I'll get gifts to your kids. They won't be there for tomorrow, but can you let your wife know?"

Hunter eyed Emory, and his heart melted even more at the compassion streaming off her face. She cared, and wanted those kids to have a nice Christmas...even if she didn't know them.

"Thank you," Jess whispered. "That's kind of you. The gifts are in a garbage bag, buried in the snow next to the compost barrel. Had to disguise the smell from the dogs."

"We appreciate you telling us." Emory turned to Hunter. "I'll get Autumn and we'll find the presents. You watch him." She hurried from the room, clearly intent on getting the gifts and playing Santa.

The kids would have their Christmas after all, but one question remained in Hunter's mind.

If Jess hadn't poisoned Rose Watson, who had?

There was still a killer among them.

~ Ten ~

Christmas Day, 6:15 a.m.

Emory slipped out of her warm, comfy bed and placed her feet on the cool hardwood floor. She peered out the window. A fresh blanket of snow covered the region, and the moon shone its beam onto the backyard. The weather had cleared. Finally. Emory rubbed her hands in excitement. It had been too long since she'd felt this way on Christmas morning. *Thank You, God, for shifting my perspective and bringing me home.*

The tension locking her shoulders over the past few months was gone and replaced by peace. Peace for her writing. Peace for her relationship with Autumn. Peace not worrying about whether she'd ever make the *NY Times* Bestseller list. Right here, right now, God had filled her with contentment and a renewed purpose for her writing—to shine His light in their darkened world. It occurred to her suddenly that she didn't hate Christmas after all. In fact, she loved everything about it.

The only question remaining stuck in her mind. Could she forgive Hunter and move on?

She shrugged off the silent question and rubbed the soft, plush, plaid material of her new pajamas. Autumn's Christmas Eve gift to both her and Hunter with the request they wear them Christmas morning.

Always the mother, but Emory didn't mind. In fact, she loved that her older sister had taken on so many of their mother's tendencies. *You'll make an awesome mom, Sissy.*

Emory stepped into her matching plaid slippers and exited her room. Seconds later, a squeal resonated up the stairway.

The kids had found the gifts Emory and Autumn had placed under the tree last night, after digging them out of the snow. Thankfully, the garbage bag had protected the wrapping. They were only cold, not wet. Joel had fixed the generator. Seemed whoever sabotaged it hadn't done a good job.

Smoke permeated the ranch, and Emory breathed in. She loved the smell of a roaring fire. Another squeal propelled her down the stairs and into the living room.

Ava, Eli, Liam, and Lacy were all hovering by the tree.

Emory clapped. "Oh, no, you don't. First, we open stockings." She raised her wrist. "And my watch says it's not time yet. You're early. What if Santa comes back?"

Their eyes widened.

A deep chuckle sounded behind her. She whirled around.

Hunter stood in his matching pajamas, arms folded and wavy hair disheveled. He looked like a cute little boy on Christmas morning. "At least let them open their stockings."

The other guests stumbled into the living room, rubbing their eyes. The children's excitement had woken the entire ranch.

Autumn appeared in the entranceway. "Kids, grab your stockings and take them over to the couch."

Once again, they squealed and did what they were told. Soon, torn wrapping paper littered the floor, and the kids happily played with the small toys from their stockings.

Ava dashed back to the tree and lifted her present. "Can I?"

"Nope. Kids, help me set the table. Breakfast first, then presents." Autumn turned her gaze to Emory. "That's the rule, right, Sissy?"

"Yup. It's tradition."

"Come, kids. Everything is ready. Just need to take the pancakes from the warming oven." They scrambled from their spots and followed Autumn into the kitchen.

The front door opened and closed. Seconds later, Mike entered the room and raised his cell phone. "Good news. Everything is back up and running. Plows have been out all night. Joel, your contractor is out there now clearing the driveway. I'll be able to take your guests back into the city by four o'clock. That's when the events end, correct?"

Joel nodded.

Emory's gaze flew to Hunter's. His contorted expression revealed the same thought as hers.

They still had a killer to catch.

If they didn't, whoever had poisoned Rose Watson would get away with it.

The cowbell clanged, announcing breakfast.

Thirty minutes later, after yummy pancakes, Autumn rose from the table. "Time to get the turkey in the oven and then the kids can open their gifts."

Their Christmas feast finished mid-afternoon after the kids enjoyed playing with their new toys. The group had scattered to finish packing, since they were leaving shortly.

"Sissy, can you get me some canned peaches from the root cellar?" Autumn asked. "I want to make a fresh peach cobbler for tonight. We're gonna have a quiet evening. Joel, can you get more firewood? Hunter, can you stoke the fire in the living room? I don't want it going out."

"Yes, Mom." Emory saluted before walking into the hallway and snatching the coat from the last hook. She put it on and stuffed her hands into the pockets.

And fingered a velvet bag. *Wait—what?*

She looked closer at the coat. Same dark color as hers, but not hers. Emory pulled the bag out and opened it, dropping the contents into her hand. Pearls. A ruby ring. An emerald necklace.

Rose Watson's jewelry, but whose coat was Emory wearing?

"I wish you hadn't done that," a sinister voice whispered.

Emory gasped and pivoted, staring down the barrel of a shotgun.

And into the eyes of the Double H Ranch's killer.

Hunter clutched the fire poker as he inched his way into the hallway. Emory's loud breath intake had alerted him to danger. Something wasn't right. He removed his slippers and padded in his sock feet down the hardwood floor. His jaw dropped at the killer's identity—not at all who he'd suspected.

Josee Drew.

He stuck the poker in her back, giving the illusion of a gun. "It's over, Josee. Give yourself up. You don't want little Ava seeing you kill an innocent woman, do you?"

She raised her hands, holding the shotgun high. When Hunter lowered the poker, she shoved her elbow into his stomach.

He stumbled backward.

Emory yelled and tackled Josee, knocking the shotgun onto the floor at the same moment the door opened.

Joel entered holding firewood. Clearly grasping what was happening, he dropped his load and rushed forward. Scooping up the discarded weapon, he aimed it at Josee. "Stand down."

Hunter regained his balance, snatched another tie from his back pocket, and yanked Josee's arms behind her back so he could secure it around her wrists. That should hold her until the police arrived. "Emory, can you ask Autumn to ensure the kids stay away?"

Emory nodded and bounded toward the kitchen. She returned a moment later.

After calling 911, Hunter grasped Josee by the elbow and directed her into the living room and onto a rocking chair. "Tell me why you killed Rose Watson. Was it for these?" He raised the jewelry bag.

She scowled. "That was just the icing on the cake."

Phil and Dick ran into the room. "We heard you caught Mama's killer." They stopped when they saw Josee sitting there, her hands behind her back.

Dick marched up to her and waggled his finger in her face. "Why did you kill my mother?"

She squirmed in her hold. "Because she cut me out of everything."

Emory sat on the hearth, petting Susie. "What do you mean?"

Josee cursed, keeping her eyes on the Watsons. "Don't you get it? I'm your long, lost sister that our dear mother discarded like rubbish." Her eyes flashed venom. "She had an affair with my father. After I was born, she didn't want me. Told my father to take me. She only wanted sons."

Phil dropped into a chair. "Wait, how old are you?"

"35. I'm your older half-sister. I was the firstborn, but that didn't matter in Rose Watson's eyes. She was despicable and deserved to die." She snarled at Emory. "I would have gotten away with it too if you hadn't put on *my* coat."

"I thought it was mine. It's the same color and was where I thought I hung mine last." Emory folded her arms. "How did you find out you were Rose's daughter?"

"My father told me on his deathbed four months ago. I started following all her social media, looking for an opportunity to get even."

"You saw Mom's post about coming here for Christmas?" Dick's normal blusterous voice held a quiver.

Josee's lips peeled back into a devious smile. "Yes, to spend time with her...how did she put it?" She rolled her eyes. "With her precious sons. How did you put up with her? She chastised you publicly."

The brothers remained silent.

The light dawned in Hunter's mind. "When you had the opportunity, you crept into her room and added the poison."

Josee snorted. "It was easy peasy. She went to the bathroom after Phil brought her the tea. I snuck in and poured multiple drops into the teapot." She leaned back in her chair. "I took her pearls but found the other jewelry when everyone was searching for the missing presents."

Hunter paced. "How did you move her body?"

"I helped." Gil Drew shuffled into the room, holding his suitcase.

"You knew about this? Were you in on it?" Hunter asked.

"No! He wasn't. He figured it out, and I begged him to help me move her body." Josee shifted in her chair. "Cal almost caught us, so we knocked him out and tried to make it look like Bucky did it. I'd seen his trophy in the kitchen and thought it would be the perfect weapon."

"But why move Rose? That doesn't make sense and had me baffled." Emory shifted her position to the window.

"Oh yes, Miss Mystery writer couldn't put all the clues together. I did it to psych you all out." Her gaze traveled from Dick to Phil. "And have fun with my *brothers*." She chuckled. "I stuffed the jewelry bag in my coat after I cut the power last night. I was afraid you would find where I hid the pieces when you were all looking for the gifts. I also tried to frame Daniel, but that didn't work."

"You're sick." Dick raised his fists. "I should punch you."

Hunter stepped in front of him. "No need for that. The police are on their way with the medical examiner. This is over." He pointed to Josee. "She'll be going away for a long time."

At last, the Christmas Caper mystery had been solved, and they could finish the day off in peace.

Christmas night, 6:00 p.m.

Emory sat on the couch in front of the fireplace hours after they'd taken Josee, Jess, and Rose away. Jess had left Emory his wife's phone number, and she planned to deliver their gifts in a few days. Santa would be a bit late, but she doubted Jess's kids would mind. The other guests had left, claiming they'd definitely be back next Christmas. Cal had asked Emory out on a date, but she made it clear she wasn't interested. Bucky and his kids had retreated to their cabin, leaving Emory with Hunter, Joel, and Autumn. Emory had contacted her editor about Daniel's claim of a leak in her office. She promised to look into it. Emory had banged out a few chapters of her book after giving her statement to the police. She had time to kill while Constable Hunter Knight conferred with his colleagues. Autumn and Joel had secretly disappeared.

Emory sipped her decaf Christmas coffee and admired the tree—the only light in the room, except for the roaring fireplace. She breathed in the aroma and relished the night's quietness, pondering what it must have been like for Mary, Joseph, and baby Jesus. Tranquility. The best gift of all.

"Penny for your thoughts." Hunter entered, carrying a mug.

"Just reflecting on how much I love the quiet. Don't get me wrong, it's been fun—except for the part about the killer and convict among us, of course."

He chuckled, lifted the pillow from the couch, and sat beside her. "Agreed. This was always my favorite part of Christmas day. Most feel let down after everything is over, but I loved to sit in front of the tree and stare at the lights. And tonight, I can do it with a beautiful woman beside me."

He sipped his coffee, his shining eyes peering over his mug.

Autumn entered. "Okay, everyone out."

Emory startled at her sister's abrupt presence. "Why?"

"You'll see." She pointed to the dining-room door. "Go in there. I'll tell you when you can return."

Emory stood. "What are you up to, big sister?"

"You'll see. Go." She nudged her to the door.

Ten minutes later, Hunter and Emory were called back.

Emory entered the darkened room. All lights were off. "What's going on, Sissy?"

Autumn took hold of Emory's hand and guided her forward. "One last present for you." She turned back to Joel, who waited in the wings. "Now."

The lights flickered on, revealing a train traveling around the tree on its tracks.

Emory's hands flew to her mouth. "Is that—"

"Yes. Joel and I refurbished it as a surprise. He got it working, and I painted the cars. All in hopes of you spending your Christmases with us." She paused before adding, "Or some of them, at least."

"Hunter, this was our father's train." Emory fell to her knees, tears spilling down her cheeks. "Where did you find it? I thought it was gone."

"Joel found it when we cleared out Mom's basement."

Emory followed the train as it circled the tree. "I absolutely love it." She hopped back up, bringing her sister into an embrace. "Thank you for making this the best Christmas."

They both sobbed as years of regret released with each choo-choo and chugalug of the train.

Emory held Autumn at arm's length. "Yes, I want to do this Christmas ranch experience every year. I love you, Sissy. I'm home."

"Finally." Autumn hugged her again. "Love you more."

"Thank you for my last present."

"Well, technically, it's not your last one." Joel opened the blinds. "Check it out."

Emory raced to the window.

Holly and battery-operated lights decorated a sleigh parked in front of the home. Two horses were ready to take their passengers. Luna and Nanook pranced around the front yard, as if they knew something special was about to happen.

"Hunter arranged this for you," her sister whispered in Emory's ear.

Emory whirled around.

Hunter held out her coat. "Shall we?"

"Yes." She turned and wiggled into the arms.

Once outside and nestled under the Christmas plaid blanket, Hunter snapped the reins. "On Dancer, on Vixen..."

The sleigh lurched forward and headed around the property toward the road leading them into the forest behind the Double H Ranch.

"I can't believe you arranged this all for me." Emory snuggled closer to the handsome man beside her.

"God helped to clear the weather. Joel and I did the rest."

Emory leaned back and stared at the sky. Clouds covered the moon again, but she didn't mind. A little snow on Christmas night would be the best ending for their day. "Thank you."

"You're welcome. You cold?"

"Nope. I'm perfect."

"Yes, you are."

Emory sighed and gazed into the blue eyes of the most gorgeous man she'd ever known. How could she have ever doubted his loyalty? "Hunter, I'm sorry."

"For what?"

"For everything. For not trusting you." She grabbed his gloved hand. "You would never betray me. I know that now. I'm sorry it took this long to figure it out."

"Thank you for saying that. I need to apologize, too."

"Why?"

"I should have been more careful. I blame myself for our breakup. I threw away the best thing that's ever happened to me." He caressed her chin. "You."

"Not your fault. How about we both forgive each other and move on?" She let her words sink in, then added, "If that's what you want."

"What are you saying?"

"I meant it when I said I've missed you. Truth is, I've realized over the past few days just how much. I want you back in my life." She bit her lip and looked away. "If you'll have me."

He guided her chin back to his gaze. "I will." He brushed his lips with hers.

She placed her hand on the back of his head, bringing him closer and intensifying their kiss. Her way of promising her commitment to a renewed relationship.

He broke away, smiled, and yanked on the reins. "We're almost there."

"Where?"

Seconds later, they exited the forest at the top of a ridge.

In front of the beautiful Rocky Mountains.

Emory sucked in a breath. "It's perfect."

Hunter tugged the reins. The horses stopped.

"Not yet." Hunter fished something from his coat pocket and raised it over her head.

Mistletoe.

She laughed. "You think we need that?"

"Work with me. It's tradition." Once again, he claimed her lips.

Lips that held her enchanted along with the season as memories of how much she loved his kisses tumbled through her mind.

He released her and wrapped his arm around her, nestling her closer.

Snowflakes floated down as if on cue.

She smiled and placed her head on his shoulder. She was home where she belonged.

In his arms.

~ Epilogue ~

December 31st, 11:55 p.m.

Hunter paced the living room, waiting for Emory to return from calling her editor. Over the past week, she'd locked herself in her room multiple times, claiming inspiration had hit her like a bull rushing toward its opponent waving a red flag. She had completed her first draft in record time and wanted her editor's initial thoughts before proceeding. Hunter had requested more time off from his sergeant, stating he required additional days to recuperate after the Christmas fiasco. Josee had confessed to her crime, and Jess had been returned to prison. Emory and Hunter had delivered an armload of presents to his kids. The excitement on their faces was worth the trip to the crazy Boxing Day sales in the mall.

As it was New Year's Eve, Autumn, Joel, Emory, and Hunter had returned from an evening out. Now it was time for the traditional countdown to ring in the new year.

"Where is she?" Hunter fingered the chain around his neck.

"Be patient, bro." Joel chuckled. "She's worth the wait."

"Hunter, are you sure you want us here for this?" Autumn poured Elderflower into their champagne glasses.

"I do. We're family."

Emory hurried into the room. "You won't believe this."

"What?" Hunter reached Emory's side in two long strides. "Tell us what happened."

"She loved it. I can't believe it. I've never written a book that fast." She ran her fingers down Hunter's cheek. "Seems you were the inspiration I needed."

He guided her over to the tree. "I'm so glad she loved it, but right now there's something important I need to talk to you about. Before the clock strikes midnight."

She grinned. "Don't worry, I'm not gonna turn into a pumpkin or lose my glass slipper."

Hunter unfastened his chain, removing the engagement ring before dropping to one knee.

Her eyes widened. "What are you doing?"

Autumn giggled.

"Emory Burke, I have never stopped loving you." He held out the ring. "I couldn't part with this and prayed one day I'd be able to put it back on your finger. I know we only just renewed our relationship, but I don't want to wait another minute. Will you marry me?"

She plopped down, meeting him at eye level. "Yes, Constable Hunter Knight. I will marry you. I love you." She held out her hand.

He slipped the ring on her finger and brought her to her feet. "I love you too." He leaned in and kissed her.

"All-righty then. It's time to celebrate." Autumn clapped. "We have thirty seconds. Grab your glasses."

Hunter released Emory. They each took a champagne flute, raising them in the air.

The group counted down to midnight.

Hunter stole a kiss. "Happy New Year, my love."

"Ditto." Emory winked.

Autumn raised her glass again. "Here's to an exciting new year!"

"And to coming home," Emory added.

"I second that." Hunter clinked Emory's glass.

He marveled at God's gifts this Christmas. Not only had He helped Hunter overcome his fear of being alone at Christmas, He'd given him back the love of his life.

Yes, home was where he'd stay.

A Note From The Author

Dear Reader,

Thank you for reading Emory and Hunter's story! I enjoyed writing this Christmas cozy mystery full of secretive guests, an escaped convict, and red herrings complete with a Hallmark vibe. Putting a writer and constable together to solve the puzzle was fun.

Emory and Hunter both wrestled with different fears, but ultimately learned to give everything over to God. He does know best, doesn't He? This is something we all can relate to, can't we? I'm so thankful He's the one in control and we can come home to Him always.

I'd love to hear from you. You can contact me through my website and also sign up for my newsletter to receive exclusive subscriber giveaways.

God bless,

Darlene L. Turner

ACKNOWLEDGMENTS

Jeff, thank you for your continued support and encouragement. I'm thankful we can do this crazy thing called life together. I love you.

Helen, Melanie, and Sara, I praise God for putting us together. I love our special times of brainstorming, writer's retreats, pouring out our hearts, and our powerful prayer sessions. We fit perfectly.

To my family, we have so many fond Christmas memories, and I had fun writing a few into this novella. You bless my life, and I praise God for each of you.

Jesus, I'm grateful You always guide my path. You've got me!

About the Author

Darlene L. Turner is a *Publishers Weekly* bestselling author known for her high-octane stories and riveting twists. Sparked by Nancy Drew, she's turned her love of solving mysteries into her writing, believing readers will be captured by her plots, inspired by her strong characters, and moved by her inspirational message. Dubbed "the plaid queen" for her love of everything plaid, Darlene resides with her husband Jeff in Ontario, Canada. You can connect with Darlene at www.darlenelturner.com where there's suspense beyond borders.

Love Across Time

HELENA SMRCEK

For Martin

To the Moon and back is too short a distance. I prefer eternity. Love you.

LOVE ACROSS TIME

Helena Smrcek

A dual timeline romance bridging the present and the past...with love.

Nick Mass is a pragmatic real estate investor with a no-nonsense approach to life. Joy Christenson, on the other hand, embraces the world with warmth and wonder. When an unexpected discovery of long-lost WWII love letters draws them together, the spark between them is undeniable. As they embark on a heartwarming quest to find the letters' surviving relatives, they uncover more than they ever imagined. Meeting Noelle Darling makes this Christmas truly magical, but it's the unfolding story of nurse Beth Merrymore and RAF pilot Gabriel Holly that touches their souls. With each letter, Nick and Joy are swept into a tale of wartime love and longing—one that stirs their hearts and kindles a romance they never saw coming. As the train circles the Christmas tree and the festive lights twinkle, they realize that love, like Christmas, always finds a way to surprise you when you least expect it. This enchanting holiday journey is filled with love, serendipity, and the magic of finding true love under the mistletoe.

And now these three remain: faith, hope and love. But the greatest of these is love.

1 Corinthians 13:13 (NIV)

~ ONE ~

RAF Coningsby Airfield, Lincolnshire, England

December 1st, 1944

During the two years of her service, Beth Merrymore had matured from a wide-eyed teenager to a highly skilled triage nurse in the small field hospital serving the RAF at the Coningsby airfield in Lincolnshire. Yet even she was startled when six airmen rushed in one afternoon carrying a stretcher.

"Nurse," one of them shouted. "We need a doctor. Now!"

She glanced at the person yelling down the hallway. A Lancaster pilot. Those men took charge, no matter what the situation. Still, this ward was her domain.

"I'll need to assess him first," she said.

"There's no time. James got hit over Germany and lost much blood. He is our rear gunner."

The countless injuries Beth had seen over the past year had taught her not to panic. Nothing would be gained by her falling apart.

"Bring him here." She opened the door to the triage room and pointed to the bed covered in fresh linen. "One of you, go get Dr. Montgomery while I evaluate the situation." All but the man who had yelled at her rushed out. She was grateful for that. The room was small, and Beth needed space to work.

"What's your name?"

"Flying Officer Gabriel Holly." The man clicked his heels and saluted her. "Ma'am."

"My name is Beth. I'll need your help, Gabriel."

He hesitated.

"Be ready to apply pressure to his leg as I examine the tourniquet." She placed her fingers under the jaw of the injured man.

"All right." Gabriel looked around as if searching for something.

"Here." She reached under the bed and pulled a white cloth from a basket. "Use this."

Gabriel placed it over the silk scarf wrapped around the gunner's thigh.

Beth reached for the sterile scissors laid out on a steel tray. "Sir." She cleared her throat. "I need to cut the fabric and examine the wound." Moving his shaking hands aside, she cut into the blood-soaked silk.

"Is this yours?" She looked up from the patient. "I'm afraid—"

"Toss it." He said, urgency in his voice.

"Now, I am going to cut his pant leg." She kept her voice low as her scissors split the fabric.

"Will he be okay?" Gabriel choked on his words.

She bit her lip. Was the man ordering her around only a few minutes ago fighting tears? "Step outside if you'd like. The doctor will be here any minute."

"I'll stay."

Beth held his gaze. "In that case, you better do as I ask. I need you to unzip his jacket and remove as much clothing as possible. The doctor must examine him to ensure we are not missing a secondary injury."

He stared at her.

"Flying Officer Gabriel Holly. Please make yourself useful or leave the room."

"Yes, ma'am."

"Be gentle," she added softly as the gunner moaned. "He's regaining consciousness."

"James?" Gabriel leaned over his gunner's face. "Can you hear me, pal?"

"He'll start registering the pain. We need to move fast," Beth said as the door flew open and Dr. Montgomery entered the room.

"You can leave, sir." He briskly addressed the pilot, then focused on the gunner.

"But—"

"Nurse. Report." He focused on Beth as if Gabriel had ceased to exist.

Beth sent a sympathetic look in the direction of the reluctant man. "I'll find you later and tell you how the patient is doing."

With a curt nod, the pilot was gone.

~ Two ~

Niagara-on-the-Lake, Ontario, Canada

December 1st, 2024

Nick Mass shifted to park and turned off the engine. The Sunday drive from Toronto had taken only two hours. Why did it look as if he had traveled at least a hundred years back in time?

He stepped out of his BMW and surveyed the house in front of him. With only six weeks until the famous Ice Wine Festival kickoff, he had his work cut out. He needed to have this place fully rented by then.

Nick walked up the snow-dusted pathway and reached for the lock-box. A quick glance at his phone to verify the code his real estate agent had texted and *voilà*, he held the key.

Buying a property sight unseen had been a major gamble. Still, he trusted Joy Christenson, even though the home inspector had given him a lengthy to-do list. Nick had renovated old homes before. What could go wrong? He chuckled. Plenty. Of that, he was sure.

He unlocked the door and walked into the small hallway. The scent of this old home surprised him. Nick could tell much about the house from the first whiff of air. If it had cats. Rodents. Mildew. Each home had a telltale smell. Nick sniffed. Wood polish and... carpet cleaner?

The pictures he had seen online featured original woodwork. That would be a bonus. Some of the old furniture that came with the property could be reused in the B&B common areas. He hoped.

The floor creaked under his leather boots, and he contemplated taking them off. Then again, experience had taught him to keep his footwear on, as it could prevent him from stepping into unexpected surprises of the worst kind.

He unbuttoned his camel hair coat and strode down the worn runner. The dark trim looked good. It was polished to a shine. Had Joy hired a cleaning service to impress him? Her commission on this sale was nothing to be sneezed at, so perhaps as a courtesy, she had.

The kitchen. He ran his hand through his thick, tousled hair, the strands falling back into place. White cabinets. Black hardware. *Complete gut. 50K for new millwork.* Nick opened the first cupboard and took a bowl to examine the floral pattern. *Garage sale or a thrift store.*

After replacing the bowl, Nick walked over to the wood-burning kitchen stove, pulled out his phone, and snapped pictures. He could sell that to a Toronto antiques dealer. Hopefully.

"Hello," a cheerful voice interrupted his calculations. "Can I come in?"

Joy. He hurried toward the front hallway. "Sure."

He did a double-take. Whoever took the picture he had seen on her website failed to capture those huge green eyes sparkling excitedly. Also, unlike her in her professional photo, her hair was down, cascading over her red winter coat.

"I thought I'd bring you a little welcome basket." Joy handed him a heap of Christmas goodies wrapped in festive cellophane.

He cleared his throat. "No need to do that."

"It's nothing." She waved him off. "I'm entering the town's baking competition and made a few extra batches."

"Well, thank you. I appreciate it. Come in. Keep your shoes on."

She shut the door and took off her boots. "What do you think?"

"Not sure yet. The kitchen reno alone will take a miracle. I want to have this place rented out by mid-January. Honestly, it's a complete gut."

"Is it?" Joy walked straight into the kitchen and stopped next to the fridge. "Looks all original. In great shape."

Nick followed her into the room and leaned against the counter. "Dated."

"It gives the house a distinct character. Pardon me if I sound patronizing. I don't intend to. But that *is* why people come here from all over the world."

"To see creaky kitchens?"

"No." She laughed. "To escape."

"Escape what?"

"Oh, come on, this is Niagara-on-the-Lake. It's all about nostalgia. We've got superb wines, gourmet foods, theatres." She ran her hand along the top of the ancient stove. "Whimsical shops, delectable chocolates, and flavored coffee. A little gem of a community. Wait until you see it in full bloom next summer."

Nick held her gaze. What was she going on about? He'd been clear about his plans. He would renovate this old house. Put up a website. List the new B&B on every platform available. As soon as the bookings came in, he would flip this baby and move on to the next project.

"Yeah, I don't do nostalgia." He folded his arms over his chest.

"Hmm," she said as she perused the contents of the cupboards. "Look at that!"

Nick froze. Was there a hole in the wall hidden behind the creaky, white door? A termite infestation?

"What?"

"Do you know what this is?" Joy held up an old lemon squeezer.

Nick's eyebrows knitted. "I'm pretty sure you're about to tell me."

"This is a Vintage Hazel Atlas Criss-Cross Pattern Pink Depression Glass Citrus Reamer from the 1930s."

"Take it. All that stuff is going to a thrift store."

"Are. You. Kidding. Me? This piece alone is worth about two hundred dollars. American."

"Great." Nick let out a short laugh. "If you find someone crazy enough to buy all this junk, I'll pay you a commission."

"I thought you wanted to turn this into a charming bed-and-breakfast."

"B&B for sure, although I think our definition of *charming* might differ. Which brings me to my next question. Do you know of an interior designer in the area who could make sense out of this old house?"

"Hmm." Joy pursed her lips. "I hate to toot my own horn, but I'm a professional interior designer. It complements my real estate license, since staging is a big thing nowadays. I can draft some preliminary floor plans."

"Will those plans include pink lemon squeezers?"

"Perhaps." She gave him a mischievous smile. "Before I make a firm commitment, let me see the rest of the house. More treasures might be hiding in all those closets and dresser drawers."

~ THREE ~

RAF Coningsby Airfield, Lincolnshire, England

December 1st, 1944

Beth took her heavy coat off the hook in the staff room and slipped into it. It was the first day of December, and the English winter had a bite. The damp weather seemed to burrow straight into her bones. She picked up the remnants of her first attempt at decorating the ward for Christmas. The men who had rushed in earlier that afternoon had knocked over the coffee tin she used as a vase and trampled over the evergreen branches. She'd toss them back into the woods on her way to the nurses' accommodations and pick fresh ones as she walked to the hospital tomorrow morning. The men in her hospital should have something festive to look at, if only twigs and berries.

Beth took her warm gloves out of her purse, then quietly closed the staff room door behind her, mindful of the injured.

As she walked to the front door, she passed the night nurse and Beth's good friend, Henrietta, carrying a tray of tea to the ward.

Beth touched Henrietta's arm. "Send for me if there is an emergency."

"It will be a quiet night. The fog is thick today. The night bombers are grounded."

"A good night's sleep sounds fabulous."

"See you in the morning," Henrietta said, her voice already weary.

They were all tired. Exhausted. The airmen, their crews, ground personnel, support staff, doctors, and nurses. How much longer could this go on?

Beth paused before turning around and walking down the hall to the third door on the left. She cracked it open and peered in. Jim, the gunner, was awake.

"Hi," she whispered, conscious of the other men in the room. "How are you feeling?" She entered and laid her broken evergreen branches at his feet.

"I'm fine, ma'am. If you see any of my crewmen, please tell them."

Perspiration on his forehead told her otherwise. Slipping off her knitted gloves, she picked up a cloth from his nightstand and dabbed his brow and then brought a glass of water to his lips. "Take a sip."

"Thank you." Jim took two gulps. "Nurse?"

"Yes?"

"How am I doing?"

She set the glass down.

"You'll be fine. Dr. Montgomery removed the imbedded object—a piece of the plane shot off by the enemy. There was no bullet in your leg. Providing we can prevent infection setting in, your leg will heal."

"Will I be able to walk?"

"Oh yes." She rested her fingers on his warm hand. "You may need to stay at a convalescence hospital for a while, but your leg will be fine."

If only we could bring this fever down.

Beth dipped the cloth in a basin of cool water again and wrung it out before placing it on his forehead.

"Try to rest. Nurse Henrietta will check on you throughout the night, and I will see you in the morning."

She picked the broken branches off the white sheets and left the room.

The damp evening air felt thick yet cold. Beth took a deep breath and let it out. If only she could let go of the day's worries that easily.

"Nurse Beth."

The masculine voice startled her, and she spun around. Gabriel pushed off a stone wall and walked toward her.

"You frightened me," she said.

"I'm sorry. I returned after supper to ask about Jim, but you were busy. I didn't want to bother you. I figured you would have to go home, eventually."

"You've been waiting out here all evening?"

He shrugged before stretching out his arm, offering her a bouquet of fresh evergreen branches.

"These are to replace those." He nodded toward the bunch in her hand. "Sorry we made such a mess bringing him in, but—"

"No need to apologize," Beth interrupted. "Thank you." She reached for the offered greenery. "It's mighty sweet of you, Gabriel."

He kicked at a pebble. "Would you mind if I walked you home?"

"Flying Officer Gabriel Holly, I'd be honored. Let me just say, though, so there are no misunderstandings later, that I came here to volunteer as a nurse." Their eyes met. "Not have my heart broken."

"But I—"

She raised her hand, still holding the broken branches. "It may be very presumptuous of me, but I've seen too many nurses crying through their shifts. I want to make that clear right from the get-go."

"Yes, ma'am." He smiled and offered her the crook of his elbow.

Beth glanced at her hands, both clutching evergreen branches, and chuckled.

"If you'll allow me." Gabriel reached for the broken twigs and tossed them in the bushes. "That should solve the problem."

She giggled and looped her arm through his.

"And I was thinking you came to inquire about your friend."

"I did. That wasn't the only reason, though."

They settled into a comfortable rhythm, following the path to her quarters. The night was still, the fog thick and damp.

After a minute or two, Gabriel broke the silence. "Everyone talks about the English weather, but one can't truly understand it until they experience it."

"I prefer a real winter. The temperature is at least minus twenty degrees Celsius in Winnipeg this time of year."

Gabriel stopped and looked at her. "You're Canadian?"

"Oh, yes."

"Me too! From Niagara-on-the-Lake. In Ontario."

"My parents took me to Niagara Falls once. The year before they died."

"Oh, I'm so sorry. You must miss them dearly."

"Yes, I do. After the Lord took them home, I volunteered as a nurse." When Gabriel didn't reply, she tilted her head to study him. "I'm sorry, are you not a Christian?"

Gabriel let out a long sigh. "I..."

When he didn't say any more, she squeezed his arm. "It was rude of me to presume. Faith is personal, and we barely know each other. I'm sorry."

"Nothing to be sorry about, Beth." He held her gaze. "It's just that every time someone mentions God, I look around, and my head is full of questions."

"It is?"

"This darn war makes me question everything."

"Everything?"

"All right. It makes me question God."

"Do you ask Him your questions?"

"Well." Gabriel drew a long breath. "God and I don't talk much these days."

"I would think that flying in dangerous missions would bring one closer to Him."

"It used to. Now I wonder why a loving God would allow all this destruction and death."

They had stopped next to the low stone wall, and Beth set the branches on top of it. "What makes you think this is His work?"

"Can't He do anything He chooses?"

"Yes," she said, her expression somber. "But I don't think God chose this."

"Then who did?"

"People."

"Why can't He stop them?"

"God gave us free will. We can't blame Him when people choose to exercise it."

When Gabriel stared off into the darkness as though pondering what she'd said, Beth picked up the branches and tugged gently on his arm so they could continue walking.

After a couple of minutes of comfortable silence, she stopped in front of a tall brick building. "Flying Officer Gabriel Holly," Beth said in a lighter tone. "These are my quarters. Thank you for your company and the stimulating conversation. By the way, I believe your friend will fully recover. It will take time, but I will say an extra prayer for him. For you, too."

She let go of his arm and turned to face him. "God still does miracles, even amidst evil."

~ FOUR ~

Niagara-on-the-Lake, Ontario, Canada

December 1st, 2024

Nick looked at his watch. "Okay, I can spare about forty-five minutes. Will that be enough time for you to get an idea of what needs to be done to spruce this place up in time for the festival?"

Joy pursed her lips. "I suppose." She slipped off her coat and draped it over a kitchen chair.

"Great," Nick snapped a few pictures of the kitchen, ensuring Joy would be in one of them. He had never seen an adult woman wearing a chic version of Mrs. Clause's suit. "Let's check out the rest of the house."

"Oh goodie." Joy playfully punched him in the shoulder. "You're practically brimming with enthusiasm."

Nick stared at her. Was this woman for real?

"Come on, there must be a little sliver of happiness hidden somewhere under that stern investor look."

Nick shook his head, then walked through the kitchen door into the living room. Hand-carved paneling covered the walls. An antique fireplace stood opposite the large window that overlooked the snowy garden. He sighed. "What am I going to do with this?"

Joy perused the room. "What do you want to do with it? It's not in a terrible shape. A little dark for my taste. But it's beautiful. Do you think the fireplace works?"

"The house inspector said the flue and chimney look good."

"Well, that's a win." She tugged at the white trim contrasting her fitted red jacket. "Imagine sitting here, drinking hot cocoa on Christmas Eve."

"Sure."

Her fingers ran over the brown brocade drapes. "We could repurpose them as upholstery for the dining room chairs."

"How about I get a couple of guys to strip the carpet and haul these medieval window coverings to Goodwill? That is, if the thrift shop would even take them."

"Have you always been such a pessimist?" Joy reached for the double French doors and opened them wide. "Look at this beauty." Her eyes rested on the large crystal chandelier hanging over the dining room table.

"Those are such a pain to clean. It will have to come down."

"Come down?" Joy walked around the room, pulled out a chair, and nodded. "Yep, these will need to be reupholstered."

"Wouldn't it be cheaper to get a new set?"

"Like from Ikea?" She glared at him.

"I'm not saying we need to assemble a set from a box. By the time you source the fabric and we find someone who can actually do that kind of work, though, it won't be worth it."

"I can do upholstery. In case you missed what I said in the living room, the drape material would be perfect for this. There is plenty of it for cushions as well. It would tie these two rooms together."

"If you say so." Nick took a few more pictures. "I'll send these to you. I would greatly appreciate it if you could come up with an estimate and a timeline. Taking in the scope of the renovations, this will be a pretty tight schedule."

"If I knew you better, I would say you tend to worry. A lot. Since I don't know you that well, I'm choosing to believe that this is one of your less positive days."

"What does that even mean?"

"It means that tomorrow will be much, much better."

Nick blew out his cheeks. If only she understood what was on his agenda for tomorrow. "Let's check the upstairs. I need to head back soon."

Joy practically leapt up the walnut staircase, reminding him of a five-year-old on Christmas morning.

"Oh, wow!"

"What?" He bounded up the steps after her.

"Look at that!"

"Is the roof leaking?"

She stuck her head out of the main bedroom. "Why would the roof be leaking?"

He crossed the distance in three fast strides. "What are you yelling about then?"

"I wasn't yelling."

"Well, you were pretty loud."

"Check this out." She extended her hand into the room.

A four-poster bed covered in floral bedding dominated the room. The pillows were propped up high between bedside tables that held lamps with matching tasseled shades.

Nick sighed.

"This is such a beautiful room." Joy spun around. "Why are you frowning?"

"You're making me dizzy."

"The budget for this room will be pretty much zero."

He raised his eyebrows. "Zero?"

"Once I make sure the mattress is good, I will confirm that." Joy tugged at the sheets.

"How about new bedding?"

"Why?" She shot him a look.

"Because it looks like some kind of botanical garden."

"Precisely. You can call this the Secret Garden Room. Your guest will love that."

"Love the old bedsheets?"

Joy shook her head. "Nick, trust me. They are not old. They are vintage." She walked toward the door opposite the enormous bed and pushed it open. "Oh, yes!"

"What?"

"Sorry to disappoint, but no roof leak here either. Only a cute ensuite. That must be a reno because houses this age usually don't have one."

"What kind of shape is it in?" Nick brushed beside her and walked in. "Oh, boy."

"What?"

"The tub. Cast iron. It will be a pain to get out."

"Claw foot! There is a guy in town who refinishes them. No need to replace it."

Nick gave her a look. "Let's check out the other two rooms."

Joy followed him down the hallway as Nick stuck his head into two more bedrooms. They were both empty.

"These two are my favorites," he said. "Paint and carpet, some new furniture, and we are off to the races. Nice and simple."

"You're the boss. Oh, there's the attic." She pointed to the ceiling where a string hung down from a small door.

Nick scanned the hallway, then opened a linen closet and pulled out a long pole with a hook at the end. He fished for the ring attached to the wooden hatch door above their heads.

"Step aside, please. Not sure what will come down." Nick tugged on the pole. Nothing. He pulled again, this time with greater heft. The wood creaked, and the small door moved downward. Then, a spring-loaded staircase unfolded.

Joy clapped her hands.

"Did you just applaud me?" Nick frowned at her.

"Come on, this is like from a storybook. A secret staircase."

"It's not much of a secret. Most old homes have something like this. Access to a storage space in the attic for all the junk no one needs."

"Has anyone ever told you that you would be perfect for the role of Grinch?" She gently shoved him aside. "If you will excuse me, I'm going to check out all that *junk* no one wants around." Joy chuckled. "You have to admit," she added as the old steps creaked under her feet. "This is exciting."

"If you say so." Nick grunted. "Turn on your phone light. The attic may not be wired."

~ FIVE ~

RAF Coningsby Airfield, Lincolnshire, England

December 2nd, 1944

The world outside her window looked milky when Beth woke up the following day. Heavy fog had descended onto the airfield. She put on her nurse's uniform, took out the curlers, and pinned her hair. With ten minutes to spare before going to the mess hall for breakfast, Beth knelt by her bed and laced her fingers.

"Dear Heavenly Father. Thank you for this day. I pray for our patients. For no one to die today. I pray for Gabriel and the questions in his heart. Please, show him you are real and good. You asked us to bless our enemies. I have a hard time with that. Especially when I see our men, like the gunner yesterday, coming back to us injured and broken. I pray for those who have not returned. Please keep them safe, so they won't fall into the hands of the Nazis. And give comfort to all who grieve. There is much pain in this world. Please forgive me for my sins and guide me through this day. In your Son's precious name. Amen."

Swiping at her tears, she rose, walked to the mirror, and smiled at her reflection. "This is the face the men need to see, Nurse Beth. Pull yourself together." She pinned her nurse's cap to her hair. Her patients needed her, and with only three weeks left before she would return to Canada, she was determined to give them all she had.

Her steps echoed down the hallway as she headed for the exit. When she pushed the door open, she drew in a sharp breath. "Oh, you startled me." Her hand flew to her chest. "For the second time."

"I apologize." Gabriel pushed away from the brick wall of her building, a sheepish look on his face.

"You did not spend the night out here, Flying Officer." She offered him a stern look.

"Only a small part of it." He grinned. "I was wondering if you would have breakfast with me."

Her right eyebrow lifted. "I'm going to the mess hall. If you want to walk with me, we can grab a coffee and a donut before I report for my shift. I wouldn't say I'm going to have breakfast with *you*, though. The entire base will be there. And men like to talk, as you well know."

He met her gaze. "Yes, I do." His eyes were sad.

"Shall we?" Beth motioned toward the mess hall. "I need to be on time."

"Of course." He tried to offer her his arm, but Beth shook her head. Limiting the amount of talk about the two of them was likely a good idea.

Their steps in sync, Beth navigated around the puddles, trying hard not to get her shoes covered in mud.

Gabriel touched her arm. "I see you forgot your bouquet."

"Oh, yeah. I did." Her mind on Gabriel and James and the war and her return to Canada, she'd completely forgotten about the evergreen branches Gabriel had given her the day before.

"No worries, ma'am," the pilot replied in all seriousness. "I shall call my florist and have a new one delivered to you before lunch."

Beth chuckled. "That won't be necessary."

Gabriel reached for the handle of the mess hall door and held it open for her. "After you." He motioned for her to enter.

Beth walked toward the counter, Gabriel at her heels. She picked up a mug of coffee, added a splash of cream, and selected a donut.

Clutching a tray in one hand, he touched her elbow. "Where would you like to sit?"

"You're not sitting with your men?"

"Absolutely not. I wouldn't get a word in. You know how airmen are." He winked at her. "All stories and tall tales to impress the ladies."

A smile broke across her face.

"How about the quiet corner back there?" He pointed with his chin.

"Looks perfect," Beth said and aimed for the vacant table.

"Wonderful. This way we can enjoy our first breakfast in peace."

They sat opposite one another, and Beth took a sip of coffee. "The entire base will be talking about us by lunch."

"Let them." He took a bite of his donut.

"Gabriel." She set down her cup. "I meant what I said yesterday."

"I'm not here to break your heart." His gaze was genuine and filled with warmth.

Which meant that, whether or not he intended to, it was quite possible he would break it anyway.

~ Six ~

Niagara-on-the-Lake, Ontario, Canada

December 1st, 2024

"Let me go first." Nick gently pushed Joy aside. "In case this contraption gives in." As if to underscore his words, the first step groaned under his weight.

"Is it safe to come up?" Joy asked as soon as he had disappeared into the darkened opening.

"You might want to get your boots first."

"I just want a quick look." She carefully took one step at the time.

"Yeah, but prepare to be disappointed. The space has been swept clean."

"Let me see." Joy's head popped through the small, rectangular opening. "Oh, wow."

Clearly her favorite word. In this case, it was completely accurate. "Wow is right." Nick whistled.

"It's enormous."

"If I can get the engineer's okay, I could fit two bedrooms up here."

"Check out that window." Joy illuminated the space with her phone as she strode to the far side of the attic.

"Be careful," Nick cautioned. "Some of these beams may not be as sturdy as you think."

"You've got to come over here."

"Why?"

"To check out this view!"

Nick joined her at the window and peered out, examining the roof structure. "I might be able to enlarge this window."

"Can you install plumbing up here?"

"Hmm." He tapped his upper lip. "Great idea. I'll have to think this through. If I can, there's enough space to add a good-sized bathroom."

Joy shone her light into a corner to their left. "Check that out." She crossed the wooden floor, bending to accommodate the sloping roof. "What is that?"

"What do you mean?"

"Right there." Her light rested on a couple of dusty planks.

"I bet you that wood's been lying there since the construction. I could repurpose it."

"That's not what I'm talking about." Joy squatted, then pushed the planks aside. "Look at that!"

"An old box?"

"Look closer."

Nick pointed his light at Joy's discovery.

"It appears to be a…" Joy shoved the planks off her find and then used her fingers to brush decades of dust and cobwebs away. "A train set?"

"That will definitely not prop up my construction budget."

"Nick!"

Joy reached back into the dark corner and pulled out another object.

"A cookie tin?" He grunted.

"It's an antique one."

"If you find cookies in that, I'm not interested."

"You are impossible." She chuckled. "Don't tell me you are not even a little excited about this."

"Excited? About an old train set and a cookie tin? Sorry, but honestly, stuff like that doesn't interest me one bit. Although I might make clothes racks out of these." Nick picked up the two rough planks. "I could make them look pretty authentic."

"Fine. What would you like to do with these?" She motioned to the train and cookie tin.

"Donate them to a thrift shop."

"What?"

"My back is killing me. I need to straighten up." Nick walked toward the window, where the roof was highest, and stretched, one hand pressed to his lower back. "You want them?"

"They belong to this house."

"And the house belongs to me. If you want them, take them. You'll save me a trip to Goodwill."

"Are you serious?" She wandered toward him, holding her treasures in both hands.

"Sure. Now let's get out of here before our phones run out of batteries, and we have to make our way back in the dark."

A few firm strides toward the folding steps and their little adventure was over. Nick took Joy's treasures from her and motioned for her to go first.

As soon as she hit the ground, she held up her hands. "Pass the boxes to me," she said.

Nick did, then rapidly descended and pushed the stairs back up. Once the latch was shut, he returned the pole to the closet.

"Well, that was well worth it." Joy was beaming. "I can't believe you let me have these." Examining her boxes in daylight, she exclaimed, "This is a Christmas cookie tin. That makes it even more special." She started to open it, but Nick held up a hand to stop her.

"I hate raining on your parade, but I have to go. Toronto traffic is terrible, and I'd like to get home in time to go over this budget and make a few calls."

"Oh, sure." She tucked the box under one arm and lifted the cookie tin into the air. "I can open this at home and message you."

"Unless it's filled with gold coins, don't bother. I'm truly not into old stuff."

They exited the house. Nick locked his newest real estate asset and returned the key to the lockbox. "In case you need to get in to take measurements or something," he explained.

"Thank you. Call me. Let me know when you'll be in town next, so I can prepare some design ideas for you."

"That would be great." Nick opened the driver's door and slipped inside. "Have a good one." He started his car. At the corner, he glanced in the rearview mirror.

Joy still stood in the driveway, hugging her treasures to her heart. Okay then. Maybe he didn't particularly like old things, but his real estate agent certainly appeared to.

~ Seven ~

RAF Coningsby Airfield, Lincolnshire, England

December 2nd, 1944

Ready to change the dressing on James' wound, Beth opened the door to the ward and halted. Gabriel stood by his gunner's bed, a bunch of evergreen clippings in his hand.

"You again?"

He turned around and grinned. "As long as the weather stays like this, I'm afraid you won't get rid of me. Besides, it's my duty to check on my crewman here."

"And bring him flowers?" She set her tray down on the nightstand.

"Flowers?" James chimed in, his voice still hoarse.

"Oh no." Gabriel lifted the bouquet. "These are for you."

"That would be the second time, Flying Officer."

James whistled.

Gabriel shot him a look. "Glad to see that you are feeling much better, pal. Right back to your old self."

James smirked.

Beth placed her hand on the patient's forehead. "The fever broke," she said, relieved. "That's a good sign."

Gabriel leaned against the bed frame. "I'll have to tell the boys. Everyone keeps asking how you're doing."

Beth turned toward him. "Why don't you do that, Gabriel? Right now. Because James and I have some work to do here. And frankly, you seemed squeamish the last time I asked you for help."

Gabriel's face reddened. He cleared his throat. "Where would you like me to leave these?"

"Right by the front door. There's a small table there with a coffee tin that should have some waster in it."

"Yes, ma'am," he said under his breath as he turned toward the door.

"Thank you," Beth said as she pulled back the sheet, exposing James's bandaged leg.

"You are most welcome." Gabriel shot her a quick smile.

"And..." She pursed her lips. "My lunch break is at 12:30, in case you don't have any prior engagements."

~ EIGHT ~

Niagara-on-the-Lake, Ontario, Canada

December 1st, 2024

When Joy got home, she kicked off her shoes and rushed to the kitchen. Jingles, her orange cat, greeted her with a loud meow.

"It's not dinnertime yet."

Setting her two items on the counter, Joy reached into the treat jar.

The cat weaved around her ankles.

"I missed you, too." Joy offered him a cookie. It vanished in the blink of an eye.

After removing her coat, she draped it over a chair, eager to open her treasures. Biting her lower lip, she contemplated her next step. Perhaps she should take pictures before opening each item. Her phone in hand, Joy snapped a few photos.

Jingles jumped onto the counter and sniffed the tin and the box.

"Nothing to eat, sorry. I'll open both to make absolutely sure." She rubbed her hands together. The sense of anticipation reminded her of Christmas days past. She would savor it.

With one touch of a button, the espresso machine came to life. Why not light a candle, turn on Christmas music, and get a tripod from her office? She could shoot a little video and send it to Nick. Would he think she was a bit much?

"He already thinks that, right?"

Jingles meowed in agreement.

Joy set everything up, then cracked a can of cat food. "How about an early dinner?" she said, hoping Jingles would stay preoccupied with his meal. That would prevent him from knocking her tripod over and stepping all over the antique containers.

"Here you go." She patted his head, and he purred approvingly.

Joy turned on her phone's camera.

"Hey, Nick. Although you will surely deny it, I think you are eager to find out what is in that box and tin, so I decided to shoot this video for you."

A latte in hand, her candle lit, soft music playing in the background, Joy sat down. "This is exciting!" She picked up the train set. "I'm willing to prolong the torture of the unknown secret in the cookie tin and open this one first. Hope that's okay with you."

She touched a finger to the top of the faded gold box featuring an engine hauling a line of cars, then looked up. "Ready?" She brushed the dust off the left upper corner. "Hmm. Hamleys?" Joy glanced at her phone. "Hold on, Nick. I'll get my laptop and Google this."

A moment later, she tapped the keys. "I thought so." Then, peering at the screen, she added, "This train set comes from Hamleys, the famous London toy store. Interesting." She tapped her bottom lip with her index finger. "How would a train set from London get to Niagara-on-the-Lake, you ask? Hmm. Let's take a peek at what's inside. That could give us some clues."

After a deep breath in, Joy began to carefully lift the paper lid. Wiggling it back and forth, she managed to loosen the aged cardboard without damaging it. Jingles jumped onto the table and sniffed around the box.

"Sorry, buddy. This is definitely not for you." Joy picked up her cat and set him on the floor. He meowed to voice his discontent before hopping onto the sofa to watch her.

"Look at that, Nick." Joy lifted the box so the camera could capture the locomotive, the caboose, and the three passenger cars nicely tucked inside. "Although it looks as though it's been well loved, the set is still in excellent condition." She ran her fingers over the stack of rails. "And it appears to be all here."

She set the lid on the box. "I'll wait for you before I test it." Joy picked up her Santa mug and took a sip of her coffee. "Now, the cookie tin. It's Walker's. My favorite Scottish shortbread. Give me a minute." Joy set down the mug before running to her kitchen sink to grab a damp dishcloth. Back at the table, she wiped off the layers of attic dust. A picture of a boy pulling a girl—bundled up with a rag doll tucked snugly in her arms—in a sled, emerged. Two sprigs of holly complemented the red-and-green tartan in the background.

"A Christmas tin. How perfect is that? Let me wash my hands before I open it." She paused the recording and rushed to the kitchen.

A minute later, she had settled on her seat again and clicked *Record*. "Since we are only a few days away from Christmas," she sipped from her Santa mug, "let's share a little holiday cheer." She waved one of the shortbread cookies she'd grabbed from her own stash in the kitchen in front of the lens. "You have a few of these in your basket, so grab one."

Joy wrapped her fingers around the red lid and pulled. Nothing. She tried again, a little harder. Still nothing.

"A friend taught me a trick. Tap around the lid with a butter knife if you can't open a pickle jar. Give me a second."

For the third time, she hurried to the kitchen. When she returned with a butter knife, Joy tapped around the tin lid.

"Hope this works."

Setting the knife aside, she wrapped her fingers around the lid again and gave it a gentle yet firm tug. The lid finally came off.

"Oh, wow! Nick! It's full of letters."

She tilted the tin towards the phone. "Look at that." Her fingers caressed the yellowed envelopes, neatly organized in two piles. "What should I do with them?"

Joy set the tin down, then placed her right hand over her mouth. After a moment, she reached for the phone and turned off the camera.

After looking up Nick's number, she attached her video to a text message.

Then, latte in hand, she wandered into the living room and sank onto the couch. Should she read them? What would Nick say?

~ Nine ~

RAF Coningsby Airfield, Lincolnshire, England

December 2nd, 1944

"When is your day off?" Gabriel asked, stirring his soup.

"I don't take days off. That is, except Sunday morning to attend the service."

"Can you request one?"

She looked at him quizzically.

"If you wanted to?" he added as he broke his dinner roll in half.

"I suppose." Her voice was tentative.

"I would like to ask you on a proper date."

Beth set her spoon down and leaned back in the chair. "Wasn't I clear about that?"

"I assure you, I'm not here to break your heart, Beth."

Avoiding his gaze, she stared at the line of service men waiting their turn in the donut line.

"Say yes, please. You deserve a bit of fun."

Her eyes rested on him. "How old are you?"

"Twenty-four."

"I'm twenty-eight."

He shoved a piece of the bun into his mouth, chewed, and swallowed. "Okay. Does that matter?"

"It might."

"Not to me."

Beth took a spoonful of her cooling soup. "We're practically strangers."

"Ask me anything."

She took another spoonful of the broth, silently observing the single pea floating on her spoon. Beth needed a moment to slow the pulse rate that had picked up when he'd asked her on a date. After swallowing, she set down her spoon and patted her mouth with a cloth napkin. "Where are you from, for starters? Do you have a family? What did you do before the war? What are your plans after the war?"

Gabriel finished his bun and swiped a few crumbs from his shirt. "I'll tell you all about that on the train."

"What train?"

"The train to London. I have a pass for Christmas Eve day. Can you take it off?"

She bit her lip. Was this man for real? He was handsome and kind, but was he trustworthy? *Could* she request a day off and spend the day with him in London? That would be crazy, wouldn't it?

"One date. That's all I'm asking for this Christmas."

At that, and the pleading in his green eyes, her heart melted. How could she say no? She felt it in her chest then, right around where her heart was pounding. A twinkle of hope. Perhaps there *was* still a glimmer of light left in this world drowning in darkness.

He reached across the table and touched her hand. A little spark threatened to ignite a fire—perhaps she should let it.

"Please," Gabriel whispered.

Beth gave up. A smile spread across her face, and she nodded. "All right. I'll ask."

~ TEN ~

Toronto, Ontario, Canada

December 1st, 2024

Nick dropped his keys on the side table. His phone pinged, and he glanced at the screen. Joy. As he slipped off his shoes, it pinged again. What was going on? His stomach growled. Joy would have to wait.

He walked to the fridge and opened it. Nothing sat on the shelves but two lonely bottles—ketchup and mustard. Not the best dinner. After closing the door with a sigh, he meandered to the sofa in the living room. Dropping onto the white leather cushions, he looked around.

Thousands of lights from the surrounding condos poured through the large window in front of him. At one time, he'd thought that was cool, but the unchanging urban landscape eventually grew boring. Had moving downtown been the best decision?

His phone pinged for the third time. A message flashed across his screen. A single question mark.

What did she want? Nick let out another long sigh. At times, his life resembled a lonely question mark. It had been almost a year since that awful Christmas Day break-up, and he'd sworn he wouldn't put himself in such a situation again. Ever.

That relationship had cost him more than he was prepared for. The last straw was her taking his dog, claiming that he was a terrible pet owner. According to her, Nick was too busy for a goldfish, never mind a pup that needed walks and attention.

He let her have him, along with the engagement ring, the furniture, and whatever else she deemed hers, figuring that would allow him to wash his hands of that toxic, manipulative, demanding woman and be better for it.

So why did he feel down today? Talking to Joy had stirred up long-forgotten yearnings. He hated to be alone, especially at this time a year.

Nick should check her messages, but he'd order takeout first. Thai sounded pretty good on a busy evening like today. He hadn't been kidding when he told Joy he still had hours of planning and estimating ahead of him. Work that would take him into the early hours of tomorrow. Only then would he drop into bed, exhausted, to wake up in four hours to another busy day.

That was how he coped. Who needed a therapist when work could keep one's mind off his personal problems? Besides, he was making good money instead of paying someone to listen to his sad story.

Nick would handle the loneliness as he had handled all other problems in his life. He didn't need anyone to hold his hand, even if the break-up had taken a lot more out of him than any previous relationship. Was that because he had genuinely thought he'd found the one? The one person God had made just for him? Well, that line of thought had proven to be as powerful as Kryptonite.

Nick scoffed. Where was God in all of this, anyway?

He tapped the screen, selected his supper, and paid. Easy as pie. No fuss, no mess, no dishes. Thirty minutes should be plenty of time to deal with whatever Joy needed. Then he would eat and get to work.

Nick scrolled through his messages. She'd attached a large file to one of hers. A video. Had she found another property for him to consider?

When she appeared on the screen, he was surprised to see her sitting in what he assumed was her house.

As she fiddled with the train box, he smiled at the jazzy Christmas soundtrack in the background. Watching her run around, first for a laptop, then a cloth, then a knife made him chuckle. This girl was all over the place. The way her eyes glistened when she finally opened the tin filled with envelopes tugged at his heart, though. She was genuine. Yes, she was a little scattered and enthusiastic over the most mundane things, but she seemed honest, kind, and thoughtful. Perhaps that was why she was great at her job.

This woman cared. Her niche was a small town minutes from the American border, and she'd done well for herself. Granted, Joy could make way more money selling Toronto condos, but somehow he didn't think that was her style.

The ringing phone started him. Her name and number flashed across the screen. Nick frowned as he hit the button to accept the call. "Yes?"

"Sorry to call you. I couldn't wait any longer."

"Wait for what?"

"I need to know what you think."

"About?" Had she already sent her design proposal? How could she, in only two hours?

"The letters, of course."

"In the tin?"

"Nick, I messaged you. Did you read my text?"

"Sorry, I just got home a few minutes ago."

"Do you want me to call you back?"

"No!"

Silence.

"Sorry, I didn't mean that I didn't want you to call me."

The doorbell app on his phone chimed.

"Give me a moment. I have to put you on hold. Someone's at the door. Don't hang up."

Nick tapped his screen and let the delivery person into the building. As he walked to the front door, he reconnected with Joy. "Someone's dropping off my Thai order. Sorry."

"It's fine."

He reached the door and pulled it open. The delivery guy was already there. After handing Nick the sealed takeout bag, he waved and took off.

Nick returned to the living room and set the bag on the coffee table before pressing the phone to his ear. "Hey, I'm back." He lowered himself onto the couch. "What's going on?"

"Are you okay with me reading the letters from the cookie tin?"

Nick unrolled the top of the paper bag with his free hand. "Why would you need to ask me that?"

"Well, they came from your house. And I think they're likely of a personal nature."

"They're old letters. I told you I don't care what happens to any of that stuff."

"This is not *stuff.* This is someone's mail. Are we breaking some kind of law by reading it?"

"How old are the letters?"

"Let me check." The sound of rustling paper filled Nick's ear. "The post stamp says 1945."

"That's almost 80 years ago. I doubt anyone would care about those letters now. Anyone who might have is likely long gone."

"What a sad thing to say," Joy replied solemnly.

Nick tugged a container free of the bag. Had he hurt her feelings? It was simple math and the only logical conclusion. Yet, from their afternoon encounter, he understood that Joy was most likely not guided by cold logic. "Hey, I didn't mean it that way."

"Hmm."

"I'll tell you what. Why don't you read a couple and try to figure out who wrote them? Then maybe we can track down their relatives if they still live in the area. We can present them with the entire cookie box, and they can decide what to do with it." Nick could hardly believe the words coming out of his own mouth. Why was he making promises to this woman? He didn't have time to traipse all over town looking for strangers so they could hand them a bunch of old, moldy mail. For some reason, he wanted to make Joy happy. Maybe because it felt appropriate, given her name. "If we can't find any family members, perhaps we could donate some of the letters to a local museum."

"That's a great idea!" The sparkly Joy was back.

He smiled.

"Thanks, Nick."

"For nothing. You found them. You're going to read them. My input is minimal. Keep me posted," he said curtly, eager to get to his dinner before he got pulled into any more crazy, time-consuming schemes.

"Sorry to keep you."

"I didn't mean it that way."

"Didn't you? Do you often say things that you don't mean?"

He frowned. "What?"

"No worries. We can work on that."

We? Where did that come from?

The aromas of ginger and garlic wafted on the air as he lifted the lid off the container. "It's just that I have a bunch of work to do after dinner."

"Understood. I'll text you if I find anything interesting."

"Sure. I'll be up until midnight."

"Great. Have a good one." She must have smiled into the phone, for her voice sounded joyful and bright.

"You too." Nick disconnected the call and reached into the bag for another container.

Loneliness returned to his condo. Who was this woman called Joy?

He contemplated the meal he'd set out on the table. Dinner for one. Nick reached for the wooden fork and dug into his pad thai. The month of December was notorious for delays. First thing tomorrow, he'd call every trade buddy he could think of and get on their schedule.

The famous Ice Wine Festival in Niagara-on-the-Lake would start on the tenth of January, and he'd better have the entire bed and breakfast booked by then.

~ Eleven ~

RAF Coningsby Airfield, Lincolnshire, England

December 24th, 1944

Beth stood in front of the mirror above her dresser, fiddling with her hair. It refused to stay in place. She stared at her reflection. How did she get here? What had happened to her promise not to get attached to any service man?

She sighed. Gabriel had happened.

The man was attentive and sweet. He'd been a teacher before the war. Like her, he had no family. Loved nature. Recited poetry and had read all the books available at the airfield library. What she liked about him the most was how he cared for his Lancaster crew.

On the days when the cloud cover broke and they scrambled to a mission, Beth could hardly concentrate on her job. She prayed for Gabriel and his men and hoped that the war would be over soon and no one else would have to die.

Today, though, she refused to think of the dangerous missions. This was Christmas Eve, and she would do her best to make it special for him.

Beth even wore the only dress she had brought and hadn't used yet. Her nurse's uniform seemed sufficient for everything she did at the airfield, including Sunday church attendance. Everyone wore a uniform. Why be different?

She smoothed the fabric around the collar. Should she iron it again? A quick glance at the clock squashed that idea. Gabriel would be here in less than ten minutes and, knowing him, he wouldn't be late.

Henrietta had insisted that Beth should wear eyeshadow and lip color. Beth dabbed her index finger on the little compact and applied the light brown powder to her upper lid. Hmm. She picked up the mascara and the applicator wand. Henrietta had said to moisten it first, so Beth dipped the applicator in the water glass on her nightstand, then gently rubbed it on the dark disk. Leaning closer to the mirror, she carefully applied the dark, pasty stuff to her upper lashes. A touch of lipstick and she almost didn't recognize herself.

Beth lifted her heavy coat from the hook, picked up her purse and gloves, slipped on her boots, and rushed out the door. Gabriel would indeed be waiting.

Her heart beat a little faster when she spotted him leaning against the wall. *Keep your feet on the ground.*

"Oh, wow." Gabriel exhaled the words as he pushed away from the wall.

Beth was thankful she had chosen not to use the rouge, for her face was instantly flushed with heat.

"Hello," she said, willing her voice not to crack.

"You look stunning." He appeared frozen to the ground.

"You wear no coat?" Beth tilted her head. "Won't you be cold?"

"I'm a warm person," he said with a grin. "And my heart is on fire."

"Oh, Gabriel." She playfully whacked his arm with her gloves. "You better get a hold of yourself, or we'll surely miss the train."

"That we won't. I got us a ride."

"A ride?"

He offered her his arm. "Let's go."

Beth was relieved when the jeep arrived at the train station with minutes to spare.

"I'm glad I let you talk me into this." She smiled, holding firmly to his arm. "I think it must be the most exciting thing I have ever done."

They settled in an empty compartment. Beth was thankful for their privacy, as she planned to have a serious conversation with him. The way things had progressed during the past three weeks scared her a little.

The train whistle blew. Then a jerk and the steam locomotive hissed. She'd never imagined her sensible self in the center of a whirlwind romance. But who could have predicted that she would meet this amazing man on an airfield in England?

"Are you comfortable?" he asked as their car slowly gained speed. He draped his arm over her shoulders.

"Yes, thank you."

Pulling her closer, he kissed her hair.

Beth gazed up at him. "I love that you thought of this, Gabriel. It's sometimes hard to remember what real life feels like."

He smiled. "This is real enough for me, Darling."

As the train settled into a comfortable rhythm and their compartment warmed up, she unbuttoned her coat. "Are you planning to return to teaching when you get back?"

"I am. How about you? What will you do? Your tour is finished in a couple of days."

She pulled away from him and half turned on the seat so she could see him. "I need to talk to you about that."

Gabriel nodded as he shifted to face her.

"I would like to enlist again and request to be stationed here. I talked to the head nurse about it, but she said there's no guarantee I would be assigned to this airfield."

"Beth." He gripped her hand. "You've done more than your part. Why take the risk?"

"Because you're here." She held his gaze. "And because I have no one waiting for me in Canada."

He frowned.

Beth touched his arm. "What is it?"

Suddenly, Gabriel got up and knelt before her.

She pressed her fingers to her chest. "Gabriel?"

"Dearest Bethany." His voice caught. "I have thought long and hard about our future together. I want to spend the rest of my life with you. You've brought much joy and meaning into my life, and I can't imagine facing the years ahead without you by my side."

Her hands flew to her mouth as tears spilled down her cheeks. *Did this man just ask her to marry him?* Warmth flooded her entire body. Her throat tight, she struggled to give him an answer in a trembling voice. "Of course I will marry you."

When he rose and sank down next to her, holding out his arms, she happily moved into his embrace.

"Today?" he whispered in her ear.

Beth pulled back and smiled through her tears. "You shouldn't joke about serious things like that."

His fingers traced her cheek, then he gently wiped her tears with his thumb. "I'm not, darling."

~ TWELVE ~

Niagara-on-the-Lake, Ontario, Canada

December 1st, 2024

Joy cozied up in her bed. Her cup of hot cocoa waited on the nightstand while the antique cookie tin rested on the pillow next to her. Jingles settled in his usual spot by her feet, staring at her dreamily. His amber eyes slowly closed. Tapping her phone, she selected a relaxing jazz re-mix of her favorite Christmas songs.

Her fingers trembled as she reached for the first envelope in the tin. Was she violating someone's privacy by reading these old letters? How would she feel if a nosy person went through her personal correspondence? Did it matter that these pages had been penned some eighty years ago? If the author had been in his or her twenties, they would be what? A hundred years old now? How many centenarians lived in this town? Likely not many. Was there any chance whoever had written these letters was still alive and living in Niagara-on-the-Lake?

Maybe Nick was right and they should donate the letters to a museum. He had mentioned trying to find relatives, though, which Joy would try her hardest to do. The descendants had the right to this find and should be the ones to decide what to do with it. After all, the letters and the train could very well be precious family heirlooms.

Fortified with purpose, Joy opened the first envelope, postmarked from England, and gingerly pulled out the thin sheet of folded paper.

January 14, 1945

My Dearest Beth,

I think of you as I soar above the clouds, the engine's hum beneath me and the vast sky stretching endlessly ahead. The world up here seems infinite and small. No matter how far I fly, though, my heart always remains with you.

The nights are long and the days blend together, but the thought of your smile keeps me going. I remember the first time I saw you at the airfield hospital, your eyes full of determination and kindness. You were a beacon of light in that sea of uncertainty. I can't believe my luck. Yes, we have known each other for only a few short weeks. Still, I feel as if we were meant to find one another. Long ago. Before this darn war started.

I will forever be grateful that you are my wife. The guys thought we were crazy, getting married only weeks after meeting. I believe that it was God who brought us together. And your prayers brought me back to Him.

Never will I forget our trip to London. It amazes me that even during these treacherous times, the Londoners took time to remember the birth of Jesus and retain a sense of hope.

Hamleys toy store almost brought me to tears—void of children's laughter, sparsely decorated, yet serving parents looking for toys to send to their children in the country.

Should our Lord choose to bless us with children, I pray that you and I will never have to be separated from them like these mothers and fathers. I pray that our sons and daughters will never have to experience such terrible evil as this cursed war.

I hope you have set our little train up somewhere in the house. Perhaps it makes you smile every time you look at it.

As soon as I can, I will keep my promise and take you on a honeymoon. I can't wait to see the Rockies with you. The Maritimes are also beautiful, especially Prince Edward Island. What I'm looking forward to the most is the old city of Quebec. We will see it all, I promise. The train is there to remind you of that every day.

Niagara-on-the-Lake must be cold this time of year. It pains me to think of you there without me. I imagine you walking along the frozen falls, the freezing mist catching in your hair, your heart full of hope for the future we'll build together when this is over. My heart is there with you. I long for the day when I can hold you close again, kiss you goodnight, and wake up to your laughter.

I can't wait to see you, to feel the warmth of your embrace, and to start the life we've dreamed of. Until that day, you are my strength, reason, and love.

Stay safe, my darling. Keep me in your prayers as I keep you in mine.

Yours forever and always,

Gabriel

Joy swiped at her tears, unprepared for the depth of emotions those few lines would stir in her heart. Who was this man, and had he kept his promise? Had Beth lived in the house Nick had just purchased? Did she and Gabriel ever see each other again?

Joy reached for her mug and took a sip of the sweet treat. She had to find out what happened to this couple.

Without further hesitation, she reached for another envelope and dove into the loving words covering the thin, yellow sheets.

~ THIRTEEN ~

Niagara-on-the-Lake, Ontario, Canada

January 10th, 1945

My Dearest Gabriel.

I hope this letter finds you well and safe, my love. First, let me assure you I'm fine, although the journey was arduous. As the winter waves of the Atlantic Ocean raged, I prayed that our convoy would avoid mines and that no U-boat would find us.

I was relieved to step on firm ground in Halifax harbor. Exhausted and still a little nauseated, I slept during most of the train ride to Toronto, dreaming of our honeymoon. It will be a wonderful time when no passengers wear a uniform and families with children take vacations once again.

I arrived in Niagara-on-the-Lake yesterday. Everything is as perfect as you described. The house is exactly as I imagined it would be from your stories. The air here is fresh and crisp, and the small-town charm is already beginning to work its magic on me. As beautiful as it is, though, it feels incomplete without you here.

I could feel your presence in every corner as I walked through the front door. I spent today cleaning and tidying up, ensuring everything was right. It felt strange to be doing it all alone. I miss you very much, Gabriel. Every room I walk into, every object I touch, I imagine you beside me, holding my hand, sharing this wonderful life with me.

As I settle into this new chapter, I've been thinking about what to do next. Everything here is unfamiliar, but I'm trying to make it feel like home.

I can't stop thinking about our time in London. It was the best day of my life. My next letter will be to the old vicar, who graciously agreed to marry us right there and then after we walked through the doors of his small church.

The roses, my beautiful wedding bouquet, the manager of the Savoy Hotel gave me, are now dry. I used one of the vases in the china cabinet and placed them in the center of the dining room table. Hope that is all right with you.

I still can't believe you would take me to such a fancy place for lunch. Never had I seen anything like it. I wonder how they manage to get fresh flowers in winter.

I loved the time we spent wandering the city, laughing and dreaming about the future. Hamleys was enchanting. I couldn't believe the size of that toy store. Perhaps, one day, we will have an opportunity to return to London. We will have to go during Christmas, for I wish to see the store decorated and full of children.

I smile as I remember how you insisted on buying me that tiny express train. A honeymoon promise that we'd take a grand adventure together one day. I have set it on the mantel for now. A small token of that unforgettable day and the dreams we have. I will look at it every morning and imagine the day we'll finally board a train together, leaving the war and all its darkness behind us.

While unpacking, I found your mother's ring in the dresser drawer. It's beautiful, Gabriel, and it means so much to me that you want me to have it. I won't wear it until you return and place it on my finger yourself, though. When you finally slide it onto my hand, that moment will be the start of our life together. Until then, I'll keep it safe, waiting for the day we can share that special moment.

I'm staying in your old bedroom. It doesn't feel right to take over your parents' room without you. With its worn furniture and memories of your childhood, this room feels like the right place for me. I've made it cozy. Added a few of my own touches. However, I won't make any significant changes until you're here.

I miss you, Gabriel. The nights are the hardest. I love you with all my heart and pray daily for your safe return. I dream of the moment when I can finally run into your arms.

I pray this war will end soon, the world will find peace again, and you'll come home to me. Until then, I'll be here, waiting for you, holding on to our love and shared dreams.

Stay safe, my darling. You are in my thoughts every moment of every day. I love you more than words can express, and I can't wait until we're together again.

With all my love,

Beth

~ FOURTEEN ~

Niagara-on-the-Lake, Ontario, Canada

December 5th, 2024

The first Thursday in December brought a little sprinkling of snow. Much to Nick's dismay, all Toronto drivers collectively forgot how to drive with the white stuff on the pavement.

The traffic stretched like taffy in all directions. To add to his misery, his favorite station switched to All-Christmas-All-the-Time mode. Coming to a complete stop on the expressway, he reached for the screen and tapped the icon. Talk show. That might do while he slowly lost his mind in this back up. The GPS reloaded. He wouldn't get to Niagara-on-the-Lake until after noon. If he had to sit in traffic for the next three and a half hours, he might as well get some work done.

He pressed a button on his steering wheel.

"Dial Joy."

"Dialing Joy," the ever-peppy synthetic voice replied.

Joy picked up on the second ring. "Hey, Nick. Are you on your way?"

"Stuck in traffic. I'll be there closer to one."

"No problem. Wait until I tell you what I discovered in the letters."

"Great." Were they romantic letters? The last thing he wanted to discuss was someone else's love life.

"I also have a few decorations in my car for the house. Are you okay with me using the spare key in the lockbox to get in?"

"What decorations?"

"Oh, just a few little things. We should start taking pictures of the rooms for the B&B platforms, even though the house isn't fully ready yet."

The car ahead of him started moving. Nick lifted his foot from the brake. The car rolled a few feet before red lights flashed in front of him, and he braked again. "You think it's okay to take the bookings? Before the renos are finished?"

"Are you on track to get the work done?"

"I think so."

"Great. Why don't you and I have a nice sit-down today and check your schedule? You might not want to take the entire place apart all at once. Maybe leave the attic addition for after the festival? March is a bit of a slow month around here."

"That's actually very sound advice." A little of the weight did lift from his shoulders. Joy was right. No need to tackle everything at once.

"Thank you."

He could hear the smile in her cheery voice. How did this woman always stay upbeat? Perhaps because she wasn't stuck on a jammed-up highway. Maybe he needed to experience some of her Christmas cheer. "Would you do me a favor and book a dinner reservation for us? My treat."

"Dinner?"

"Sure. We can discuss the schedule. Bring your designs as well if they're ready."

"Okay. Where would you like to go?"

"I'll leave that up to you."

"Hmm." She paused for a moment.

"Is there a problem?"

"Is there a budget?" she quipped back.

He tapped the steering wheel. "Let's go somewhere nice."

Joy chuckled. "I can definitely find nice in this town."

The traffic inched forward again.

"All right then. It's a date."

A brief silence filled his car.

"Joy?"

"Still here. A date it is," she added tentatively. "I've got to run now. Lots to do before you get here."

She disconnected the call.

What was he thinking? A date? Nick grunted. The last thing he wanted was to mislead her. In no way, shape, or form was he ready for any kind of date, especially not with a cute and delightful person like Joy.

~ FIFTEEN ~

RAF Coningsby Airfield, Lincolnshire, England

February 2nd, 1945

My Dearest Beth,

Your letter arrived yesterday, and I can't tell you how much it meant. I've read it over and over, each word bringing me closer to you, even though I'm far away. I can almost picture you in our little Niagara-on-the-Lake house, making it a home like we dreamed. It comforts me that you're settling in, even as the world remains in turmoil.

Our missions have been relentless, Beth. The skies over Germany are more dangerous now than ever before. We are bombing the Nazi V-rocket locations, but I can't write about that.

The Luftwaffe is still fighting back. You would think that with the Allies pushing the Nazis toward Germany, they would have the sense to give up. Every time we take to the air, it feels like we're playing a deadly game of cat and mouse. The weather has been unpredictable, too—one moment, clear skies, the next, we're flying blind through thick clouds. It's a test of nerve and skill, and I won't lie, there are moments when I feel the weight of it all pressing down on me.

But thoughts of you, my love, keep me focused. I fly with the hope that each mission will bring us one step closer to the end of this war. Then I can finally come home to you.

The other night, we were caught in a terrible storm. The winds tossed us around like rag dolls, and for a while, I wasn't sure we'd make it back. Somehow, we did. Afterward, as I lay in my bunk, trying to calm my racing heart, I thought of our time in London. I could almost hear your laughter echoing through the narrow streets, and I clung to that memory to chase away the fear. That express train from Hamleys, our little token of the future, means more to me now than ever. It's a promise, Beth. One I intend to keep.

Hearing about my mother's ring made me smile. I'm glad you found it. And I'm even more delighted that you're waiting for me to put it on your finger myself. I think about that moment often. It keeps me going, knowing that when this is all over, we'll have the life we've dreamed of. I miss you so much it hurts.

I understand why you've chosen to stay in my old bedroom. I'm glad it's giving you some comfort. That room was my sanctuary when I was a boy, and now, knowing you're there makes me happy. We'll make the rest of the house ours when I return.

I miss you more than words can express. The nights are long here, too, especially after a mission when the adrenaline fades and all that's left is the quiet and the cold. I lie awake thinking of you, wishing you were here or, better yet, wishing I was there with you. I love you more than I've ever loved anything, my dearest. The thought of holding you again, of finally being able to live the normal life we've been denied for so long, is what keeps me strong. Just think, Lord willing, I'll be home in a few months. We will decorate our first Christmas tree together as we celebrate our first anniversary. I long for that day with all my heart.

Pray for me, Beth, as I pray for you. This war can't last forever. When it ends, I'll be on the first plane home to you. Until then, I'm with you in spirit, and your love is my shield against the darkness.

Stay safe, my love. I'll write again as soon as I can. Until then, keep the faith. You are my heart and my soul.

With all my love,

Gabriel

~ SIXTEEN ~

Niagara-on-the-Lake, Ontario, Canada

December 5th, 2024

When Nick finally parked in the driveway, he climbed out of his car and stood there, staring at the house. The front door of his newest project was decorated with a charming Christmas wreath. Two matching planters flanked the entrance. A long string of lights had been draped over the shrubs in the front garden.

When Joy said *a few things*, he hadn't imagined she would bring an entire craft store. The photos should be more general, as the bookings were for January. By then, all this Christmassy stuff would be tired, ready for a storage room.

He would have to have a serious talk with her about this. And about *the date*. He blew out his cheeks. The word had just slipped out. Unfortunately, she'd noticed. Now he had to go into damage control mode. How would he explain that he didn't mean a *date date*, only a dinner? With a friend. A business associate. Yes, those were the correct words to use. A business meeting. With an associate.

He pushed the door open. Before he could even step inside, the sweet scents of spices and all things Christmas enveloped him. What was the woman up to?

"Joy?"

"Come on in," her voice chimed from some room on the first floor. "Great timing. I just finished decorating. We can use your phone to take a few pictures."

Nick slipped his shoes off and walked toward the kitchen, passing a smiling Frosty the Snowman holding a sign that said *May Christmas Warm Your Heart* as he started down the hall. The railing leading to the second floor was wrapped in a festive garland adorned with plaid bows. Oh boy. How could he tell her the railing was scheduled to be refinished next week?

"Do you like it?" She practically bounced into the hallway. "I think it's splendid. I was thrilled when I found the ribbon matching the cookie box's tartan."

He blinked. Her pants suit was perfectly cut, yet he wasn't sure what to think of it. "Do you always wear red?"

"In December? Yes."

Nick struggled not to stare. She did look great. "Uhm. What cookie box are you talking about?"

"The tin we found up in the attic, of course. Give me a sec." Joy zoomed into the kitchen and returned with the old tin.

"Great." He grunted.

"Grinch."

Nick drew his eyebrows together.

"Well, you definitely lack enthusiasm. Christmas decorating is my favorite thing to do. Come look at the living room." She skipped ahead of him.

He clenched his fists. Was she ten years old? He reluctantly followed her to the next room, then stood in the doorway, gaping.

A tall Christmas tree stood next to the fireplace, adorned with identical bows to the railing and a million other things. His eyes had difficulty taking in all the little planes, small British flags, and shortbread cookies dangling from the branches. Walking closer, he picked up a small envelope.

"I made those," Joy said with notable pride. "There is a YouTube tutorial on fake-aging paper. I figured we should go with the theme."

"What theme?"

"The love letters, of course."

"Love letters?"

"That's what was in the tin. A bunch of old love letters from the Second World War."

"Have you read them all?"

Joy lowered her gaze as if caught stealing cookies from the jar. "Most of them. Once I started, I couldn't stop."

"What did you find out?"

"It's a beautiful story."

"Great." Nick strode into the kitchen. The counters were covered with trays displaying an appetizing assortment of cookies. "Where did you get these?" He reached for a gingerbread star.

"I baked them. Remember? The competition?"

He contemplated the white icing before taking a bite. "You're a woman of many talents."

"Thank you," she said, smiling. "The only thing I didn't get a chance to do was set up the train under the tree."

His eyebrows rose.

"Would you help me?"

"Me?"

"It's your house. Your tree."

"But—"

"But what?"

He reached for another cookie, stalling for time so he could come up with a good reason for not encouraging her in this madness. "These are good."

Joy's quick fingers plucked the cookie out of his hand. "You can have this one after the train is done."

"What?"

"Yep, you heard me right. We need to finish decorating and start taking photos. I made the reservations for six-thirty, which means..." she glanced at her phone, "we better get cracking."

"About that." Nick cleared his throat.

"What?" She halted. "Did you change your mind? I can cancel." She held up her phone.

"No. I don't want you to cancel. I only want to make sure you didn't misunderstand me."

"Misunderstand you?"

"When I said—"

"What?"

"*Date.*"

Joy burst out laughing. "Are you worried I thought you were asking me out on a date?"

Warmth crept up Nick's neck. "I mean, I guess I was."

She planted her hands on her hips. "Trust me. If you were to ask me on an actual date, I would expect much more than a quick call ordering me to make dinner reservations."

~ Seventeen ~

Niagara-on-the-Lake, Ontario, Canada

February 14th, 1945

My Dearest Gabriel,

Your letter arrived this morning, the best Valentine's Day gift I could wish for. It filled my heart with much joy and relief. Knowing you are safe, even amidst all that danger, brings me peace. I miss you, Gabriel, and I long for the day when we can finally be together again.

I'm surprised to see the first signs of spring. It is too early, even for Niagara-on-the-Lake, but the garden is beginning to wake up. The snowdrops and crocuses are peeking through the soil, their delicate leaves promising warmer days ahead. They're beautiful. I spent the morning raking out old leaves and trimming the hedge along the fence. I imagined us out there together, planting new flowers and making it our little haven. I wish you could see the warm sun rays and the way the light filters through the trees. It feels like nature is whispering that the long, hard winter is ending. I pray that it's a sign this terrible war will be over soon, too.

The weather has been unusually mild. I took the opportunity to wash all the drapery. The fresh air did wonders for them, and it felt satisfying to see them drying in the breeze, fluttering like flags of hope. I took them in before the night's frost and am drying them by the fireplace. The whole house smells of sunshine and fresh linen.

I've been keeping up with the news through the newspapers and the radio as best I can. Every report sounds more promising than the last. The Allied forces are pushing the Nazis back, and it seems that soon they'll be crossing the borders into Germany itself. There's talk of victory, the tide finally turning in our favor, filling me with much hope. We're not there yet, but I can feel it—the end is near. This war can't go on much longer, and I pray every day that soon you'll be coming home to me.

I've been thinking a lot about what our life will be like when you return. The simple things—cooking dinner, going for walks along the lake, starting a family. It's those thoughts that keep me going, even on the days when I miss you so much it's hard to breathe. I love you, Gabriel, more than words can say. Every moment we've been apart has only deepened that love, and I can't wait to share every part of my life with you.

I still keep your mother's ring tucked safely away, waiting for the day you will place it on my finger. I think about that moment often.

The nights are still lonely, but knowing that you're out there, doing everything you can to come back to me, gives me strength. I lie in your old bed and imagine you beside me, your arms around me, keeping me safe. I love you, my darling, with all my heart, and I can't wait for the day when we'll never have to say goodbye again.

Until then, stay safe, Gabriel. You are always in my thoughts and prayers. I'm counting down the days until you're home, where you belong.

With all my love,

Beth

~ Eighteen ~

Niagara-on-the-Lake, Ontario, Canada

December 5th, 2024

"Hope you like this place," Joy said as she met Nick at the restaurant entrance. It had been her decision to take their own cars. Honestly, she'd had enough of his downer attitude and planned to head straight home after their meal.

"Looks okay," he said as he held the door open for her.

"It might not be your Toronto-style dining venue, but all you asked for was *nice*. Queen's Landing definitely fits the bill."

She walked through the door into a bar area paneled in dark wood and decorated in a fancy English pub style. The stained-glass windows created a nice division from the hallway beyond the bar.

"I see what you mean," he said quietly behind her.

"Follow me." Joy smiled and marched through the space toward the back door. "This is not where we eat."

"Yes, ma'am."

A beautiful foyer opened before them, warm and bright and decorated with white Christmas trees featuring purple ornaments. Oversized bouquets of roses added to the festive feel.

"Wow, what is this place?"

"That's a banquet hall to the left. The wedding season is always on at Queen's Landing."

"Even at Christmas?"

"You bet. The hotel does a fabulous job with decorations. Who wouldn't want to be married here?"

Judging from the look on his face, him. Joy narrowly resisted rolling her eyes as she stopped in front of the maître d'. "Good evening. We have a reservation for two."

The uniformed man smiled. "Your name, please?"

"Joy."

He picked up two menus. "Follow me."

A grand dining room opened before them, framed by large windows overlooking a garden sprinkled with fresh snow. The sconces on the walls infused the space in a golden hue. Their server was already waiting for them at the table. He pulled out one of the high-backed leather chairs and motioned to Joy.

"Thank you." She sat down as the man behind her tucked in the chair. Nick took the chair opposite her, reached for the linen napkin, shook it out, and spread it over his knees.

"Nice enough for you?" She smiled across the table.

"It is. Thank you," he said and looked her in the eyes. "It's been a while since I've had the chance to enjoy a lovely meal in a place like this." Their gazes locked. "With wonderful company."

So, he can be polite when he chooses to.

Joy reached for her napkin and laid it over her lap, buying a few precious seconds before she sorted out how to reply. The server came to her rescue, handing her a large, opened menu.

When they were alone once more, she looked over at Nick. "The food here is great, and the local wine is fabulous, too." She tilted her head.

"And now that we both understand that this *date* is not a date, we can relax and discuss more important matters."

"The renovation?"

"The letters and the train, of course." She chuckled.

"Oh, that."

"I promised to tell you the entire story over dinner. We'd better order."

The appetizer plates cleared, Joy glanced at the kitchen door, anticipating their main course. They had both ordered filet mignon, medium rare, with a side of vegetables. Perhaps they had more in common than an old house needing major TLC.

"Tell me." Nick broke the silence. "How long have you lived in this area?"

"About five years." Joy reached for the butter knife and spread a dab of the whipped artisan delicacy onto her crisp roll.

"You like it here?"

"I do." She set the knife on the table. "I fell in love with this town, the community, the farmers, and I found an amazing church here. What's not to like?"

Nick lifted his shoulders. "I guess."

So, their little town hadn't won him over yet. Fine. Joy enjoyed a challenge. "How about you? Had you always lived in the great TO?"

"Yes. I was born in the Davenport area. My parents still have a house there."

"How do you put up with the traffic?"

He shrugged again. "It's a daily grind you get used to."

"Is that why you're always..." She took a bite of the crusty roll.

"Why I'm always what?"

Was that a hint of defensiveness in his voice?

Joy chewed slowly. "How do I put it?" She set the rest of her bun on the bread plate. "Rushed? Perhaps a little angry?"

He stayed silent.

"Sorry, I don't mean to offend you. But I don't think I've ever met anyone who disliked Christmas as much as you seem to."

"Why do you say that?" He reached for his glass of water.

"I saw it on your face. You hated the garland, didn't like the tree, and putting together the train was a chore you would rather not do. Am I right?"

He set his glass down. "I don't like doing things that waste time."

"Waste time?" Did the man have absolutely no sense of childlike wonder?

Thankfully, the steaks arrived, and the rich aroma of their meal tangibly decreased the tension between them.

Joy cut into her meat and took a bite, closing her eyes to enjoy the intense flavor.

"This is one of the best steaks I've ever had," Nick said.

She opened her eyes. "Honestly?"

He nodded and cut another piece. "Why don't you tell me about those letters?"

She welcomed the change of topic with a smile. "You were right about them."

"I was?"

"They should be archived in a museum. They're beautifully written love letters, filled with details about the house, the town, and the last months of the war. Her name was Beth, and his Gabriel. I imagine them coming to this hotel to celebrate special occasions."

"Is that why you made our dinner reservations here?"

"Aside from knowing that the food would be great? Yes."

He smirked, then forked another piece of steak.

"Let me tell you more about their story," Joy said between bites. "They met in an airfield hospital in England. That was December 1944. And get this." She waved her fork. "They were married within three weeks of their meeting. On Christmas Eve."

"You're kidding."

"Nope."

"How could someone marry a person they didn't even know?"

"Maybe they knew each other enough."

"What do you mean?" Nick set his cutlery down.

"I think that the moment we meet the person God intended for us, we know."

He swiped the burgundy cloth napkin across his mouth. "That only happens in Hallmark movies. Real life doesn't work that way."

"It did for them."

"Well, it didn't for me." He tossed the napkin onto the table before cutting into his potato with unnecessary vigor.

Whoa. Obviously a sore spot. "Want to talk about that?"

"Not really."

"Is that why you dislike Christmas?"

His fork clattered onto his plate as he reached for his glass of water and took a swig. When he set the glass down, several drops sloshed onto the table.

"I'm sorry." She grabbed her napkin and dabbed at the spill. "I didn't mean to get personal."

"Why don't we just stick to the old letters?"

Joy laid the napkin across her knees again. "Fine. Beth and Gabriel got married on the twenty-fourth of December 1944. Afterwards, they went to the Hamleys toy store in central London where Gabriel bought Beth the train set we found in the attic."

"Instead of a ring?"

"No, as a promise to take her on a honeymoon after the war ended. She'd always wanted to take the train across Canada, so they decided to do that as soon as he returned home."

"Don't tell me this is a Nicholas Sparks story. He got shot down, or she wrote him a Dear John letter."

Nick watches Nicholas Sparks films?

"Has anyone ever told you that you might be a cynic?" Joy dabbed the corners of her mouth with her napkin and set it on the plate.

Nick grinned.

"Let me tell you what happened. Gabriel got shot down towards the end of the war and was taken prisoner."

"Here we go." Nick tossed his napkin onto the table. "You can stop right there."

Joy held up a hand. "Listen. Beth waited for several weeks, not knowing if he was dead or alive. She wrote to his base commander, and when she got no response, she traveled to Europe to look for him."

"Are you kidding?"

"No. If you can believe it, she signed up with the Red Cross. Boarded a ship and went on a search and rescue mission for her husband."

"Did she find him?"

Joy was about to answer his question when the server came to collect their plates.

"Would you like a peek at our dessert menu?" he asked.

Without glancing at Nick, she nodded, remembering how fast he had scarfed down her Christmas cookies.

"Sure." Dessert would be nice. Besides, she wasn't quite finished with her story yet.

~ NINETEEN ~

Niagara-on-the-Lake, Ontario, Canada

February 28th, 1944

My Dearest Gabriel.

I hope this letter finds you safe, but my heart is heavy with worry as I write. It's been weeks since I last heard from you, and every hour without word feels like a lifetime. I understand that the missions are demanding, but I can't help the fear that's crept into my thoughts. Please, my love, if you can, send me a letter as soon as you're able. I only need to know that you're okay.

Every time the postman arrives, my heart leaps in hope, only to sink when there's nothing from you. I remind myself constantly that no news is good news. That you're likely caught up in the intensity of your work. Still, it's hard not to imagine the worst. You're my whole world, Gabriel, and the thought of something happening to you is more than I can bear.

The town is much the same as ever, though the mood seems to have shifted lately. Everyone here is on edge, anxious for any news from the front. The local papers have been full of updates about the Allied advances, and the radio crackles with reports of progress in Europe. They say we're getting closer to victory, that the Nazis are being pushed farther back every day. Still, it all feels far away from where I am, alone in this little house, waiting for your news. There's talk that the war could end soon, but I don't dare let myself hope for that just yet—not until I'm sure you're safe.

I love you, my dearest, and every day without you feels like an eternity. I'm trying to stay strong for both of us. Please, Gabriel, write to me as soon as you can. I'll be waiting by the window, watching for the postman, hoping with all my heart that he will bring a letter from you.

Take care of yourself, my love. You are in my thoughts and prayers, and I'm here, waiting and loving you with all that I am.

With all my love,

Beth

~ Twenty ~

Niagara-on-the-Lake, Ontario, Canada

December 5th, 2024

The decaf lattes, cheesecake, and tiramisu arrived, much to Nick's joy. He loved his sweets, and clearly the woman across the table did, too. Perhaps they had more in common than he'd realized. If only she didn't seem to perceive things that were none of her business. Things he would rather keep to himself.

Joy was pretty, intelligent, and funny. Still, she had this irritating way of getting under his skin with all that positivity. It hadn't taken her long to figure out that he didn't like Christmas. Of course, had she experienced a holiday like he had a year ago, she wouldn't either.

"Tell me." Nick sank his spoon into the creamy tiramisu. "Did they find each other?"

"I will, but only if you agree to share the desserts. I had a tough time deciding between the two."

He grinned, then gently pushed his plate toward the center of the table. "As long as you don't wolf the whole thing down before I get to taste it."

"I'll try to behave myself," she said solemnly as she nudged her cheesecake closer to him. "Here. Have a taste. This might be my favorite."

"I thought mine was your favorite."

"Can't a girl have two favorites?"

Nick smirked, then went for the cheesecake. The silky texture of the cake with a slight hint of cherries melted on his tongue. "Oh, my goodness." He groaned. "Now I understand."

"See? I told you."

He wiped his mouth with the napkin and set it next to the plate. "So? Did they?"

"Did they what?"

He held her gaze. "Find each other."

"That's still a mystery."

He wrinkled his forehead. "What do you mean? You said that they came here to celebrate their anniversaries."

"No. I said I *imagined* them coming here."

"I don't believe that you don't know. You're stringing me along."

She lifted a hand in the air. "I'm not. None of the letters say."

Nick pursed his lips. "Did you just trick me into ordering dessert?"

"What if I did? Are you regretting your decision?"

"Nope." Nick scraped the last bit of the tiramisu out of the dish. "You?"

"No." She set her fork on the empty cheesecake plate. "For a date that wasn't a date, I had a great time."

"I did, too."

She studied him a little too long for his comfort.

Nick cleared his throat. "What comes next?"

"Next?" Her eyebrows knitted together. "I think I'm going home next." She paused before adding, "Alone."

"That's not what I meant," he stammered. Nick leaned forward. "Joy, I have a feeling you've misunderstood this entire evening. I hope I didn't mislead—"

She raised her hand. "Relax. I was kidding. Her blue eyes held a mischievous glint. "For a cool Toronto investor, you get your knickers in a knot very easily."

Nick was trying to keep things professional, and this girl was baiting him? He let out a sigh. "To be clear, I meant, what are you planning to do next with the letters?"

"I'll use my real estate agent powers to check the property's history. I should be able to perform a search for past owners."

"And then?"

The server appeared at their table. "Is there anything else I can get either of you?"

Nick looked across the table at Joy and raised his eyebrow.

"I'm fine, thank you," she replied.

Nick nodded. "Just the bill, thanks."

When the man set it on the table in a black faux leather folder, Joy reached for it. "We can go Dutch."

Nick grabbed it before she could. "I said this was my treat." *Did she think he couldn't afford this place?*

"Thank you," she said with a smile. "The next dinner is on me."

Next dinner? He tugged the wallet from his pocket and pulled out a credit card. Actually, he would like that. Joy was delightful company. Aside from being excited about the simple things in life, she also had the uncanny ability to keep him on his toes. If he was honest with himself, he'd have to admit he rather enjoyed that. Naturally, he'd never tell her. That could potentially open a door he was not ready to walk through. Yet.

~ TWENTY-ONE ~

Niagara-on-the-Lake, Ontario, Canada

March 10th, 1945

Group Captain Reginald Thompson Conings by Airfield, Lincolnshire, England

Dear Group Captain Thompson,

I hope this letter finds you well. My name is Beth Holly, and I served as a nurse at the airfield hospital some months ago. I write to you now not as a former colleague but as a deeply concerned wife.

My husband, Flying Officer Gabriel Holly, is a member of one of the squadrons under your command. It has been several weeks since I last received a letter from him, and I am growing increasingly worried. I understand that communication can be difficult, especially during intense operations. Even so, the silence has become unbearable. I am writing to you with the hope that you might be able to provide me with some news about his squadron and his well-being.

Gabriel is everything to me, and these past few weeks without word have been the hardest I've faced. I understand you are responsible for many men and cannot attend to every personal matter. I ask you, though, as someone who has served alongside your men, someone who has seen firsthand the toll this war takes on those who fight it. Could you please look into this for me?

I would be eternally grateful for any information you could provide, even if it is only to say that he is safe or still out on a mission.

I realize that asking for this favor may be an imposition, but I don't know where else to turn. The uncertainty is consuming me, and I find myself imagining the worst. I have always respected the work you and your men do, and I know Gabriel is proud to serve under your command. If you could find it in your heart to help ease my fears, I would be forever in your debt.

Thank you for taking the time to read this letter and for all that you do for the men in your care. I hope and pray that you can provide some news about my husband.

With sincere respect and gratitude,

Beth Holly

Niagara-on-the-Lake, Canada

~ TWENTY-TWO ~

Niagara-on-the-Lake, Ontario, Canada

December 6st, 2024

Sitting cross-legged on her sofa, Joy energetically tapped the keys on her laptop. This information hunt was exciting. She couldn't wait to update Nick.

Nick. The man who liked to hide behind a calm exterior but who had evidently had his heart broken and decided not to trust... anyone. Still, there were a few cracks in that well-maintained façade. As much as he loved to denounce anything even remotely related to Christmas, she had noticed the quiet joy in his eyes after she'd coerced him into helping set up the train set and the toy actually worked.

And there were the beautiful Christmas trees in the Queen's Landing lobby he'd paused by when he thought she wasn't paying attention. Had a nostalgic look crossed his face, or had she imagined it?

What had happened to cause him such pain?

Lord, please help me find a way to help him heal. I don't know if he is a man of faith, but you know his heart.

Joy paused. When had she begun to pray for Nick? Talking to God was natural to her, but she didn't keep an account of her conversations. Still, Nick had been on her heart since they'd met.

She scanned the old census records. As her friend at the land registry office had suggested, Joy had signed up for an online platform tracking genealogies. And there it was. Gabriel Holly had been the sole owner of the house on Maple Leaf Avenue since 1942. Joy looked at the next census record. Beth Holly had been added to the deed, a wife to Gabriel. That meant their quick London marriage had been recognized as legal in Canada. She scrolled down the document and found the next set of records. Beth, Gabriel, and Noelle Holly were registered at the address.

Joy grabbed her phone and stabbed the buttons, drumming her fingers on the arm of the couch as she waited through three rings.

"Hello?"

Finally. "Nick!"

"What's going on? Are you okay?"

Unable to sit a second longer, she got up and paced the living room carpet. "I found her!"

"What?"

"She was in the census records."

"Joy, can this wait? I'm in a meeting with my contractors right now."

"Sure. Sorry." She frowned. When and how, exactly, had he gained the power to instantly douse her enthusiasm? "I'll call you back later today."

"Fine."

Joy disconnected the phone. Why had she expected him, Mr. Grumpy, to share her excitement? She tossed the device onto the couch next to Jingles, who meowed his displeasure at being disturbed.

"It's not my responsibility to make others happy." Joy ran a hand along the back of the disgruntled kitty. "Right?" The cat meowed again, in agreement this time. "Now that I have a name, I can check the current real estate records, see if I can find Noelle Holly on the deed."

Joy clicked on her realtor portal and entered her password. Once the site loaded, she typed in the street address, and there it was. Noelle and Rudolf Darling were listed as the property owners. "She married Rudolf, and they took over the house." She petted Jingles' head. "I wonder if that was an inheritance or if her parents sold it to them." Unfortunately, such information was not available. The Darlings had sold the house to the Stevens five years ago, and Nick had purchased the property from them.

"Let's check some of the social media platforms," Joy said to Jingles. "Noelle and her husband would be in their 80s now, but many seniors are on Facebook. We could strike gold."

She typed Noelle's name into the Facebook search bar. A short list came up. Joy scanned the suggestions and eliminated everyone who looked under fifty. One profile remained. She clicked on the picture of a sunflower. Skeptical of any page without a person's face, she wasn't keen on exploring that option but, much to her surprise, it wasn't a fake account.

The page offered many posts, mostly photos of various activities. She scrolled down, read a few comments, and gasped. She knew exactly where to find Noelle.

Joy checked the corner of her screen. It was 2:35 p.m. Should she get into her car and simply drive to the River's Edge Retirement Home, fifteen minutes away? Or should she try again to tell *him* that she'd found Noelle?

Joy glanced at her phone. Nick was far more interested in gutting and modernizing the old house than in uncovering its history and preserving the memories.

Was there a way to convince him to change his mind? Unsure why, she felt an attachment to the old furnishings and dishes that had been left in the kitchen. The scent of old polished woodwork and the rustle of fading drapery brought her an unexpected sense of comfort. If only she could afford this home, she would buy it from him before the hammers hit the tiled floors.

Her phone rang.

"Hey." She tried and failed to disguise the surprise in her voice at seeing Nick's name at the top of her screen.

"Sorry to be short when you called, but I had a bunch of guys here looking at the plans."

An apology?

"No problem."

"Tell me, what did you find out?"

"Nick," she said, the enthusiasm he'd doused earlier returning full force. "I think I found *her*."

"Who?"

"Noelle."

"Who is Noelle?"

"Oh, sorry." Joy stopped pacing and rested a hand on her head. Obviously, she was getting ahead of the man. "I need to explain."

"Please do."

"Noelle Holly was registered on the census. I think Gabriel and Beth had a baby, which would mean he came home." Her voice broke. Good grief. She was becoming far too attached to these people she had never met and who wouldn't even be alive anymore.

"Are you all right?"

"Yeah." Joy sniffed. "Anyway, I think I found Noelle's Facebook page. I believe she lives in a nearby retirement home."

"Are you for real?"

Was that a hint of interest in his voice? Joy would take it. She lowered her arm to her side. "We should visit her."

"We?"

"Yes. We can give her the letters and the train set. They may mean something to her, and I think she should be the one who decides what to do with them."

"Sure, but do I have to be there? Can't you just drive over and give her the stuff?"

Joy took a deep breath.

"Hello?"

She blew out her cheeks. This man, indeed, didn't have a heart. "Still here." There had to be a way to make him understand how significant their find was. "You're the owner of the house. I think you should be the one presenting the items to her."

"You found them."

"It's your house."

"Joy." Silence filled the air. "I..."

"What?"

"I'm kind of busy. We're working on a very tight timeline."

A spark of an idea flashed through her brain. "Don't you see? This is a prime opportunity to get some media exposure."

"What do you mean?"

"Why don't we plan a Christmas open house and invite Noelle? I can contact the town newspaper, the chamber of commerce, the historical society, and the local museum. We can make it a thing."

"A thing?" The interest she'd caught in his voice had turned into trepidation.

"Yes, don't you see? The social media exposure alone will surely bring a bunch of bookings."

"Hmm. You may be onto something."

Give it a business twist, and he's all in. "I believe I am."

"Let me think about it first."

"Oh, come on, it's already mid-December. There are only two weekends before Christmas, and most people are super busy."

"Tell me about it."

"You get how important this is, right?" She meant how important it was to reunite the train and letters with Gabriel and Beth's daughter, but let Nick think she meant it was important to his B&B business. Whatever it took to get him on board.

"Okay. Go for it."

"Yes!"

Joy disconnected the call before he could change his mind. A Christmas open house would be fun. How hard could it be? The house was already decorated. She still had several batches of cookies, which she should hide before Nick polished them off. All that was left to do was print the invitations and e-mail a press release. And visit the River's Edge Retirement Home.

~ TWENTY-THREE ~

RAF Coningsby Airfield, Lincolnshire, England

March 23rd, 1945

12 Maple Leaf Avenue
Niagara-on-the-Lake
Ontario, Canada

Dear Mrs. Holly,

I have received your letter and wish to extend my sincerest sympathies for the worry you must be enduring. It is indeed challenging to await news during these uncertain times. I'm sorry that I do not have better information to provide to ease your distress.

Flying Officer Gabriel Holly's Lancaster, regrettably, came under fire during a recent operation over Germany. The aircraft sustained considerable damage, necessitating the crew's evacuation. A report from an escort aircraft indicates that five parachutes were observed deploying safely, though this does leave two crew members unaccounted for.

Given the current situation on the ground, with intense fighting as German forces are pushed back towards Berlin, it is unfortunately impossible to undertake a search and rescue mission at this time. The conditions are perilous, and the area is fiercely contested.

I can only offer my prayers for the safety of your husband and his crew. Whilst the situation is uncertain, I urge you not to lose hope. It is possible they have been taken prisoner or have found their way to safety.

We are doing everything within our power to monitor the situation closely. You will be informed immediately should any further information come to light.

With the deepest respect and hope,

Group Captain Reginald Thompson

Royal Air Force

~ TWENTY-FOUR ~

Niagara-on-the-Lake, Ontario, Canada

December 7th, 2024

This time, Joy agreed to go with Nick in his car. Was that a step in the right direction for the two of them? As usual, Joy radiated excitement. Was it possible her enthusiasm could be contagious? If it was, so far he hadn't caught it. After all, they were going to a retirement home, not a rock concert.

"Thanks for dressing up for the occasion," she said, glancing at him.

"I didn't."

"Sorry, I was trying to compliment you, Mr. Grumpy."

He grunted.

"Exactly."

He signaled to turn at the next corner. "Did you call them to make sure your Noelle is an actual resident there?"

"Yes, but they wouldn't confirm or deny that. Privacy protection."

He shot her a sideway look. "Are you telling me we could be going on a wild goose chase?"

"Call it an adventure." Joy reached for the central console.

"Don't touch that."

Her hand froze mid-air. "Don't touch what? The fan?"

"I have it set on auto. If you turn the dial, it will change the settings."

Joy lowered her hand to her knee. "Excuse me. I wouldn't want to change your settings. How about I let the cold air blast my face instead?"

Wow. For the first time he could recall, her voice held a tinge of frost. Maybe he should let her turn up the heat a little. "It will warm up in a few seconds."

"Sure, but it can do that without freezing my nose."

He grunted again as he reached for the climate control icon on the screen and tapped it. "Better?"

Joy studied her nails. "Note to future self. Always take my car."

"I didn't mean to be overly controlling."

"Yes, you did. At least you could own that."

In no mood for a lecture, Nick focused on the road ahead. Thankfully, the nursing home wasn't too far.

She half turned in her seat to face him. "Let me just say that I think you're a good guy."

He glanced at her.

"Somewhere deep inside, that is."

"Thanks. I think."

"The only thing is, you're super guarded."

"I have my reasons."

Joy unclipped her hair and brushed it out with her fingers. "Nick, every one of us has been hurt at one point in our lives."

"Who says I've been hurt?"

When she smiled at him, he fought the urge to pull to the side of the road and suggest she call an Uber.

"I don't mean to pry, but—"

"So don't." He glanced at the GPS. They were almost there.

Silence filled the car.

Nick signaled left and pulled into the parking lot. "Let's just hope we won't discover that this Noelle has passed on and that the trip here was a total waste of time."

The place looked more like a fancy resort than an old folks' home. The Christmas music that seemed to be playing everywhere he went these days filled the air, pumped into the space through invisible speakers.

Nick leaned back against the high counter of the reception desk and scanned the dark wood paneling. Someone had spent a boatload of money on this place. The carpets were custom-made to fit the hallways, and the high-back chairs had been upholstered in a complementing pattern. All the window coverings, light fixtures, and hardware also appeared to be custom. What did Joy think of this place? Nothing old or dated. There *were* Christmas decorations everywhere—which she would like, even though she likely secretly hated *the lack of character*, as she would call it. He turned around as she came up to stand at the counter next to him.

"Hi." Joy smiled at the woman minding the front desk. "We're here to see Noelle Holly."

The woman shook her head. "We have no one here by that name."

Nick gazed up at the ceiling. As he'd predicted, this was a total waste of time.

"Do you have anyone here named Noelle?"

"Yes, we do, but—"

"I'm afraid I might have given you her maiden name. Her married name would be Darling. Noelle Darling."

"Still, we're not supposed to—"

Joy rushed on, obviously not about to let the woman refuse to help them. "I'm a realtor, and Nick here is my client. He purchased a home on Maple Leaf Avenue, and we found some family heirlooms in the attic. We would like to ask if Mrs. Darling wants to keep them."

This entire intro without taking a breath? Nick chuckled. Although it was the poor woman behind the counter who appeared almost dizzy.

Before she could speak, Joy leaned over the counter and tapped the top of the computer. "I'm quite certain Noelle Darling is here. Would it be possible to see if she is available?"

Conceding defeat, the receptionist picked up the phone. After dialing, she waited a moment and then said, "Mrs. Darling, I have a couple of people here asking for you. Would you be able to come down for a few minutes?"

A brief pause.

"If you're uncomfortable, you don't need to see them. You can say no."

Nick glanced at Joy. Her smile dropped.

"Okay, dear. I will tell them to wait in the coffee shop. Take your time."

Joy was instantly beaming. Nick shook his head. This woman was deeply invested in that old box of letters. Why was it so important to her? The old couple was long gone; if this was the right Noelle, she might not even care about some correspondence penned before her time.

"If you'll wait there," the woman pointed toward a glass door adorned with frosty lettering spelling out the words *Coffee Shop*. "Mrs. Darling should be along shortly."

They entered the large room staged as Starbucks and smothered with Christmas décor. The holiday tunes followed them.

Nick spotted an automated espresso machine. "At least the coffee here should be good," he said, picking up a paper cup covered in a silver snowflake pattern. "Care for one?"

"Sure."

"A latte?"

"Yes, please."

He pressed the appropriate buttons. Why did her smile make him feel—feel what? Happy?

The coffee machine hissed, and in seconds the entire place smelled simply divine. The milk trickled into the double-shot espresso. As he picked up the full cup, ready to carry it to the small table in the corner, a blue-haired lady, leaning on a walker, shuffled in.

"Hello." Her voice was a little raspy. "Young man, are you the one looking for me?"

"Hi." He set down the coffee and shook her hand. "Are you Mrs. Noelle Darling?"

"I am."

"Then yes, you're the one we're looking for. My name is Nick, and over there is my friend Joy. Would you have a few minutes to chat?"

Cold, bony fingers wrapped around his hand. "I suppose I do, since I came all the way down here."

Nick smiled. "I'm pretty good at making coffee," he said, motioning to the machine. "Would you care for one?"

"I don't drink coffee, but if you could make me a cup of hot chocolate, that would be wonderful."

"One hot chocolate coming up. Do you need help to get to the table?"

"Don't fuss over me. I get around just fine," the woman said, approaching Joy.

"Hello." Joy stood and moved a chair away from the table, motioning for the older lady to sit down. "Thank you for making time to see us."

"I'll say I was a little surprised when Sandra called me, but then I thought, why not see what you are here about?" Mrs. Darling slowly lowered herself onto the chair as if not trusting that it would support her weight.

"Here are your drinks, ladies." Nick set two paper cups in front of them. "I see some shortbread in the display unit. Should I bring some?" He winked at Joy.

"That would be lovely," the lady said.

It only took him a minute or two to bring over three cookies and his cup of coffee. After sitting down, he took the cling wrap off the shortbread and took a bite.

"Not bad." He waved the cookie in the air. "I'll have to stop by here more often. This place beats Starbucks any day."

~ TWENTY-FIVE ~

Niagara-on-the-Lake, Ontario, Canada

April 7th, 1945

Beth sat by the window, the early morning light filtering through the drapes. The garden outside was still, the last frost of the season slowly disappearing in the morning sun. The scene's beauty was wasted on her, however. Her thoughts were far away, somewhere over the battle-scarred fields of Europe, where Gabriel was lost to her.

It had been a week since she had received the letter from Group Captain Reginald Thompson. The news had shattered her world, leaving her in numb disbelief. Gabriel's Lancaster had gone down, and while five parachutes had been counted, the crew's fate remained uncertain. Two men were unaccounted for, and no one could tell her if Gabriel was among them. The waiting, the not knowing, was unbearable.

Beth felt as if she were living in a dream or, better yet, a nightmare. She tried to keep busy—tending the garden, sewing, and writing letters that she could never bring herself to send. The ache in her heart only grew.

She could no longer sit here in Niagara-on-the-Lake, waiting for news that might never come. *God, what if Gabriel is injured or imprisoned?* If there was any chance that Gabriel was alive, she had to do something. She had to find him.

Beth rose and rushed up the stairs to Gabriel's old bedroom. There was no time to waste. The war was reaching its final stages. Every day, the situation in Europe grew more chaotic. She was a nurse, and now she would use those skills not only to tend to the wounded but to find her husband.

Pulling her old suitcase out from under the bed, she started to pack, the plan solidifying in her mind as she worked. She would enlist with the Red Cross. They were desperate for help, especially in the field hospitals near the front lines where the need was greatest. It would be dangerous, but it was a risk she was willing to take. She couldn't sit idle any longer, not while Gabriel might be out there somewhere.

Beth walked through the house to make sure everything was in order. Bundled in her warm coat, she locked the door and placed the house key under the planter. Exactly the way she had found it a few short months ago.

If she walked fast, she would get to the station in time to catch the Toronto-bound train that would take her downtown. The Red Cross building was across the street from Union Station.

As she scurried to meet her train, Beth felt a sense of purpose she hadn't experienced since her departure from England. The uncertainty was still there, the fear of what might happen, but it was tempered by the knowledge that she was doing something, that she had a purpose. She would go to Europe, and she would find Gabriel.

~ Twenty-six ~

Niagara-on-the-Lake, Ontario, Canada

December 7th, 2024

Joy was dumbstruck. Who *was* this charming man? What had happened to the grumpy Nick who drove her in his fancy car she wasn't allowed to touch? She sipped her latte and watched him closely.

The old lady clearly liked him, and he seemed to bask in her attention. She told him that Beth and Gabriel were indeed her parents. Noelle had lived with her husband on Maple Leaf Avenue after her parents passed. Once he was gone, the house was a bit much for her, so she sold it to the Stevens with everything in it.

Joy should have been happy with the turn of events. And she was happy, thrilled even, that they had tracked down Beth and Gabriel's daughter. Still, her thoughts wandered. Nick was sweet to Noelle. It must be Joy then. Why did he dislike her? After seeing him with Noelle, she couldn't help but notice the dramatic shift in his attitude. He wasn't grumpy or pessimistic, didn't chirp back every opportunity he got, and definitely didn't tell her what not to do.

Joy nibbled on the cookie, feeling a little left out of the conversation as the other two chatted about the weather and activities at the home.

God, why do I feel this connection to a man who obviously despises me?

She couldn't take it any longer.

"Noelle," Joy interrupted their conversation. "We came because we found a tin box with war-time letters written by your parents."

Noelle set her hot chocolate down so fast it sloshed over the rim and spilled onto the table.

Nick got off his chair and rushed to get a handful of napkins.

The woman's hand shook slightly when she rested it on the table between her and Joy. "You don't say. Where?"

Joy studied her. Were there tears in the old woman's eyes? "In the attic of your old home. Nick bought it off the Stevens, and I found the the letters during the walk-through."

"I looked everywhere for them before I sold the house. Those were the only things I wanted to take with me. The letters and the train. Did you find it, too?"

"Yes," Joy said softly as Nick wiped the table with a crumpled handful of white paper napkins. "We did."

Noelle's bottom lip trembled, and Nick sat down and reached for her hand.

A lump formed in Joy's throat as she watched this unexpected moment of tenderness.

Her pale blue eyes glistening, Noelle gazed at Joy. "How will I ever thank you? Did you bring them with you?"

Joy shook her head, fighting the emotions. "No. I'm sorry. We weren't sure if you were the one we were looking for."

"Oh." Noelle reached for a napkin and dabbed at her eyes. "Would you? Please?"

"How would you like to visit your old home?" Nick asked.

Noelle looked at him, eyebrows knitted. "How can I?"

Nick smiled and rested a hand on Joy's arm. "Joy is planning a Christmas open house in your honor. We would very much like for you to come and collect those wonderful family heirlooms. Right?" He looked over at Joy.

Joy tore her gaze from the fingers still touching her arm and cleared her throat. "Yes, absolutely."

~ TWENTY-SEVEN ~

Southern England

April 1945

The ship rocked on the dark waters of the Atlantic, the sound of waves and the hum of the engines a constant. Beth stood at the rail, gripping the cold metal and praying. She stared out over the endless expanse of ocean. *God, please, don't let me be too late.*

Every mile brought her closer to her husband but also closer to the dangers that lay ahead. Their ship was part of a convoy, escorted by naval vessels. The German U-boats were never far from her mind. Each night, she lay in her narrow bunk, praying.

Finally, after what felt like an eternity at sea, she sighted land. They docked at a port in southern England, and the passengers disembarked into the bustle of the harbor. Beth's heart raced as she stepped onto solid ground. *God, please guide me.*

The Red Cross official in Toronto had instructed her to report to their London office for further orders. But her mind was already focused on her true destination—the RAF Coningsby Airfield.

The train journey to London was a blur of countryside, fields, and villages passing by in a patchwork of green and brown. The war had left its mark even here, in the heart of England. Bombed-out buildings and makeshift repairs were a common sight, a testament to the devastation that had reached these shores. Even so, the people's resilience was evident. Despite the destruction, life continued.

London itself was a maze of activity, as she had remembered it. Beth made her way to the Red Cross headquarters. After confirming her orders, she took another train north.

When she finally arrived at the Coningsby Airfield, the sight of it brought back a flood of memories. The rows of hangars, the planes lined up on the tarmac, the distant sound of engines—everything was familiar, yet different. The base was busier than ever, and the atmosphere was tense.

Beth entered the command center, stopping at long last in front of the office of Group Captain Reginald Thompson. Her heart pounded as she knocked on the door.

"Come in," a voice called from within.

Beth stepped inside. Reginald Thompson had not changed. His uniform was crisp, and his expression was one of practiced calm. He looked up from the papers on his desk when she stopped on the far side of his desk.

"Mrs. Holly, I presume?" he said, standing and extending his hand. "I received word that you were on your way."

"Yes, sir," Beth replied, shaking his hand firmly. "I'm here to find out what happened to my husband, Flying Officer Gabriel Holly."

Group Captain nodded, his expression softening slightly. "Please, have a seat." He gestured to the chair in front of his desk. "I understand your concern, Mrs. Holly. Gabriel was a fine officer. I assure you that we are doing everything possible to find out what happened to him and his crew."

Was?

A steel claw gripped Beth's heart and squeezed all her hope out of it. A cry escaped her. *God, he has to be alive.* She wouldn't let herself panic. That never helped anyone.

"Pardon me," she said, taking a handkerchief out of her purse.

The officer, ever the gentleman, gave her time to pull herself together. When she could trust her voice again, she looked into the officer's eyes. "His Lancaster went down over Germany," she said, her voice steady despite the turmoil inside her. "What are the chances he survived?"

The Group Captain sighed, leaning back in his chair. "His aircraft sustained damage during an operation over the Ruhr Valley. They were on their return flight when they encountered heavy enemy fire. The area where they went down is fiercely contested, with intense ground fighting as the Allies advance towards Berlin. Their exact whereabouts are unknown."

Beth had known the situation was terrible, but hearing it spelled out even more plainly than in the letter Group Captain Thompson had written her made it all the more real.

"Is there any way to find out if he was one of the men who parachuted out?" she asked, her voice barely above a whisper.

"We have no means of knowing for certain. The Germans are in retreat, leaving devastation in their wake. All we can do is hope and pray that Gabriel and the others somehow managed to survive and find shelter."

Beth took a deep breath, her mind racing. "Then I need to go there," she said, her voice firm.

Group Captain Thompson shook his head. "Mrs. Holly, I appreciate your resolve, but the front lines are no place for you. The situation is highly dangerous, and you would be placing yourself in considerable peril. The war is drawing to a close—soon we shall have more information, and you can make decisions at that time. For now, I must strongly urge you to remain here, where it's safer."

Beth clutched in both hands the bag she'd set on her lap. "With all due respect, sir, I can't wait any longer. Every day that passes, every moment, could mean the difference between life and death for Gabriel. I've come this far, and I won't stop now. If there's even the slightest chance I can help him, I must take it."

The Group Captain looked at her, his expression a mix of admiration and concern. "You're a brave woman, Mrs. Holly, and I can see you've made up your mind. But please consider the risks. The front lines are unpredictable, and the situation could change at any moment."

Beth lifted her chin. "I've thought about the risks, sir. But I couldn't live with myself if I didn't do everything I could to find him. If Gabriel is out there, I must go."

Group Captain Thompson sighed, nodding slowly. "Very well, Mrs. Holly. I can't stop you. Let me make a few inquiries and see if we can arrange for you to be attached to a field hospital near the front lines." He stood. "I would implore you, though, to please be careful. The war may be ending, but it's not over yet."

Beth rose and shook the hand he held out over the desk. "Thank you, sir. I appreciate your help."

~ TWENTY-EIGHT ~

Niagara-on-the-Lake, Ontario, Canada

December 7th, 2024

"I would call that a total success," Nick said as soon as she buckled up.

She shifted to face him, her blue eyes probing his.

He turned on the engine, then glanced at her. "What?"

"I'm confused," she said softly.

"About what?"

"You. Have I done something to offend you?"

"Offend me?" His brow furrowed. "Why would you ask that?"

"Why? Because in all the time we've spent together, I have never seen you this happy."

Nick shifted the transmission into drive and peered over his shoulder as he reversed out of the parking lot. How could he answer that?

She didn't wait for him to respond before saying, "That leads me to only one conclusion. You don't care to have me around."

He left the parking lot and turned toward Maple Leaf Avenue, his mind racing. He didn't understand himself how he felt; how could he explain it to her?

When silence settled in the car, Joy took her phone out of her purse and checked her email.

Say something. Make this better. "I..."

She ignored him.

How could he explain that the opposite was true? He did enjoy having her around, and every time they met, he struggled to—to do what? Hide his true feelings?

"Joy." Nick cleared his throat. They were almost at the house. He had to say what was on his mind because, if he was reading her right, she was hurt. If he left things unsaid, she would most likely shut him out of her life as soon as the open house was over.

"It's not you." He winced at the words that came out of his mouth, since they made it sound as though he was breaking up with her or something. Normally he was pretty good with his words, but right now, with her glaring at him, they just wouldn't come.

"Oh, sure," she said sarcastically.

"Let me finish, please."

She wrapped her scarf tighter around her neck.

He sighed. Might as well come clean. "I went through a terrible breakup a year ago. Actually, she broke up with me last Christmas."

Joy's features softened as they pulled into the driveway.

"And took my dog."

Her shoulders slumped. "That's terrible. But what does that have to do with me?"

"Absolutely nothing. It's just that—" He shifted into park.

"What?"

"I..." Nick reached for her hand. "I've never met anyone like you."

She slowly wiggled her fingers out of his grasp. "That's why you're miserable every time we meet?"

"I'm not miserable every time we meet. I'm miserable all the time. I have a hard time even thinking about..."

"What?" The hope in her voice dug into his chest.

"I haven't dated anyone since last Christmas. And I don't know if I'm ready to now."

She nodded silently.

With nothing left to say, Nick pulled at the door handle and stepped out of his car.

~ TWENTY-NINE ~

Somewhere in Europe

May 1945

The air was thick with the smell of smoke and earth, a bitter reminder of the battle that had raged here not long ago. Beth moved quickly through the makeshift field hospital, her hands steady despite the chaos. Wounded soldiers filled the cots. Outside the tents, the rumble of distant artillery was a constant backdrop, a reminder that the war, though nearly over, was still claiming its final victims.

Beth had arrived two days ago and quickly fallen in step with the other volunteers and doctors. The work was grueling, but it allowed her to ask about a Lancaster that had gone down in late March. Most shook their heads, but a few offered snippets of information—rumors of a crew that had parachuted out, whispers of prisoners taken by the Germans.

It wasn't much, but it kept her going. Gabriel was out there somewhere, and she would not rest until she found him. Beth clung to the hope that he had survived.

On the fifth day of her service, a group of infantrymen arrived at the field hospital. Their faces were etched with exhaustion and something else—an urgency that caught Beth's attention.

"What's happened?" she asked one of the soldiers, a tall man with a bandaged arm.

"The Germans are retreating," he said, his voice rough with fatigue. "We've been pushing them back for days, and we're closing in on one of the camps where they've been holding POWs. We've heard the Germans are evacuating, leaving the prisoners behind. It's hell on earth out there."

Beth's heart skipped a beat. "Which camp?" she asked, trying to steady her voice.

"Can't remember the name," the soldier replied. "But it's not far from here. We've been told to prepare for an influx of prisoners—hundreds of them. They'll be in bad shape."

Beth nodded, her mind racing. If Gabriel had been captured, he could be one of those prisoners. With the camp being liberated, she might finally find him.

That evening, the head nurse gathered the Red Cross volunteers for a briefing. Her face was grave as she addressed them. "We've received word that a concentration camp nearby has been liberated," she said. "The conditions there were worse than we'd feared. We must prepare to receive the prisoners who were held there—many will desperately need medical attention and proper nutrition. This will be one of the most challenging tasks we've faced, but it will also be one of the most important. These men and women need our help to survive."

Beth listened intently, her heart pounding in her chest. She was ready to face whatever came, although the thought of Gabriel being one of those prisoners made her stomach turn.

The following day, trucks rolled in. The Red Cross volunteers stood ready, their hands laden with supplies—blankets, food, and medical kits. As the soldiers began unloading the first group of prisoners, Beth felt a surge of anxiety. She scanned the faces of the men as they were helped off the trucks, and her heart broke. She willed herself to stay on task. Assess, administer first aid, and remain calm and collected. She was a nurse.

These men and women needed her. Yet, her eyes searched desperately for Gabriel.

The last truck pulled in as the sun set below the horizon. This had been one of the most challenging days of her service. Exhausted, she grappled with a deep sense of despair. Gabriel hadn't been among the prisoners. Where was he?

Movement behind the last of the trucks caught her eye. A group of men. Unlike the others, these prisoners moved with purpose, helping others off the truck.

Beth's breath caught in her throat as one of the men captured her attention—a tall, lean figure with a familiar gait. His tattered clothes hung on his thin frame, but something about him made her heart skip a beat.

She stepped forward, her eyes fixed on the man as he helped another prisoner down from the truck. She struggled to breathe as the world seemed to narrow to one person. Almost afraid to speak his name aloud, she whispered, "Gabriel?"

As if he could hear her, the man turned. Their eyes met, and Beth pressed a hand to her chest. It was him. He looked different—thinner, worn, with lines of exhaustion etched into his face. But it was Gabriel. He was alive.

"Gabriel!" Beth cried out, her voice breaking as she started toward him, tears streaming down her face.

Her husband stared at her, blinking as if trying to convince himself that what he saw was real. And then, suddenly, he staggered forward, his own eyes glistening.

"Beth?" His voice was hoarse. "Beth, is it really you?"

Her hands trembled as she reached him and touched his face.

"It's me." She choked out the words, her throat so thick she could barely speak. "Oh, Gabriel, I thought I'd lost you."

He pulled her into his arms. "I kept hoping, praying..."

Beth clung to him, tears of relief and joy streaming down her face. For a long moment, they stood there, holding each other, oblivious to the surrounding chaos. They had each other. That was all that mattered.

~ Thirty ~

Niagara-on-the-Lake, Ontario, Canada

December 14th, 2024

Joy had decided that she needed to focus, no matter what personal problems Nick refused to deal with. The open house on Maple Leaf Avenue would be the best in town.

The invitations to the media had gone out. The Chamber of Commerce confirmed that several of their board members were coming. She had even hired three theatre actors to dress up in 40s fashion and sing traditional Christmas carols.

A busload of seniors was coming, and Noelle had assured them she would be thrilled to revisit her former home.

The whole place sparkled and smelled like Christmas. A childhood sense of wonder filled Joy as she did the final walk-through a few minutes before 3:00 p.m.—the official start of the festivities.

She had spoken to Nick only a couple of times since the day they had visited the senior home. If she were honest with herself, she missed him. Even so, his past was something he had to deal with by himself, and until he was ready to move on, she would stay out of his way. A rebound relationship was a recipe for disaster. As much as she would like to take him out for another no-date date, she promised herself she wouldn't bring it up.

Joy straightened the few carefully wrapped packages under the tree and ran her fingers over the antique cookie tin. For better or worse, Nick should be here. This was his house, his find, and his party.

At that moment, the door flew open, and in he walked, hands filled with boxes, bags hanging off his arms.

"Joy," he called out. "Would you get the door, please?"

"What is all this?" She brushed by him to close the door and shut out the gusting wind.

"Secret Santa."

"What are you talking about?"

"I called the retirement home manager and asked if there was anything the residents could use. Then I got a few things."

Yet another side of Nick she would never have expected.

"Can you help me place these under the tree?"

"Sure." Unable to keep from smiling, she took a few boxes from his arms and arranged them next to the roaring fireplace.

Ten minutes later, the presents were neatly displayed. Joy's Christmas playlist filled the home with music. She lit the scented candles on the coffee table and stepped back to survey the room. Everything was perfect as a knock on the old door announced their first visitors.

Nick welcomed the group of seniors and their activity director. When Noelle stepped over the threshold, her eyes glistened with tears.

Joy filled a few cups with Christmas punch and walked around the house with a tray of cookies, encouraging their guests to taste them.

A few minutes later, the Chamber of Commerce president came in, followed by several local business owners. The house was getting full. Once the singers arrived, the party was in full swing.

About an hour into the festivities, Nick asked Noelle to sit by the Christmas tree in the high winged chair. The local paper was already there, and the photographer was ready. Nick gave a short speech, retelling the story of their discoveries in the attic and Joy's determination to find Beth and Gabriel's relatives, which had led them to Noelle.

"Which brings us to this special moment. Joy." Nick turned toward her, his face beaming. "Would you kindly do the honors and present Noelle with her parents' letters?"

"I would love to," she replied, fighting tears as she picked up the tin and gently handed it to Noelle. "These are yours," she said and smiled.

"Thank you, dear." Noelle ran her wrinkled hands over the lid, then carefully opened the container. "You've made this old woman very happy. I thought these were forever lost, much like that little train set my parents set up under the tree every year." She pointed to the engine circling the Christmas tree.

"Lost and found." Nick lifted his glass. "I would like to propose a toast to Beth and Gabriel. The local war-time heroes who found love in the most unlikely place. Despite thinking all might be lost, they found each other again. Cheers."

"Cheers," the guests said in unison.

"Now, if you don't mind, Noelle, would you please share your parents' story with us?" Joy asked. "I've read the letters, but they stop as your father was shot down over Germany. How did he make it home?"

"Of course, dear." Noelle rested her fingers on the pile of yellowed envelopes. "My mother went after him."

"And found him?"

"Of course! How else did you think I came into the world?" The old woman laughed. "She used to say she went to Europe the first time to find her purpose and the second time to find her heart."

Cameras flashed, the guests applauded, and Nick refilled Noelle's punch glass. As the guests trickled out the door, Joy couldn't help but wish that she might, one day, find her heart too.

~ THIRTY-ONE ~

Niagara-on-the-Lake, Ontario, Canada

December 14th, 2024

“That should do it,” Nick said as he tied the last garbage bag. “This was one of the best Christmas parties I’ve ever attended. And it’s all thanks to you.” He carried the bag into the front hall.

Joy sat in the winged chair, letting her eyes take in all the twinkling lights. If he ran a B&B here, there would most likely be more Christmas trees in this window, but would any of them encompass as much history, love, and hope as this one?

“What are you thinking?” Nick asked as he handed her one last cup of apple cider.

“I was thinking that this was such a wonderful, whimsical evening I don’t even have the words to fully describe it. The entire community came together to remember and celebrate two people who truly made a difference. Not only that, but they also loved. Fully. Despite the terrible times they lived in.”

Nick sipped his drink, eyes on her.

“I have to admit I’m a little sad that this house filled with memories will become another cookie-cutter interior design project with fake antiques and muffins made from a box.”

He lowered himself onto the footstool in front of her. "What if I were to tell you I might have reconsidered the reno project?"

Joy stared at him.

"After hearing the story today, I realized how important this house is. To this town, to Noelle, to you, and to me."

She was about to say something, but he lifted his hand. "Please."

Joy nodded.

"I've been thinking about the courage it took for Beth to cross the ocean teeming with U-boats and mines. Then, traveling from bombed-out London across the English Channel to war-torn Europe. All the way to Germany, still full of Nazis desperately trying to escape justice. To go to the end of the world for the one you love. To find him and bring him home. That is..." he choked on the words. "That is true love."

Joy's throat tightened. What was he saying? "I want that." Nick's eyes glistened with tears. "No matter the past hurts. No matter the risk."

She covered her lips with her fingers, fighting back tears of her own. This was the Nick she wished to know—honest, open, and vulnerable. She mustered a smile. "So, Mr. Grumpy, if I were to ask you right now on a *not a no-date date*, what would you say?"

He cleared his throat, then reached for her hand. A smile broke across his face. "I'd say you owe me a fancy dinner."

"It might be hard to get a table this late at Queen's Landing." She glanced at her phone as she stood up. "They'll be closing in about an hour. But we can always try."

"No worries." Nick pushed to his feet and reached for her. "I'll bet the 24-hour Tim's down the street has a table available for us." He wrapped his arms around her and drew her to his chest. "See, I don't want to rush our first *not a no-date date,*" Nick whispered into her ear.

When she looked up at him, her heart full of hope, he tucked a loose strand of hair behind her ear. "Because I think I might have found my true love in this old house full of memories." Then he gently kissed her. "Merry Christmas, sweetheart."

~ EPILOGUE ~

Noelle finished the story, leaned on her cane, and pointed to the gallery display on the dining room wall.

"Here are my parents' letters. Joy and Nick had them framed by an archivist."

"Are these the originals?" Jeannette, a guest from Switzerland, leaned in to examine the framed letters up close.

"Oh, yes."

"Really?" She stretched out her hand, almost touching the glass. "And you're okay with us reading them?"

"Of course. But I'll sit down while you do that. Come and see me if you have any more questions."

"Thank you." Jeannette smiled at her.

Noelle walked over to the winged chair and slowly lowered herself onto the seat. Who would have thought that a visit from two strangers only a year ago could bring her this much happiness. She glanced up. The Christmas tree sparkled, lights reflecting off the tiny airplane wings. Joy had gone to a lot of trouble to find the collectible Spitfires, Hurricanes, and, of course, the Lancaster models.

Noelle inhaled the scents of Christmas. The delicious aroma of freshly baked cookies mingled with pine and Joy's festive candles on the mantel. Bright flames danced in the fireplace hearth. This was something she had never dared to hope for. The young couple who'd bought the house a year ago had made her life delightful.

She tapped her fingers to the rhythm of "The Little Drummer Boy" on the armrest of her oversized chair. Noelle had never imagined that she'd be sitting in her father's chair again, let alone spending her last days here in the home where she'd had such a wonderful upbringing.

"Would you like me to refill your apple cider?" Nick walked over to her, careful not to trip over the little choo-choo train running in endless circles under the tree.

"Oh, would you, dear." She picked up the antique tea cup from the side table and passed it to him. "And please tell that sweet wife of yours to get off her feet. We have enough cookies to host two open houses."

Nick chuckled as he walked toward the kitchen. "I'll do my best, but you know Mrs. Mass. No matter how often I tell her to sit down and rest, she won't stop until everything is perfect."

Everything is perfect. Noelle glanced toward the dining room. Jeanette's husband had joined her, and the two held hands as they whispered to each other. At times like this, Noelle missed Rudy, but the loneliness no longer suffocated her.

Noelle hummed along with "God Rest Ye Merry Gentlemen." The faces of each of them—those she had loved the most—drifted through her mind. Her parents, Beth and Nick, and of course her Rudy, celebrating the birth of Jesus in Eternity. Waiting for her.

A tear rolled down her cheek. She missed them. Noelle brushed the tear away. The last thing she wanted was for Nick to return and fuss over her. He was very good at that.

She filled her lungs. The retirement home bus would be here soon. Her friends were on the way, excited about the open house.

When this day ended, she would rest in the little room upstairs filled with memories. But before she let sleep overtake her, Noelle would pray. She would thank God for Nick and Joy and ask for His blessings for the new year that was just around the corner. God willing, by the time next Christmas came along, she would be bouncing not one but two babies on her old knees.

Noelle closed her eyes and silently thanked the Lord. Yes, she was home for Christmas.

A Note From the Author

Dear Reader,

Thank you from the bottom of my heart for joining me on this journey through Nick and Joy's story. I hope their adventure, from uncovering long-lost WWII love letters to discovering love in the most unexpected places, brought a little extra magic to your heart this Christmas season.

But what happened to Nick Mass last Christmas that left him such a Grinch? If you're curious to learn more about the events that shaped his character and why love was the last thing on his mind, I have a special treat for you! Visit my website at , where you'll find exclusive bonus content that dives into Nick's story from the previous Christmas. Trust me, you won't want to miss it!

Your support and time mean the world to me, and I hope this story reminded you that love has a way of finding us—even when we least expect it.

Thank you again for reading, and may your days ahead be filled with joy, hope, and a little bit of holiday magic.

With warmest wishes,

Helena Smrcek

www.helenasmrcek.com

P.S. Don't forget to check out the bonus content for a little more holiday fun!

ACKNOWLEDGMENTS

Cec Murphey, a man of extraordinary talents whose heart always champions the underdog. Thank you for helping me to tell stories that change lives. Your love has changed mine.

God loves to surprise me, and so He did with not one, not two, but three amazing friends. This collection of novellas was written from our hearts after many conversations, countless messages, and prayers from our hearts directly to the Father. Fab Four, I'm thankful for our friendship, support, and most of all, love.

These acknowledgments wouldn't be complete without mentioning the men and women who did what was right and necessary. These WWII heroes stopped the evil that threatened our civilization. Millions have laid down their lives so we can celebrate this Christmas with those we love. May they never be forgotten.

Jesus, thank you for sending a group of missionaries in 1986 to a lonely refugee teenager, uncertain of her future. The Christmas gift they brought wasn't in a shoe box. It was in their hearts.

About the Author

With a passion for storytelling sparked by her grandparents, Helena Smrcek weaves heartfelt tales that explore themes of faith, love, and redemption. She finds inspiration in the beauty of nature, often hiking and gardening to connect with the world around her.

A devoted dog lover, Helena cherishes the companionship of her furry friends and believes they bring unconditional joy to life. Her mornings are incomplete without a strong cup of coffee, and she loves exploring new coffee shops for that perfect brew.

History is another passion, fueling her imagination with stories from different eras and inspiring the characters she brings to life. Traveling to new places feeds her creative soul, providing fresh perspectives and experiences for her writing.

An avid baker, Helena enjoys sharing homemade treats with family and friends, making every occasion a little sweeter.

Through her writing, she hopes to create a sense of wonder and connection for her readers, much like the stories that first enchanted her.

Where My Heart Belongs

MELANIE STEVENSON

For Ralph

In your love, my heart found a home.

WHERE MY HEART BELONGS

Melanie Stevenson

When dreams take a detour, love finds its way.

Having given up the better part of her twenties climbing the corporate ladder and crushing on her dashing boss, Porsha jumps on the opportunity to impress him by giving a keynote speech, even if it is in a language she hasn't spoken since high school. One obstacle after another to getting a promotion (not to mention gaining her boss's affection) stacks up, and her Christmas plans quickly unravel. When she bumps into a handsome, bell-ringing street Santa, not only her plans but her entire life just might change.

"Yes, everything else is worthless when compared with the infinite value of knowing Christ Jesus my Lord."

Philippians 3:8 (NLT)

~ ONE ~

If embarrassment were personified, it would come in the form of me in this moment, standing here on this stage in my underwear. That's how bad this whole debacle has gone. And I'm not exaggerating.

Neither am I in my underwear.

Still, if the stage were a lake and I was in the middle of it treading water for dear life, that might come close to describing my situation. At this moment, I'd welcome the Loch Ness Monster to swim up from the depths and swallow me alive.

Right now, preferably.

Make your move, Nessie, here I am!

Not surprisingly, there is no monster to save me. I finish my speech—using the French I haven't spoken since high school—and stumble off the stage into the black-curtained wings. At least they do a decent job of swallowing me alive. How long can I hide here? Until the audience has filed out of the auditorium to their homes and hotel rooms?

Trust me, it's that bad.

Any sane person would have said no. Would have never come to Quebec City on December the twenty-third to give a speech to a segment of the population that doesn't speak her language. If her boss had asked her, a person in charge of her mental faculties would have passed it off as a joke and said something pithy like, *not until hell freezes over*.

And it may very well have, because this feels pretty close.

Did I mention the temperature? It's minus thirty. Degrees Celsius. And yes, for you Fahrenheit people, that *is* as cold as it sounds. You think I'm kidding? I am not. Welcome to Quebec in December. Did I also mention I hate winter?

But I digress.

I yank the black sail of a curtain off my face. It's fused to my lips, thanks to the lip gloss I generously applied minutes before stepping on this stage in a fake-it-'til-you-make-it moment of boldness. If I was about to make a colossal fool of myself, may as well look decent doing it. Sadly, no amount of lip gloss or matching fuchsia power suit could make up for what just happened out there.

I can almost hear my colleague and best friend, Barbie, (not her real name but Margot Robbie's doppelganger, thus the nickname) saying, "What were you thinking?" Or, more accurately, hissing the words in a stage whisper fit for this moment.

Barbie's not here, however. She's in Toronto, where I should be. At the office. Where I should also be.

I can already see the disapproving look on my boss's face. And he, unlike my bestie, *is* here. Which is more than a tad unfortunate.

You're late to the show, though, so let me catch you up on why I won't see the disapproving look on my boss's face.

I'm about to be fired.

Wait. Let me wipe off this lip gloss I fear smeared across my check when I extricated the black curtain from my lips. No sensible person can possibly have a conversation, let alone be taken seriously, with lip gloss smeared across her cheek.

Entirely distracting and highly unprofessional.

Because I don't have a tissue, I go ahead and use the black curtain to wipe off the Picasso impression it's made of my face.

Since we don't really know each other yet, picture me leaning across a table in a diner, a forkful of scrambled eggs half raised to my mouth as I launch into this account of my disastrous speech.

You need to know that I'm usually pretty good at this whole public speaking schtick. I was that drama kid in school. You know, the one most people either admired or found endlessly annoying. I like attention. No, scratch that, I *love* attention. If you're a psychologist, hold off on the analysis a sec, and let me finish.

This is good.

About an hour ago, I was in a green room a few meters behind these curtains, applying the aforementioned traitorous lip gloss, when a knock sounded on the door. I thought it might be the stagehand giving me the five-minute warning, so I got up and swung open the door. It was not the stagehand.

It was my boss.

If we were sitting across the table from each other at the diner, I'd hold up a finger while I stuffed a forkful of scrambled eggs in my mouth and chewed. I'd try not to talk with my mouth full, but seriously, how are you supposed to have brunch with a girlfriend and tell her a crazy story without doing that?

So yeah, I'd hold up a finger, stuff in the eggs, and you'd wait while I chewed because heaven forbid I should talk with my mouth full. Which makes the dramatic pause that much weightier.

After swallowing, I'd launch into this part.

The part where my boss—correction, painfully attractive *French* boss—is standing at the door to my green room, smiling. He does that a lot and believe me when I tell you that it's enough to make a non-swooning-type-girl swoon.

That would be me.

Only now I'm swooning. I shouldn't be because in approximately five minutes, if the backstage manager is doing her job properly, I'll be at the podium, making a career-collapsing speech and wishing those curtains would swallow me up.

Even now, I can smell my boss's cologne as he leans one shoulder on the door frame. What does it smell like, you ask? A mixture of hot summer night and fresh pine trees. Did I mention he's smiling?

At *me*.

The smell, the smile, and the suit are disarming enough, but then he says (I'd reach across the table at this point to take your hand for emphasis if you and I were besties), "You're the best I've got, Porscha. Go out there and show them how it's done."

Oh yeah, that's my name. Porsha Ivy.

My dad was, and may still be, a car freak, and my mom said there was no way she was going to name her first-born daughter after a car, so they made a compromise in the spelling of my name. Turns out she should have given in because there were no more car-name compromises coming down the pipe.

I'm an only child.

I'd hold up a hand here because if you were a psychologist you'd want to ask about that. My family situation is another drama entirely to unpack, however, and would take more time than we have, not to mention ruin our pretend brunch. Besides, I'm just getting to the juicy part—my boss.

I know what you're thinking. *Porsh* (that's what Barbie calls me, and after our hypothetical brunch I might let you too), *boss-swooning is dangerous and potentially career ending.*

And you'd be right, although might I remind you that I have both the career-ending and dangerous parts covered?

But I'll get to that.

In the meantime, back to my boss. He's leaning on the door frame, his plump lips turned up at the corners as he compliments me. Then he hits me with, "How about a drink back the hotel after?"

He did not! you'd say.

Yes. He did! I'd assure you while asking, *could you ease off on your grip*?

You're squeezing my hand across the table a little too tightly. The same one I haven't let go of so I could impart the appropriate amount of gravitas to my story.

How did I respond? Hang on while I swallow. By the way, isn't this bacon to die for?

I said, *Sorry, I have plans.*

You say, *you did not!*

I did, I swear. I reach a pinky finger across the table. Are you into pinky swearing? I know it's juvenile, but it's a lot better than actually swearing. Sometimes.

He looks at me as if he's viewing the previously mentioned Loch Ness Monster and straightens, pressing his lips together. Which, I might add, I have no idea how he manages, since they are like mini feather pillows stacked one on top of the other. I won't lie and say I haven't dreamed of running and diving into them a time or two.

Why didn't I say yes? Are you kidding? Aren't *you* supposed to be the psychologist? And I thought you were against office romances. Everyone, including you and I, knows it's a bad idea to date your boss. In hindsight, though, (I flick my brown hair over my shoulder) I should have said yes. Because after what just happened, I won't be seeing him ever again.

What happened? I'm getting to that. I was filling in a bit of backstory so when I get to the part about why I'm hiding back here, it will add more weight to the story.

Did I mention I'm dramatic?

So, my boss (I take an imaginary sip of coffee) is looking at me the way I described, and because a) I can't take it anymore and b) I will likely back down and say *yes* any second, I turn away from the doorway he is standing in and begin to apply another coat of lip gloss. Not because I need any more lip gloss, but because it's a way out from under his pouty-lipped gaze. And trust me, (I dab the imaginary ketchup from my lips with my imaginary napkin) you would turn away too. He's that magnetic, and we've agreed I can't afford to be drawn in.

Which is how I came to apply the copious amount of lip gloss that glued me to this curtain.

Is it all off my cheek yet? Great. If we were at the diner, I'd say, *Let's get a refill of coffee.* Did I mention I love coffee? As in, I'm involved in a full-blown love affair with the stuff.

What I do not love is winter, in case I haven't already mentioned that. In fact, right after this I'm heading to the train station to return to Toronto where I will catch a flight to the Bahamas.

You're wondering if I'm spending Christmas alone? Indeed I am. I intend to spend it in the warmth. Not here in this hell-has-indeed-frozen-over place. Sorry, but minus thirty Celsius? I know Toronto is just as bad sometimes—precisely why I'm going somewhere hot. Isn't my boss hot enough, you ask? Why yes, he is. Again, we've established he's off limits. I can't afford *him*, but I can the Bahamas.

There it will be nothing but me and the sea and the sun.

Did I mention I also hate Christmas? Definitely more than I hate the cold, although not because of the snow. Let's not get into that right now. I'm trying to tell you about the debacle (I point stage left) because we're actually here and not in the imagined diner where I wish we were. If that were the case, the nightmare that has become my life would be over, and I'd be describing to you how I got fired.

Instead, here we are. I'm still standing backstage, and my heart rate is only just returning to normal.

My boss, by the way, doesn't take no for an answer. That's probably why he's the CEO of Imagine Marketing. Back at the dressing room, that trait of his was vexingly annoying because he stood there watching me overapply lip gloss with an unsteady hand instead of accepting defeat gracefully and walking away. While I should have been rehearsing the first line to the talk I was about to give in front of a thousand colleagues, I was wondering what this lip gloss would feel like when transferred from my lips to his.

Yes, I just said that.

You've caught me at a particularly weak moment. Hiding in these curtains is not my finest hour, I can assure you.

Could you just peek out and see if anyone is coming? Namely a good-looking guy in a navy-blue suit and bow tie?

Why did they ask me to speak at this black-tie event? Thanks for the vote of confidence. Oh, you're kidding (insert awkward laugh). I don't know you well enough to know your sense of humor yet. Plus, I'm a tad frazzled, in case you haven't noticed. Even so, I quite like you already.

At this moment, we hear footsteps. Instinctively, we dive deeper into the curtains because if you're found, so will I be, and no one wants that right now.

The stage manager whisks past. I exhale deeply. Maybe a little too loudly.

I undo the bottom button on my tailored blazer. *Why am I wearing a pantsuit to a black-tie event?* you whisper. Because I don't like dresses, and besides, as a female provincial marketing manager, I need to be taken seriously. Like that will happen after today.

I hold my breath when more footfalls echo backstage. Men's dress shoes, hitting the black floor.

It's him.

I'm not ready to hear my boss tell me I no longer work for the company I have given the better part of my twenties to, so I stuff my backside deeper into the curtains as he passes.

Do you smell that? Yup, that's his cologne. I know, isn't it sooo good?

So, that's him. The one who doesn't take no for an answer and who, after smirking while watching me apply lip gloss like a kindergartener coloring outside of the lines, says, "See you in the hotel bar at ten." He then turned to go—too late to be of benefit to me—and was replaced by the stage manager giving me the five-minute warning (also too late to be of benefit to me).

I pause my storytelling to check my Versace watch. It's 5:15 PM. I've gotta go. My train leaves in forty-five minutes. If you want to join me on the walk—correction, run—(we grin at each other) to the *Gare du Palais* station, I'll get you fully up to speed.

First, though, would you mind checking to see if the coast is clear?

~ TWO ~

At this point you're probably wondering how old my boss is, although you're likely not nearly as interested in him as a side character as I am. To be honest, I should be much less interested in him as well. I promise I was trying my darndest to do just that when he asked me for a drink.

Who am I kidding? I've been crushing on the man for six years. I *know*. The same amount of time that I've worked for Imagine Marketing. Which is why, although I'm a slightly dramatic individual, the self discipline it required for me to decline his drink invitation cannot be underestimated.

All I need to do is make it out of here without seeing him, and I'll be on my merry way. See what I did there? A little Christmas reference for your benefit. You've no idea how much it pained me.

If I time it right, in approximately forty-five minutes, I'll be settling into my seat on the Via Rail train back to Toronto Pearson International Airport. That will allow me to make my 6:30 AM flight to Bahamas where I will spend seven blissful days in the sun and sand while all you crazies slip and slide your way through the holidays.

So, is the coast clear? I just need to get to the green room to grab my case.

I try to walk normally. Try to act like the adult in high heels I haven't yet managed to become. I slink—correction, stride confidently—along the hallway that leads to the green room. As I round the corner, I run smack dab into, you guessed it, my Mr. Why-do-you-have-to-look-like-a-Calvin-Klein-underwear-model boss.

"Porsha." He's smiling in what I take to be a sympathetic way.

Suddenly I'm fourteen and have just crashed into Michael Barret in the hallway. My books, all of them but one, have tumbled onto the floor at his feet, and I have no words.

"Can I have a minute?" my boss asks. His gaze shifts to the door of the green room I had nearly made it to undetected.

If anyone needs a minute, it's me. My insanely handsome boss is about to fire me.

"Actually, no. I have a train to catch." Mentally, I'm bending to pick up the "fallen books" of my childhood.

"It will only take a sec." He's following me now. I don't know how I do it, especially in these four-inch stilettos, but I make it to the green room a full three meters ahead of him and slam the door behind me.

I know what you're thinking. I'm a baby. You're not wrong. I am, indeed, a baby at this moment. But darn it all, I want to make the train, get on that plane, and be in the Bahamas by Christmas Eve. Preferably before getting fired.

While I hide, breathless, behind this door, let me fill you in on a few details. For a Type-A personality, getting the promotion is paramount, which explains how I came to be embarrassing myself on that stage. I cannot begin to count the hours I've poured into Imagine Marketing to get where I am. Even so, when I pictured my late twenties, I thought I'd be much further along in my career.

I imagined myself running my own company, or at least considerably higher up on the food chain. I'd be married, or at least comfortably attached to a significant other. I'd be able to keep my condo neat, or at least be able to find my keys. Most days, I'm doing well if I manage to grab my coffee at the café on the corner and make it to work on time with my blouse tucked in. Despite all this, at Imagine, I'm somehow remarkably put together.

I know. Hiding behind curtains and in green rooms doesn't exactly exude late-twenties *or* put together. Which brings me back to this predicament. My boss.

A knock sounds and I hear his voice. It's a hide-and-seek game gone sideways. Mostly because he saw me come into this room and therefore hiding is not an option. "Porsha?"

I don't want to answer, obviously, but I suppose I have to, seeing as how he does know I'm here. "Yeah, um, I'm in a real rush. Can we chat when I'm back?"

What am I so afraid of? Good question, doctor.

We pause this cringy interlude to look at why Porsha was, moments before and again currently, hiding. I said I would tell you before we were interrupted, so Jeremy can wait.

Yes, that's my boss's name. I forgot to mention it? There's a lot going on right now, and as you can tell, I'm having trouble focusing.

How far back do you want to go? Just kidding. I'm not giving you my life story, yet (insert a giggle and a swat on your shoulder). But I will tell you, finally, what happened before you turned up in the wings.

Why am I in Quebec City in the middle of winter two days before December 25th?

I was asked—or, more accurately, selected—by the great and wonderful Mr. Fox. Yes, that's *actually* Jeremy's last name. *I know.* How appropriate. Anyway, as I was saying, I was selected to give the keynote address at our annual event. Normally, I thrive in this situation, as mentioned. But here's the kicker. After I accepted his offer to speak—granting me, presumably, the chance to be applauded by my peers, promoted, and adored by Jeremy—he asked, "How's your French?"

In his French accent.

"Oh, fine. Yeah, fine," I said with a nervous laugh. Which it isn't. Anymore. Like I said, I haven't used it since high school.

"Great, because the audience will be mostly Francophone."

I know I should have confessed right then, but heaven help me, I didn't want to disappoint him. Or, more accurately, I didn't want him to be disappointed in me.

So, for the past half hour, I stood on that stage bumbling my way through a speech in a language I can't even claim as a second. I'm sure that performance has not only lost me a promotion—not to mention that peer applause and the adoration of my boss—but my job.

Another knock. "Porsha?"

Even now I like the way he says my name, placing the accent on "sha" and rolling the "r" slightly.

I know, I need to get it together.

I sigh. My forehead is against the door, my hands pressed against the cool metal. I should be brave. I should swing open the door and let the proverbial books fall where they may at this grown boy's feet, but I'm too proud.

Or too afraid.

The way I bumbled my way through my talk using basic, poorly executed French was excruciating. And if that wasn't bad enough—here's the real kicker—I went ahead and said something that, as soon as shocked laughter rose from the crowd, I realized was the wrong word—like a really wrong, X-rated word. I would have given anything to have been able to disappear in a puff of smoke at that moment. And now, the very person I cannot face is standing outside this door.

"Can I come in?" he asks.

No, you certainly may not. "I'm in a real rush. I'd love to catch up with you later, though." Of course I don't mean it. I'm lying, and I don't make a habit of fibbing. Still, desperate times call for desperate measures.

"It will only take a minute." His voice is remarkably clear from the other side of the door. Notice how he doesn't take no for an answer?

I hear a second voice. It's the stage manager, and she's telling Jeremy it's his turn.

"Okay, I gotta run, but we'll talk as soon as I'm done my speech," he says and presumably walks down the hallway and disappears past the black curtains to take the stage for the final hurrah. You know, the good old pep rally talk that big bosses give to quell any ill will of the masses toward their company and garner their unwavering trust and undying respect.

Near fatality averted, I exhale.

As I gather my things, I hear the clapping. It works every time.

I slip out of the room and the event space before he's finished his oration. I don't hear the final applause. The one where everyone springs to their feet hooting and hollering and clapping in time with the heavy bass music pumping out of speakers on stands near the stage.

Nope. I don't hear it because, before the fanfare, I'm already stepping through the doors of The Chateau Frontenac and into the biting cold.

Except for one small glitch.

A storm blew in while I was giving my talk, and it's not the one raging inside me. I look down and find my recently purchased heels are buried in a snow drift. I have no other shoes except a pair of flip flops for my sunshiny trip. I'm traveling light because, as I've established, I'm *not* staying here.

On that note... I take a deep breath and say, "Here goes nothing" before plunging a snow-covered heel forward into the storm.

~ THREE ~

I brave the biting wind, take another step forward, and slip onto the sidewalk. There is no way to walk in this, so I decide to hail the lone taxi inching by. Mercifully, it pulls over, and I throw my suitcase and myself inside and say, "Train station, please."

Not in French.

Minutes later, I fall—literally fall—out of the taxi. As soon as my heel hits solid ground, aka the ice-covered sidewalk, it comes out from under me, and just like that, I'm down.

As I clutch onto the taxi door to right myself, I consider taking off my traction-less heels that are causing me to skid like a comic book character on the pavement. That would inevitably invite frostbite, though, and I've had enough torture for one day, thanks very much. Still, I'm undeterred. I'm getting out of this frozen city and onto a tropical island come hail or high water or, in this case, come ice and deep snow. No one, not slick Jeremy Fox or this foul weather is going to stop me.

Oh, don't feel sorry for me. And please, you keep your winter boots. Kind of you to offer, though.

I use my carry-on case as a crutch and slide into the train station without another incident and relatively unscathed, except that my feet are wet and frozen, and my shoes are likely damaged beyond repair. Did I mention they are suede Gucci? Even so, I'm here, and I haven't missed the train, so things are looking up.

For about ten seconds. Then I hear this coming over the loudspeaker: "Due to a province-wide ice storm, all trains are canceled until further notice. We apologize for the inconvenience and will alert you as soon as we resume service. Merry Christmas."

Wait. What? Did they just cancel my ticket out of here and end with Merry Christmas? In the same announcement? You've got to be kidding.

I stifle a scream. Modern life isn't conducive to screaming outbursts in public just because you're frustrated by the transit system. Still, I'm pretty close to not giving a crap right now.

I haven't had a day like this since the books-at-the-boy's-feet incident, which, incidentally, was followed by a math test slapped on my desk with a 49% scrawled across the top (no hand-drawn teacher's happy faces for me) and ended with the news that my lost cat had been found dead on the train tracks behind our house.

This day is stacking up to be on par with that, except I'm a grown up now. Ot at least trying to be.

Oh yes. I was going to tell you my age. Or did I already? I'm pretty sure I have undiagnosed ADHD. So far, apart from forgetting to show up for a handful of coffee-shop dates with friends, losing personal items, and an underlying feeling of dread, it's worked in my favor. Almost a superpower, in fact, with the laser focus I can apply. Except not in French class, apparently.

Darn it all.

I'm twenty-eight, although most days I still feel like I'm eighteen. Some days, like this one, I wish I were. Aforementioned boss is twenty-nine. The kind of twenty-nine that is charmingly confident and runner muscular. No heavy-around-the-middle for this guy.

How do I know? Well, for starters his fitted dress shirts leave little to the imagination. And once (here I'd cup my hand around the side of my mouth if you were beside me, even though I'm in a train station with a whole host of people who are, like me, ready to riot) I saw him shirtless in his swimming trunks sitting atop a makeshift wooden plank inside a dunk tank.

I'm not ashamed to admit that I studied him like a specimen inside a petri dish until someone tossed me the ball. It took three tries while he smirked at me with those plush lips and menacing, dark eyes until I hit the bullseye and glimpsed the fleeting, and oh-so-satisfying, look of shock as it washed over his features before he plummeted into the ice-cold water.

Okay. Back to my age because I'm stalling dealing with how I'm going to handle the newly delivered information that I am stuck in Quebec City the day before Christmas Eve in a snowstorm.

At twenty-eight, you'd think I might have had a serious relationship by now. Instead, I've had a string of disasters. More on that later. Maybe. Suffice it to say that I am legitimately the worst at girl-friending.

Whether with a boyfriend or a best friend.

Ask Barbie. She'll tell you. I don't know how she's even stuck around this long. You see, if you're not in front of me, I'll forget you exist. No offense. It's an ADHD thing.

For example, if I'm working on a project, you'll think I fell off the face of the earth. And one day, or, more likely, one night when I'm dropping off to sleep, you'll come to mind, and I'll think, *gosh it's been a while. I should call her.* Then I'll forget for another two months until you think I've completely abandoned the friendship. Which, I assure you, I have not. However, I might have to do so once I finally call, full of apologies, and you're like, *what the heck?*

The same is true for boyfriends. I'm hopeless. But Jeremy *is* in front of me every day. For six years! Making him infuriatingly hard to forget.

Until today.

I'll be able to forget him now, since I am virtually unemployed.

As for the others, I won't bore you with the details. Think *La La Land* meets *Jerry Maguire* and you'll get the idea. Basically, I don't have the constitution for conventional relationships. I'm more the romanticizing-my-twenties-away kind of gal, lacking any and all prospects of lifetime cohabitation with a member of the opposite sex in the near future.

Especially now.

Within the course of an hour, I've managed to get asked out for a drink with the man of my every-waking dream and nearly be fired by the same man.

Oof.

Hang on a sec. They're making another announcement. Never mind. It's a repeat of the last one canceling the trains.

I'd better come up with a plan. Everyone will be clamoring for a taxi and a hotel room, so I need to put on my big girl shoes and get walking.

I squeeze through the doors, along with a few hundred other disappointed travelers, and step into the biting cold. Minus thirty-two-plus-wind-chill cold now, making it feel as though I've stepped into a life-sized deep freezer with a massive fan. All I know is that I'm out here for three seconds and I may as well be naked for all the good this lightweight dress coat is doing me.

After ten minutes, I give up getting another taxi. I'm liable to freeze if I wait any longer. I consider my options. I would rather get hypothermia than go back to the hotel.

I turn towards a coffee shop, head down to block the wind, intending to step inside to call an Uber. I may as well have ice skates on, as I have taken to sliding my shoes along the ground instead of actually lifting them. The last thing I need is a concussion.

It's in this assumed position that I skid into a post, which knocks me off balance. I grasp it to right myself, but it's not attached to the ground. Both me, the post, and whatever is hanging from the post tip over.

Now I'm laying prostrate in an ice puddle among, inexplicably, a barrage of coins and bills. I lift my head to watch my suitcase skid down the hill, bump over the sidewalk, and launch off the side of a staircase. It disappears over the edge alongside the plastic ball of money.

Hello day of the fallen books, my old friend.

As if that isn't bad enough, I look up and, wait for it... the snow boots in my line of vision belong to an exceedingly tall Santa Claus who, mid-ring of a bell dangling from his hand, is staring down at me with dazzling blue eyes.

~ Four ~

Before I know it, Santa is bending—correction, kneeling—in the snow-slush beside me.

"Are you okay?" he asks.

I turn my head and yep, there they are again. Those startlingly blue eyes. Like the Bahamas water I should be close to swimming in instead of this frozen sludge.

Santa's hat slides off his head and falls into said sludge beside my soon-to-be-frozen fingers. He holds out his hand, but when I oblige him and pick up his hat and pass it to him, he takes it in his other hand, leaving the first one extended. Oh. He wants to help me up.

I have no options, so I take his hand. Not until he pulls me to my feet do I realize that one of those said feet is sans high-heeled shoe.

So, here I am, standing lopsided but upright, looking into the face of a shockingly handsome, Santa-suited stranger.

"*Merci*," I manage to squeak out. I don't ever want to use this Latin-based language again, but my mother drilled politeness into my bones, so I make one last allowance.

"You're welcome," he says, and I cringe. My accent is so bad that he speaks to me in English. "Can I help?"

It's at this moment I realize that the money scattered around where I'd been lying must have been formerly inside the plastic ball that hung from the pole I grabbed to try to steady myself. A piece of the broken ball also lies nearby, its Salvation Army logo half submerged in snow.

Perfect.

But Church Boy—let's change his name to something less Christmasy for now—grins. Not the sympathetic type of smile that assures you you're pathetic. More of a this-is-crazy-but-also-funny one.

I'm not going to lie, because I already told you I don't make a habit of it, but I swoon a little.

I know what you're thinking. What about your boss? And you'd be right to ask. After all, only an hour ago, I was in a fight-or-flight predicament regarding him. But Church Boy, despite any religious bias I may have formed over the years, is the type to make you forget your boss. Or that you swore you would never set foot in church again.

I smile back, in a not-quite-so-dazzling-as-him sort of way. After all, it's not easy to look elegant with ice balls fused to the ends of your eyelashes.

I would flick my hair over my shoulder, but it's plastered to my face and neck. Frozen, in fact. Not a look I'd recommend.

Church Boy appears unruffled. More than that, he appears perfect. Feels perfect too, since he's still holding my frozen hand. Which I notice because he begins rubbing it between both of his.

What is happening? A complete, yet gorgeous, stranger wearing a Santa suit is rubbing my hands to warm them. Any moment he'll probably blow on them.

He *does*.

I should be grossed out, or think it's creepy, but this random act of kindness deserves some respect. Let's be honest, I'm a damsel in legit distress. Okay, *damsel* is a bit of a stretch, seeing as I'm sure I look more like a drowned rat.

Church Boy must have an affinity for rodents.

He stops rubbing my hands. I would stuff them inside my flimsy coat pockets if I didn't need them to walk. To balance. To survive these elements. It's genuinely looking as though I may have to crawl from here and be forced to embrace my new rodent-like attributes.

He asks a question emphatically enough to suggest he might have asked it before. Even so, it doesn't register. Somehow, I'm still smiling. A lunatic trapped in a woman's body. A gust of wind rips the singular button off my coat and sends it flapping behind me.

This would be the part where my last book hits Michael Barret's toe.

At this point, I am beyond caring. Come on, storm. Take it all. (Picture Rose standing at the bow of the Titanic, arms flung wide, except way less glamorous). Instead, I think about his money and bend to pick up a couple of toonies. I *know*. He's barely finished warming my fingers, and I go and plunge them back into liquid snow. Sanity is scarce these days. Mine, anyway.

"Please don't worry about it. Here, take this." He's removed his Santa coat and is placing it over my shoulders.

I don't protest because I have started to wonder if this is the day I die. Frozen in French Land. The last words off my lips will be "*Au revoir*" in a horrific French accent.

"Thank you," I manage. The Santa coat is big enough to cover my coat with room to do up the buttons, which I attempt. Unfortunately, my fingers aren't working. Ironic that I detest Christmas, and now I'm clamoring to fasten a Santa coat around myself.

A nearby clock strikes seven. The exact time I was supposed to be inside a warm train cabin peering out the window at this wintry mess instead of being in it.

Church Boy moves my hands away and starts doing up the buttons.

"Come with me," he says when he's done.

He may be a serial killer disguised as a Santa, but I could not care less. Surviving this storm is the only thing on my mind right now.

I follow him. Actually, I let him lead me. He's holding my hand again, and I'm pretty sure the look just before he grabbed it was him considering carrying me.

At least I'd like to think so.

I don't even know him. Still, I'm worried about this kind, jacket-less Santa getting sick from the cold.

He leads me to the top of the staircase, the one my suitcase and his money ball disappeared over. "Wait here, okay?" He clutches the handrail and makes his way down the stairs. I peer down after him to see my suitcase splayed open like a banana split at the bottom. Bras, underwear, and bikinis are scattered in the snow—a colorful crime scene of fabric.

There is no way I'm going to let a gorgeous stranger handle my underwear and string bikinis, so I start down the stairs after him to rescue my beachwear and, hopefully, my dignity. If I weren't on the brink of hypothermia, I might have the wherewithal to appreciate the narrow street below lined with quaint shops and Christmas lights. It's all I can do, though, to keep my teeth from rattling together. I know my lips are purple, and not because of the shade of lip gloss that is frozen to my mouth. I swear if I speak my lips will crack.

Church Boy has begun gathering up my personal items. Under normal circumstances, I'd be mortified. But wait, I spoke too soon. A large gust of wind flings my fluorescent pink thong into the air and across Church Boy's face, making him look like some sort of masked bandit. He peels it from his eyes and tosses it into the suitcase.

As if that wasn't bad enough, my last existing piece of footwear is yanked off my foot halfway down the staircase when the heel jams into one of the cracks. I can't tell how deep it's stuck because the snow has covered everything, including said heel.

I choose not to dig it out, only resume the descent. Unfortunately, I'm distracted by this whole fiasco and lose my footing. Without warning, I'm tobogganing down the icy stairs on my behind. By the time I reach the bottom, where Church Boy is bent over closing my case, I careen into his backside, and we collectively tumble into the snow. Now I'm on top of him, certain this could not get more awkward.

It does.

Because now my misty breath is meeting his misty breath like an airborne kiss, our faces inches apart, and I do some weird cough thing to break the tension. To my horror, spittle flings from my mouth and hits him square in his eye. Yes, you heard right.

I have no words.

After a quick swipe of his eye, he reaches for my shoulders. "Are you okay?"

I attempt to clamber to my feet, but slip on the ice and end up splayed on top of him.

Heaven, help me.

This time I let him push me up, and, somehow, I'm vertical again.

"Your zipper's broken," he says calmly as he bends to tuck the irreparable case under his arm as though none of that had just happened. How is he more worried about my belongings than his money?

When he straightens and turns toward me, for the first time shock contorts his face. I'm guessing he's just noticed my naked feet.

~ FIVE ~

"What happened to your shoes?"

I'm too cold to speak.

Church Boy makes an executive decision. He lifts me from behind and plants me inside the entry of a nearby shop. Once he retrieves my case, he sets it next to me and says, "Wait here."

This time I listen.

A couple of minutes later, a white SUV pulls up and Church Boy steps out. If this were a western, he'd be the cowboy skidding into town on a white horse to save me.

He contemplates me shivering in the alcove of the shop, as if assessing what to do, then wordlessly lifts me up again and carries me over the snow in his arms. My ribs are against his chest, his body blocking me from the hungry wind. I don't know where to put my hands, so I wrap one around his neck and let the other dangle in front. If I weren't deliriously cold—not to mention life-threateningly mortified—this might be romantic.

Seconds later, he sets me on the passenger seat of his SUV and jumps in beside me on the driver's side. He turns the heat to full and the vents towards me, and in no time warm air infiltrates the space.

"I'm Grant," he says, reaching out his hand.

My voice gets stuck in my windpipe, and I forget all decorum.

Did I mention I'm not at my best around tall, dark, and handsome? Blue eyes are my absolute kryptonite, and his, specifically, are making me melt despite the freezing temperatures or the nagging detail that he could be a serial killer. But let's put that behind us for now, in favor of his ridiculous beauty.

When I don't reach out and don't speak, he rubs his hands together and blows on them. Like he did mine but a lot less carefully.

The car windows are getting fogged up, and I try not to think about the reasons car windows get fogged up as I peer out the side window. The snow races past, and we're not even moving yet. I can't see the people I suspect are trudging past the vehicle in search of shelter or a hotel room.

Speaking of which, I need a hotel room. Although, based on my luck so far, an igloo might be in my immediate future.

"Porsha," I blurt, turning around to face him.

His head swings to the side, and once again I'm undone by his adorable, miniature frown mixed with a crooked half smile.

"Your favorite car?"

"No, my name."

"Oh, got it. Nice to meet you, Porsha." The smile inflates, and I'm not looking away. It's like he's a neodymium magnet, and I am a miniature shard of metal. Let's skip the way he says my name and not mention that it's enough to make a frozen gal melt.

Instantly.

"I'm sorry about your money globe thingy," I say, trying to extricate the strands of hair from the side of my mouth I notice only when I started talking and because my lips are defrosting now.

I hold my hands up to the vents, and the tips of my bright pink fingers sting.

"Don't worry about it. The money goes to help people, so the way I see it, you helped spread Christmas cheer."

Huh. That's refreshing.

I bite the side of my lip. It feels like I've been to the dentist for a filling and the freezing is wearing off. I'm nervous. Not because I think my life may be at risk, but because being in this confined space with such perfection is making me jittery. I haven't felt like this in a very long time.

Maybe ever.

Not even around my boss.

"I need to find a hotel," I say, rubbing my frozen toes. They ache so badly now I think I could cry.

"I was about to ask you if you did."

"The trains are canceled. Can you believe that?"

"That's crazy, although they did say this would be bad."

I'd been too busy cramming a second language to follow weather reports.

"Since when can't trains go through snow?" I ask in an *isn't-that-ludicrous* tone.

"There's been freezing rain, which can cause the switches to get stuck. I guess they're taking precautions."

I nod. Of course the storm of the century had to happen today.

He's studying his phone screen. "The radar shows there's going to be a small break in about ten minutes." He tips the screen toward me, but I'm not accustomed to reading radars. I have other strengths. Radar reading and French speaking don't qualify.

"We can wait a few minutes until the snow lets up, and then I'll take you to a hotel if you like."

I gaze out the windshield. I have no idea how that's even possible. Either the break in the weather or the driving in it. I don't have a car in Toronto, so what would I know, but this appears especially impassible.

"I have a parka and a spare pair of boots in the trunk."

"Oh, you mean walk to a hotel." I let out a nervous laugh. I don't want to look like an idiot in front of him, although it's likely much too late for that. "That'd be great."

We sit in silence for a minute. The kind of gut-wrenching quiet that always lures me into saying regretful things. I pray I don't succumb, and I'm not even into praying like I assume Church Boy, now renamed Grant, is.

"I was supposed to be on a beach tomorrow." I kick myself for being hopeful about answered prayers.

He stops tapping the steering wheel. "I'm sorry about that." He does look sorry, and somehow that lessens the sting of the lost holiday.

"Were you going away for Christmas with your family?"

"Nope... with myself."

"Yourself? Really?" He may have winced when he said that, but it's kind of dark, and I don't know him well enough to be sure.

"The thing is, I hate Christmas."

Yeah, it's a wince. I'm certain now because the expression didn't change except to grow more pronounced.

"Who hates Christmas?"

I raise my hand like I've been found guilty of the worst possible crime.

"Fascinating. I've never met anyone who hates Christmas. I love Christmas. It's my favorite time of year."

"I get that response a lot."

"Why do you hate Christmas? What's to hate?"

I let out a brief hissing sound. The kind the Via Rail train should have made about thirty minutes ago as it was pulling away from the station. "Don't get me started."

"Please? I'd like to hear."

"Okay, you asked for it. Don't hate me for making you rethink the season."

And I say the same to you, because I like you and there's a chance we'll be friends after all this is over.

"For starters, it's commercialism to the max. People rushing around like madmen to find the perfect gift, then buying a bunch of stuff they can't afford and getting themselves into ridiculous debt just to one-up people. The gluttonous eating and the absurd amount of weight gained by said gluttonous eating, only to drain the rest of their savings a couple of weeks later on a gym membership they'll never use." I pause to come up for air and to measure how he's taking my rant.

He's smiling. Honestly. Can you believe this guy?

I continue, because self-restraint is also not in my repertoire of strengths. "They shuffle off to the obligatory once-a-year church service, light a candle, swing it around while singing off tune and coming precariously close to burning the blue hair of the old lady in the pew in front, then rip open an absurd number of presents, leaving them with gift hangover, not to mention a food coma."

"You've given this a lot of thought."

"Mmm hmm." I say it as though I've won.

Obviously, I have.

When the unnerving silence returns, I come this close (picture me holding my thumb and index finger half an inch apart in front of my face) to blurting out the real reason I hate Christmas. Thankfully, I'm saved by a gust of wind so strong that it rattles the car. I rub circles over the misted window and peer outside. The snow appears to have calmed down, but the wind is making a tornado of whatever has fallen.

Even so, we decide to take a chance in the pause to find me a place to stay.

The nasty whiteness is ankle deep, and I'm grateful for the puffer jacket Grant grabbed from his trunk and gave me (after taking back the Santa coat) and the oversized snow boots he laced up around my feet as I hung them out the car door before we braved this chaos. I am not, however, grateful for the wind, which continues to whip my frozen hair in my face. I'm certain that by the time this is over I'll have multiple lacerations across my cheeks.

It's that bad.

Grant scrutinizes me before stopping to zip the coat he gave me to wear all the way up under my chin. My hands are inside the pockets, so I don't even attempt to help. I'm like a helpless child, and I feel like one, relying on him in this storm.

I follow him through the streets, dodging other pedestrians slogging their way through this force of nature. We're collectively caught, but it's every man, woman, and child for themselves. Except for the stranger beside me who has taken it upon himself to be my Sherpa guide.

Truly, this curving hill feels as though we're scaling Mt. Everest. Before I know it, Sherpa Grant has offered his arm, and I have looped mine through his and stuffed my hand back in my pocket.

We move as one under a stone arch. We aren't speaking because all our effort and concentration is on this task of survival, or at least mine is. Besides, the ravenous wind would swallow and carry off any words we could possibly form.

Then I realize something. I've stopped being afraid. Weird, right?

With the strength of his stride and his arm linked in mine, I'm no longer scared of blowing away in this storm, and I have all I need to survive. I know, it sounds dramatic. I honestly have no idea, though, how I would have managed by myself in a thin coat and heels. Or worse, bare feet.

But this Good Samaritan took it upon himself to help me. There's no way he needed to do this.

We reach the top of the hill, and the Chateau Frontenac comes into view. The same hotel I recently ran away from. If he means to take me there to get a room, I can't and I won't. I'm not joking. Call me what you will. A coward. Crazy. I don't care. I can't go back in there, and I tell Grant as much.

He has no idea why and he doesn't ask, bless his dear heart. Instead, he takes a detour, trying five different boutique hotels. It's no surprise that they all have no vacancy. Some even have line-ups outside the door.

We take a minute to warm up inside the vestibule of one of them. In the confined space, I turn to find there's a mirror right next to my head. According to my reflection, it's worse than you tried to tell me. I look like I've gone through an apocalypse, and I'm the zombie.

In desperation, I do a three-finger swipe under my eyes to try to wipe the mascara away. There is nothing to be done for my hair. It's a saturated mass of brown, matted tangles.

I catch Grant's reflection over my shoulder, and he doesn't look away. Strangely, it's not uncomfortable. It's kind of nice, even if I look tragic. A warm tingle works its way up my spine, and my zombie face smiles.

He doesn't look like he's in an end-of-the-world situation. He looks as though he's skipped through a summer's day, minus the Santa suit, his cheeks flushed from the sun and his wavy hair dripping from a mere dip in a lake.

A mischievous grin hijacks his lips, and he shakes his head. The "lake" water from his hair sprays around the small space, on the mirror, and me. Now we're laughing. No, cackling. The front desk workers and hopeful patrons turn as one to glare at us.

Of course, that only makes us laugh harder.

"We should go before we get kicked out," he says.

I nod and wipe the side of my eyes, likely smearing more mascara under them. What do I care? This guy has seen me at my worst, which means it can only go up from here, right? Besides, why should I worry what a complete stranger thinks of me? Except he's such a cute complete stranger.

"I have an idea," he says and takes my hand.

~ SIX ~

We run out into the snow to find there is a lull in the storm and the wind has taken a break. Minutes later we reach Grant's car, and I don't question climbing in after he opens the door.

"What's the plan?" I ask.

"I know another place. It's outside of town, but there will be room."

I think about the canceled trains and the fact that I won't make my flight even if they start up again tomorrow and so I agree. If I'm going to be stranded in the Artic on Christmas, I may as well find a warm bed for the night. Still, I'm leery about driving in this weather, even if it is in an SUV.

As if hearing my concern, he says, "I have chains on my tires."

I have no idea what that means, but I assume it's helpful, so I go with it.

Before you get the idea that I'm one of these weak women who does anything a man says, I feel the need to tell you, I am not. I'm also unused to not being in control. This entire hour and a half has been entirely out of character for me. The guy-rescues-girl debacle and the ensuing follow-the-leader bit. I'm normally the leader. I've only ever been the rescuer. Of myself, and others.

To a fault.

See Exhibit A. My formerly frozen hand has a white-knuckled grip on the car door handle. Even though I've never seen this much snow,

I would rather be the driver. Thankfully, there aren't many cars on the road, and Grant takes it slow.

In the spirit of vulnerability (thank you, Brené Brown), I feel inclined to add at this point that my job has been my life. I'm ashamed to say I've been fixated on working my way up the corporate ladder. The same one I fell to the bottom rung of today. You say, *I thought you were fixated on your boss?* And you wouldn't be wrong. But can't a girl have more than one fixation? Job? Clothes? Make-up? Hot yoga? Handsome Boss? You get the idea. Why get too specific?

I wonder if Grant has any fixations. Perhaps helping people is one of them.

"Why were you standing in a snowstorm beside a see-through ball of money ringing a bell?" I turn sideways in the seat to ask him. I know what it is, but I'm poking fun. Or trying to. I'm relieved when he smiles.

"I was filling in for my dad. It's usually his thing. Does it every year, but he had an appointment, so I said I'd cover for him."

"Is that your church?" I'm referring the logo on the broken-open money ball that rolled down the hill along with my suitcase.

"Yeah." He nods, and I hope that talking to him won't break his concentration on the road. Although the snow has eased off for now, the roads are terrible. You can't even see the middle line on the highway.

"It's nice of you to help me like this." I've already said thank you, twice, but his treatment of me is more than anyone could ask for, and I'm beyond grateful.

He smiles, and I notice his profile is just as spectacular as the front view of his face.

"What are you doing in Quebec City the day before Christmas Eve?" he asks.

"Staff Christmas party and year-end event. Oh, and getting fired."

He glances away from the road a sec to eye me. "Who fires someone at Christmas?"

"Well, I'm not technically fired yet, but close enough."

"What happened?"

"Let's just say my command of the French language could stand some refinement."

He raises his eyebrows.

"Yeah, I said something on stage during a keynote talk I shouldn't have. Something really awkward. Super bad form and highly unprofessional." I'm rubbing my forehead as I say this, reliving the event I want to forget in my mind.

"It can't be that bad."

"Trust me, it was. And the worst part was that I didn't retract it. I just kept going." I can feel my insides cringing as I recount it.

"Then what happened?"

"Oh, I just barreled right through the rest of the speech and ran off the stage like an idiot and hid."

"Hid?"

"Yes, hid." I flash him one of those stiff, clenched-teeth smiles.

Although he smiles at my attempt to gloss over the whole mess, he doesn't say anything more. I'm glad about that because I really don't want to rehash a second more of my recent thirty-minute nightmare.

"Are you warming up a bit now?"

I nod. I should have spoken instead because he looks over again. Even though I'm a little on edge about the roads, this one glance, filled to the brim with concern, speaks volumes. I melt a little more. If he keeps up the smiles and the concern I'll become a puddle, like Frosty the Snowman in the greenhouse. Of course, I'm hoping this story ends better.

Snow-laden conifers line the sides of the highway, acting as sentinels to keep us on the road. Once again, I briefly question the wisdom of hopping in a car and letting a stranger drive me into the Canadian wilderness in a blinding snowstorm. I have no idea where I am or where we're going. If I hadn't been so desperate, I'd never, in a million years, be doing this. I console myself with the fact that he's a churchgoer.

After about thirty minutes of driving, we turn down a narrow, tree-lined road, barely wide enough for his SUV. It opens to a small clearing where the most adorable log cabin sits in the snow like an ornament on top of an ice cream cake.

"Is this where you *live*?"

"Sometimes."

"I guess that's why there are vacancies?" I wait for the smile. It doesn't make an appearance.

"Is this okay? I mean, if you..." His voice trails off. We both know there are no other options. Under normal circumstances this would be far from okay. But these are far from normal circumstances.

As if to punctuate that sentiment, the snow starts up like someone turned the precipitation dial to the maximum setting.

He smiles then. The kind that says *what can I say* without saying anything.

I smile back. The kind that says *I'm okay with it.* Which we know I shouldn't be. But my "Spidey senses" are giving me the green light. He seems like one of the good guys.

Grant gets out and pulls my salvaged suitcase from the backseat. I follow him up the steps to the cabin door where a fresh wreath hangs and wait for him as he wrestles a key out of his pocket.

He opens the door, and we step inside. It's warm, well, at least warmer than outside, and smells of pine and woodsmoke.

"Welcome to my humble abode." He sets my case down and lights an oil lantern on the table next to him, which he uses to show me to a bedroom.

The *only* bedroom.

After placing the lantern on the bedside table and my case inside the door he says, "Make yourself comfortable. There are towels in here if you want to take a shower." He points to a wooden wardrobe at the end of the bed. "The bathroom's in the next room. Take your time."

He leaves the room, closing the door behind him, and I'm left standing in a strange room next to an oil burning lamp.

Go ahead and call me Laura Ingalls. And while you're at it, hand me a floral pinafore.

I open the wardrobe and reach for a towel. I don't know why, but I bury my damp face in it and take in the clean laundry smell that is a different fragrance than my own. I decide I like it better.

When I open the wooden bedroom door and step out, Grant lifts his head to smile at me from where he is bent in front of a fireplace. Logs are piled on top of birch bark, and he has a box of matches in his hand.

By the time I am done the most wonderful hot shower of my existence, I exit the bathroom and am met with a fire crackling in the hearth and the aroma of woodsmoke and cooking.

Grant's wearing an apron (yes, you heard me correctly) over top of jeans and a woolen sweater he must have changed into while I was in the shower. Steam is rising into his face from whatever he's stirring in the pot. I notice all this as I slip into my room. I don't stop or say a word because I've taken a chance and wrapped the delicious-smelling towel around me instead of putting back on my wet, filthy clothes. I'm hoping he doesn't notice. I don't want him to think I'm one of "those girls."

Unfortunately, there's a small problem in paradise.

All the clothes in my suitcase are soaked. More than that, they are beach clothes. However, as soon as I enter the room, I hear Grant call, "Those are for you" before I close the door.

I look down to see a pair of gray trackpants, a plaid flannel button-up shirt, and a handknit pair of woolen socks lying neatly on the bed.

Are you kidding me?

Everything is much too big. Thankfully, the track pants have a drawstring, and I cinch it as tight as it will go. The clothes feel like a warm hug, as if caring has been worn into the fabric by the previous wearer. Maybe some of it will vicariously rub off on me, since I've only been looking out for number one for a while now.

Maybe for as long as I can remember.

I materialize from the bedroom and stroll into the kitchen. Grant turns from the counter, two plates in hand.

"Thanks," I say, holding up my arms where two extra-long sleeves envelop my hands and flop over the ends of my fingers.

Augh. His grin. I can't even. It warms me more than that fire ever could.

He sets the plates on a rustic wooden table and moves to stand in front of me. "May I?" he asks, pointing to the sleeves.

I nod, and he reaches for the end of the fabric and begins rolling. When his fingers slide along my wrist, a tingle shoots up my arm and down the other. I don't know where to look, so I watch his fingers work. He's close enough to smell the mixture of woodsmoke and cologne that emanates from his skin.

"Go ahead and have a seat," he says now that my hands are properly visible. He drags a wooden chair out from the table and waits for me to sit before pushing it in and taking a seat across from me.

I peer down at the food the same moment the smell of warm beef stew enters my nose, and I realize I haven't eaten all day. I never eat before a presentation. Nerves and food don't mix well with me. Even though the lunch buffet the Chateau Frontenac provided for our group looked incredible, none made it into my mouth.

I let out a moan, and he chuckles. If heaven exists, it better include food.

Suddenly, he's saying something in a soft voice, clearly not to me. His head is lowered toward the table, and he's uttering a prayer into the quiet, smoke-scented air. I shouldn't be surprised because he was collecting money for his church, after all. Still, I haven't said grace before eating in years. Not since dinners at my girlfriend's as a kid.

In his deep voice, he gently and humbly gives thanks to a God I doubt exists. Even so, it's sweet and I don't fault him for it, although I think it's highly unnecessary. God didn't provide the food. Grant did, with the labor of his hands doing whatever he does for work.

If you believe in God, forgive me. We can discuss that later too, if you want. To be honest, I'm being polite. I don't actually want to discuss religion. I've made my own conclusions about the "Big Guy upstairs" and I've also made my peace with it. But since you're a new friend, I'll make allowances (insert winky face) and maybe we can chat later if, like Grant, it's your thing.

"Dig in." He opens his eyes after the *amen* part.

I never closed mine. I watched his lips move while he prayed and the way the candlelight flickered over his perfectly angled features, and now I'm embarrassed at being caught. I wince-smile and pick up the fork beside the spoon. I don't know if the spoon is for dessert or an alternate utensil for the stew.

I vote for dessert.

As soon as I take the first bite, I moan again. I don't even try to stop it. I've never in all my life tasted anything savory this delicious.

"You like it?" he asks, even though it's obvious there's no need.

"It's amazing. How did you whip that up so fast?"

"I usually make up a large pot and freeze smaller portions for later."

I wonder if *smaller portions* include a significant other. I decide not to ask. Even if he is single, it would be foolish to consider showing an ounce of interest. By tomorrow morning, the storm will have moved on, and so will I. Besides, I don't make a habit of dating church goers, even if they are perfection in human form. And he probably doesn't make a habit of dating heathens.

I laugh at the thought.

Who said anything about dating? My mind sometimes.

"What's so funny?"

Oh my gosh. I laughed out loud. Whoopsie.

"Oh, nothing," I say as my mind grasps for a safe topic.

~ SEVEN ~

"How often do you come here?" I ask. Wherever *here* is.

I scan the room. Timber beams brace the roof, wedged into the log walls that surround us like a warm hug. A pair of wooden skis are criss-crossed on the wall above a comfy-looking sofa facing the fireplace. A stunning photo of an elk's head hangs over the fireplace, and a fur pelt of some sort lies on the floor in front (I'm trying not to judge).

"Whenever I can, but more often in the winter. I also have a condo in Montreal."

"It's so peaceful." I reach for the spoon. To heck with dessert. I want every last drop of this rich stew sauce. "This is amazing."

A little gravy seeps out of the side of my mouth with the confession, and I scold myself for talking with my mouth full. Old habits die hard. I wipe it off with the paper napkin that had been folded under the fork and spoon.

"Yeah, it's a great thinking place. A couple days here, and it all comes into focus."

"All?"

"Life. Problems. Priorities. Being here has a way of clarifying things."

"I'll bet," I say, even though I have no experience with this. I'm sure one night won't make an ounce of difference in clarity for me. I'm missing my holiday. And I'll need to get on the job search train ASAP.

What problems does this guy have that require clarity? Any thought of that flees when he looks up over his half-full bowl and smiles. It warms me more than the stew and the fire combined, and I get busy scraping the bottom of my bowl with my spoon.

Grant stands and brings over the pot, asking with his eyes if I want some more.

I nod and he refills my bowl.

I feel his eyes on me as we eat. As if he has a million questions he's not asking or already knows the answers to. This doesn't make me self-conscious or worried he's a psycho. I'm beyond caring.

Sort of.

The thing is, I'm dry, warm, and wrapped in hot-guy clothes, eating the stew of my life. Shockingly, right now I don't feel the need to fill the silence. Apparently, neither does he. It's actually refreshing.

We finish eating at the same time, his one serving to my two, and he reaches for my bowl.

I have no idea what time it is, and for the first time since fleeing the hotel I look at my phone while he rinses our dishes in the sink. When the screen lights up with the time, 7:05, I notice there is one missed call and two text messages from Jeremy. I take in a breath and open my phone.

5:05: Porsha, can you please give me a call.

6:02: Where are you? The front desk said you checked out.

In the middle of nowhere with a gorgeous stranger, I consider typing back.

Grant looks over his shoulder, and I force a smile. I can't help noticing how different he and Jeremy are. People serve Jeremy. Not the other way around. Grant has been doing nothing but serving me these past two hours. It's not just that, though. It's the way he carries himself—with a sort of quiet assurance far beyond craving attention or praise or working hard to be liked. He looks to be my age, but I wonder how old he is to have become this self assured and peaceful. I could stand to be more like him.

To be fair, I haven't seen him interact with others apart from multiple hotel clerks who told us there was no room at the inn. When he heard that, he didn't grow angry or loud and demand his own way like I've seen Jeremy do on multiple occasions. Until now, I've always admired Jeremy. Now that I'm witnessing this quiet strength, I think it takes a lot more character and self-control to behave this way.

Maybe Grant was raised by good parents. Or maybe there's something to all that churchy stuff. Either way, my boss is really starting to pale in comparison.

I place my phone face down on the table next to a dog-eared Bible.

"How do you feel about hot chocolate?" he says while wiping his hands on a tea towel.

"Hypothetically or right now?"

He shoots me a lopsided grin. "Right now."

"Do you even need to ask?"

"With or without whipped cream and marshmallows?"

Can you believe him? I've become the heroine of a Hallmark movie. He's killing me with kindness and food, not to mention his looks.

"Again, do you even need to ask?"

His smile widens as he turns to take two mugs off a live-edge wooden shelf. Since his back is to me, I steal a glance. His Nordic sweater hugs his broad shoulders and arms, and his jeans fit perfectly.

We sip hot chocolate with marshmallows piled on top of an extravagant mound of whipped cream in front of the fire. I like him even more for not being stingy about the whipped cream. I also like these pottery mugs.

For reference's sake, Grant's sitting on the floor directly in front of the fire, poking at it with a stick. I'm curled up on a leather chair wrapped in the warmth of the fire, a wool blanket he handed me before he sat down, and his clothes. Which, when I think about it, is shockingly intimate for not knowing the guy. Still, what choice did I have? Wet clothes or hot-guy clothes? Which would you choose?

The storm has resumed raging. It uses wind as its accomplice, tossing the snow up and blasting it on the frosted-up windowpanes as though, with its insatiable appetite, dissatisfied with all it has consumed.

Including my vacation plans.

Inside this adorable cabin, though, as the sweet, warm liquid hits my tongue, I moan. Again. It's that good. Who is he, Gordon Ramsey's brother?

I don't need to know. In fact, the less I know about Grant the better. I don't want to end up crushing on a guy who lives in the back woods of Quebec. Not only is it too far off the grid to make a relationship work, but I'm a high-rise and coffee-shop-on-every-corner kind of gal. Besides, I've already alluded to my lack of finesse in the dating department. Despite my attempts to avoid it, I'm somehow drawn to Grant, in every way imaginable. Maybe this could be different?

I'm rushing ahead of myself. My track record with members of the opposite sex isn't exactly stellar, so it's better to nip any thoughts of a future for the two of us in the bud. Besides, the second this storm blows by, I'm out of here. If I'm lucky, I can still grab a last-minute flight and be on a beach sipping a piña colada by Boxing Day.

Right now, though, I'm curled in the chair with my legs pulled up under me, staring into my mug at the melting whipped cream and thinking about all this as soft jazz music drifts from a hidden speaker.

"What do you do besides rescue random people from snowstorms?" I scold myself for my lack of discipline. Didn't I just say the less I know the better?

He stops poking and turns his head toward me. Under his warm gaze, I feel like I've been injected with a shot of extra-strength adrenaline.

Get it together, Porsha.

"I work at an ice hotel."

"Brr, that sounds chilly. No wonder you made this storm seem like a walk in the park."

He laughs. "I do love winter."

I blink slowly. Who loves winter? Forget everything. He's not perfect after all.

I want to ask more about his job and what he does in the off season when the whole thing melts to the ground. I leave it for now. Like I told you, I'm intent on keeping my distance, and the more I know, the harder that could be.

"How about you?" he asks.

"I work for a marketing firm. We have offices across Canada and the US, and I work out of the Toronto one."

"Is that what brings you here?"

I nod. I don't want to think about why I'm here so close to Christmas or that I should be on a train bound for Toronto. Not getting snowed in at a cabin in the wilderness.

And yet, watching him poke at the fire as though he hasn't got a care in the world is strangely comforting. He's not trying to make this less awkward because a) he either doesn't seem to find it awkward, or b) he's an exceptional actor. He seems... peaceful. Like this is the most natural thing ever.

"Do you make a habit of carrying people over the snow and bringing them to your cabin?" I'm teasing, although there is an undertone of seriousness to it. Maybe he's so calm because people in Quebec do this sort of thing all the time. Help each other out in snowstorms and do whatever it takes. Maybe everyone here goes the extra mile.

He tamps out the glowing end of the stick on the hearthstone and rotates toward me.

"No, this is a first."

"It's a bit risky. I could be a serial killer."

He laughs and I enjoy the sound, the way his eyes crinkle at the sides, and the lingering smile that accompanies it all. But the way his eyes meet mine when it fades? Gulp. There goes my heart again. I just need to make it through this night. How hard can that be?

"You could be, but you're giving off more of a highly-underprepared-for-winter-storms vibe. I'll take my chances on the serial killer part."

"Not afraid to die, eh?"

"Not in the least."

"You sound pretty sure about that."

"I am." One knee has fallen to the side and his forearm hugs the other near his chest. "Are you afraid to die?"

"Yeah, of course I am. I'm waaay too young to die."

"Fair enough," he says.

I pinch my brows together. Judging by the prayer, the philanthropy, and the well-used Bible on his table, he's likely confident about where he's going. I, on the other hand, am sure about nothing—except his eyes. They produce a flurry of feelings within me more tumultuous than the snowstorm outside.

Despite my holiday plans having been turned upside down and the fact that I will be jobless the second I answer Jeremy's texts, this moment—and the handful of ones preceding it since I fell—feel like a taste of heaven. This time I'm not being dramatic. I'm warm and dry, my tummy is full, and I have a place to lay my head tonight. My basic needs have been met, thank you, Maslow. The rest of the hierarchical triangle will have to wait.

I attempt to conceal a yawn by forcing my mouth closed, but the sound escapes.

"If you're tired, feel free to turn in for the night."

Grant rises from his place at the hearth, and I'm surprised how disappointed I am about this. As tired as I am, I don't want this evening to end. He must not feel the same way, as he's already taking the cushions off the pull-out couch.

It crosses my mind how his churchy friends would feel about him picking up a woman he's never met and spending the night with her, even if she is sleeping on his couch. I'm not beyond thinking about the optics.

Which is also why I had never accepted a drink invitation from Jeremy. If I was going to earn a promotion, it would be fair and square. No back-stabbing office gossip about me sleeping my way to the top. At least I don't need to worry about that anymore.

I stand to help him fix the sheet around the corners of the pull-out mattress and smooth the quilt overtop.

"This looks handmade," I say, tracing the stitches.

"Yeah, my grandmother's handiwork."

I run my hand over the patchwork of fabric. Quilts aren't my style. They don't work with my modern, minimalist apartment. Still, I can appreciate the work and the love that must have gone into making it, even if I never knew either of my grandmothers.

Grant stands on the other side of the bed with an odd look on his face. I don't know him well enough to read it, so I simply say, "Good night."

He doesn't move.

I let out an awkward laugh and lower myself to the side of the bed. I don't need tucking in like a three-year-old, but I wouldn't put it past him at this point, after all he's done for me.

"Porsha, that's your room in there." He points to the bedroom he showed me to when I arrived. The room he apparently means me to sleep in. The room he has given up for me, I now realize.

My cheeks burn. I'm an idiot. I can only hope he didn't think I was making a move on him.

"Oh right, of course. I thought... I mean, you didn't need to give up your room," I stammer.

A fleeting look of relief crosses his face, and I see that he did indeed think I was planning on climbing into bed with him.

I feel compelled to explain. "I wasn't... uh, meaning that..." I attempt to clarify while pointing to the couch, but I come off sounding as though I've forgotten how to speak and give up.

He nods and rewards my blundering with that adorable lopsided smile. "It's okay. Goodnight, Porsha. Sleep tight and don't let the bed bugs bite."

I giggle like a schoolgirl. Do people still say that?

He throws another log on the fire, then pulls back the side of the quilt.

"Thank you for everything, and don't you worry. I'll be out of your way first thing in the morning." I punctuate this with a super-awkward, bent-arm swing in front of my body.

So ridiculous.

He's pulling his sweater over his head. I'm transfixed because his white T-shirt lifted with his sweater and forgive me, but I glimpsed his washboard abs and I'll never be able to unsee them. He yanks the fabric down and runs his fingers through his dark curls. I close my mouth and hope by some miracle I'm not physically drooling because I am internally.

"My pleasure." He folds the sweater and places it on the leather chair I was sitting in a moment ago. His eyes, as though catching the light of every candle in the room, gaze back at me.

Why aren't my feet moving?

"Do you need anything else?" he asks.

When my legs remember how to walk, I trip over the edge of the carpet. As I attempt to regain my balance, the over-sized woolen socks slip on the wooden floor, and I fall backwards onto the bed. I scramble to my feet, although not before his strong hands reach around my shoulders to steady me.

Now we're face-to-face, his inches from mine. I'm breathing heavily from that added display of clumsiness, certainly not because I'm looking into the face of sheer perfection. Heaven help me, I almost kiss him but gather my rapidly waning reserve of strength to stop myself even though every fiber of my being wants him to kiss me.

Don't say it. *I know.* I don't even know his last name. Even so, nothing else matters in this moment.

He lets go of me, like the gentleman he has shown himself to be, and my racing heart sags in my chest.

"I'll just..." I point with both hands toward the bedroom, and he nods.

"Good night," I pause to say at the doorway to the bedroom.

"Good night, Porsha," he says. "And, for the record, you're not in my way."

~ EIGHT ~

Inside the bedroom, I rest my head against the closed door and let out a long sigh. I don't move, only stand there, trying to breathe normally. Then, as if I haven't caused enough carnage for one day, I turn and fling open the door.

To my surprise, there he stands, arm raised and hand poised to knock.

"Do you want to..." we say at the same time and laugh.

"Stay up and chat a while?" he finishes.

I nod but internally squeal.

"I'd really like that," I manage to say somewhat normally.

After I follow him to the living room, he moves his sweater from the chair so I can sit back down and lowers himself onto the matching one beside it. Bing Crosby's voice swells over the crackling fire, the lyrics to "White Christmas" filling the room.

I search for a place to bury my feelings as I focus on the flames. My face grows warm. Although I tell myself it's because of the fire, it's more than that. Grant has ignited something inside me that I don't want to extinguish.

Sixty seconds in, and I'm already uncomfortable in the silence. This time I swear I'm not going to be the one to break it. It's so much safer being the question-asker, though. What if he thinks up something I don't want to answer?

Why should I care, you ask? I guess I shouldn't. After all, didn't I say I'm out of here the moment this storm lets up? Somehow it matters more than I can explain.

"I don't know your last name," Grant says beside me.

"Ivy," I tell him and hear an immediate chuckle. "What?"

"It's funny you hate Christmas with that last name."

"I know, right?" I look over to see his eyes twinkling with mischief. It's a good thing I'm not standing, or I wouldn't be for long. The look on his face is making me weak.

"Good thing your parents didn't name you Holly."

"I wouldn't put it past them with their precedent on first names."

He lets out a belly laugh. I join him, warmed that he enjoys my dry humor. Then our laughter fades, and I grow nervous.

"What do you think you'll do after this job?" he asks, referring to my pending dismissal.

I exhale a breath I didn't know I was holding, thankful for a safe topic. "Maybe take the trip I'm currently missing," I say, attempting to keep it light. Besides, the creases around his eyes when he smiles are irresistible, and I can't get enough of his lopsided grin.

"How about you? What do you do for work during the summer?" I ask.

His gaze shifts to a basket between the chairs holding several magazines, then makes its way back to me. I take both the look and the pause to mean he's contemplating how much to tell me. I get it. I'm in the exact same position.

Finally, he lifts one of the magazines from the basket and hands it to me. I have no idea why or what to do with it, so I peer down at the front cover. My breath catches when I see the full-size photo of him with a camera around his neck and his name centered under a National

Geographic logo. Even in two dimensions, his piercing eyes take my breath away.

"Grant Hazelton," I read aloud. "Wildlife Photographer? Are you kidding me?" I look over at him.

He runs his fingers over the shadow of stubble on his jaw, looking as though he's given away a secret.

"I never would have guessed that." I shake my head, still taking him in.

He offers me a what-can-I say shrug before reaching for the magazine. I snatch it away and start leafing through it to find a several-page spread depicting his work. He's captured photos of lynx and bear and moose and loons, and they are stunning in their vibrancy, color, and the way Grant has framed them in their surroundings. I'm enraptured. Because of my job, I can appreciate masterful photography when I see it.

A foreign sense of pride wells in my chest. I know how hard he must have worked to not only hone his craft but to capture these shots, not to mention make a living at it. Still, I don't know how to file these feelings. I'm not used to caring about, let alone celebrating, the success of others. Like I mentioned, I've been too busy crafting my own.

At some point, we move to the floor and sit side by side on the fur pelt. Our backs rest against the chairs, our faces are warm and golden from the fire.

"So that's your work then?" I point to the elk photo above the fire.

He nods.

"What about this?" I run my hand over the pelt, puzzling over the incongruity between this and his photography.

"Handed down from my great-grandfather, like this cabin."

I shoot him a wistful smile, trying to grasp how it would feel to be attached to my past in any form, let alone to inherit pieces of it. "It's so nice here. Too bad you only come sometimes."

"I come whenever I can. Keeps it special. Besides, I travel a lot with my work."

"Of course," I say.

Then Grant hits me with, "What's the one characteristic you like most about yourself?"

Yikes. Back to me.

"Umm," I stammer. I've honestly never given it much thought, as I've been too busy for any sort of existential meanderings. I chew the inside of my cheek.

When he sees me wrestling to form an answer, he adds, "How about one exterior and one interior characteristic."

"I like my hair," I say and flick a few strands over my shoulder.

He rewards me with a smile that makes me feel like a helium balloon is expanding inside my chest. "Fully understandable."

I'm still absorbing his compliment and hoping my playful answer was enough of a distraction when he adds, "What about on the inside?"

Oh boy. Here we go. I gaze at the ceiling and struggle to find something commendable I like about myself while watching the shadows cast from the flames dance over the wooden beams.

"How about I go first," he says, rescuing me. I'm waiting for him to tell me about himself when he says, "I like your spunk."

I have no idea how he knows that about me. I don't ask, only go ahead and say, "And I like your kindness." I reach over to give his arm a squeeze and decide to leave my hand there.

He places his over mine and says, "And I like you."

That stops me in my tracks. I hear my pulse in my ears and grow much too warm under his fleece shirt and consuming gaze.

"I like you too," I manage to say as I grasp the front of his fleece shirt and tug it away from my skin. How difficult will it be to say goodbye to him tomorrow? When one side of his lips lift, ten times more weight gets piled on top of that sentiment.

After a few quiet minutes, I blurt, "I like my drivenness" into the silence.

When he doesn't speak, I glance sideways to see him grinning. Even though I've only known him a few hours, I swear this smile is one of pride, which gives me the courage to say more. "I've worked really hard to get where I am."

"I love that," he says. "I'll bet there were some decent-sized sacrifices along the way."

"You're not kidding. It's all been worth it, though."

I expect him to respond similarly about his work. Instead, he looks reticent. Almost sad.

Although I'm sure there's a reason for that, Grant doesn't offer one. I start to regret exposing myself and pull back my hand as if physically retracting my words. From now on, I'm sticking to surface topics.

I'm doing just that, searching for something light, when he says, "My ex-girlfriend didn't admire my drivenness." Leaning forward, he pokes at the logs.

"No? What happened?" I dive in. So much for sticking to surface topics.

He shrugs again. "Let's just say she didn't appreciate my work schedule."

Pain stabs my chest. "I'm sorry."

"I'm not. At least, not anymore."

I bite the side of my bottom lip. How could anyone let this guy go? "I'm sure she regrets it."

He tilts his head. "I doubt it. She married the producer she ran off with and lives in LA."

His words sting even me. I let out a stiff breath and slowly shake my head. The fire cracks and spits out a few sparks as if punctuating my sentiment. I have no words. This time the silence is fitting.

After a few minutes, he says, "What about you?"

My muscles tighten. Aren't we done with that subject? I know I am. "What about me?"

"What's your story?"

"Not much to tell," I say, still trying to circumvent talking about myself. "I got a degree in business from Laurier University and have been working in marketing ever since. Nothing too exciting."

Dare I hope this will suffice? When I glance over, I'm met with eyes that are prying the lid off places I've hidden. I'm not ready to rehash my past, and I'm leery about sharing anything about the present. Which doesn't leave much.

"Tell me about your church." I spin the conversation back to him. "I don't know anyone who goes to church anymore."

"No?" He raises his eyebrows. "I take it you don't either."

I shake my head. "It lost its luster for me a long time ago."

"Care to share about that?"

"Not really. Frankly, I just don't see the point of it all." How did the conversation get back to me? I take the stick from him, shift closer to the fire, and give the coals a jab, desperate for a reprieve from this God talk, not to mention Grant's heady gaze.

"I get that."

"You get that? How would you?" As that was the last response I'd expected from him, I stop prodding and shift to face him.

When my eyes find his, it feels as though someone took the hot end of the stick I'd been stabbing into the fire and used it to poke at my heart.

Grant lifts both hands. "I've had to work through my own stuff with God."

"What do you mean?"

"Let's just say I avoided him for a long time."

I go back to poking the fire. I don't want to admit that I've been avoiding God. Even if I hadn't been, I don't have time for God, and I especially don't want him interfering in my life. I've been doing fine on my own, thank you very much.

Grant seems to sense I need a minute and goes to the kitchen. I hear clanking dishes, but I don't turn around. I'm still thinking about what he said, not to mention that I'm experiencing conflicting emotions I'd rather keep hidden. Concerning both God and Grant.

I know. It's kind of a lot.

After several minutes, Grant returns carrying two mugs overflowing with whipped cream.

"I took a chance you might like seconds." He hands me a mug with whipped cream spilling over the edges. I lick my way around the sides to stop it overflowing. Seconds is exactly what I need. And not just of hot chocolate.

After settling on the chair, he takes a sip. A blob of whipped cream ends up on his nose, and I instinctively reach out to wipe it away with my fingertip. It takes all my effort to retract my hand. I continue to peer at him over my mug, soaking in the warmth of his reciprocated gaze.

When it becomes too much, I busy myself by taking a gulp of my drink. It's not easy navigating around the whipped cream, and I get a dollop of it on my own nose. Before I know it, Grant's thumb passes over the end of it.

We remain like this, transfixed, until we both let out an awkward laugh and take a simultaneous sip.

"So... no one of significance?" he surprises me by asking.

"Nope. I'm much too busy for relationships." Although you and I know I would have made an allowance for Jeremy. The way I'm feeling right now, I'd make several for Grant. I finger the handle of the mug and its smooth glaze.

Grant nods and looks thoughtful. His eyes on the fire, he says, "Maybe your circumstances have changed now?"

When I catch the hint of a grin at the side of his lips, I say, "Maybe they have."

~ NINE ~

We end up talking most of the night. At some point, I must've dropped off to sleep because when I open my eyes, I'm horizontal on the floor in front of a quiet fire with grandma's quilt draped over me.

I sit up and find Grant asleep sideways in the chair. He even looks adorable while sleeping. *Help me.* I silently mouth those words, not sure to whom, as I drag the back of my hand over my mouth to wipe away sleep drool.

Except this morning, with the dull crackle of the nearly spent fire and dim light filtering through the windows, and after our hours-long conversation last night, I don't want any such help. Quite the opposite.

When Grant spoke about his family, his friends, and his faith, a tsunami of emotions washed over me, and I found myself drowning in admiration and a touch of envy. His life, and the intentional way he's living it, is so far removed from mine. The stark contrast between us and the countless choices that have made up our lives this far were highlighted to me.

I've been so busy climbing the corporate ladder, racing around the country, distracted by a six-year romance that doesn't exist, that I've lost myself.

Maybe I never found myself in the first place.

But Grant is solid. He's certain of who he is and where he's going, and I don't just mean in the afterlife. None of this is fixed for him. He lives in the present, in some kind of Zen flow state, if you will, not striving or surviving like I am, but listening, as he calls it. I have to admit, that sounded a tad far-fetched. If it works for him, though, who am I to judge? I'm choosing not to hold the God stuff against him, even though I wholeheartedly disagree. It may be the only red flag, although I've only known him for twelve hours.

Even so, I don't want to fall in love with a church boy. I definitely don't want to spend the rest of my life sitting in a pew in a floral dress, even if it is beside Grant. I know I'm racing ahead again, but shouldn't one examine these sorts of scenarios ahead of time before diving in? Though there's a lot I'd like to dive into (wink wink), church boys are off-limits. Even ones that seem heaven sent.

Maybe there's more to it than stuffy church pews, though. Maybe God can be found anywhere.

In a church, in a cabin in the woods, or even in the wilderness.

Which is where I am both physically and metaphorically at this moment, minus the pew.

Maybe God isn't limited to a place or time, but is somehow everywhere all at once, like Grant said last night—including in his heart. That part went a little too far, but he said it with such a calm assurance and sincerity, I took note. Obviously, or I wouldn't be recounting it to you now.

Grant opens sleepy eyes, and a smile stretches over his mouth at the same time his muscled arms reach over his head. I've been staring at him ever since I woke up and don't bother to stop. Why would I, when I'm daydreaming about what it would be like to wake up to this scenery every day of my life? So here I sit with a goofy smile, gazing at him like an adoring puppy.

"Good morning," he says as he swings his legs around to sit up.

"Morning." I gather some crumbs of self-respect and the wool sock that slipped off my foot in my sleep and begin sliding it back on my foot.

He's suddenly on his knees next to me, and my heart is set alight, like the match he strikes and holds to the kindling he's tossed into the fireplace. Just the feel of his arm brushing mine as he reaches forward is enough to make me to retract everything I said about keeping my distance. I'm not moving out of the way.

The closer the better.

After he refreshes the fire, he turns to face me and asks, "Coffee?"

A vision of me cupping his adorable face—which is half an arms' length from mine—between my hands and pulling him in for a caffeine-laced kiss, flashes through my mind. I restrict myself to saying, "Yeah" with a do-you-even-need-to-ask intonation.

On his way to the kitchen, he peers out the window and says, "Oh man."

When I join him, a snow drift is piled past the window ledge. "Are you kidding me? Is this normal?"

"It has happened, but no, not exactly normal."

I nod slowly while peering out. Mammoth flakes fall from the gray sky. If he exists, and I'm still not sure about that, what is the big guy upstairs up to? If he does exist, he must be in charge of the weather and has, for some reason, arranged for me to be stuck here.

I smell coffee and turn away from the window and those thoughts. It might be a good idea for me to practice being present like Grant. It's doubtful he has racing thoughts like I do. His are probably more the float-down-the-river-in-nature sort while mine are like a screamer music video montage on fast-forward.

"I thought we could go for a walk after breakfast." He hands me a mug of coffee.

I belly laugh. Until I realize he's serious and then hiccup/grunt to reel it back in. I'm the epitome of attractiveness. "Sorry. Not used to going for a walk in ten feet of snow."

"I get it. It'll be beautiful though," he says as he moves back into the kitchen. "Apparently the power is out across the province."

Hence the candles, I deduce, as I follow him, stopping near the counter and propping my hip against the side.

"I have a generator, so it's all good, and we have the fire, of course." He takes a sip of coffee.

Interesting. The candles were just a nice touch then.

I try to stay with him while he explains that he checked, and the trains are obviously still not running. "I'm cool if you need to stay longer," he says.

I open my mouth to speak, but no words come. Although I don't know what other engagements he would normally have on Christmas Eve, or what or who he's missing to help me, I'm exceedingly grateful. I'm overcome by his kindness. Not to mention speechless. Besides, I really have no choice.

"I have two sets of snowshoes." He says this as if it might elicit an "oh goody" along with the clapping of my hands, but I'm mulling over the fact that not only am I not going to spend Christmas Eve solo on a beach, I'm going to spend it with a stranger in sub-zero temperatures.

I know. It could be way worse. I could be sleeping inside an igloo.

Grant opens the fridge, while I return to the former thought about what he might be missing out on by being stuck here with me. Why does he have two sets of snowshoes? He didn't mention a person of significance, although that doesn't mean there isn't one.

"What do you feel like eating?" he asks, peering over the open fridge door with his magnetic eyes.

"I make a mean omelette."

"Omelettes it is," he says and sets a carton of eggs on the counter.

A few minutes later, I'm still thinking about who Miss Second-set-of-snowshoes might be while whisking the eggs. I try to ignore the knot of disappointment in my stomach. It's fitting that I'm crying while chopping the onions. Fitting and ridiculous. I've only just met Grant and already I'm sad about losing him. I turn to see him setting the table and folding red plaid napkins at the sides of the plates. I've never in my life wanted my omelettes to taste incredible more than I do now.

"They smell amazing," he says, returning to the kitchen for the coffee carafe. He offers me a refill, then pops two slices of bread in the toaster.

When everything is ready, we load our plates and carry them to the table. Even as he bows his head to pray, I'm still turning over the possibility of Grant having a girlfriend. She's probably some goody-two-shoes church girl who is breathtakingly beautiful even in a floral, up-to-the-neck dress. Another reason I need to keep my distance. Who could compete with that?

I laugh to myself. When Grant lifts his head, I press my lips together. Even I know that laughing while praying is poor etiquette. I take a long sip of coffee.

Once breakfast is cleared away (I help this time), he brings me a woman's jacket, a scarf, and a pair of winter boots.

"Try these," he says, and now I'm sure he isn't single. She even leaves clothes here.

They all fit, even the shoes. I'm mildly upset she isn't fat. Yes, I actually thought that.

He looks up from lacing his boots. "Do they fit?"

I nod. Should I be wearing his partner's clothing? She might waltz in here any moment and question everything, which would be even messier than this snowstorm.

"I knew they would. You looked to be about the same size as my sister."

"This stuff belongs to your sister?" I accentuate the word sister.

It's his turn to laugh. "Yeah, she's always forgetting things when she comes to visit. Drives my brother-in-law crazy."

I follow him outside with a notable bounce in my stride, and he hands me a pair of snowshoes. I sit beside him on one of the snow-covered chairs on the porch and attempt to copy the way he puts them on.

When he sees me struggling with the straps, Grant asks, "Can I help?"

"Please," I say, and he kneels in front of me.

King-sized snowflakes pummel us, even under the covering, and one smashes into my eyeball. I close one eye but leave the other one open to watch how he threads and tightens the straps in case I ever need to do this again. Which I highly doubt. At least, not by choice. Within a few seconds he's strapped them on.

We trudge toward the forest of fir trees behind his cabin, passing through a small opening in the bush. Sans snowstorms this may be a path, but we settle with making our own. It's Narnia on steroids. Any moment Mr. Tumnus may skip by, or the White Witch might pull up and offer us Turkish Delight and a ride on her sleigh.

Grant leads the way. He tells me that it will be easier for me if he goes first so he can compact the snow. Since I've never done this winter activity, I agree. Besides, I assume he knows where he's going, even in the snow.

After several minutes of walking—I mean snowshoeing—I may as well be in a hot yoga class. I'm about to ask how much longer when we come to a clearing and there, laid out in front of us, is some sort of village composed of white buildings. As we draw closer, I see that the structures appear to be made of ice.

"Wait a minute. Is this where you work?" I ask.

"It is." His chest puffs out a little, and I know enough to be excited, even if I'm staring at a life-sized igloo village. "It's still under construction. Do you want to see inside?"

I follow him under a tall ice archway. It's quiet and still inside and a welcome reprieve from the storm. A cavernous lobby leads to a bar carved out of ice, complete with drinking glasses also carved out of ice. We take a right. In front of us, a staircase winds up the left side of the wall, stopping just below the ceiling. Grant holds out his hand palm up, and we start up the steps. When we reach the top, an ice slide stretches out beneath us.

I turn to face Grant, open mouthed.

"Go ahead," he says.

I don't need to be asked twice. I lower myself onto the slick ice. Down I go, and once I'm at the bottom, I immediately stand up to take another turn. On the third try, I've forgotten about the storm, the missed train, and my holiday. I'm having the time of my life.

On the fourth, I decide to change it up and go down backwards. Unfortunately, at the bottom, I bump my head against the ice wall. It takes me a second to move out of the way because I'm rubbing the sore spot. Grant is already on his way down, his legs splayed to the sides to avoid kicking me, and he ends up on my lap. We are chest to chest and when our steamy-breath laughter fades, I do the unthinkable.

I *know*. I shouldn't have, but I do. What can I say?

As soon as I press my lips against his warm, soft ones, I melt into him. I lose all sense of space and time, ushered into the fairy tale this ice hotel depicts, carried into a dream of being kissed by a handsome knight who has saved me. Nothing else matters. Nothing.

For about three seconds.

Until he pulls away and mumbles, "Sorry."

I'm not sorry. I am, however, certain that if I stand close to a wall, I'll cause irreparable structural damage by melting the ice supports. My lips are tingling, and I can't see straight. I don't know what kind of spell this guy has placed on me, only that I've never felt this way, and I don't want it to end. With both hands, I reach for the back of his neck and draw him closer.

When he immediately separates his mouth from mine, I come to my senses and jolt back as though someone has thrown a snowball down my back. As I stare into the empty space he'd occupied seconds before, I internally curse myself for my lack of self-control.

I've made a fool of myself. Again.

When I dare to look up, his arm is extended towards me. I take his offered hand and am drawn up from the ice slide to face him. "I shouldn't have done—"

His finger covers my apology.

I stand warm and numb, sucking in fragments of icy air to reinflate my lungs. As I do, Grant pulls me into a sweet, reassuring hug. One that both holds me up while I recover from the most intoxicating human exchange I've ever experienced and wordlessly assures me I'm so much more than a stolen kiss with a stranger.

I rest my head between his jaw and shoulder, drowning in the faint smell of his cologne.

Too soon, he shifts backwards and peers down at me. I lose the breath I was concentrating on taking when he grins.

The hug, this moment, that grin. All of it somehow manages to make me smile. You'd think I'd never been kissed before.

After that, it feels like it.

~ TEN ~

Grant takes my hand and leads me through sculpted ice passageways where multiple rooms shoot off the sides, each with different themes carved into the walls. This place is like a temporary art gallery, and I'm mesmerized.

We enter an elaborately carved room displaying a heart-shaped bed with a canopy of folded ice curtains surrounding it. He grabs my hand and pulls me over to sit on top of the ice bed in the center of a private little sleeping cave.

"This is the honeymoon suite," he says. "What do you think?"

"It's beautiful." I run my fingertips over the elaborate and intricately carved headboard. "Whoever the artist is, he or she is definitely skilled at sculpting."

He's beaming now.

"Wait a sec. This is your work, isn't it?"

He nods.

"Grant, it's incredible." I scan the intricate carvings of fleur-de-lis and the folds of ice fabric around the four-poster bed frame. This was not what I was expecting when he told me he worked at an ice hotel. "I'm impressed. How did you learn to do this?"

He helps me to my feet, which is well-timed because sitting on this bed with him has me thinking thoughts I have no business thinking.

"Ice carving has been a hobby of mine since I was a kid, so I decided to turn it into something meaningful."

As he shows me the rest of the ice hotel, he explains his craft and how he learned it. I'm wonderstruck by the idea that he is both a well-known photographer and a gifted sculptor. Of course he is. When he goes on to tell me that people come from all over the world to stay here during the winter, I have no words.

We end the tour inside a chapel which, no surprise, is also his design and making. We stand side-by-side in the center aisle, our heads tipped back so we can survey the vaulted arches that form the nave, our misty breaths meeting above our heads. I shiver and clench my teeth together to stop them from chattering.

"You're cold." He rests a hand on my back.

"Yes, but I don't want to go yet," I surprise myself by saying. It's been a long time since I set foot in a church, if this can be considered one, and it's so peaceful and sacred—even if it is sub-zero—that I'm compelled to stay.

Grant leads me to a pew covered in, you guessed it, a fur pelt. After wrapping a wool blanket over my shoulders, he draws me into the circle of his arm, which warms me more than the blanket.

We're in an enormous church igloo, and I want to stay here forever. What is wrong with me?

I hear his soft, steady breathing, feel the slight rise and fall of his chest, and see the mist of air that forms when he exhales. He rubs his hand along my arm to warm me.

"Do you mind if I ask why you were going to spend Christmas in the Bahamas instead of at home with family?"

I shrug, working to appear casual. "I like the warm weather."

He raises his eyebrows but doesn't say a thing.

I scratch above my ear, even though there is no itch there. I try to keep silent. Unlike Grant, though, I'm nowhere close to perfecting that yet, and I revert to filling the silence like I always do.

Within seconds I say, "As I mentioned, I don't like Christmas."

This time he hides the wince.

What I don't tell him is that I've tried to ignore Christmas ever since my dad left. On Christmas Day. And went on to immediately set up shop with a new family. I also refrain from telling him that my mom was so sad, she didn't put up a tree that year or any year after that.

Sorry, I know that's a little depressing. Which is exactly why I'm not unloading this on Grant.

"Just prior to meeting you, I made a colossal fool of myself giving a keynote address on marketing strategies to an audience full of colleagues in a language I don't recall how to speak." I know I've already mentioned this back in the car, but I'm grasping for a change of topic.

"That's why you got fired?"

"I'm not technically fired yet, although I'm one phone call away from it. So yeah, I may be running away."

'You should call him back."

"Who?'

"Your Hot Boss."

I let out a short, huffing sound. "How do you know he's hot? I never said—"

"Your phone rang while you were asleep. A notification flashed on the screen, and I couldn't help but notice."

My shoulders slump. Note to self: change Hot Boss to Jeremy Fox on phone.

"So, you like the heat, and you hate Christmas. Fair enough. I'd go to the Bahamas for Christmas too, if I were you."

"Would you?"

"Yeah, except my family wouldn't let me forget it. We're big on Christmas."

Red Flag number two. A God *and* Christmas lover.

Short side bar, and I promise to make it quick. Bear with me a sec because it may be pertinent to the story.

I'm a runner. Both literally and figuratively. I run for exercise and stress relief, and I run from uncomfortable things. I probably didn't need to tell you that, as you already figured it out, didn't you? It strikes me that *psychologist* is too boring a title for you. I'll call you Sherlock from now on (insert winky face and we laugh together because you already understand my weird humor).

I ran away from home at seventeen, after my parents' ugly divorce and after my mom's newest boyfriend at the time got a little too handsy. I've been running, and occasionally hiding behind curtains, ever since. This may be the first time I'm not only fully cognizant of this repetitive pattern of behavior but also the first time that I feel safe enough *not* to run. Which is slightly unnerving, considering that in less than twenty-four hours I not only had a sleepover, I also shared a kiss (a very delicious kiss, I might add) with a complete stranger. I did say I'd make this quick and look at me rambling on.

Back to right now where Grant is performing open heart surgery on me, boring a hole into me with his eyes and peeling back barriers with pinpoint precision. I hope I make it out alive.

"Know what I love about this place?" He gives my shoulder a small squeeze. "How quiet and peaceful it is. I often come to work early, so I can come in here to be alone and pray." His words startle me out of my daydreaming (I won't tell you what else I was thinking about), and I do the unthinkable.

No, I don't kiss him again. I choke laugh. *Lord, help me.*

I cannot imagine a situation in which I'd come to work early to pray. Maybe he can shoot a few prayers heavenward for me while he's at it because, clearly, I need it. I'm about as pious as a church mouse dangling from the overhead ice chandelier, hanging on for dear life. If I met a perilous and untimely demise today, I have no idea where I'd end up.

Unlike Grant.

He's studying me, although not with the kind of disappointed gaze I received from the Sunday School teacher at my girlfriend's church when I was a kid. Grant's is full of understanding. How can he be so utterly unoffendable?

"Hey, are you thirsty?"

I nod and he says, "Okay, I'll go get us a drink. Be back in a minute. You okay here?"

I give him two thumbs up, and he disappears through the chapel doors. As soon as he leaves, I notice how quiet and peaceful it is, like he said. I sit in it a moment and take it in. It may be the most peaceful place I've ever been. So peaceful, I'm tempted to try a prayer of my own.

"God... are you there?" I have no idea what else to say. I'm pondering how to continue when something shifts inside me. Something unseen but real. It washes over me and through me, and I begin to weep, heaven help me. I'm crying while seated on an ice pew, questioning my sanity as massive tears stream down my face from below closed eyelids. It strikes me then that, even though Grant left, I'm not alone. God *is* here with me. And that is when I begin to pray.

I squeeze my eyes shut tighter. I don't know what to say to the God I have run from since childhood. The God whose existence I persistently denied, who I believed couldn't be trusted. But I've heard the way Grant prays, like God is right in front of him, and I think I can do the same.

"Dear God," I begin in a wobbly voice. "I'm sorry I've been avoiding you all these years. I know we haven't been on speaking terms, but if you'll forgive me, I'd like to change that. I'd like us to be... friends. Thank you for forgiving me and showing me that you are real."

I utter a shaky *Amen* and open my eyes to find Grant standing in front of me holding two ice goblets. He sets them on the pew before lowering to his knees in front of me.

He doesn't speak, only takes my hand and folds it in both of his.

At this point, I'm ugly crying. Snot is dribbling out of my nose, and I taste it when it crests my upper lip. I'm a watery mess, fluid coming out of every orifice on my face. After a long time, I lean back and wipe my nose with the back of my free hand. I know it's gross, but what choice do I have? If I don't, I may end up sporting snot icicles.

Grant takes his thumbs and wipes them over my cheeks. The look on his face speaks infinite kindness and compassion with the quiet assurance that I am safe. Tenderness radiates through his touch. His eyes close, and I take a moment to study his face. The flicker of a frown graces his forehead as he opens with, "Dear God."

I've never been prayed for before, and I can barely tell you what he said, but what struck me was he thanked God for me. Can you imagine?

When he finishes, he stands and tugs on my hands to raise me to my feet. We stand face to face and, as I look into his eyes, nothing is the same as it had been minutes before. Over his shoulder, my eyes fall on an ice-carved cross at the altar I hadn't noticed until now. Everything looks and feels different. My heart has wings. I'm full of joy and peace and love and they're exploding out of my chest like a Fourth of July fireworks display, all of it escaping from every cell of my being. I'm forgiven and loved. I'm completely and fully alive.

I draw Grant in for a massive hug, squeezing him with an unspoiled passion I've never before known, and I hear a puff of breath escape his nose. He squeezes me back, and we cry happy tears in the sacred silence beneath icy arches.

Strangely, nothing matters, and everything matters. My worries, cares, and doubts have lifted, and all this unseen beauty has come to the foreground. As though I had been living in black and white and now the world is shimmering in technicolor.

I guess this is how it feels to truly be alive and unafraid.

If you already know this feeling, I'm ecstatic for you. I'd also be happy to have that conversation with you about God I previously poo pooed.

"You okay?" Grant asks.

"I've never been better." And I smile for what feels like the first time in my life.

~ Eleven ~

"Can I take you somewhere else?" Grant asks.

"As long as it involves food." I grin, feeling like a five-year-old who has just jumped off a swing into the arms of her daddy.

In truth, I have.

I also feel famished, although I'm no longer cold. I'm warm from the inside out. Glowing from the God encounter I just experienced. I will never be the same.

"It does. Loads of it," he says and reaches for the hand I just finished using to flick a frozen tear from my cheek.

We walk out of the chapel and into the icy air where silent snowflakes descend from the sky. One lands on the end of my nose, another in my eyelashes, and one more on my sleeve. I glance down to see its intricate shape and am awestruck by its complexity and beauty. It's as if someone slid glasses onto my face, and I can finally see.

Grant looks up from strapping on my snowshoes. "All set?"

"You bet."

He starts blazing the trail.

From behind him, I scoop up a pile of snow and form it into a ball. When it hits the back of Grant's jacket, he turns and flashes me an enormous grin that transforms into a mischievous one.

I waddle-run like a penguin towards the woods for cover, giggling and gathering handfuls of snow to toss at him from behind a tree while snowballs explode all around me. When I launch one into the air and it lands inside the collar of his coat, he drops his and runs toward me. Because he is much more accomplished at this winter sport, in no time he scoops me up, flings me over his shoulder, and plunks me in a soft snowdrift. Except he loses his balance on the release and falls toward me, bracing himself by planting his arms on either side of my head to hold himself, push-up style, over me.

I reach up and pull him in and we end our snow fight with a "make up" kiss. This time he reciprocates, his lips softly searching mine and gently calming my devouring ones. Unlike the last time, he doesn't pull away too soon, and I discover that, like everything else about him, the affection he offers is strong, loving, even peaceful. Being with him dissipates my A-Type fear and striving. His kisses, like his presence, make me feel safe, calm, and warm. His tender embrace is like a rugged, protective shelter from the storm.

He feels like home.

When it's over, much too soon for my liking, he rolls off me and takes my hand. We lie side by side in the snow, grinning like two kids who have just unwrapped the best gift they've ever received, letting the flakes fall wherever they please. He's in no rush and neither am I (for once). Not until my stomach growls, and he hears it.

"We should get going. You're hungry."

"I'm okay," I say because, even though it's true, I like it here, lying in the snow with him. I may even like winter. Heck, I like everything right now.

Especially the man at my side.

I know what you're thinking. Whirlwind romances never last. But I'm *not* thinking about that right now. Instead, I'm thinking about the man next to me and how miraculous it is that I met him. And that, because of him, I've also met God, and my life has been entirely transformed in a few short hours. *I know.* It's *a lot.*

The smell of woodsmoke is in the air. Have we made it back to Grant's cabin? Apparently not because after a five-minute walk we come to clearing, another cabin resting in the center. Smoke is curling out of the stone chimney attached to the side of the wood building, and candles flicker in the windowsills as if to welcome weary travelers.

"What is this place?"

Grant squeezes my hand and leads me up a pathway carved out of the snow. As soon as we set foot on the porch, the door swings open and the sound of laughter spills out alongside the aroma of turkey. In the doorway stands a near duplicate if grayer version of Grant. It all becomes clear when a woman of the same age and hair color joins him at the door.

"You made it, son," his dad says, drawing him in for a hug.

"And you brought a friend," his mom adds.

They don't try to hide their surprised delight and their smiles, a similar warmth radiating from them as it does from Grant.

"Come in, come in." His dad swings the door wide.

I step forward, and his mother gathers me in for a warm hug.

"This is Porsha," Grant tells them.

His dad clasps my hand as another woman, who looks to be my exact age and, as Grant suggested, my exact size, sidles in between Grant's parents.

"Hey, I'm Giselle, Grant's sister." Her smile makes her appear more attractive than should be legal. These are some powerful genetics. "Nice coat." She winks, and somehow I know we'll be fast friends. She turns to her right and introduces her husband, Pierre. And just like that I'm surrounded by family on Christmas Eve.

We're singing Christmas carols by the fire. Our tummies are full of turkey and stuffing and sweets, and the fire warms the space with a flickering glow that, along with the Christmas tree lights, illuminates the faces of Grant's family gathered around me. Laughter is freely shared, as is good-natured teasing, directed mostly toward Grant. Listening to their stories and jests (his parents are trying their best to speak in English for my sake), I have learned that Grant is adventurous, fiercely loyal, and protective of those he loves.

What I notice most is that they are treating me as though I belong here. As though I'm not intruding on their familial gathering. I've never felt this sense of belonging or witnessed such acceptance and love.

Grant reaches for my hand and gives it a squeeze on the chorus of "O Come All Ye Faithful." When I turn my head to the side, I meet his warm smile. If this is a dream, I never want to wake up. I snuggle against him, and he draws me in. Any closer and I'd be sitting on his lap.

Grant's mother places Christmas cookies on the table in front of us, and they begin passing presents. Tradition dictates one gift each on Christmas Eve, Grant tells me. Of course, I'm not expecting a gift. I've already got all I need. A newly discovered love of God and a brand-new, very handsome friend, but Grant hands me a rolled piece of paper. Turns out it's a birch bark scroll.

I scrunch up my face in a way that says *you didn't have to give me anything* while at the same time going ahead and unrolling it. I swing my head to the side to look at him. Does he mean what he's written on the bark page?

He searches my face for the response I haven't given and then says, "What do you think, Porsha?"

I want to hear my name on his lips for the rest of my life. Don't worry, he isn't asking *that* yet. He is asking me out on a date, though, according to the charcoal script on the bark. I have no idea about the logistics or anything else, for that matter. All I know is I have no doubt of the answer to his question, this priceless gift in the form of time with him.

"Yes, I'd like that," I say.

His shoulders relax, and his lips brush my cheek.

Everyone is smiling but they don't pry, and I'm amazed by that. They've let us have this sacred moment without demanding the details.

I reach for a Christmas cookie. Shortbread dipped in chocolate. As the combined deliciousness melts over my tongue, I sigh. It doesn't get any better than this. I offer Grant a bite. Somehow, I want him to experience everything with me, and I'm delighted when he takes the cookie directly into his mouth from my hand. He's probably tasted this family recipe a million times, although never with me.

When he gets up to help his mom in the kitchen, Giselle takes his place beside me on the couch and leans in conspiratorially to whisper, "What was your gift?" We giggle over the birchbark scroll, our heads close together like giddy seventh graders as I show her. She already feels like a friend.

"I'd love the chance to spend more time with you. Would you like to accompany me to dinner and the symphony in Toronto?" Giselle reads from the scroll. "How romantic. We didn't know Grant had a girlfriend. When did you two meet?"

"Yesterday," I say with grin, then fill her in on the unusual details of how I've come to be sitting beside her on her parents' couch on Christmas Eve.

"Wow, how fortuitous." She winks. If she shares the faith of her brother, and more recently mine, we both know our meeting was not merely happenstance.

There is definitely a higher power at work here.

After a few minutes, I go to the kitchen and tap Grant on the shoulder. He turns from scraping a plate, and I melt from his 1,000-watt smile.

"I'm going to make that call," I tell him.

"Okay," he says and squeezes my shoulder. Both his touch and nod of understanding lend me strength.

I slip my phone from my pocket. I've been ignoring every vibration, so four notifications from Barbie and three additional ones from Jeremy await me.

Although I'm prepared for the worst, I'm no longer fearful, which is both odd and refreshing. I don't bother to read Jeremy's messages. I just press on his name to call.

He picks up on the first ring. "Porscha, are you okay? Where have you been?"

"I'm fine. Merry Christmas, by the way," I offer, noting that the flutter I always get when I speak to him is strangely absent.

"Merry Christmas," he says in a way that dismisses the holiday as inconsequential. He sounds a little breathless. Maybe he went snowshoeing, too. "I've been trying to reach you."

"I've been a little busy." I peer through the doorway into the kitchen at Grant who has his hands in dishwater while laughing about something with Giselle, drying the dishes beside him.

After a pause, Jeremy says, "I wanted to tell you this in person, but you were already gone. With this insane storm and your vacation, I'll go ahead and tell you over the phone."

I brace myself. It sounds like the intro to a breakup, even though I know it's laying the groundwork for my work dismissal.

"First, I wanted to commend you on your talk."

My mind reels as though someone pushed the rewind button on a movie, wanting to ensure they heard the lines correctly. As he's still talking, I force myself to focus.

"You simplified a complex topic and delivered the material with ease, authenticity, and boldness. Except maybe the X-rated part." He chuckles through the phone. "From the feedback I received, it was a hit. Everyone loved it."

I don't say anything because my brain is having trouble computing let alone forming words.

"Second, and the reason I wanted to speak with you in person—"

"Wait!" I say through the receiver. I can't absorb what he's said, and I'm not even sure I heard him correctly. "Did you say everyone loved it?"

"Yeah."

"Even with my infantile French and the mess-up?" I downplay the wording, even though I'm thinking *catastrophic* mess-up.

"Yes, Porsha. They were touched by how hard you tried and the heart behind it. I'm not kidding when I say they loved you."

Crazy, right? All this time I'd been thinking I failed miserably.

"I'd like to offer you that Marketing Director position."

I know I should speak, but the shock is crowding out words.

"Porsha, are you still there?"

"I'm here," I manage. But what hits me is that I'm here in a simple cabin on Christmas Eve, embraced by strangers. Most importantly, I've found something more precious than praise or promotions.

I've found love from God.

Jeremy is still speaking, so I wrinkle my forehead in an attempt to concentrate. "And third, I'd like to make a date with you for that drink." When I don't respond, he laughs and says, "Sorry, that was a lot all at once. I just... I was worried. You always answer my texts."

All the things Jeremy is saying used to be everything I ever wanted to hear. Accolades, advancement, and for him to notice me. Now that it's happening—incomprehensively all at once—it pales in comparison to these past twenty-four hours.

This moment, in this place, with these people.

"I'm here," I repeat. And there's nowhere else I'd rather be. Not on a stage or a sandy beach, not higher up the corporate ladder or the object of Jeremy's affection.

I've found what is truly important, and I'm never letting it go.

"So, what do you think?" he asks.

"How about we talk more when I get back?"

There's a pause on the other end before he says, "Uh, yeah... sure."

I know he's not used to getting put on hold or me not being available at every waking moment. Even during my holidays.

"Great," I say. "Let's chat then."

I hang up and stare at my phone a few seconds. Then I open my contacts and scroll until I find the name I'm looking for. I push the edit button and change "Hot Boss" to "Jeremy Fox" before I join Grant and Giselle in the kitchen.

~ TWELVE ~

I'm hesitant to admit to you that this is the best Christmas I've ever experienced, for reasons too complicated to get into on Christmas Eve. Suffice it to say, my backstory has left me with the propensity to not only avoid this particular holiday but to speak vehemently against it (I'm sure you recall my earlier rant). Still, it has taken on new meaning for me now that I believe in the Child's birth that this season is supposed to celebrate.

Giselle, Pierre, Grant, and I have stayed up late chatting by the fire. Looking around the room at these people who have welcomed me like family, I feel I belong. And as Grant slides his arm around my shoulder and draws me closer to him on the couch, a thousand sandy beaches can't compare to the warmth I feel now. Sinking into his embrace, I'm as at home as I've ever been.

When Christmas Eve turns into Christmas Day, Giselle and Pierre offer a final "Merry Christmas" and slip off to bed. Grant doesn't make a move to go, and we remain side by side on the couch, watching the fire. How is it that I feel this comfortable with someone I've just met? It makes no sense.

When I yawn, he shifts over and places a pillow on his lap. I rest the back of my head on the pillow and stretch out on the couch. He gazes down at me, his luminous eyes dancing in the flickering glow from the fire. Warmth radiates from them and draws me in.

"Do you believe in miracles?" I ask him.

"Tonight, more than ever," he says and winks. "What about you?"

"I once heard someone say, 'A miracle is something only God can do.' I never fully understood what they meant until now."

An adorable frown pinches the skin between his eyes. "Why do you understand now?"

"Well, he used a snowstorm and a plastic money ball to get me to you, and you and a chapel to get me to him. I'd say that qualifies as a miracle."

"What about Christmas? Any change in that department?"

"Let's just say that I'm starting to see what the hype is about."

His smile illuminates the room more than the tree, the candles, and the firelight ever could. It also illuminates my insides.

"Thank you for everything you've done. I don't know anyone else who would have—"

He presses his index finger to my lips. "No need to thank me. It was my pleasure."

Instead of drinking in this moment, I mumble under his finger, "What will we do?"

His thumb makes its way across my lips, and his eyes twinkle. "Don't worry. We'll figure it out, one day at a time."

The fire crackles and a few sparks dance up the chimney in a mini fireworks display, a reflection of how Grant makes me feel when he leans down and kisses my lips.

We fall asleep in front of the fire and wake Christmas morning to the smell of coffee. Grant lifts his head from the back of the couch the moment my eyes open, and our gazes lock.

"Merry Christmas," he says, in a soft, sleepy voice.

"Merry Christmas." The clattering of dishes in the kitchen draws my attention, and I glance over. Giselle is leaning against the counter, cupping a mug. I sit up and stretch my arms over my head while Grant straightens. How had he been able to remain in a sitting position all night? All I know is I hope that, somehow, we can wake up next to each other forever.

And no, I'm not apologizing for rushing ahead this time.

Soon, the rest of the family crowds in, and I'm gently introduced to my first family Christmas morning in years.

After a cooked breakfast, compliments of Giselle and Pierre, I thank Grant's parents for the meal and slip from the table to step outside onto the front porch, coffee mug in hand.

Snowflakes float in the air as though gravity has gone on Christmas break, and I follow one on its sleepy descent until it lands on the sleeve of the sweater Grant loaned me.

One tiny miracle of millions simply waiting to be noticed.

How could I have been so blind for so long? About everything.

I gaze up into the sky and see a patch of blue between the gray. The storm is over, and the sun is trying to break through the clouds.

I whisper the second prayer of my life into the air, my breath drawing misty words and carrying them to the unseen God. I know not everything needs to be seen to be believed, but I'm thankful God tapped me on the shoulder in the chapel to introduce himself, and I tell him so now.

His timing was perfect.

Meeting Grant is more than I could have asked for, but the gift of God's presence is a priceless treasure no earthly gift could match.

I set my mug on the wooden railing and pull my phone from the pocket of Grant's trackpants, determined to do what I came out here for.

Something I should have done years ago.

I press the name *David Ivy* in my contacts. It rings three times before a voice I hadn't heard in eleven years says, "Hello?"

I grip the railing with my free hand and take a deep breath before saying, "Hi, Dad… Merry Christmas."

~ Epilogue ~

Isn't it funny how the worst things in life often lead to the place you're meant to be? Like walking through a blinding storm to where the sun waits on the other side? Sometimes you just need to keep moving forward or, better yet, let yourself be led by someone who knows the way.

After that call with my dad last Christmas, I stood on the porch watching snowflakes drift to the ground. I was thinking about how many years it had taken me to call him when a lone wolf howled in the distance. Seconds later, the call was answered from another direction. I smiled because I had been like a lone wolf, running through the wilderness. Little did I know, I wasn't actually alone. At any moment I could have called out, and my cry would have been answered.

I'm so glad I finally did.

I'm not only talking about my dad. I'm so glad I called out to God.

Now I'm surrounded with a sense of peace, my soul has found rest, and my striving has ceased. Hope has taken flight, and I'm excited to find out where God is leading me.

Most of all, I'm never alone.

But let me catch you up, since it's been a bit.

Two days ago, I met Grant for the last time at Union Station.

I didn't end up accepting Jeremy's invitation for that drink, but I did accept the promotion and have been Lead Marketing Director at Imagine for the past eleven months. I don't answer Jeremy's calls or texts on weekends. He knows this, but he still tests my newly instituted work/life boundaries, even though I've made them abundantly clear.

My weekends and heart are reserved for the man who makes my breath catch in my throat and my heart beat double time. The one I'll never again need to meet at the train station to spend a weekend together because, as of two days ago, on precisely the same date we met last year, he moved to Toronto to take the position of curator at the Art Gallery of Ontario. And who, after today, I will live with in our newly renovated house in the Beaches. The man I'm standing beside at the altar of the Ice Chapel in front of a handful of guests at this very moment. I know! (Here you and I would grasp each other's forearms and squeal while jumping up and down).

The same man who rescued me last year so I could be saved.

It's Christmas Eve, our second Christmas together, and our wedding day.

But right now, I need to pay attention. I'm getting sidetracked, and that's not something you should do when you're about to say your vows.

Pierre gives Grant the wedding band, and I hand my bouquet of ice roses, carved by my fiancé, to my Maid of Honor, Giselle. I place my hands in Grant's.

"Porsha," Grant says, facing me. When I meet his eyes, my heart surges in my chest. "I'm so glad you bumped into that ball of money last year."

I laugh and so does the gathered crowd, especially Barbie who is sitting in the front row, my parents on one side of her and you on the other.

"These past few months with you have been the happiest of my life. You're a God-gift that keeps on giving."

I squeeze his hands and begin to feel as if we're the only two in the chapel.

"Porsha, when you said yes to being my wife, I felt like I'd won the lottery ten times over, although no amount of money could replace what you've come to mean to me. I love your goofiness, your resilient approach to life, your drivenness," (he winks) "and your sense of adventure. I especially love your clumsiness. Without it, we might never have met. I thank God every day for that storm and the high heels you were attempting to maneuver your way through it in."

He's gazing at me with those eyes of his, and I'm even more captured by them than the day we met. "I love your eyes and the way they reach into my soul. I love you more than words do justice, so I'll just say that I'm so excited for you to be my wife and for us to spend our lives together." He slides the ring onto my finger, and I brush a tear from my cheek, thankful I let Barbie apply waterproof mascara when she did my makeup.

Grant's smile wraps around me, and I draw in a shaky breath as I take the wedding band from Giselle. "Grant, I never knew true love until you. I love your selflessness, your kindness, your gentleness, and *your* drivenness." (I wink back.) "I love the way you set aside your own interests to help others, especially the way you helped me last Christmas. Because of you, I fell in love with Jesus, and that changed everything—my outlook, my goals, my life here, and my eternity. I can't wait to spend our lives together loving God and each other. I'm honored to be your wife and can think of nowhere I'd rather be than with you for the rest of my life. I love you."

I slide the band on his finger, the pastor pronounces us husband and wife, and we exchange our first kiss as a married couple. His soft, sweet lips find mine and, even though we are in an ice hotel in December, I'm warmer than I've ever been.

Guess where we are spending our first night? In the honeymoon suite with a freshly carved heart-shaped poster bed created by my new husband whose lips are pressed to mine this very moment.

In case you haven't noticed, I've become rather fond of Christmas. I've even developed an affinity for winter. I'm working on my French (I whisper that part in your ear because I don't want anyone getting too excited about that yet). Grant and I have found an amazing church downtown Toronto where I don't have to wear floral dresses unless I want to (we laugh together because you get it).

I'm still a runner. Instead of running away, though, I run towards people, the unknown, and hard things.

I especially run to God.

And you? I'm so glad you're still here. I want to hear more of your story, so let's get that coffee we're always talking about, okay? Until then, keep taking the next step of faith. He's only a whisper away.

NOTE FROM THE AUTHOR

Dear Reader,

Thank you for reading Porsha and Grant's love story.

Porsha demonstrated the way we often struggle on our own trying to earn accolades, acceptance, and love. The way we often ignore God while trying to forge our own path and exhaust ourselves in the process, to find that, in the end, He is the only one who can give us the peace and contentment we're striving for. Porsha realized everything that she was chasing after paled in comparison to being loved by Grant, but especially being loved by God. Like us, God's love transforms her heart and her thinking and gives her more than she could have asked for or imagined. Porsha's story is my own. Maybe it's yours too.

Grant depicted the love of Jesus by laying down his life to protect and help Porsha, setting aside his own schedule and comfort, and showing her what true love looks like. Grant is someone I aspire to become, someone who I hope God continues to shape me into—a likeness of Him.

My hope is their story encouraged you that no matter where you find yourself, "in a church, in a cabin in the woods, or even in the wilderness," God can be found.

I'd love to hear from you. Feel free to contact me through my website www.melaniestevenson.com where you can also find my blogs. You can also subscribe to my newsletter to receive writing updates, exclusive content, and giveaways.

God's blessings on your journey, and, in the words of Porsha, "keep taking the next step of faith. He's only a whisper away."

Melanie Stevenson

ACKNOWLEDGEMENTS

To Ralph, thank you for always believing in me and listening to my stories. You're my biggest cheerleader and embracer of my weird humor. I love you (and our Christmas traditions).

To my kids, Kurtis, Konnor, Elanna, and Keira, my daughter-in-law, Mariana, and my grand-babies, Montgomery and Emilia. I'm so glad God gave me each of you. Your lives and love inspire me. You've made my world so full and beautiful. I love each of you.

To Mum and Dad, thank you for your self-sacrificing love and care throughout my life. I love you both.

To the Birthday Girls, who listen to my stories and cheer for me in my writing life. Your friendship is so precious to me, and you reflect God's love and goodness.

To my Fab Four ladies, Darlene, Helen, and Sara. I'm so thankful God put us together. It's been a joy to collaborate with you on this project. I'd been working mostly alone at my writing until you invited me in. You opened a whole new chapter to me—the most exciting one yet! I love our writing retreats, our road trips, and our prayer times. What a blessing each of you are!

My Lord and Savior, thank you for showing me you exist and for loving me through this life.

ABOUT THE AUTHOR

Melanie is an award-winning author and speaker and lives in Ontario, Canada, surrounded by her husband and four children. She attended the University of Waterloo and obtained her Bachelor of Fine Arts. Melanie's first book, *One More Tomorrow*, was shortlisted in the Word Alive Press publishing and was published in 2019. In 2020, she won Best Romantic Fiction for *One More Tomorrow* and Best New Canadian Author at The Word Awards—Canada's top Christian literary awards. Melanie writes with sensitivity and discretion, often tackling complex topics to kindle compassion and hope. She weaves in beauty with unusual depth while encouraging the reader and listener that although collectively flawed, hope and goodness can be found. Her mission is to create stories of excellence that impact hearts and lives. Paper, canvas, and dirt are her favorite blank pages. You can find her at www.melaniestevenson.com and @melaniestevensonauthor or visit her blog at www.scentofheaven.me

WELCOME TO AVONLEA
Just a Gilbert Blythe Kind of Girl
SUGAR
SARA DAVISON

To Michael

Who will always be my Gilbert Blythe.

Just a Gilbert Blythe Kind of Girl

Sara Davison

Lucy May McQuaid has spent her whole life trying to follow in the footsteps of the mother she lost when she was seven years old. Playing Anne of Green Gables on the same stage her mother had would almost make it feel as though her mom was with her this Christmas.

Then a shocking revelation shakes everything Lucy ever believed to be true. Will finding her Gilbert Blythe help ease the ache, or will the man she is losing her heart to turn out to be as fictional as everything else in her life?

"You never know what peace is until you walk on the shores or in the fields or along the winding red roads of Prince Edward Island ... when the dew is falling and the old stars are peeping out and the sea keeps its mighty tryst with the little land it loves."

~ Lucy Maud Montgomery

~ ONE ~

"I know I chatter on far too much, but if you only knew how many things I want to say and don't."

~ Anne Shirley

Lucy burst through the double doors of the workshop hard enough they slammed against the wooden walls on either side. "I'm in!"

"Lucille May McQuaid!" August Dorey—her closest neighbor since he and his family had moved onto the property next to hers when they were both five—ripped off his safety glasses and tossed them onto a nearby table. "If I'd been running the saw, I could have cut my hand off."

She waved that away. "I listened quick before I came in."

"Even so," August grumbled, kicking a piece of wood beneath the table, "you entering this place like a normal citizen once in a while would be nice."

"And you showing me how happy you are to see me once in a while would be nice."

"I'm showing you *exactly* how happy I am to see you. At my place of business. Without warning. When I'm busy working. Was I not clear enough?" He swiped at the sawdust on his black T-shirt before tugging off his work gloves and firing them one at a time onto the top of the table, sending papers covered in scribbled plans and blueprints scattering onto the floor.

Lucy waved that away too. Honestly, the man could be such a grump. He wouldn't rain all over her good mood today though. "Aren't you going to ask me?"

"To leave? I'm pretty sure that was implied. But if you need me to spell it out ..." He planted a hand between her shoulder blades and guided her toward the door.

Lucy ducked away from him, and he exhaled. Loudly. "Fine. If it will get you out of my hair, I'll ask. What, exactly, are you in? And if the answer is someone else's way for a change, trust me, I have no problem with that." He leaned against the edge of a table saw and crossed his arms over his chest. As usual, he wore his dark hair in a short ponytail, although one curl had escaped to brush his shoulder

"No, silly. I mean I'm in as Anne. They called me a few minutes ago. Jessica Lewis broke her leg in a car accident and can't perform in The Avonlea Christmas Show. Isn't that amazing?"

"I'm guessing Jessica Lewis doesn't think so."

"I mean, it's not amazing that she broke her leg, of course." Lucy plucked a dead leaf from the *Just a Gilbert Blythe Kind of Girl* sweatshirt she wore under her unzipped winter jacket. Likely she shouldn't have dived into the woods between their family properties the second she got the news, desperate to share it with August. Hopefully the scratches on the backs of her hands from shoving bare branches out of her way would disappear before the show. She sighed. Maybe it wouldn't hurt for her to start thinking about things more before jumping in headlong, like August and her dad were constantly suggesting.

Lucy tossed that thought away like she had the leaf from her shirt. "I certainly wouldn't have wanted it to happen, even if I have tried out for that role for five straight years and not gotten it because Jessica's uncle is on the board."

"Doesn't she have an understudy?"

"Her understudy was driving the car. Two cracked ribs." Lucy wiped the smile from her face. "Which is terribly sad, of course."

"Yeah. I can see you're all broken up about it," August said dryly. "So you're going to Cavendish?" He dragged the toe of one work boot across the concrete floor, making a small pile of wood shavings, his gaze fixed on the pile and not her.

"Well, yeah. That's where the show is. I leave tomorrow morning. The rest of the cast has been rehearsing for more than a month already, so I'll be jumping in for the last two weeks before the big performance December twenty-third. They do it on a stage in the barn on the L.M. Montgomery National Heritage site, right next to Green Gables, and the Christmas ball is held outside under the stars after the show. Doesn't that sound romantic?"

"It sounds cold."

Lucy crossed her own arms, ignoring the prickle of a burr that must have latched onto her shirt digging into her arm. "You know this is my dream, right? I fell in love with Anne of Green Gables as a kid when my mom read me the books. She loved Anne so much that she named me after the author." The prickle grew too much to bear, and she uncrossed her arms. "If I perform the same role, on the same stage she did, it will kind of be like she's here with me for Christmas, you know?"

August expelled a breath. "I do know all that." He looked up long enough to nod curtly at her shirt. "And you'll be spending the Christmas holidays with the legendary Gilbert Blythe. Like you've always wanted."

His voice held a slight edge. Lucy frowned. "You don't have to sound so churlish. I have good news for you too."

"And here I thought you leaving for a few weeks *was* the good news." Still not meeting her eyes, August shoved away from the saw and strode over to grab his work gloves.

"Ha ha. No. The good news is they want you to come too."

Clutching his gloves in one hand, he spun around to face her. "What are you talking about? I'm not an actor."

"I know that. They're short of people to repair the sets, and they asked if I knew of anyone who could, you know, hammer a nail. I told them I'd ask you."

August raised his eyebrows and gaped at her. "Hammer a nail? Do you have any idea what I actually do here?"

"Well, yeah, I mean ..." Lucy scanned the expansive space. Probably something she *should* know. Her gaze swept across piles of neatly stacked wood and every kind of tool known to man before she swung back in his direction. "Something with ... planks, right?"

"Planks."

"Yeah. Planks and saws and ... stuff."

His jaw tightened. "Don't you have some packing to do?"

She clasped her fingers together and took a step backwards, towards the door. "Yes. But you'll think about coming with me, right?"

"No." August used his gloves to herd her like a border collie toward the exit. "Does your dad know you're doing this?"

Lucy stepped outside and turned to face him. "Not yet. I wanted to come tell you first."

That softened his dark-stubbled Mi'kmaq features. Slightly. "Ah."

"He's on a business trip for a few days. I'll call him when I get home."

He contemplated her a moment. "Don't you think you might be a little ... not teenagerish for this role?"

She planted her hands on her hips. "Are you trying to say I'm old?"

"No. I'm trying *not* to say that."

Lucy harumphed. "They knew I was twenty-nine when they offered it to me. Gilbert's a couple of years older."

"The guy *playing* Gilbert, you mean."

"That's what I said."

"It isn't. You said ..." August closed his eyes briefly and drew in a steadying breath. "Never mind."

"Besides, you're only as old as you feel."

"Oh, right. Definitely the motto of the entertainment industry." He touched a lock of her hair. "You don't think you might be a little too blonde?" He pulled his arm back and stuck his hands in the front pockets of his jeans.

Lucy shrugged. "I'll dye my hair tonight."

"Well, all right then." He lifted his shoulders. "Hope it doesn't turn green on you."

Her eyes widened. "Did you just make an Anne of Green Gables reference?"

"I don't think so. That doesn't sound like me at all." August withdrew his hands from his pockets and grasped the edge of both doors. "Well, bye." The doors began to move toward her.

"Wait." Lucy pressed a palm to each to hold them open. "You really won't consider coming with me?"

"Definitely not. This is my busiest time of year. I can't just walk away from my life to go with you to *hammer a few nails*."

"This is Cordial Cove, August. There is no life here."

"I'm sure your dad, *the mayor*, would love hearing you say that."

She shrugged. "My dad knows I have big dreams, like my mother did. This could be the first step toward reaching mine. To getting out of this Podunk town."

His dark eyes met hers. "If that's what you want, then I hope it works out for you."

The doors inched closer. Lucy shoved one unlaced, faux-fur-lined winter boot into the opening to stop them. "What if I told you I needed you?"

August rested his forearm on the edge of one of the doors, his face unreadable. "*Are* you telling me you need me?"

"I'm just asking if, hypothetically, I said something along those lines. Would you change your mind?"

"Come right out and say the words; see what happens." When she didn't answer—she wasn't about to beg the guy, for goodness' sake—he lowered his arm. "That's what I thought. How are you getting there?"

"Penny, of course."

August shook his head. "That car is a hundred years old. I wouldn't trust her to get me across the street let alone across Prince Edward Island."

"She's a classic."

"She's worth about as much as her name."

Lucy scowled. "Well, she's my only option, if you aren't coming."

"Which I'm not."

"Fine."

"Head out early. There's talk of dirt comin' by nightfall."

Lucy hadn't heard that talk, but it was good to know. "I will. Penny's not the best in bad weather."

"Or weather in general, from what I've observed."

She pulled her boot out of the doorway as August slowly moved the doors toward her. He peered out through the diminishing opening. "I'd say break a leg, but I'm sure whoever said those words to Jessica Lewis last is deeply regretting it. So, best wishes, Cordelia."

Cordelia? "Was that another Anne of Green Gables reference?"

"Definitely not. You can't quote from something you haven't read or seen, Lucille." The opening had nearly disappeared. "I'm going back to work now. Lots and lots of planks to take care of with my saws and stuff."

The last few words were largely muffled as the doors clicked shut.

Lucy clenched her fists as she stared at the red-painted wood an inch from her face. Argggh. The man was so infuriating. Why couldn't he just once follow the script she'd written in her head for the two of them?

She spun around and stomped toward the overgrown path through the woods. Likely because, as August had said, that didn't sound like him at all.

~ Two ~

"My life is a perfect graveyard of buried hopes."
~ Anne Shirley

Lucy tossed the final bag into her trunk and eased it closed. The last thing Penny needed was to lose any more of her paint job. She shot a glance in the direction of August's property and then straightened her shoulders. She didn't need him. This was a huge opportunity for her. Possibly even her big break. If she hoped to become a Broadway star one day, she needed this acting credit. And she needed to get it by standing on her own two feet.

With a curt nod, she tore her gaze from the chimney she could barely catch a glimpse of above the trees and slid behind the wheel of her car. *Okay, Lord. This is it. Let's go.*

When Lucy turned the key in the ignition, the old engine turned once, twice, and then died. No problem. Penny was not a morning person and sometimes needed a little cajoling to get going. Lucy waited a few seconds before turning the key again. This time, her beloved car—a secondhand high school graduation present from her dad—emitted several screeching, groaning noises even Lucy had never heard before and then fell silent, an unnecessarily dramatic puff of dark smoke exploding from beneath her hood.

"Nooooo!" Lucy stared at the noxious cloud rising into the air before dropping her forehead to the steering wheel. Penny let out a last, lamenting toot of her horn before it, too, dissipated in the cool morning air.

The first rehearsal was in two hours. How was she going to get there? Uber? Lucy snorted softly into the steering wheel. As if Prince Edward Island had Uber service. A cab would cost an absolute fortune, and passenger trains had stopped running in the province long before she was born. Could she hitchhike?

Lucy shuddered at the thought of what her dad—and August—would have to say about that. She did know exactly what Anne Shirley would have to say about this situation. *This is the most tragical thing that has ever happened to me.* A tear of frustration slid down her cheek and onto the steering wheel, leaving a splotch in the dust. Like her dreams. Crumbled to death in the dust. Her forehead still pressed to the center of the wheel, Lucy sighed. No doubt her mother, and every other person who'd achieved success on the stage, had faced far bigger obstacles than this. Did they sit around crying? Of course not, and neither would—

A soft rapping against her window yanked her from her thoughts, and she swiped at her cheek as she straightened. August. Lucy reached for the manual handle and lowered the glass an inch. "I'm fine."

"Clearly." His lips twitched. "Anything I can do?"

His amusement was not contagious. She pressed her shoulders back. "Thank you for your offer of assistance, Mr. Dorey, but it is not required."

He let out a short laugh. "Getting into character already, I see." Resting a hand on the roof of the car, he ducked a little to peer through the window. "Look. I was wrong to say this car was worth a penny."

"Thank you," she said archly, both hands still on the steering wheel.

"And by wrong, I mean generous."

Oh. She gripped the wheel tighter. "Did you come all the way over here solely to mock me?"

"Nope. That part's a bonus." He straightened and lifted his hand. Car keys dangled from one finger.

Lucy let go of the wheel and shoved the door open so quickly August had to jump out of the way to avoid getting hit. She flung her arms around his neck. "You're coming with me?"

"I'm *driving* you," he corrected, reaching behind his head to grasp her wrists and untangle her arms from around him. "Then I am turning around and coming back home."

A ridiculous amount of disappointment flowed through her. What happened to standing on her own two feet? Besides, even if he wasn't coming with her, his offer was better than nothing. Helped her over one of those hurdles to her dreams. Her throat tightened. "Thank you."

August bent a finger and swiped another tear from her cheek with his knuckle. "There's no need to cry about it," he said gruffly. "It's the least I can do when you're in the *depths of despair*." He stepped back. "And no, that was not a reference. It's a perfectly normal thing to say to someone who's upset."

Lucy grinned. "Of course it is."

August nodded toward the back of her car. "Open the trunk and I'll grab your stuff. Carrots."

She made a face at him. The dye job had turned out pretty well, in her opinion. Although, after what August had said, she *had* held her breath a little before removing the towel. When she'd looked at herself in the mirror this morning *Anne* had stared back, which had sent shivers of delight all through her.

Thankfully, when Lucy hit the button to release the trunk latch, Penny complied for once, and they managed to move all her bags—the number of which, remarkably, August didn't comment on as he worked—into the back seat of his bright-blue Dodge Charger.

"Why not the trunk?" she'd asked when he opened the rear passenger door and slid the first bags in.

"We can unload you faster from here," he said shortly.

Lucy didn't respond to that, only winced as he lifted the final bag out and slammed the trunk, sending a cascade of copper-colored paint chips scattering across the snow like a mini blizzard. "Don't." She shot August a heated glance, and he clamped his mouth shut.

Although they were traveling halfway across the province, Prince Edward Island was small enough the trip only took them an hour and a half. August had turned on the radio as soon as they started driving—clearly an attempt to ensure she didn't talk non-stop on the way there. He turned into the lane leading to the house the legendary Green Gables had been modeled after—the place where relatives of Lucy Maud Montgomery had lived and where she had spent a lot of time while growing up—and pulled into a spot in the largely empty parking lot. "Where can I dump your stuff?"

Being on this property where the author had been inspired to write the Anne books filled Lucy with such joy that even August being August couldn't bring her down. Still, she glared at him as she lowered her sneakered feet from the dash. "You could at least pretend you're not thrilled to be getting rid of me."

"Pretending's your thing, not mine." He shouldered open the door and climbed out of the vehicle.

That better be an allusion to her chosen career, not her character. Almost too pumped up to care, Lucy scrambled out of the car after him.

"I'm supposed to bring my bags to the main office, and they'll give me directions to my room."

"Got it." August slung the handle of her toiletries bag over his shoulder and reached into the back seat for one of her suitcases.

Loaded with bags, they started for the main building. As they struggled through the doors, a woman with dangly earrings and sandy-brown hair cut in a chic style around her jawline jumped up and rounded the desk. "Lucy McQuaid?"

"Yes, ma'am." Lucy set her second suitcase on the floor.

"Welcome! Mr. Arsenault is anxious to meet you. I'll let him know you've arrived." The woman waved toward a door off the lobby. "There's a storage room there. Put your things inside for now and you can take them to your room later."

Which meant that August could get going faster, which was great. Just great.

The two of them brought in the rest of her things and set them in the small room. When he'd unloaded the last bag, August pulled the door shut behind him. "I guess I'll head ..." His eyes narrowed as he let go of the knob and strode over to a wall of windows along the back of the lobby area.

Lucy came up to stand next to him. From this vantage point, they could see the barn behind the main building and three men working in front of it constructing what might, if someone were to squint and use her exceptional imagination, look a little like a dance floor raised three or four feet off the ground.

Planting a palm on the window frame, he leaned closer. "What in the name of all that is good is happening out there?"

"I think that's where the Christmas ball is going to be held."

August winced. "Good luck getting that to hold up a bunch of people without collapsing." He pushed away from the frame and brushed his hands together as though ridding himself of any obligation regarding the debacle outside. "Well, I'm off."

"Seriously? You're going to walk away and let those guys mess things up out there?"

"Not my circus, not my monkeys, Lucille." He strode for the rear exit.

Technically true. Even so, there had to be some way to get him to stay.

Own two feet. Own two feet.

Those same two feet dragged a little as Lucy trailed him to the door. August gripped the metal bar and then, his back to her, said, "For the record, I'm not."

"You're not what?"

"Thrilled to be getting rid of you." He leaned into the bar and the door cracked open. "See ya."

"Wait." Lucy grabbed the sleeve of his coat. "You can't say something like that and then just leave."

"Watch me." He covered her hand with his, tugged it away from his coat, and then glanced over her shoulder. "What are they doing now? If they think they can ..." August dropped her hand like a microphone and whirled around to grasp the bar again. "Not my problem."

Who was he trying to convince—himself or her?

"Mr. Dorey?" A man in navy dress pants and a navy-and-red-striped shirt strode toward them.

August hesitated as though seriously contemplating pushing through the exit and fleeing. Then he blew out a loud breath, turned around, and stepped forward to allow the door to close at his back. "Yes?"

The man held out a hand as he reached them, and August shook it briefly. "I'm Corbin Arsenault, the director of The Avonlea Christmas Show."

"Oh. Then I think it's Miss McQuaid here that you want." August lightly grasped her upper arms from behind and eased her forward. "She's your new Anne."

"Ah." As though noticing her for the first time, the director glanced down at her. "Lucy McQuaid. A pleasure to meet you, too, of course. I'm looking forward to working with you."

Before she could respond, he'd turned back to August. "Mr. Dorey—"

"It's August."

"August. I couldn't help but overhear you when you were over at the window next to my office. You seem to have some idea of how to construct a stage."

"No."

Lucy glanced up at him. Seriously, was that simply the default answer the man went to every time?

August met her eyes before rolling his a little and clearing his throat. "That is, I do have construction knowledge, yes, but I've never built a stage. And, as I told Lucy, I'm too busy at work right now to take time off."

"Oh." The director looked crestfallen. "That's really too bad. As you can see ..." He waved a hand toward the window. "Our crew is woefully short-handed and in desperate need of someone with actual experience. I'd been hoping ..." He pursed his lips. "You wouldn't be willing to stay for a few hours, would you? At least set them on the right track? We'd hate to see anyone get injured due to poorly built sets."

Zing. Lucy mentally applauded the director for landing that shot so perfectly. August shifted behind her, as though he could sense her approval and took it for the ganging up against him that it was.

A loud cracking sound and several shouts from outside drew their attention to the window. Part of the makeshift dance floor had broken off and now hung dangling from the rest of the wobbly structure. Perfect timing. Lucy pressed her lips together to keep from smiling.

August mumbled something under his breath she couldn't clearly make out but that sounded a lot like *you've got to be kidding me* before saying, "Fine. I'll stay for a few hours. Then I'll need to head back to my *life* at home."

Okay, that one zinged *her* a little. Lucy was too happy about him staying to mind. Not that she couldn't do this on her own. It was just that everything was ... better when August was around. It always had been.

"Understood." Mr. Arsenault reached around Lucy to grasp August's hand again and pump it enthusiastically. "Thank you."

This time she did catch his mumbled *whatever* before he said, a little louder, "You're welcome."

"Okay then." The director took a few steps in the direction of his office before seeming to remember she was there and turning back. "Lucy. I'll see you in the barn for rehearsal in a few minutes?"

"Yes, sir." She waited until he had returned to his office before whirling around to face August, her hands pressed together in front of her chest.

He scowled at her. "You can wipe that smug look off your face, Lucille. I only agreed to stay for a few hours because I don't want ... anyone getting hurt. I'm out of here tonight. And you and your wheedling ways are not going to stop me."

"You know, for someone who's never seen the series or read the books, you sure quote them a lot."

"I have no idea what you're talking about. That's an expression my grandmother used to use is all."

"If you say so."

"I do say so, for all the good it will do me when you never listen to a thing I—"

Another cracking sound followed by more yelling cut him off. August rolled his eyes again. "I better get out there before someone gets killed." He backed toward the door, shoving it open as he pointed in her direction. "Tonight."

As soon as the door closed behind him, Lucy allowed herself the smile that had threatened to cross her face since he'd agreed not to go right away. Sure, she could stand on her own two feet. But, for a few more hours at least, she wouldn't have to.

~ THREE ~

"But really, Marilla, the flying part is glorious as long as it lasts... it's like soaring through a sunset. I think it almost pays for the thud."

~ Anne Shirley

A stillness had fallen over the December afternoon, the kind of hush that carried a warning of *dirt* coming.

As much as Lucy had wanted August to stay, as much as she loved looking out through the open side of the barn while she and Diana practiced their scenes to see him hauling wood or standing with the other men, showing them the kinds of scraps of paper that littered the table in his workshop, her mood lowered along with the heavy clouds gathering at the horizon.

Mallory Stone, who played Diana, turned out to be a decent scene partner, although when the director had excused himself for a moment and gone over to the main building, Mallory stopped chatting about makeup mid-sentence to peer around Lucy. "Whoa. Who is *that*?"

Lucy turned around to look. August was hammering a nail into a plank on the dance floor. So why'd he get all bent out of shape when that was what Lucy suggested he did? She flapped a hand in his direction. "Oh, that's just August."

"August? Cool name. Are the two of you ...?"

"Together? Oh, no." A little flustered, Lucy shot another look in his direction. "We're friends. He drove me here, but he isn't staying."

"Hmm." Mallory sashayed to the edge of the stage and propped a hip against the side of the schoolhouse, staring outside. "What's his situation?"

"His situation?" A heat as prickly as that burr caught on her shirt drifted through Lucy, despite the cold wind sweeping in through the open barn doors.

"Yeah, you know. Is he involved with anyone?"

"August?" Lucy almost laughed. Although it had seemed as though every girl in school liked him, August didn't date. "No. He's married to his work."

"Interesting." Mallory bit her ridiculously pouty lower lip as she gazed out the open doors.

Lucy contemplated her. Mallory was beautiful, with long, dark hair that didn't even appear to have been dyed that color. She seemed nice enough too. So why was the idea of her going after August tightening up Lucy's chest until it hurt to draw in a frost-tinged breath of air? Maybe it wouldn't be the worst thing after all if he left in a few hours.

Before she could lose herself completely down that rabbit trail, the director returned. Lucy and Mallory jumped into the scene where Diana asked Anne if she would be okay if Diana turned her sights on Gilbert. After their earlier conversation, Lucy didn't have to call on her acting skills to convey Anne's mixed and very complicated response to the idea.

"All right, Lucy, Mallory, good job." Mr. Arsenault clapped his hands twice as he strode onstage. "Mallory, you're free to go. Be back at nine tomorrow morning, please. Lucy, Jack should be here any minute. I'd like the two of you to practice the scene where Gilbert tells Anne he is giving up the Avonlea school for her. All right?"

"Sure. I ..."

Someone strolling in from stage left caught her eye. Whatever Lucy had been about to say was carried away as though the wind that had picked up from the north had gotten hold of the words and snatched them from her mouth. The man walking towards her *was* Gilbert Blythe. As the leading man in this play, he was perfect. Maybe even as the leading man in her life.

Shaking her head to free it of the *romantic notion*, as Marilla would call it, Lucy straightened to her full five foot five as Jack approached. The director met them in the middle of the stage. "Jack Miller, this is Lucy McQuaid."

Jack reached for her hand and held it in both of his. "Lucy. It's a pleasure. I'm looking forward to working with you."

Although she rarely lacked for words—very rarely, if what August constantly informed her was true—Lucy could only manage a slightly garbled, "So am I," in response.

His smile broadened as if he was well aware of the effect he had on her. That he likely had on every woman he met. That jolted her back to reality, and Lucy lifted her chin and tugged her hand free. His lips quirked.

Mr. Arsenault continued as though completely unaware of the subtext happening between the two stars of the show. "There will be time later to get to know each other. Right now, since the temperature is dropping, I'd like us to dive in before it gets too cold to be out here."

Lucy's nod was stilted. "Of course." As she turned away from the two men, she caught a glimpse of August, who had jumped down off the platform and stood watching her and Jack. He held her gaze a moment, the look on his face as indecipherable as usual, before turning away to respond to a guy who'd crouched at the edge of the broken stage to ask him something.

What was that about?

A snowflake swirled through the air to land on her cheek. Uh oh. August had a tendency to get completely caught up in his work. Likely why he protested so vehemently when she burst in and disrupted him. Did he remember a storm was coming? Should she warn him, suggest he head out before the roads got bad?

"Lucy?"

She blinked and looked over at Mr. Arsenault, who was frowning. Had he been trying to get her attention? "Yes?"

He held up the script. "Could we ...?"

"Oh, right. Of course." Lucy glanced at the script, although she didn't need to. The first line was hers. As she spoke the words, the rest of the world faded away as it always did, and she became Anne.

By the time the director was satisfied with the scene, a couple more hours had passed. Snow swirled thick and white, and Lucy couldn't see anything past the open barn doors. Had August left? Farewells were not his thing any more than *pretending* was, so he wouldn't have waited around to say goodbye to her.

"Dinner in the cafeteria in thirty minutes," Mr. Arsenault announced as he headed for the wing. "Good job, you two."

Jack smiled at her. "That was great, Lucy. You know all the lines already."

"Yeah, well, I've been wanting to be in this production for a while, so I kept myself prepared."

"In case every other actress broke a bone or two, you mean?" Jack's grin was spot-on Gilbert Blythe, although his amusement at the misfortune of the two women who'd been in the car crash was off. Not that she'd been as *broken up* about the news as she should have been either.

A little of the stardust dancing around in Lucy's head dissipated. "Well, I wouldn't have wished for that, but yeah." She peered outside again but nothing—not workmen or the precarious dance floor or anything else—took shape in the swirling white. August should definitely not be out in this. *Lord, if he is, keep him safe.* "I think I'll go find my room and then get ready for dinner."

Jack nodded. "All right. I'll see you in the cafeteria."

Lucy nodded and headed for the rear of the barn, to the exit closest to the main building's back door. She was still wearing her sneakers, and she slipped and slid her way across the twenty-foot expanse of snow and ice until she was able to fling open the door and step inside. Brushing snow from her hair and the shoulders of her sweatshirt, she crossed the lobby to retrieve her things from the storage room and find out where she would be staying for the next two weeks.

The storage room was empty. Where was all her stuff? Had someone stolen it? Heat rushed through her. What kind of security did they have in this place, anyway? She closed the door and stalked across the lobby to stop in front of the counter. Nothing she'd brought with her—or left at home, for that matter—was valuable to anyone other than her, but still.

The woman who'd greeted her when she arrived was talking on the phone, and she held up a finger in Lucy's direction. Lucy nodded. The woman droned on and on with the person on the other end of the line, a call that sounded suspiciously personal to Lucy. She didn't realize she was drumming her fingers on the counter until the woman frowned at her.

In an attempt to take her mind off her missing possessions, she wandered into the next room and started looking at all the pictures and artifacts from the life and career of Lucy Maud Montgomery.

The woman was fascinating. Although she was familiar with the story, Lucy read about all the rejections for her work Montgomery had received, including five for her first book, *Anne of Green Gables*. Bet those guys were kicking themselves when the sixth publisher released the book and it became an instant, worldwide success.

One of the author's quotes, written on a card attached to the wall, struck Lucy. "Oh I wonder if I shall ever be able to do anything worthwhile in the way of writing. It is my dearest ambition."

Lucy almost laughed. Do anything worthwhile? If anyone ever needed proof of the impact one writer could have, they didn't have to look any farther than her little province. The handprints of Anne—of Lucy herself—were everywhere on this island. More than a hundred years after the book was published tourists from all over the world still streamed here every summer to soak up all things *Anne of Green Gables*.

Lucy Maud Montgomery's dearest ambition had certainly been achieved. Would Lucy May McQuaid's be? She wrinkled her nose. What *was* her dearest ambition? Acting? For most of her life she'd been focused on getting to this point—playing Anne in The Avonlea Christmas Show like her mother had. Now that she was here, it was falling a little flat. Why was that? Was it because August had gone?

She gazed at the picture of the other Lucy. So much of what she'd done she had accomplished on her own after the death of her mother when Lucy Maud Montgomery was a toddler. August might be her oldest friend, but that didn't mean Lucy May McQuaid couldn't do anything without him. That was ridiculous. He had his own life, his own *dearest ambitions*. Whatever those might be, he'd made it clear—repeatedly—that they were more important to him than being here with her.

"It wasn't stolen, in case you were wondering."

Lucy spun around so quickly August had to grab her elbows to keep her from going down. She stared up at him. "You're still here."

"Uh, yeah." He let go of her. "The roads are slippy as all get out. I missed my window to leave, thanks to my misguided belief I might be able to impart in a few hours enough knowledge to those lunkheads out there to make any difference."

Slippy. August was usually so well-spoken that hearing him use the slang term so many in their little fishing village did made her smile. "Do you have a toothbrush or anything?"

"I might or might not have thrown a bag into the trunk just in case."

So he'd at least been open to the possibility of staying here with her. The rush of joy at seeing him dispelled the last of the heat drifting through Lucy since discovering someone had taken her … "Wait. What wasn't stolen?"

"Your stuff. I carried it all up and put it in your room."

"G'way with ya."

His lips twitched. "I'm not kidding. It wasn't any trouble, even if you did bring enough bags for three people and twice as long a stay. At least."

"Well, thank you."

As usual, he shrugged off her gratitude. "You were busy, looked like."

That edge was back in his voice, and she narrowed her eyes. "I *was* busy. Busy working."

"Yeah. It appeared to be hard work."

Uncomfortable heat drifted through her chest again. What was his problem? "August."

He lifted both hands. "You're right. Not my business what you do. Or who you do it with."

"Speaking of which, *Diana* was having a little trouble concentrating today."

His forehead wrinkled. "Diana?"

"Yeah. She wanted to know what your situation was."

"Is her name actually Diana?"

"Right now it is. But no, it's Mallory Stone."

"Huh. What did you tell her?"

"That you were married to your work."

He studied her. Lucy might have known him almost her whole life, but so often—like now—she had no idea what he was thinking. He lifted a hand, palm up. "As beautiful a relationship as my *planks* and I have, could be time for that to change. I'll be stuck here a day or two. Maybe I should talk to her."

"Maybe you should."

"Unless, of course, you can think of any reason I shouldn't."

The only reason that would come to Lucy's mind was a completely crazy one. Certainly not one she could share with August. She lifted her shoulders. "Nope. No reason."

He nodded slowly, his lips slightly pursed. "All right then."

It *was* all right. Mallory and August were welcome to each other. Lucy certainly wouldn't stand in their way. She had big plans. Big dreams. She was getting out of her little hick town and becoming somebody, exactly like her mother had done.

And nobody, not even August Dorey, was going to get in her way.

~ FOUR ~

"That's the worst of growing up, and I'm beginning to realize it. The things you wanted so much when you were a child don't seem half so wonderful to you when you get them."

~ Anne Shirley

And then Gilbert kisses Anne.

Lucy ran her fingers over the words in the script. The scene they would rehearse the next day. Five innocuous little words, and yet they captured the moment everyone watching would be waiting for, the moment the entire story built toward. Was she ready?

After she and August had spoken at the Lucy Maud Montgomery display, he'd been trapped on the grounds for three days. Despite the weather, he and his crew had managed to get a decent amount of work done. Not that Lucy had been paying particular attention to what he did. She was a professional. Unlike Mallory, who could barely take her eyes off him, much to Mr. Arsenault's—and the rest of the cast's—annoyance. Definitely not a kindred spirit, even if the two of them played bosom friends in the story.

When Lucy and August had gone to dinner that first night, Mallory had waved as soon as he walked into the cafeteria and pointed to the empty seat next to her. August had lifted a hand to her before grabbing a tray and sliding it along the rollers. Despite what he'd said to Lucy in the museum, he hadn't gone over to sit with Mallory once he had his food.

Instead, he'd joined his crew without a backward glance at Lucy. Was he upset with her for some reason?

Lucy hesitated with her tray until Jack grasped her elbow. "Join me, Anne," he'd whispered in her ear before directing her across the room to a table for two in front of the window.

Jack had been as charming at dinner as he'd been at their first meeting, and they had laughed their way through the meal. In the days that followed, he sought her out at every opportunity.

Like her, Jack preferred to remain in character, so Anne and Gilbert getting to know each other, discussing *that pesky Josie Pye* or the latest Avonlea *news* from Mrs. Lynde as they ate or relaxed before the fireplace in the lounge every evening, was a really good thing. For the play, of course.

The storm abated on the third day, which meant August should be able to return home the next morning. He'd barely spoken to Lucy since she'd told him to go ahead and talk to Mallory, so what difference would that make to her?

She was attempting to convince herself that it made no difference whatsoever as she said "Night, Gil" to Jack and headed up the stairs leading to her room. When she reached the top and turned the corner, she nearly ran headlong into August.

He grasped her upper arms lightly when she skidded to a stop inches in front of him but let go of her almost immediately. "You okay?"

"Yeah. Sure. Fine."

He peered around her. "Where's Jack?"

Lucy frowned. "Do you seriously think I would bring him up to my room?"

"No, of course not. It's just that, ever since we arrived, everywhere you've gone Jack has been sure to follow. It's weird to see you on your own."

"Do you have a problem with Jack, August?"

"Why would you think that?"

"Well, for starters, the ck in his name doesn't have its own syllable."

August propped a shoulder against the wall and scrubbed his face with both hands before exhaling. "You're right. Sorry. I've had a lot on my mind the past few days, thinking about stuff back home. Now your director has begged me to stay on for the rest of the week."

"Really? What did you tell him?"

"I told him no, of course."

"Of course." August saying anything other than no would be as weird as he'd told her seeing her without Jack was. "So you're leaving in the morning?"

"No."

She blinked. "You're not?"

"I did say no, but he practically begged until, foolishly, I gave in. I shouldn't have, since I really need to get home. We've actually been making progress, though, and I do hate to leave the job half-finished."

"You'll be here until Saturday then?"

August pushed away from the wall. "Can you put up with me that long?"

"Your presence hasn't killed me yet."

"Week's not over." He bushed by her and started down the stairs. "Good night, Lucille. Get some sleep. Tomorrow is a new day."

"With no mistakes in it," she mumbled quietly, always glad for Anne's wise words when she needed them.

"No mistakes in it yet." August's voice drifted up the stairs behind him.

Although Lucy stared at his retreating back, he didn't turn around. When he'd disappeared through the lobby doors, she shook her head and started for her room. Whether or not that boy would admit it, he had definitely read those books.

"Weather's better today, Anne. Want to go for a walk?"

Jack and Lucy had finished Friday lunch and had an hour until rehearsals started again. She shot a look toward the back corner of the cafeteria. Mallory had plopped herself down across from August and was talking away to him, one hand gesturing dramatically as she flung her long, dark hair over her shoulder with the other.

August didn't appear to be speaking. Shocker. He also didn't appear to be trying to get away. Lucy shifted her attention to Jack. "A walk sounds great."

They headed out of the main building, across the newly fallen snow that had built up in the courtyard outside the barn. "What are your plans for after the show?" Jack followed her along the side of the nearly finished dance floor and across the lawn to the Green Gables house.

"After the show? I, uh, haven't really thought that far ahead, to be honest."

They rounded the far corner of the historic house. Although they'd only been walking a few minutes, Lucy was breathing heavily from the effort of pulling her booted feet out of the soft snow she'd sunk into over and over, and she slowed her steps when they reached the sheltered side of the house.

"Want to take a break?" Jack came up to stop in front of her.

"Sure." Lucy leaned back against the wall, grateful for the reprieve.

Jack tugged his gloves off, stuck them in his coat pockets, and pressed a palm to the wall next to her head. "You should think about coming to New York with me."

Lucy's eyes widened. "To New York? With you?" Neither of those statements would register. Although, New York *was* the dream. She had quite a bit of money saved up—from allowances and her after-school job in the one little hardware store in town that had become full-time after she graduated. She'd kept almost every dollar she had ever earned in her New York Dream Fund. If Jack was serious, Lucy could simply withdraw that money from the bank and be on her way to stardom. That was what she'd always wanted, wasn't it? So why didn't she feel even a niggle of excitement at the idea?

"Yeah, I mean, I'm getting involved with the theatre scene there. I'm already booked for a show in January, and I think they're still looking for people to fill a few roles. It's not exactly Broadway, but it's not that far off, either. It's the Diamond Theater, where a lot of big-name stage actors got their start."

"I've heard of it. I'm not ready for anything like that, though."

Jack's hand inched closer to her. "What are you talking about? You're really good. Better than you think. If I put in a word for you ..." He lifted his hand from the wall and brushed a strand of long, red hair back from her cheek. "... I'm sure I could get you in. We could play opposite each other." He leaned in closer. "Don't you think we have good chemistry?"

Lucy swallowed. Jack was cute, no question. Every time she looked at him, she had no trouble thinking of him as Gilbert. As August had said the day she told him she'd gotten the part of Anne, she *had* always wanted to spend Christmas—or any day of the year, really—with Gilbert Blythe. Now she was. It sounded as though they could spend a lot more days together, if she only said the word.

Why did that thought fall flat too? Had she simply built up this experience so much in her head that reality could never compare?

"I do think we have chemistry, actually. And I've enjoyed doing this show with you. But ..."

"Please say yes."

Oh man. Lucy groaned inwardly. Now he was speaking Gilbert to her. Her kryptonite. Although, for some reason, it didn't have the effect on her she might have expected.

"This doesn't have to end, Luce." He touched a finger to her lower lip. "I'm getting out of this province, going somewhere. You can too."

Luce. Did that mean they were themselves in this moment? Jack was saying all the right words, promising her everything she'd always thought she wanted. So why ...

He pressed his lips to hers.

Lucy was so shocked that, for a few seconds, she couldn't move. Then she pulled back, abruptly enough that she bumped her head against the wood siding of the house. "Jack, I ..."

A noise to her right caught her attention and they both glanced over. A pile of lumber sat at the entrance to the Balsam Hill Trail, the pathway through overhanging branches that Lucy Maud Montgomery had called *Lovers Lane*. As she watched, someone yanked two pieces of wood from the pile and hefted them onto his shoulder.

August.

~ FIVE ~

"... but wouldn't it have been more beautiful still, Anne, if there had been no separation or misunderstanding . . . if they had come hand in hand all the way through life, with no memories behind them but those which belonged to each other."

~ Gilbert Blythe

Jack stepped back. "Sorry, Luce. I shouldn't have done that."

Lucy waved away his apology. "It's okay. I can see how you might have thought ..." She shot another look to her right in time to see August disappear behind the house. When she turned back, Jack was watching her.

"I guess that answers one of my questions."

"One of them?"

"Yeah. The one I didn't ask with words." He offered her a sheepish grin.

"I'm sorry." It answered a question or two for her as well. Questions she didn't even realize she'd been asking herself. And it ignited a fireworks' display of others blazing across the sky. August? When? How? She barely refrained from burying her face in her hands and moaning. This couldn't be happening.

Jack waved a hand like she had done. "Can't blame a guy for trying." He pulled his gloves from his pockets and tugged them on. "Will you think about my other question, at least?"

"I will. I promise." Did she seriously have to think about New York? The goal she'd been working toward her whole life? She had no idea why she wasn't jumping all over the opportunity, only that something was holding her back. Something she needed to figure out sooner than later.

"All right then, Anne. Time to get back to work."

Him returning them to a professional level relieved a little of the tension between them. Now she just had to talk to August, find out what he'd seen. And what he thought about what he'd seen. And where the two of them should go from here.

"You go ahead. I'll be right there. I need to ... freshen up."

"Yeah, okay." Jack gave her a knowing look. "Say hi to your construction guy for me."

"He's not my ..."

Jack had already disappeared around the corner of the house. With a heavy sigh, Lucy headed the opposite direction. At the back of the building, she found August's footsteps and attempted to stay in them to avoid sinking into the snow, but his legs were too long for her. Trudging through drifts, she made her way to the open door of the workshop next to the barn.

"August?" She stepped onto the threshold right as August fired up the saw. He glanced over and pointed to his noise canceling headphones before flicking his fingers toward the door. Then he leaned down and began feeding one of the pieces of wood into the saw.

Lucy winced at the grating noise. He wasn't going to talk to her. Fine. Did that mean he'd seen her and Jack? Either way, she'd track him down later, make sure she explained everything before he left tomorrow.

Spinning around, she nearly walked straight into another man. Seriously, she really had to stop doing that. "Sorry." Her eyes on the snow, she started to walk around him.

"Lucy?"

She glanced up. "Dad?" His presence was so unexpected that she couldn't keep from launching herself into his arms.

He held her for a moment before easing her back and searching her face. "You okay?"

"Of course. Why wouldn't I be?" Even to Lucy, her voice sounded too bright, too high. No way her father would buy it.

He glanced through the open door of the workshop and his face cleared. "Ah." He held out his arm. "Let's walk."

Although she should be getting to work, Lucy needed a few minutes with her father more. She hadn't seen him in days, and she had missed him. Missed his dad jokes and the way he always chuckled after sharing one with her. The red knitted hat she'd made him for Christmas like ten years ago that he still wore all winter even though it was old and bits of wool poked out all over it. The way he knocked softly before sticking his head into her room every night to wish her sweet dreams. His homemade macaroni and cheese. Everything, really.

She slid her hand through the crook of his elbow, and the two of them started off across the snow. When they passed the spot on the far side of the house where she and Jack had stood, Lucy kept her eyes straight ahead. *And then Gilbert kisses Anne*. The culmination of the story. Except that Jack's kiss hadn't felt like the culmination. Not even the start of something potentially beautiful. More like a threat to something else—something far more valuable.

They waded through the soft snow down the sloping lawn to the bridge that led over to Lucy Maud Montgomery's *Haunted Woods*. Halfway across the bridge, her dad stopped, and Lucy's hand slid from his arm. He turned and rested his forearms on the wooden railing. Lucy joined him, and they stood a moment, gazing out over the white, silent world. Then she cleared her throat. "Not that I'm not thrilled to see you, but what are you doing here?"

"I was sorry to miss you before you left, so I thought I'd drive up and check on you."

"You didn't seem surprised to see August here."

Her dad brushed a little snow off the railing with the side of his gloved hand. "I'm not."

"Why?"

"Well, for starters, he called me when I got home from my trip and asked if I would check on his place occasionally while he was gone."

"Oh." What was there to check on? August's parents had moved to Florida three years earlier, and his older brothers and sister all had their own homes, so he was alone on the family land. Not much there to worry about, though, other than the old farmhouse and that workshop of his filled with planks.

"Also, August has always looked out for you, from the time you were kids. Even if you're both adults and perfectly capable of taking care of yourselves, he still does it. So no, it doesn't surprise me that he's here."

Lucy bit her lip. Was that true? Every one of her memories was inextricably entwined with August. She couldn't remember a time when he hadn't been part of her life. Sure, he was usually grumpy and pushing her toward the door. Even so, she had always known he would be there when she wanted to talk to him, the way she had when she'd gotten the news about Anne. He was the only one she had thought of. The one she had to see. "I watch out for him too."

The assertion fell as flat as her time here at Green Gables. *Did* she watch out for August? Given the way her chest ached now at the thought that she might somehow have hurt him, she wanted to. So maybe she hadn't always watched out for him like she should have. Now that she felt the sudden, driving need to do so, was it too late? Had she taken for granted one too many times that he would always be there for her?

"Of course you do."

Her father's words, slow to come, were far less emphatic than she would have liked. The truth hurt, apparently.

Still, Lucy doubled down. "Isn't that what friends do for each other?"

"Friends are there for each other, yes."

But? She was too scared to voice the question, so it only hung in the frosty air between them.

"It's not like it's a big deal, him taking a bit of time away from his work, right? I mean, what does he do, anyway, build decks and stuff? It's not the time of year for that."

Her dad shifted around to face her, his eyes suddenly as unreadable as August's. "Any chance you could get away for a few hours? There's something I'd love to show you."

Could she? They were supposed to rehearse the kissing scene today. Suddenly that was the last thing she felt like doing. Since she was in almost every scene, she was the only cast member who hadn't taken a break all week. "Hold on." She tugged the phone from her pocket and sent a text to Mr. Arsenault. After a minute or so, the device vibrated in her hand, and she scanned his reply before returning the phone to her pocket. "The director says it's okay for me to take the afternoon off. He'll work with Matthew on the puffed sleeves scene instead of the one we'd been planning to rehearse today."

"Great. I'd like to take you home for a quick visit. We'll grab a coffee for the road, since there's still no decent place to get a cup in Cordial Cove. Although I'm working on that."

"You are?" Lucy had long bemoaned the fact that there was no good coffee shop in her little hometown. Had her dad and the town council managed to entice one of the big chains to build a franchise there?

"Yep. Nothing's for sure yet. I'll let you know." He tugged his red wool hat down over his ears before holding out his arm again. "Shall we?"

An afternoon with her dad was exactly what Lucy needed right now so, not even caring where he was taking her or why, she grasped his elbow. "Let's go."

~ SIX ~

"The world calls them its singers and poets and artists and storytellers; but they are just people who have never forgotten the way to fairyland."

~ L.M. Montgomery

The whole, winding route home, Lucy pulled an August and stayed mostly silent, staring out the window as her dad talked about his trip. They grabbed coffee and biscuits at the Prince Edward Island Preserve Company in New Glasgow, ten minutes from Cavendish. Her mother had taken Lucy there once, for her seventh birthday. They'd ordered high tea and sipped from china mugs with their pinkies out while wearing fancy, wide-brimmed hats.

Afterwards, they'd gone to nearby North Rustico, one of Lucy's favorite places on the island. As waves crashed onto the sand, they had wandered along a driftwood strewn beach, gathering shells and glittering, worn-smooth rocks. Lucy's birthday was October twenty-second, and the beach had ended at a stand of trees ablaze with red, gold, and orange. Her mother had picked up handfuls of leaves from the ground and tossed them into the air, and they had laughed as the leaves rained down on them.

Her hands raised to the sky, her mother threw back her head and quoted Anne Shirley as they twirled in circles on the beach, the leaves crunching beneath their feet. "I'm so glad I live in a world where there are Octobers." The joyous words had danced too, lifted and carried by the breeze swooping in from the ocean.

A perfect day.

Even now, the warmth that had filled Lucy from the tips of her toes to the top of her head—despite the nip in the air—as she and her mother danced on the beach that day curled through her like soft, comforting woodsmoke. Although it had made what followed that much more unbearable, she wouldn't trade a moment of it.

That memory was the most vivid Lucy had of them together. So many other memories had slipped into a haze of fog as the years passed by. Even now, Lucy struggled to call her mother's face to mind. What remained were moments—a word or a touch, reading together at night, she and her mom dressing up and performing skits for her dad—moments that were beginning to darken and curl around the edges like a photograph tossed into the fire.

Melancholy drifted through her at the thought. Lucy took a sip of the rich, hot coffee and rested the side of her head against the back of the seat, catching glimpses of the ice-green Atlantic ocean between the trees and listening to her dad's voice. Not until he mentioned how excited he'd been to receive her message that she had gotten this role did she turn away from the glass to face him. "Like Mom, right?"

A shadow passed over his face. Did he still mourn his wife? Come to think of it, the two of them rarely spoke about her mother. That memory of Lucy and her mom dancing on the beach on Lucy's birthday was the last one they had created.

A few days later, her mother had returned to the theatre, promising to see Lucy at Christmas. As the holidays approached, Lucy began eagerly counting the days until her mother returned from a stage production in New York City. Then, the night she was finally to arrive home, her father had trudged into Lucy's room, shoulders bowed. He sat on the edge of the bed, took Lucy's hand in his, and told her in the gentlest voice she'd ever heard him use that the plane her mother had been flying in, trying to get home to them, had crashed, and Mom had gone to Heaven.

He reached over now and took her hand, the way he had that night. "Yeah, Lucy May. Like Mom."

When he let go of her, chills rippled through her. Lucy ran her hands up and down the sleeves of her down jacket. She hadn't thought about that night in a long time. What was bringing it to mind now? Didn't she have enough to think about with Jack and August and this role she had to get perfect to honor her mother, maybe follow in her footsteps all the way to New York?

Before she could analyze her continued lack of enthusiasm at the thought, her dad pulled into their lane, drove around behind the house, and parked. When they got out of the car, he held a hand toward the opening in the woods. "Let's take the shortcut."

"We're going to August's? Why, when he isn't here?"

"I have a key. Like I said, I want to show you something."

For some reason, the walk to August's place felt momentous, every step weighed down with apprehension. Was it because Lucy might have ruined their friendship that afternoon and might not be taking this path through the woods again after today?

The thick snow that had fallen since she left had draped a winter hush over their little corner of Prince Edward Island. The tromping of their boots on the iced-over cement pad outside August's workshop, the jangling of keys as her father tugged them from his pocket, the creaking of the door when he pushed it open all felt like an affront to the stillness, as though the two of them were trespassing on sacred ground.

She stepped over the threshold, tiptoeing after her father into August's workshop. Unlike the last time she'd been here, everything was in its place—stacks of wood piled against one wall, saws powered down and covered over, papers cleared off the table, shavings swept up from the floor. She'd never been here when August wasn't. As silent and cranky as he usually was, the place still felt empty and cheerless without him.

Lucy dragged a gloved finger across a spotless shelf. "What did you want to show me?"

"It's back here. Come with me."

She followed her father through the work area and waited as he unlocked another door. Where did this one lead? For all the times she had been in the building, August had never taken her in here.

"I discovered this room by accident a couple of days ago." Her dad pushed the door open. "So you know, yes, August does build decks and houses, beautiful ones. I'm guessing that's only to pay the bills, though, to finance what he really loves to do. Which is this." He reached to the side to flick on the light before moving out of her way. "Go ahead."

Lucy hesitated before stepping into the room. And stopping abruptly. Her mouth dropped open. What in the world? She slowly scanned the space, her mind refusing to take in what she was seeing. All four walls of the six-by-ten room were lined with shelves, and every shelf was filled with wooden carvings—animals and people and trees and games, including at least two chess sets. The pieces were shined to a gleaming polish and each one was a work of art.

"What is all this?" Reverently, Lucy reached out and lifted the nearest piece—a monkey hanging from a tree branch by one long arm. Every leaf was intricately carved with veins running through it. Had she ever seen anything more beautiful?

"This is August, Lucy. His heart and soul on full display."

She pressed a palm to her abdomen. "August made these?"

"That's right." He pointed to a tiny *A.D.* etched into the base of the monkey figurine.

How had she described what August did—*something with saws and planks*? No wonder he'd tossed her out of the place. She pressed her eyes shut. How could she have been so blind? How did she not know this was what her best friend did? Who he was?

Another quote from Lucy Maud Montgomery drifted through her mind. "How we all love to create! It is a little bit of the divine in us." This small room held evidence of the divine in every square inch.

"I had no idea. He never told me."

"Did you ever ask?"

Had she? Maybe not. She was forever going on to him about her dreams and her plans. It was entirely possible she'd never stopped to ask—or even wonder—what *he* did. What *his* dreams and plans were. She set the monkey down, shoved her palms against her eyes, and moaned. "I'm the worst friend ever."

"There are eight billion people in the world. It's statistically unlikely you're the *worst* friend out there."

Her dad's voice held laughter, and Lucy lowered her hands and opened her eyes. "Thanks. That makes me feel so much better."

"Look, Lucy." Her dad rested a hand, warm and strong, on her back. "I know things haven't been easy for you since your mom left."

Her head jerked. "Left?"

"Died, I mean. Although I tried to be both mom and dad to you, I know it's not the same. Losing a parent at a young age like that, it has to affect a person. You turned out to be this strong, amazing, talented woman I'm immensely proud of. Even so, you've spent your life desperately trying to find a way to connect with your mother. It's become a single-minded focus for you, and sometimes that has meant you haven't been as aware as you might have been of the other people in your life, the ones who are still here."

Tears pricked her eyes. The truth really did hurt, even though her dad was speaking it in that same gentle voice he'd used the night he told her that her mother would never be coming home. "You're right, I have. Although I didn't realize it, suddenly I can clearly see that's exactly what I've done. To you and August especially." She wrapped her arms around his waist and laid her head on his chest. "I'm so sorry."

Her dad held her close for a moment before stepping back. "I forgive you, and so will he."

"I don't know if he will now."

Her dad studied her a moment. "Something's changed with you and August, hasn't it?"

It felt as though, in the span of a few short hours, everything had changed. Or maybe it was more like one of those beautiful things inside the piece of wood that had always been there, waiting for the artist to clear away the parts that weren't needed. Now that beautiful thing had emerged, as warm and glowing as any of August's pieces of art. "It has, yes."

"What happened?"

Warmth crept into her cheeks. "Jack Miller, the actor playing Gilbert, kissed me earlier today, right before you arrived."

"Of course he did. That's the big moment in the play, isn't it?"

"Well, yeah, only we weren't rehearsing at the time. We were around the side of the Green Gables house, and I think August saw us. I felt bad about it, like I might have hurt him somehow. I'd just tried to talk to him when you saw me at the workshop. He only turned on the saw and waved me away."

"Why do you think it might have hurt him, seeing you with someone else?"

"I don't know, except that maybe I've started to realize I might think of him as more than a friend. If he feels the same way, which I doubt, then him seeing that kiss could've really messed things up. A kiss with someone I realized immediately was not the right person, even though he's *so* Gilbert Blythe."

Her dad rolled his eyes in a very August Dorey way. "What is it with you women and Gilbert Blythe?"

Lucy clasped her fingers in front of her. "He's incredibly cute and sweet and adorable and he really gets Anne and he's always there for her and he's—"

"Fictional?"

Her shoulders slumped. "There's that."

"Of course, take out Anne and insert Lucy and you might have someone who sounds an awful lot like August."

"Huh." Lucy had never thought of August as a Gilbert type—if a much grumpier version—but now that her dad mentioned it ...

"Anyway, it's all made me think that I might actually ... care about August." She wasn't nearly ready to use the *l* word. Was she?

"Finally."

Lucy blinked. "Finally?"

"Yeah. I don't doubt August feels the same way, and I don't think, deep down, you doubt it either. I've known how you guys feel about each other for years."

"What? Why didn't you tell me?"

Her dad laughed. "I thought it best to wait for the two of you to figure it out."

"But every time I get close to August, he pulls away."

"I'm pretty sure I know the reason for that, and I'm ninety-nine percent convinced it isn't because he doesn't want to be close to you. Still, I'll let the two of you figure that out as well."

Yeah, she was already pushing the boundaries of comfortable, discussing physical affection between her and a guy with her dad. She'd always been able to approach him about anything, though. Something she appreciated, since her mom hadn't been there for her to talk about this stuff with. Was that something her mother had thought about as the plane plummeted to the ground, that she would miss all these moments, all these talks, with Lucy? Her heart ached even more than it already had been.

Lucy pressed her hands to her cheeks. "What if it's too late? What if I've blown it?"

"Look around you, Lucy."

She complied, struck again by August's skill and creativity. Where had this talent, this love of coaxing a breathtaking piece from a chunk of wood come from, his Mi'kmaq ancestors? It was clearly a God-given gift, but his heritage might play into it as well. Something else she'd never really asked him about and should have.

Her dad slid an arm around her shoulders. "Only a thoughtful, extremely sensitive man could produce works of art like these. When August feels, he feels deeply. And the way he feels about you? I suspect that, second only to his relationship with God, those feelings are so much a part of him it would pretty much destroy him to try and untangle them, yank them out by the roots, and toss them away. I do encourage you to discuss it with him, though, before that hurt grows."

The small room spun around her. Could what her dad was saying possibly be true? Did August actually—

"Lucy?"

She blinked. "Sorry, what?"

"I said, let's head back to Cavendish. Maybe you can still talk to August tonight."

Lucy took one more lingering glance around the room before walking into the workshop. Her dad locked the door and touched her arm. "There's something else you should know."

She was pretty sure her head was too full at the moment to take in even one more thing. Even so, she followed him across the room to a phone and answering machine on a desk in the corner. The number 45 flashed in the little screen on the machine. Her dad hit the button, and Lucy listened to the first three messages, all people trying to place orders for August's pieces in time for Christmas.

Her stomach tightened. August's words, that he couldn't simply walk away and leave his work, that this was his busiest time of year, finally sank in. Some of those people sounded pretty ticked off. Would him staying in Cavendish solely because she and Mr. Arsenault had, selfishly, begged him to do so for their sakes result in a huge loss of business for him? Judging by these messages, of course it would. So why had he agreed?

The possible answer to that was more than she could take in. Still, after everything August had done for her, everything he had given up, it was time for her to think about him for a change.

"Dad." She grabbed his arm and turned him to face her. "There's something I desperately need you to do."

~ Seven ~

"This is a wound I shall bear forever."
~ Anne Shirley

Lucy stared out the window at the fields of white and trees dripping with melting snow as they made the trek back to the Green Gables property. Her father's words ran through her mind over and over. She couldn't argue with any of the charges he had gently leveled against her. And it made sense what he'd said about Lucy dedicating her life to trying to forge some kind of connection to her mother after she died.

Or what was it her father had said? That her mother left? That was an odd way to put it. It implied some kind of intent, which was impossible when she had been killed in a plane crash. And she *had* been killed in a plane crash. Right?

Furrowing her brow, Lucy slid her phone out of her pocket and held it up. "I should check my messages. They might want me back at a certain time for rehearsal."

Her dad nodded. Likely he was mulling over the request she'd made of him—deciding on the best way to carry it out.

So that what she'd said wouldn't be a complete lie, Lucy did check her messages. Nothing from Mr. Arsenault or August, only a short text from Jack. "You OK?" He was a good guy, just not the guy for her, as Gilbert Blythe-like as he might be.

As surreptitiously as possible, she called up the search box and entered *plane crash, 2002.* A plane crash always made headlines, didn't it? And the death of a woman who'd achieved at least a modicum of success on the stage surely merited some coverage. Why hadn't Lucy ever tried to look her up before?

Only one crash came up that matched the year, although it had happened in March, not December and had been a small five-seater. Neither of those details fit. Why wouldn't there have been any coverage of a crash with so many fatalities?

A hard, cold ball formed in her stomach. Lucy shifted in her seat to face her father. "Dad, what airline was Mom flying with when she crashed?"

He didn't take his eyes off the road, although his fingers did tighten around the steering wheel. "Airline?"

"Yeah." The phone shook a little when she lifted it in his direction. "After we talked about her earlier, I thought I'd look up the details, since I've never done that. I can't find any major crashes that happened in December of that year. Which is weird, right?"

He exhaled a long, slow breath. "Is there any chance you will let this go, Lucy May?"

"I think you know me better than that."

"Okay. Hold on. There's a rest stop ahead. I'll pull over so we can talk."

She nodded, her throat tightening at the resignation in his voice. What was happening?

They drove in silence for five minutes, tiny zaps of electricity shooting through every part of her body. Then her father flipped on the turn signal and eased his car off the road and into a newly plowed lot overlooking the ocean. After stopping the car and killing the engine, he turned in his seat to look at her. "I should have told you this a long time ago."

He stopped and drew in a long, slightly shuddering breath as though gathering strength before blurting out, "Your mother didn't die the night I told you she was never coming home."

The zaps of electricity grew stronger. Lucy's eyelids flickered as she tried to make sense of the words. "She didn't die? Then why did you tell me she did? And where is she?"

Her dad's eyes closed briefly before he opened them and met her gaze. "She is dead now. She died eleven years ago. From a drug overdose." He reached out, but when Lucy curled her fingers into a fist and pressed it to her chest, he pulled back his hand. "I'm so sorry."

"Sorry?" She had no idea how to feel. Angry? Betrayed? Grief-stricken? The only emotion she could clearly identify was confusion. What in the world was her father saying? "Sorry for what? Her death? That you have been lying to me for twenty-two years? Or that you kept my mother from me my whole life?"

His head jerked. "I didn't keep your mother from you, Lucy. I would never have done that. The night I told you she died I had just gotten off the phone with her. She was supposed to be on her way home for Christmas, but she called to tell me that she couldn't do it. She couldn't be a wife or a mother. Couldn't live in a small town in Prince Edward Island. She had to be free to pursue her own dreams, unencumbered by anything to do with her past. She left me, Lucy. She left us."

Okay, hurt was rising to the surface fast. "Why didn't you tell me the truth?"

"Maybe I should have, but I couldn't. I couldn't bring myself to rip your life apart like that, to allow you to believe for one second that you were someone anyone could simply walk away from. I couldn't do it. Even if you never forgive me, I won't regret that decision. The truth would have shattered you, and my number one job in life is to protect you, to keep anyone or anything from hurting you. I did my job."

His chin lifted a little at that, an uncharacteristic defiance in his voice.

Lucy pulled her feet up onto the seat, propped her elbows on her knees, and pressed the tips of her shaking fingers to her forehead. "What happened to her?" The question came out in a raspy whisper.

"I don't know a lot of the details, since she didn't keep in touch. From the little I heard from friends of hers, she got the odd acting job here and there, nothing big. Apparently, the offers became fewer and further between as she got older. She struggled, got into drugs. And eventually that's what killed her."

"I was *eighteen* when she actually died. Didn't you think I could handle the truth then?"

"I didn't hear about her death until a few months after, and you had just started university. I did wrestle harder with that decision, and maybe it was pure cowardice, but you were doing so well. Every time you came home, I was determined that would be the visit I'd come clean, tell you everything. In the end, I sent you back without having done it. God forgive me. I have no real excuse for that except my desire for you to be happy. To believe that you'd had a mother who loved you and wanted the best for you. And you did believe that."

"But it was a lie."

He sighed. "Yes. That was a lie. It was also her loss. She missed out on seeing you grow up, on sharing every moment of your life with you, on watching you reach every milestone and become this incredible woman. I can't feel anything but sorry for her for that. And blessed and grateful for myself that I was there for all of it."

Lucy closed her eyes. Her chest ached so badly it hurt to draw a breath, and her entire body trembled. *Lord, are you hearing this? What am I supposed to do with it?* For several minutes, neither of them moved. The memory of that day on the beach slammed into her, knocking the breath from her lungs. Their perfect day. Had her mother known, even then, that she would never see Lucy again? Had that day been her farewell gift to the young daughter she would abandon weeks later?

The thought tainted that beloved memory like a few drops of strychnine tossed into clean, sparkling well water.

Lucy lifted her head. "Even though I kind of get it, I'm going to need a little time to deal with the fact that you have lied to me for so long."

Her father nodded. "I understand. Take all the time you need." He ran a finger under his eye. "Do you still want me to take you to Green Gables?"

Did she? Could she possibly go back there, get up on stage and act, pretend that her entire world hadn't been rocked off its foundation? *Pretending's your thing, not mine.* Lucy lifted her chin the way her dad had. Even if he'd said it facetiously, August hadn't been wrong. Pretending *was* her thing. If every single other part of her life had changed today, that hadn't. She could still act.

On stage, she could become someone else—Anne with an e, with all her quirks and eccentricities and the people who loved her and chose her when her own mother and father had been taken away. People who accepted her for who she was. And her happy ending with Gilbert. "Yeah. I need to go back. I have to see this through."

A sad smile turned up the corners of her dad's mouth. "That's my girl." He leaned forward and turned the key to start the engine.

Twenty minutes later, he pulled into the parking lot of the heritage site and stopped at the curb in front of the entrance to the main building. She pushed open the door.

"Lucy?"

She shifted around to face her dad. "Yeah?"

"Is it still okay if I come to the performance?"

His face held such a mixture of apprehension and hope that her anger toward him slipped through her fingers. Maybe he should have told her the truth a long time ago. As he'd said, though, he had only been trying to protect her. She reached over and covered his hand, still clutching the steering wheel. "You've never missed a performance of mine in my life. I don't think I could do it if I looked out and didn't see you there. So yes, I'll be watching for you."

His smile quivered a little. "Then I'll be there. Front row."

~ EIGHT ~

"I've just been imagining that it was really me you wanted after all and that I was to stay here for ever and ever. It was a great comfort while it lasted. But the worst of imagining things is that the time comes when you have to stop and that hurts."

~ Anne Shirley

Rehearsals were over for the day by the time Lucy wandered around the main building to the barn. No one appeared to be around. Likely they were all at dinner, but she couldn't bring herself to go in, to face her castmates. Or August. After what her dad had shown her in the workshop, she'd been determined to find August that night, talk to him. Now she wasn't sure she could handle one more difficult conversation. So many emotions had coursed through her earlier. Now all she felt was numb.

Twilight had fallen over the property. Still, there was enough light in the barn for her to see the large, wooden mural of the train that Anne—full of the hope that she had finally found a forever home—had taken to Bright River. The train she'd climbed off of believing she was stepping into her new life with Matthew and Marilla. Until she found out they had been expecting a boy.

Was that simply life? If you allowed yourself to dream, to believe, were hopes always dashed because the people you thought would love you, would want you, were always looking for something or someone else?

She stopped in the doorway and contemplated the mural. If only she could board that train right now and take it … Her eyes narrowed. Where would she go? Home would be ideal, except where was home for her? Her dad had never suggested she get a place of her own, but it was time. Past time, really. What had she been waiting for? The answer, as distant and hidden in shadow as the Green Gables house across the property, began to form in her mind.

From the barn opening, Lucy glanced at the sky, darkening to cobalt. One star, hovering above the trees that surrounded the heritage site, glimmered against the blue. *Show me what to do, would ya?* She froze. Had she really spoken to the Almighty God of the universe that glibly?

Lucy thought back. Was that how she typically prayed? Firing off random requests—borderline demands, really—without a lot of thought? Certainly without a lot of reverence.

The truth struck her, and she squeezed her eyes shut. Her whole life, she'd taken God for granted the same way she had taken her dad and August for granted, hadn't she? As though all three of them existed solely to be at her beck and call. To follow her script, as it were. Lucy pressed the fingers of both hands against her mouth. *God, forgive me.*

The three-word prayer was the most heartfelt one she could remember praying. It had barely left her soul before the oddest sensation filled her, as though someone was wrapping arms around her and holding her close. Did that mean God hadn't given up on her and walked away like her mother had? *Thank you for being faithful when I was not. When the one who should have loved me the most was not. I'm going to do better. I promise. Can you help me do better with Dad and August too?*

Lucy drew in the first deep breath she'd taken since walking into the little room filled with August's artwork.

A bench sat on the makeshift train station platform in front of the mural, and she stumbled to it and sank down. The howl of a wolf, far-off and melancholy, rose above the trees. Footsteps crunched on the snow before August wandered through the opening into the barn. She bit her lip, not moving as he closed the distance between them and lowered himself onto the bench next to her. In the dim light, his dark eyes, filled with concern, probed hers. "I saw you walk by the building. You doing okay, Lucille?"

"I don't know." The words came out almost as a sob.

August frowned. "What is it?"

She pulled her feet up onto the bench and wrapped her arms around her knees. "Remember when my mom died?"

"Of course. When we were seven, right? A plane crash?"

"That's what I thought. Today my dad let me know that the night he told me she died, she really only called to say that she didn't want to be a wife or mother, that she was walking away from us to pursue her own dreams."

"Seriously?" August's voice held a mixture of anger and disbelief. "Who walks away from their own child? From you?"

When Lucy didn't offer the obvious answer—her mother—his shoulders slumped. "Sorry. That's not helpful." He slid a little closer. "So she's alive?"

Lucy shook her head. "Apparently she died eleven years ago from a drug overdose."

August exhaled. "Wow. I'm really sorry."

She rested her head on his shoulder. For once, August didn't pull away. "I realized today that I've spent my whole life trying to get close to someone who couldn't get far enough from me."

"She was a fool, Lucille. She had no idea what she was walking away from."

That helped. A little.

They sat in silence for a few minutes, the forest darkening around them. In the distance, a wolf howled again and then a clump of snow slid from the roof above the open barn doors and landed on the ground with a soft thud. Birds cooed up in the rafters. The sounds of night falling.

"One can't stay sad for very long in such an interesting world, can one?" August's voice was as soft as the moonlight casting a silver glow over the courtyard.

Lucy almost smiled. "I'm not sure if anything in the world makes me happier than you quoting *Anne of Green Gables* to me."

"I'm not ..."

She lifted her head and looked at him, and he rolled his eyes. "All right. I admit it. I might have read the books. And watched the mini-series."

"I knew it!" She bumped his shoulder with hers. "Why did you?"

"Because it was important to you."

Oh. In her new, unselfish life, August's example might be a good one to follow. Lucy rested her head on his shoulder again. *I'm so glad I live in a world where there are Augusts.* She closed her eyes, drawing comfort from the hard muscles, the warmth of him against her cheek. "Say something else."

After a moment, he said, "Those who knew Anne best felt, without realizing that they felt it, that her greatest attraction was the aura of possibility surrounding her... the power of future development that was in her. She seemed to walk in an atmosphere of things about to happen."

A little of the ache in her chest eased. "So you've what, memorized the whole series?"

"Only the parts that most reminded me of you."

She did smile then. "I think you may be a kindred spirit after all."

"We're not as scarce as you might think."

Lucy sighed. "I don't want you to leave tomorrow."

"Why not?"

"Because ..." Because you're my best friend, she'd been about to say. Which was true, except that, after today, she understood it wasn't the whole truth. August was more than that to her. Much more. Did he feel the same way? If she told him and he didn't, their friendship would be ruined. She couldn't lose that. Couldn't lose him.

"Because why?"

"Because I ... do."

He drew in a slow breath, as longsuffering as he always was when dealing with her. "You do what?"

"I need you."

A heartbeat of silence passed between them and then another.

Lucy straightened and turned her head so she could see his face. "You told me to say those words to you to see what happens."

In the pale moonlight, a gleam ignited in his eyes. "I did, didn't I? Very well then, Lucille May McQuaid. I'll stay."

Joy ignited deep inside, doused quickly by thoughts of that room of wooden pieces of art. Of the messages on the machine. "You know what? I really appreciate you agreeing to stay for me, but I shouldn't have asked you to. It was selfish. You need to go home."

A little too much surprise flashed across his face for Lucy's liking. Was it that unusual for her to think about the people she cared about more than she thought about herself?

"Really?"

Given the hint of shock in his voice, apparently it was. "Yeah. I mean, I don't want you to go. I'm starting to see how much I've taken you and my dad for granted, though. God too. I'm truly sorry. I've asked God to help me do better, to think about others more, and I'm really going to try. So, as much as I want you here, I want you to do what's best for yourself even more."

"Huh."

"Have you ever noticed one encouraging thing about me? I never make the same mistake twice."

A smirk crossed his face. "I don't know as that's much benefit when you're always making new ones."

August quoting Marilla gave Lucy the best kind of heart palpitations. So much so that her *train of thought* nearly derailed. She pressed her fingertips to the mural, forcing herself back on track. "Can you forgive me?"

August studied her a moment before touching her cheek with his finger, maybe the first time he'd been the one to reach out to her—when he wasn't trying to run her off his property, anyway. Just as quickly, he pulled his hand away, but the warmth of his touch lingered on her skin despite the deep chill in the air. "I do forgive you. And I appreciate you telling me to go home. I actually am going to stay, though. I already told Mr. Arsenault I would."

"You did? Why?"

"Because when Marilla dumped that twenty-pound bag of brown sugar on the kitchen table today, two of the table legs broke through the stage. So, rehearsals are moving to the dance floor while the guys and I shore up the main stage this week to make sure the next thing to go through the wood isn't someone's foot. Or worse."

"Oh. Wow." Her head weighed a thousand pounds. Thoughts as countless as snowflakes drifted through it to land on a growing pile like the ones that had built up outside the barn this week. Lucy shifted closer to lean against him. She lowered her feet to the ground until her knee rested against his, testing the limits of his tolerance. When he didn't move, she said, "Even if I shouldn't be, I'm really glad you'll be here."

"So am I. Since we're being all honest and everything, I need you too."

The fluttering started up in her chest again. "You do?"

"Of course. I know I've never said this before, but you're my ..."

Lucy held her breath. She was what, the woman of his dreams? The love of his life? His Anne?

"Best friend."

Oh. Best friend. Right. Good answer. The one she should have given him earlier. Lucy swallowed the sudden lump in her throat. "You're my best friend too." It wasn't a lie. He *was* her best friend. Which would be a great foundation on which to stack, like bricks, all those other feelings coursing through her. Except that when August said *best friend*, it didn't sound as though he meant the words as a foundation. More like the whole house. One of those tiny houses, maybe. Or a shed. Not big enough, in any case. Not nearly big enough for her.

Which meant she might need to build a house of her own.

"Jack asked me to go to New York with him."

August's arm tensed. He didn't speak for a moment, then he eased away from her. It had grown too dark in the barn for her to read on his face what he was feeling. Or maybe he'd gone into August lockdown again.

Her knee was cold where his no longer touched, and she repressed a shiver. "What are you thinking?"

"I'm thinking that you should go with him."

That was definitely not the line she had written for him in her head, the script for how this conversation between the two of them would go. The hurt she'd felt when her father told her that her mother had chosen to walk away from her rose to the surface again. Lucy pressed a palm to her chest. "You do?"

"Yeah. I mean, it's your dream, right? Not everyone gets the chance to live their dream. You shouldn't pass that up. Besides, Jack seems like a decent guy." He smacked his knees with both hands before standing. "I wish you all the best, Lucy. I hope you find everything you're looking for."

Lucy. Although it was actually her name, August had never called her that in her life. Of all the words he was throwing at her, him calling her that hurt more than anything. It closed a door, changed everything between them. It also answered the question he'd asked earlier about who could walk away from her. After her mother, his name had just been added to the list.

He didn't wait for her to respond, merely nodded curtly before striding out of the barn.

Lucy didn't move, only sat there in the darkness and watched him go.

~ Nine ~

"I am well in body although considerably rumpled up in spirit..."
~ Anne Shirley

August barely spoke to Lucy all week. The odd time she caught his gaze across the cafeteria or when she glanced into the barn to check on the progress there, the dark eyes that met hers were cold, detached, as though they were strangers instead of life-long friends.

Former life-long friends, maybe.

That look intensified the iciness drifting through her that hadn't gone away since the conversation she'd had in the car with her dad. Lucy began to feel like Frosty the Snowman in reverse—as though little by little she was freezing up inside, and there was nothing she could do to stop it.

August and his crew were working hard to make sure the stage was ready for the performance. Lucy and Jack and the rest of the cast were working hard too. Working hard was the only way Lucy could get through this, could banish thoughts of her mother's abandonment and August's rejection.

They rehearsed the scene where Anne invited Diana for tea and mistakenly served her bosom friend current wine instead of raspberry cordial. Mallory was so hilarious as an inebriated Diana that Lucy couldn't help but laugh, which lifted a little of the heaviness pressing down on her. It helped, too, that even Mallory seemed to pick up on the *stay away* vibe August was giving off and rarely approached him, focusing instead on getting ready for the show.

Lucy shouldn't care about that, since clearly anything she might have hoped would happen between her and August wasn't going to happen. Still, she was glad. Her heart would ache even more than it already did if she had to watch the two of them together.

Jack didn't press her to tell him if she'd made a decision about New York. Not in words, anyway, although she caught him watching her sometimes, the question lingering in his eyes. As she had no idea what to tell him, she'd only smile and look away. Other than the hint that his mind was occasionally on what would happen when the show was over, he stayed in character.

Whether or not the charming, funny, perceptive persona was real, Jack in character was a constant reminder to Lucy of why she'd always been a Gilbert Blythe kind of girl. Even if, as her dad had reminded her, Gilbert was fictional. Maybe fictional men were her lot in life. At least they did what the author told them to. Followed the lines in the script. And they were always there when you lifted the cover of the book.

She shot a glance at August, hammering yet another nail into the stage. He'd shed his coat, and his long-sleeved white T-shirt stretched across his broad shoulders. Biting her lip, Lucy glanced away.

Her gaze collided with Jack's, who was watching her, a small smile on his face. The two of them were alone up on the dance floor, waiting for Mr. Arsenault to signal that they were finally to rehearse their big kissing scene.

Jack lifted a hand. "Why don't you just ask him?"

Lucy frowned. "Ask who what?"

"How he feels. And you know who."

She blew out a breath. "I know how he feels. We talked a few nights ago. He made it clear he thinks of me as a friend."

Jack snorted. "Sorry, but there's no way that guy thinks of you as just a friend."

"I told him you'd invited me to go to New York with you, and he said you were a decent person and I should go."

"Did he seem happy about it?"

Her forehead wrinkled as she thought back. Had he? August had tensed and pulled away from her when she'd mentioned it, then kind of ground the words out before wishing her well and taking off. "No. I guess he didn't. So why would he tell me to go?"

Jack waved a hand through the air. "You ever hear of the old *if you love something set it free* thing?"

Was that what August had been doing, setting her free? And was that what her father meant when he said August not touching her wasn't because he didn't want to? That he was letting her go instead of doing anything that might hold her back from the life she wanted?

And wait, did that mean August might actually think of her as more than his *best friend* after all?

Why don't you just ask him?

Jack's words echoed in her head. To be fair, she never had done that with August. If she'd poured her heart out to him, told him how she actually felt, and *then* he'd left, she would know he didn't feel the same way. What if she poured her heart out to him and he *didn't* leave? What if he told her his feelings for her were deeper than friendship, too?

The joy that flowed in like the Bay of Fundy tide at the thought helped wash away the confusion about one thing, at least. "Jack." She met his gaze again.

He offered her a sad smile. "You're not coming with me, are you?"

"I can't."

"Even if he doesn't feel the way you hope?"

"Even then. Everything that has happened to me this week has shown me that acting isn't really my dream. It was the thing I thought would keep me close to my mother. But I have to let her go too. At least, I have to let go of the idea I've always had of her, which was never even true. I need to find my own dream. Although I'm not entirely sure what that dream is yet, I do know where I'll find it. I have to go home."

He nodded. "You'll figure it out, Luce." He shot another look in August's direction. "And if he doesn't, then he's an idiot."

Before she could respond, the director clapped his hands. "Jack? Lucy? Ready to walk through the big scene?"

August didn't turn around at that, merely kept hammering. She lifted her chin. "Yep. All set."

"From the top, then."

She and Jack stood next to a row of wooden sawhorses they'd set up to represent a bridge for rehearsal. As always, Lucy allowed the role to swallow her up. In the shadow of the fabled Green Gables house, she *became* Anne. She was only vaguely aware of it when the hammering stopped. Then she stood on an actual bridge, water flowing and sparkling beneath her as she and Gilbert talked, as he warned her that the next few years wouldn't be easy, and as she spoke the iconic line, "I don't want diamond sunbursts and marble halls. I only want you."

And then Gilbert kisses Anne.

Even as lost in the moment as she was, Lucy sensed it when Gilbert briefly became Jack. When the lips pressed gently to hers weren't promising a future; they were saying goodbye.

Then Mr. Arsenault called out, "That's it. Thank you," and she and Jack broke apart.

For a moment, neither of them moved, as if he was fighting as hard as she was to return to the present moment. Or maybe to cling to the one that had just passed. Then Gilbert's easy grin crossed Jack's face, and the spell was broken.

The hammering started up again, more forceful this time, although Lucy didn't glance in August's direction. Instead, she peered down at the director, standing in ankle-deep snow in the courtyard. "Okay if we take five?"

When he nodded, Lucy headed for the stairs. She needed to call her dad. She had one more favor to ask of him, and she couldn't wait a single minute to do it.

As he'd promised, when the curtain rose on the newly shored up and repaired stage, Lucy's dad sat in the front row. Although the performance was sold out, no one had taken the seat next to him. Was that supposed to be for August? Had he even stayed to watch the show or was he already gone? Lucy shoved the thought from her mind before it carved out an emptiness in her chest that would keep her from losing herself in her role.

Her father looked a little uncertain until Lucy smiled at him. Then his shoulders relaxed, and he beamed at her before she spoke her first line and he and the rest of the audience disappeared.

Only when Gilbert leaned in to kiss Anne and the spectators rose as one to their feet, applauding madly and encouraging her and Jack to take bow after bow, did she come back to reality. Her father stood at the foot of the stage, clapping, cheering, and, once, sticking his thumb and finger into his mouth to let out a piercing whistle. The seat next to him remained empty.

Jack held Lucy's hand tightly, likely as aware as she that their time together was slipping away. Not once since she'd told him she wasn't going to New York had she regretted that decision, though.

The clapping finally died away and the live music started up. The crowd drifted out to the courtyard where the ball was set to begin. Anne and Gilbert, who always danced the first waltz to kick off the evening, met in the middle of the floor. Jack circled her waist with one arm while clasping her hand in the air with the other. The night was clear and cold, the sky a dark sapphire canopy of twinkling gold stars.

Gilbert whisking Anne around the dance floor would have been magical, a perfect moment, if not for the ache creeping back into Lucy's chest now that the performance was over. Had it only been two weeks since she'd left home? Somehow she had managed to lose both her mother and her best friend in that amount of time.

Lucy gazed up at the night sky. *Thank you, Lord. For the time I had with my mom, for a dad who stepped in to be both mother and father to me and did it beautifully, and for the friendship I will cherish for the rest of my life, even if it has ended. Help me to never take a gift from you for granted again.*

The song ended, another one started up, and suddenly the dance floor was crowded with people. Good thing August had strengthened it, or the night could have ended in disaster. A sad smile crossed her face as Jack squeezed her fingers. "It's been a pleasure, Lucy McQuaid. Wherever you end up, whatever you decide to do with your life, I truly hope you are happy."

"Thanks, Jack Miller. I hope you are happy too. I look forward to the day I can tell everyone I knew you when."

He leaned in and kissed her on the cheek and then he was gone.

Lucy made her way down the steps, scanning the courtyard.

"August left, sweetheart." Her father waited for her at the bottom of the stairs.

Although she'd suspected as much, it still hurt. Hopefully the phantom pain of August's absence in her life would ease in time. She smiled as her dad handed her a beautiful bouquet of wildflowers and then held out his arm. "Shall we head out too, Lucy May?"

Clutching the bouquet in one hand, Lucy slid her other through the crook of his elbow. "Yes, let's. I'm ready to go home."

~ TEN ~

"Mrs. Lynde always says, 'Blessed are they who expect nothing for they shall not be disappointed.' But I think it would be worse to expect nothing than to be disappointed."

~ Anne Shirley

Christmas Eve day dawned crisp, cold, and with a light scattering of flakes drifting down from an Arctic-blue sky. Perfect.

Lucy made her way along the pathway through the trees connecting her house to August's. Her steps faltered a little as she approached the two cement stairs leading to his rear entrance. Would he come to the door? They hadn't had an actual conversation since the night she'd told him Jack had invited her to go to New York, so it was quite possible he wouldn't if he suspected it was her.

She lifted her chin. He was in for a battle of wills, then, because she wasn't leaving until they spoke. After climbing the stairs, she pulled open the screen and rapped her gloved knuckles against the blue wood. Although August was a morning person, it wasn't eight yet, so he might still be eating breakfast or even sleeping in after a couple of weeks of hard manual labor at the heritage site.

Lucy made a fist and pounded harder on the door. After a minute or so, she finally caught the distant thudding of feet on the stairs that descended from the second floor to the living room. Her heart rate picked up.

Seconds later, the door flew open. August stood in the kitchen. He wore jeans and a long-sleeved black T-shirt, but he clutched a red plaid blanket around himself as though she'd pulled him from his bed. His dark curls fell around his shoulders, and for a moment she couldn't breathe. The only thing in the world she wanted was to fling herself into his arms. He'd push her away, though, and she couldn't take that. Not again.

He scowled. "What?"

"Did I wake you?"

"Of course not. It's eight in the morning." Despite his words, his eyes looked heavy and red-rimmed. Had he not slept well last night? Before she could ask, August unwound the blanket and tossed it over the back of a kitchen chair. "What do you want?"

The answer that flitted through her head was far too dangerous to speak out loud. She settled for, "I want you to come out to the workshop with me."

"No."

August started to shut the door on her, but Lucy shot out a hand to stop it. "Please, August. There's something I need to show you."

He ran a hand over his face and exhaled loudly. "Look, Lucy. I can't keep doing this."

"What, calling me Lucy? Because I swear if you don't stop, I *will* break a slate over your head."

Nothing in his way-too-handsome face softened at her weak attempt at humor.

"All right. I promise no more Anne jokes if you come with me."

He hesitated a moment before shaking his head and reaching down to tug on his sneakers. "Five minutes and then you go home and enjoy Christmas with your dad. Got it?"

"Who are you going to enjoy *your* Christmas with?" His family had all been here in November, before their parents left for Florida. Had that been their holiday celebration? Would he be alone the next couple of days? The thought was unbearable.

"None of your business." August brushed the curls from his face before snagging a coat from the hook by the door. He yanked it on and then waved for her to go ahead.

Lucy started along the neatly shoveled pathway to the barn. When had August found time to do that? It would have been dark by the time he got home the night before. Maybe her dad had done it, although he'd been pretty busy running around town for her the last few days.

August trudged along behind her. "Not sure what you think you're going to show me in my own workshop, but whatever."

"You'll find out if you stop grumbling and just come along."

Although he was behind her, she *felt* him roll his eyes. If a deep sadness hadn't cast a shadow over the morning, she might have laughed. It was entirely possible that, as Anne had said to Diana, after today she and August might be strangers living side by side. Which would break her heart, although she couldn't blame him for ending their friendship.

They reached the workshop doors and August came up to stand next to her. The raucous strains of "Grandma Got Run Over by a Reindeer" drifted out through the cracks, and his eyebrows drew together. "What's going on? Is someone in there?"

"You'll have to go in and see, won't you?"

With a frustrated huff, he lifted one of the handles and then planted his palm on the door to shove it open. Lucy stepped inside and he followed her, stopping so abruptly one running shoe skidded a little along the floor. All the saws and other equipment and tools had been moved to the left side of the room. Along the other two walls and in front of the pile of planks, her dad and whoever he'd recruited to help him had set up tables. Every surface held a display of August's wooden art pieces. Strings of twinkling lights had been wound around every rafter, and a massive, decorated tree towered in one corner, the shiny gold star on top nearly touching the roof. With Christmas music playing in the background and the sweet, spicy aroma of hot apple cider floating in the air, the place had been transformed into a festive wonderland.

"What is all this?'

Lucy tried to decipher his tone. Was he in shock? Confused? Angry? Hopefully once he understood what was happening, he would no longer be any of those things.

Her dad came out of the small room holding one of the chess sets in both hands. "You're here!" he exclaimed as he carried the game over to the last table with a bit of space on it and set it down. "Everyone else is in the office getting the food and drinks ready."

Deep furrows appeared in August's forehead. "Everyone else?"

"Yes. The volunteers. Come join us."

"We'll be right there." August ground out the words the way he had when he'd told Lucy to go to New York with Jack. Which wasn't good. Her dad waved and headed off to the office area. August wrapped his fingers around Lucy's upper arm and directed her toward the small room where he stored his artwork. Not exactly the kind of touch she wanted from him. Even so, she didn't protest as he guided her into the room, let her go, then turned and closed the door. When he whirled around, his face had settled into granite again.

"Lucy."

"Yes?" Her voice came out overly bright and cheerful, as it had with her father.

"What is happening here? In *my* shop. With *my* work."

Suddenly her brilliant idea didn't seem so brilliant. August was right. This was his place, and these were his pieces. She shouldn't have assumed he would appreciate the idea she'd come up with for them. "Umm. Since you sacrificed the opportunity to sell your work by coming up to Cavendish, we thought we could do a pop-up store today. For the locals and anyone else interested in driving here to look at it."

"A pop-up store."

"That's right."

He stared at her a moment before he said, "No *locals* will be interested in my stuff. Why do you think I never tell anyone around here what I do? These are fishermen, Lucy. Good, decent, hardworking people who don't have any interest in spending what little money they make on art. Which I understand."

"You don't know that."

"I do know that. My dad, who is the best man in the world but who thinks exactly like all the other men in town, told me as much when I finally got up the nerve two years ago to show him what I was making out here."

"Oh, August." His dad had trampled all over his dream? Was that why August was so determined for Lucy to pursue hers? And why he kept his incredible pieces locked up and hidden away in this little back room?

His jaw tightened. "Don't do that."

"Don't do what?"

"Feel sorry for me. Not you."

"I don't feel sorry for you. I *feel* for you. It's completely different. You can feel sorry for any stranger on the street, but you can only deeply feel for someone you care deeply about."

Although he contemplated her a moment, he didn't acknowledge her confession, only said, "I guess I appreciate the thought, but you and your dad and *everyone else* out there have wasted your time. I'll help you take the decorations down and put them away and then you can all go home and be with your families for Christmas."

The ache in her chest that hadn't fully gone away in days intensified. Was he right? Had they wasted their time? Would all their efforts result in August only feeling more rejected as an artist?

He glanced around the small room as though noticing the empty shelves for the first time. "Where are the rest of my pieces?"

Caught up in the tumult of emotion his words had stirred up, Lucy couldn't make sense of what he'd asked. "The rest?"

"Yeah. I only saw about half of them out in the workshop. Have you moved the other ones somewhere?"

"Oh. No. We, um ..." Would he be mad about this part too? She bit her lip.

"You what?"

"Sold them."

He cocked his head. "What do you mean you sold them? To whom?"

"All those people who called you with orders."

August drove his fingers through his thick curls. "I do not understand what you are saying to me. How could you have sold them? You were with me the whole time. And how did you know what to charge or how to ship them?"

"My dad and I were in your shop a week ago. He showed me your pieces and then we listened to a couple of the messages on your machine." Which, hearing the words out loud, sounded like an egregious invasion of his privacy. August was a deeply private person. How off-the-charts enraged would this make him?

Before he could speak and let her know the answer to that, she rushed on. "We also found a price list on your desk and shipping materials in the cupboard in the office. You were missing out on all that business because of me, so I gave my dad money to hire Emily Packard, who's home from university for the holidays, to listen to all the messages, take the orders, arrange for payment, and ship them out."

August opened his mouth to reply. Before he could, someone rapped on the door of the small room. Grateful for the reprieve, Lucy spun around and opened it.

"Sorry to interrupt." Her dad lifted his wrist in the air and tapped his watch. "They're starting to arrive, and everyone is looking for August."

"Who is starting to arrive?" August came up to stand behind her.

"Your customers. There's quite a crowd already."

"But ..."

Lucy grabbed his arm and dragged him from the room and out into the workshop. Although it wasn't yet nine—the start time they'd advertised on flyers in their little town and the neighboring fishing villages—a dozen people milled in front of the tables, carefully lifting pieces or leaning in to examine them more closely. One woman held a gorgeous stallion with a flowing mane in one hand while waving her credit card in the other. "Who do I pay for this?"

Lucy's dad pressed a hand to their backs and propelled Lucy and August forward. "Go, you two. Take their money. Gwen and Caroline are over at the packing table, ready to box the pieces up and gift wrap them. The rest of us will take care of serving the refreshments in the other room."

As they took their places behind the tables, Lucy shot a look at August. For once, she had no trouble reading the emotion on his face as he surveyed the line of people forming to talk to him about his work. Wonder.

They kept busy all day. It seemed as though everyone in their little village—all those *good, decent, hardworking people* August had assumed wouldn't be interested in his art—had shown up needing last-minute Christmas presents for their kids or parents or friends. A reporter from *The Guardian* newspaper in Charlottetown even dropped in for a quick interview with August.

Since Lucy had told him about this event the night before, Mr. Arsenault came by on his way to Halifax to spend Christmas with his family. For his daughter, he bought a cat and two kittens stretched out on a piece of wood so light and polished it appeared to radiate sunshine.

Lucy might have suggested the monkey piece to him, but she had snagged that one for herself, paid for it, and already spirited it up to her bedroom so she would never forget the awe she had felt the moment she realized what August had done. What he was capable of.

By the time they closed the door on the last person, Lucy was exhausted. All that remained on the tables were a few scattered ornaments and a couple of wooden squirrels. As soon as Christmas was over August would have to start replenishing his stock. The thought of him out here doing what he loved, following his dream, made her so happy that it was worth every bit of the money and effort it had taken to pull off the event today, no matter what happened between the two of them.

Lucy's dad wandered behind the table and slung an arm around both their shoulders. "Well? Good day, right?"

"Incredible day." August sounded a little breathless. "I'm not sure how to thank you and the rest of the volunteers for what you did."

"You don't have to thank us, August. That's what we do in this town. We're here for each other. Believe me, I didn't have to twist any arms to get anyone to help or to drum up business. You and your work were the draw."

"Still, I appreciate it."

Her dad slapped him on the back a couple of times. “It was our pleasure. Now, I’ve got a turkey in the oven and pies cooling on the counter. You’ll have dinner with Lucy and me tonight.”

It wasn’t a question, which was smart on her dad’s part. Kept August from having the opportunity to say *no*.

“Thanks, Dad. We’ll be there shortly. August and I need to run one errand first.”

August narrowed his eyes. “What errand?”

Lucy only lifted her shoulders. “You’ll have to come with me to see, won’t you?”

~ Eleven ~

"It's lovely to be going home and know it's home."

~ Anne Shirley

"I can't believe you did all that for me." August turned the Charger onto the road at the end of his driveway and headed toward Cordial Cove.

"You're not mad?"

They reached the point—guarded over by a towering red-and-white lighthouse—and he veered right, following the ocean. "I mean, I kind of was at first. Then I realized what was happening, and I couldn't believe it. I'm grateful, Lucy. Truly."

Not grateful enough to stop calling her Lucy. She hid a wince. Clearly, they still had a ways to go. "I'm thrilled it turned out so well. Although I'm not one bit surprised. Your work is incredible, August. Why didn't you ever show it to me?"

"I was going to. Then I told my dad about it, and he reacted the way he did. After that, I couldn't bring myself to show you in case you felt the same way. That would have destroyed me."

"I wouldn't have."

"I know that now. I think, on some level, I knew it then too. It shook me though, what my dad said. Made me question whether what I was doing, what I was so driven to do, was actually worthwhile. That's why I've pushed you so hard to follow your dreams. I never want you to feel that way."

"Is that why you told me to go with Jack to New York?"

"Yeah, I guess it is." August flipped on the signal before turning onto the main street of their little town.

"Not because you were trying to get rid of me?"

He jerked his head in her direction. "Why would you think that?'

"Oh, I don't know. Maybe because every time I come to your workshop you try to get rid of me."

"That's not because I don't want you there. It's because I do."

Lucy furrowed her brow. "That makes no sense."

He blew out his breath. "In my mind, it does. Where are we going, anyway?"

She gestured through the front window. "Half a block up on the right." They drew close to the shop front she was watching for, and she pointed to the empty spot in front of it. "Pull over here."

When he complied and turned off the engine, Lucy undid her seatbelt and turned to face him. "Explain it to me. Why do you always try to get rid of me if you actually want me to stay?"

"Because I never want to hold you back. You have these big dreams, dreams of getting out of this town and making something of yourself in the theatre world. So, I'm glad you're going with Jack. I'm happy you're pursuing your goals."

"Are you?"

"Well, *glad* and *happy* might be overstating it a bit. It's what you've been longing to do, though, so I wouldn't want anything different for you."

"What if I've realized I want something different for myself?"

His dark eyes probed hers. "Have you?"

"Yes. After my dad told me the truth about my mom, I realized that the theatre was her dream, not mine. I would never have been able to achieve my hopes and goals and dreams in New York."

"Then where do you think you can achieve them?"

"Here. In Cordial Cove. If I ever doubted that, the way the town came together today to celebrate and support you and your work drove any misgivings away. This is where I want to be. And this is what I want to be doing." She inclined her head in the direction of the shop.

"Which is what?"

"Come see." Lucy pushed open the door and hopped onto the sidewalk.

"Hi, Lucy." A woman pushing a baby stroller waved from across the street. "Loved you as Anne!"

Lucy waved back. "Thanks, Chloe. Merry Christmas!"

August rounded the front of the car and stepped onto the sidewalk. A man striding past stopped long enough to clap him on the shoulder. "Great job today, August. Looking forward to giving my wife the tiger you made to add to her collection."

"Thanks, Tom."

"I'm putting in my order now for two baby tigers to go with it for her birthday in March."

"You got it. Enjoy your holidays."

"You too." Tom lifted a hand before continuing along the sidewalk.

Lucy made her way to the front entrance of the store, her heart full. How could she have ever thought she wanted to leave this wonderful little town? She tugged loose from her shirt the key she'd hung on a string around her neck and unlocked the door. Bells jangled when she pushed it open and stepped inside. Crumpled paper and empty boxes were strewn around the floor and dust coated every surface. The place needed work, for sure.

Still, she could see it. People at each table, the rich aromas of brewing coffee and fresh-baked cinnamon buns permeating the air. The hum of conversation. The *aura of possibility and the atmosphere of things about to happen* as August had quoted to Lucy that night on the makeshift train station platform.

He stopped in the middle of the floor. "What is this place?"

"It's going to be the coffee shop that Cordial Cove has needed forever."

"Whose coffee shop?"

"Mine."

He swung his gaze to meet hers. "Yours?"

"Yes. My dad and the council decided the town needed one and designated this space for it. They were accepting tenders until a couple of days ago, and I barely got my application in before the deadline. Turned out it was the only one, so I put down the deposit and signed the lease this morning."

He took a few steps closer to the counter and braced himself with a palm pressed to the dusty top of it. "You paid someone to ship out my orders, too. Where is all this money coming from?"

"My New York Dream Fund."

"Then you're really not going to New York?"

"That's right. *This* is my dream, August. Remember when you questioned why I was doing a business degree when I thought I wanted to be an actor? I wasn't even sure myself, but now I know why. I want to run this business. I have all kinds of ideas for it, including a huge display of work by local artisans in this corner here." She spread out her arms to indicate the space. "I'm planning to commission from you a whole

Prince Edward Island line—Green Gables characters, lighthouses, ships, whales, potatoes, anything you can think of that those *hardworking fishermen* and the rest of the world will want to purchase as souvenirs of the most beautiful place in the world."

August rubbed his temple with the palm of his hand as though trying to absorb everything she was saying. "You're not going to leave me much time to work with my *saws and planks*, are you?"

Lucy grinned. "Nope. Although, I might be able to help you run your business more efficiently so you have time to do both."

"How?"

She walked over and stopped in front of him. "Well, you *must* have a website, for starters. No one takes orders through the phone anymore. You need to offer online ordering, so people from all around the world can purchase your pieces. And you have to keep better books, come up with an itemized list of inventory, take advantage of tax breaks, apply for grants, adver—"

August groaned. "I hate all that stuff."

"I know. But I love it. That's why I'm going to do it for you. Eventually we'll hire an accountant and any other staff we need. You'll be free to simply create."

"What about your acting? Even if it's not your big dream, you still love it. And you're really good at it." He reached out and rubbed a strand of her red hair between his fingers. "You were amazing last night. You *were* Anne."

"How do you know? I didn't see you there."

"I stood at the back and took off right before the big kiss. Definitely didn't need to watch *that* again."

Lucy tried to rein in the thrill of hope his words sent tingling all through her. "Well, Mr. Arsenault says I can play Anne for the next year or two, even though I'll be even less *teenagerish*"—she shot him a mock glare—"than I am now. After that, maybe I'll try for Rachel Lynde. I've always wanted to play her. That will be more than enough to scratch my acting itch."

He turned slowly, taking in the space before stopping and gazing at her. "I can see it."

Warmth flowed through her, melting the ice that had begun to form the day she'd found out her mother had abandoned her. "You can?"

"Absolutely. It will be the hub of the whole town. What will you call it?"

"I was thinking about The *Epekwitk* Café."

In the language of the Mi'kmaq, August's people, *Epekwitk,* the original name of Prince Edward Island, meant *something lying on the water.* According to the little museum on the Green Gables heritage site, Lucy Maud Montgomery had loved that name for her beloved province—which she translated as *cradled by the water*—and believed that was what they should have continued to call it. Lucy was inclined to agree.

"Really?" August's features softened, something she was determined to spend her life making happen, since it sent such tendrils of delight curling through her.

"Really."

August grasped both sides of her unzipped jacket and gently tugged her closer. "Are you sure about all this, Lucille?"

"I've never been more sure about anything." Especially since he was back to calling her Lucille. Not to mention looking at her in a way he never had before. His beautiful *heart and soul on full display,* as her father had described it. She gave up trying to contain the hope and simply let it spread through her like sunshine filling a dark room when the curtains were flung open.

He let go of her jacket. "Then I know what I want to spend part of the proceeds from today's *pop-up store* on."

"What?"

"You're going to need a car to get to work."

Lucy stuck out her lower lip in a very *Mallory Stone* kind of way. "I don't want to get rid of Penny."

"Heaven forbid. I was only going to suggest we put some money into her. Try to get her value up to fifty or sixty cents, anyway."

"That's good enough for me."

He grinned. "You don't ask for much, do you?"

"Part of the new and improved Lucy."

August touched her cheek with his finger, sending another wave of warmth coursing through her. For once, he lingered instead of pulling away immediately. "Don't change too much, okay?"

As she so often did when emotions ran too deep for her to conjure up words of her own, Lucy fell back on the wisdom and eloquence of Lucy Maud Montgomery. "I'm not a bit changed—not really. I'm only just pruned down and branched out. The real me—back here—is just the same."

~ Twelve ~

Perhaps... perhaps... love unfolded naturally out of a beautiful friendship, as a golden-hearted rose slipping from its green sheath.

~ Lucy Maud Montgomery

Lucy sank onto the couch, her stomach as full as her heart had been since seeing those first customers admiring August's handiwork. By the time they had arrived home from their trip to the coffee shop, her dad had dinner on the table.

August had eaten his share, although he'd been his usual quiet self. Was he still trying to take in everything that had happened? Or maybe he was working his way toward telling her that, even if she was staying in town, it would be best for them to remain friends. If that.

After they'd helped her dad clean up and he had excused himself to go to bed, Lucy fully expected August to flee. Instead, he followed her to the living room, the papered walls glowing softly in the twinkling lights on the tree and the flames flickering in the woodstove. He settled at the other end of the couch from her.

Lucy leaned back against the arm, her sock feet propped on the cushion. "I need to ask you something."

He looked a little apprehensive, although he nodded. "Okay."

"Why did you really send me away?"

His brow furrowed. "Send you away from where?"

"Your workshop. You told me earlier that you were always ordering me to leave even though you actually wanted me there because you didn't want to stand in my way. But how would me hanging around your shop keep me from pursuing my dreams?"

"It wasn't the hanging around." August took a slow, deep breath. "It was the fact that, if you stayed very long, I didn't know if I would be able to keep from pulling you into my arms and begging you not to go."

"Oh." Warmth crept into her cheeks, and she pressed her fingers to them. "If you had done that, I definitely wouldn't have gone."

"Which was why I couldn't do it. If I had, and that was the reason you stayed, I would have been the one keeping you from the life you wanted. I refuse to be that person."

Lucy swung around and lowered her feet to the floor. Padding across the carpet, she made her way to the tree and reached into the branches to retrieve the gift she'd stuck there earlier. "Can I give you your present now?"

He stared at her a moment as she walked back, as though attempting to follow the abrupt change in topic. Then he reached for the brightly wrapped box. "You don't have anything to say about what I told you?"

"I do. This gift is my response."

August scrutinized the package as she sank onto the couch next to him. Carefully, he unwrapped the paper, set it on the coffee table, and lifted the lid off the box. For a moment, he only gazed at the object inside. Then he tucked the lid under the box and picked up the small, silver, three-inch-long train before setting the empty container on the coffee table. The corners of his lips quirked as he held the train up in her direction. "This is your response to what I told you?"

"Yes." Lucy ran a palm over the couch cushion, imagining the cold, wooden bench in the barn. "Remember that night when we sat on the bench in front of that mural of the train?"

"Every detail."

She smiled faintly. "I'd found out that afternoon about my mom leaving, and I was feeling badly about that and about you seeing me and Jack kissing behind the Green Gables house."

August grimaced, and she reached over and touched his arm lightly. "*He* kissed *me*, and when I immediately pulled away, he apologized. It meant nothing to me, except that it showed me he was not the one I wanted to be with."

"No?" Interest sparked in August's dark eyes. "Then who is?"

"I'm coming to that part."

"Well, get on with it then."

Lucy grinned. "I stared at that train, thinking about Anne traveling to Bright River on it, anticipating that she was going to her new home in Avonlea, that she would have a family. Even though her going there was a mistake, in the end, that was exactly what she found. People who loved her and accepted her for who she was." With one finger, she traced the top of the train resting on August's palm. "I started wondering where I would take that train if I could climb aboard it. Where was home? And the answer came to me. It's you, August. *You* are home for me."

August gazed at her a moment before leaning over to set the train on the coffee table next to the box. "Can I give you your present now?"

Lucy watched as he got up and walked away from her, crossing the room toward the door. "You don't have anything to say about what I told you?"

He stopped when he reached the chair inside the entrance where he had slung his coat when they came in. After rooting around in the pocket for a moment, he withdrew a small package. "I do." He came back and held out a gift about the same size and shape as the one she'd given him. More beautifully wrapped, though, in gold and black paper and a gold bow. "This gift is my response."

With trembling fingers, Lucy took the box and ripped the paper off, tossing it onto the floor.

When she lifted the lid, she considered the items inside—two rolls of candy nestled on a bed of soft, white tissue paper. A pack of Starbursts and one of Halls.

August sat next to her, bending one knee so he could face her, and rested a finger on the edge of the box. "Starbursts were the closest I could come to sunbursts, since I have no idea what diamond sunbursts are. Or marble halls, for that matter. Still, I want to give them to you, Lucille. I want to give you everything. Everything you want. Everything you need. Everything you dream of."

Those lovely palpitations in her chest started up again. "Then you only have to give me yourself," she said.

August took the box from her and set it on the coffee table next to the train. "Done."

Unable to keep from doing it a moment longer, Lucy brushed the curls back from his face, her fingertips rasping over light stubble. "Did you really watch the mini-series?"

"Yes. It was agonizing."

"Will you watch it again with me?"

"No."

Lucy offered him her best *wheedling ways* look, and he rolled his eyes. "Probably."

She laughed. "Does this mean you'll be my Gilbert Blythe?"

"No." He slid closer to her on the couch, until his knee touched hers. "But I'll be your August Dorey. Will that be enough?"

"More than enough."

"Good." He took her face in his hands, his fingers strong and warm against her skin. "You're home for me too, Lucille May McQuaid. You always have been."

For once in his life, he followed the script she had written in her mind for this exact moment between the two of them.

And then August kisses Lucy.

A Note From The Author

Dear Reader,

When my Fab Four sisters and I first started talking about doing an anthology together and setting our four stories in four different provinces, I knew right away that I wanted to set mine in Prince Edward Island.

Although I have only visited the island twice, it's one of my favourite places in Canada—breathtakingly beautiful with wonderful, friendly people and the sweet scent of Anne (and fresh fish and frying potatoes) drifting on the air everywhere you go.

So, this story is a love letter to PEI and to Lucy Maud Montgomery and the creativity and breathtaking imagination that gave the world Anne, Gilbert, Rachel, Matthew, Marilla, and so many other unforgettable characters.

Although her life was hard, the author found beauty everywhere she turned, especially in her beloved Prince Edward Island—a beauty that comes out in every word she put on paper.

My hope for each of you, dear ones, is that you will experience that beauty for yourself and be reminded of the one who created it, the one whose birthday we celebrate this time of year.

And I pray that, like Anne on that train to Bright River, you will find your way to the place, the people, who will be home for you this Christmas and every day of the year.

Sara

P.S. I would love to connect with you further! Find me on Facebook at Author Sara Davison or visit www.saradavison.org for more on my life, faith, books, and to sign up for my short, once-a-month newsletter.

Acknowledgments

To my Fab Four sisters. When Darlene, Helena, Melanie, and I took a road trip to a writer's conference in North Carolina earlier this year, the idea for this book was formed. It's been a fun journey to completion, mainly because everything is more fun when the four of us do it together. I'm so thankful for the three of you. For the laughs, prayers, support, and encouragement you unfailingly give me in my writing and in my life in general. You are a precious gift from God!

Speaking of gifts from God, my husband, Michael, is truly one of my greatest and most cherished. I'm so thankful that you have supported me through this up-and-down, two-steps-forward-one-step-back writing journey. I could not do what I do if you were not always on my side.

And always and above all, to the One who gives the stories and who made a way for all who believe to live with Him forever in our eternal home. It is all from You and for You.

ABOUT THE AUTHOR

Sara Davison is the author of the romantic suspense series The Day Draws Near, The Night Guardians, The Rose Tattoo Trilogy, In the Shadows, and two sparrows for a penny, as well as the standalone speculative, The Watcher. A finalist for more than a dozen national writing awards, Davison is a Holt Medallion, Cascade, and two-time Carol Award winner. She currently resides in Ontario, Canada with her husband, Michael. Like every good Canadian, she loves hockey, poutine, and apologizing for no particular reason. Get to know Sara better at www.saradavison.org.

Made in United States
Orlando, FL
19 November 2025

72726956R00243